Eyes In The Dark

Vance Albright

LIGHT AND DARK NOVELIZATIONS

AUTHORS NOTE

AUTHORS NOTE

Novels by Vance Albright

Depths of Paradise

How I Survived A Nightmare

Author's Note

Eyes in the Dark shares a universe with *Depths of Paradise* and *How I Survived A Nightmare*. You don't have to read any one book to understand what is happening in another. Though I do encourage the reader to do so to catch Easter eggs I occasionally hide. My goal is to create a world were all my stories share a world but at the same time does not force the reader to follow every story to understand what's going on in future books, unless it is a direct sequel to a story.

Vance Albright can be contacted at the following links.

Website:

https://lightanddarknovelizations.com

Business E-mail:

lightanddarknovelizations@gmail.com

Facebook:

https://www.facebook.com/lightanddarknovelizations

Thank you to my amazing book editors and designer

Spelling and Grammar: Jerome Otte

Cover Designer: Brandi Doane McCann.

https://www.ebook-coverdesigns.com

Developmental Editor: Savannah Gilbo.

https://www.savannahgilbo.com

ISBNs

E-book: 978-1-7340628-5-4

Paperback: 978-1-7340628-4-7

PROLOGUE

Kyle Nottingham stumbled, then fell face down in the snow. He slowly got up, clenching the deep gash on his right arm. He focused on the outline of the small, two-story red building only a few yards ahead of him. The safe haven he had left to find his friends. Through the darkness, the wind howled in his ears, large snowflakes hitting his reddening face. The sound of snow crunching in front of him caught his ear.

"Brian, Michelle?" He yelled softly, fearing whatever was out there would hear him. He again heard the sound of crunching snow, this time from his left. He turned his flashlight to the diamond-shaped holes in the animal barrier that wrapped around the foundation of the radio station. Through them, he saw the outline of a large, furry body lying on the ground. The head looked up at him. Its large eyes reflecting in the light. That sent him sprinting towards the stairs that led to the radio station door. He pulled it open, then quickly slammed it shut. The room was dark inside. A single wall separated the radio broadcasting area from the small office, break room, and bathroom areas. Lockers and shelves of spare equipment lined the wall. He flicked the light switch back and forth; as he expected, nothing happened. He took off his wet gloves, tossing them onto a table, then moved a large shelf to barricade the door. *Got to get help.* He thought knowing it was only a matter of time before whatever was out there made it inside. He walked over to his locker to grab his truck keys. For a moment, he thought about rushing for his truck but decided against it, knowing whatever was out there was close by. He put them in his pocket and grabbed his cell phone. Right away, it felt odd, like it was too light. He pulled it out, spun it around, opened the back, and saw the battery had been removed. In a panic, he screamed.

"Leave me alone! I have a gun in here!" Hoping whoever was out there would get scared off by his bluff. Reaching into a nearby drawer, he grabbed a cleaning cloth. He gritted his teeth in pain when he tightened them around his bleeding wound, then went into the broadcasting station. Maneuvering around the equipment, he grabbed a battery-powered radio and flashlight from a shelf. He sat the radio down, turned it on, and picked up the microphone. "This is radio station K572, Alaska," he said in a desperate, shaky voice. "I need help! There's something outside the station!" He paused for a moment to regain his composure. "A little less than half an hour ago, our phone lines went out. My cohost, Brian Clint, went out to see if the snow had knocked the lines down. After he didn't come back, me and Michelle went out to see if he was injured. This is no joke. If anyone is receiving this, send help!" Nothing but the crackle of static came through. From outside, he heard the boom of a gun, followed by a man screaming. "Damn it!" He screamed. Losing control of his senses, he threw the microphone at the wall. A loud knock on the window sent him stumbling out of his chair.

"Kyle, let me in! Open the window." A frightened woman's voice cried.

"Michelle!" He yelled, rushing to it. He pulled open the curtains. A shriek of terror left his throat; he nearly lost control of his bowels when he saw what was staring back at him. In a panic, he stumbled backwards, smacking the back of his head on the wooden table. He laid on the floor, moaning at the throbbing pain coming from his head. He glanced at the window again, fearing what would happen next. To his relief, the horrible face that had been staring back at him was gone. He started to get to his feet when he heard a loud thump against the wall. The panic he felt was getting stronger. The dark room seemed to be getting smaller. "Somebody help!" He screamed out of desperation. He got up, grabbing the only weapon within reach: a large steel snow shovel. "I've got a shotgun. Go away or I'll shoot," he yelled, hoping his bluff would work.

"*Goooo ahead*." A woman's voice replied in an eerie tone.

"Who are you? What do you want?" he yelled. This time, the window shattered in response. The wailing wind poured into the room. It's eerie howl making his skin crawl. His fingers fumbled with the flashlight before finally managing to turn it on. He unlocked the studio door and slowly opened it. Right away, he saw the outside door was broken inward. The large cabinet lay on the ground. Breathing heavily, he moved to the entrance, gripping the shovel tightly, ready to attack anything waiting in the darkness. To his surprise and relief, all he could make out was the snow-covered landscape. He peered out the doorway, but still he saw nothing. Taking the chance he was given, he rushed down the steps. On the third and last step, he felt his foot slip on ice. He yelled as he fell down the stairs. The shovel and flashlight flew from his hands. He lay on the ground, moaning for a moment. Remembering his situation, he quickly got up. His breathing increased as his hands frantically searched for the flashlight. The feeling of terror in his heart was only amplified by the wind's eerie howls. After what felt like an eternity, his hand brushed against the flashlight. He smacked it a few times, trying to get it to turn back on. Suddenly, he saw his shadow in front of him. A dim light behind him became brighter, lighting up the area. The smell of smoke filled his nostrils, and he heard the crackling of wood. He turned to see the radio station in flames. *What's going on?* He thought. Watching the fire climb up the structure. He ran for the parked cars, desperate to reach his truck. He didn't know where his cohosts were, nor did he care. Right now, all he could think about was getting out of here alive. When he reached his truck, his frozen fingers fumbled into his pocket, searching for the keys. His body froze when he heard a sound that was not the wind but a low guttural growl directly behind him. For a few seconds, Kyle's screams could be heard against the waling wind, then silence.

CHAPTER 1

Mariah Forester slowly opened her eyes, her successful fantasy life as a pet stylist living in a five-story mansion transforming back into her one-bedroom apartment. Her dog, Blaze, sat on the edge of the bed. The sound of her phone's alarm was ringing in her ears. Mariah turned off the alarm, then felt Blaze's warm tongue move across her face. "Alright, I'm up," she said, tiredly giving Blaze's head a rub. "I was enjoying my dream quite a bit." Blaze ran out of the bedroom, returning a few seconds later with her empty food bowl. "OK, OK! I'll get you breakfast." Mariah reluctantly sat up and got out of bed, she went to the kitchen and put a bacon and egg toaster strudel in the toaster, then filled Blaze's food bowl with kibbles and laid it on the ground. She looked at her weather app and gave a slight huff of annoyance, seeing that five inches of snow had fallen that night.

"What a great way to start the morning," she said in a sarcastic tone. Blaze finished her breakfast quickly, then started whining at the door. "Alright," Mariah said, placing her strudel on a plate next to a banana and a glass of orange juice. "I'll take you out as soon as I get my coat on," Mariah continued as she slipped into her snow boots and put her coat on. Blaze brought her leash to her. Mariah took it, attached it to Blaze's collar, and opened the door. The cold hit her skin instantly. She wrapped her arms around her chest as Blaze sniffed and pawed at the snow. *I wanted to live in Florida or Hawaii; why am I still here?* She asked herself. Two years ago, she was attending the University of Fairbanks with dreams of becoming a wildlife biologist exploring the world's rainforests. She had gotten through the first year with average grades, then failed several of her core biology classes. In frustration and because of medical issues, she dropped out of college. Still determined to follow her dreams and wanting to get her own place, she moved to Snowy Hills, mainly because the rent there was cheaper than getting a place in Fairbanks. She hoped to intern and eventually get a job with Alaskan Fish and Game. Those dreams also ended in disappointment. Finally, her luck changed when she managed to get hired by Snowy Hills Kennels as a kennel attendant. She did well at her new job, getting the surprising news last week that she had been promoted to team supervisor. She was grateful for the promotion and enjoyed working with and caring for the dogs, but the bitter cold made her want to transfer to a kennel or dog grooming position in warmer climates as quickly as possible. She remained with Snowy Hills because due to its remote location and sled dog training program. Snowy Hills pay rate was much higher than the standard kennel in the lower forty-eight states. Mariah had tried for high-paying positions in the lower forty-eight states, but all of them needed considerable management experience, none of which she had. *A few years of experience, and this snow will be warm sand.* Mariah thought envisioning it. After Blaze finished her morning bathroom break, Mariah went back inside. Her exposed, fair skin had turned a light red. She went over to the breakfast table and noticed the strudel was missing from its plate. She looked under the table. Blaze lay there, chewing something. She sighed in annoyance. *I didn't do anything*, Blaze's look said. *It was your fault for leaving the strudel out.*

"Thank you," Mariah said with annoyance. She remade her breakfast, ate, and then went into the bathroom to shower. Around twenty minutes later, she came out.

"Did you pack for mommy while she was in the shower?" Mariah asked, looking at Blaze, who was lying near the heat vent. Blaze opened her eyes momentarily, then went back to sleep. Mariah laid her three travel bags on her bed and put in fourteen different outfits and three sets of work uniforms. Enough to cover her two-week shift. She closed the first bag. She opened the second, smaller bag, placing toiletries and snacks inside. Blaze got up and started sniffing when Mariah put several of her favorite toys in the bag. "No, we can play later," Mariah said, gently pushing Blaze's nose away from the bag. Knowing the kennels internet was well known for lagging and pausing during video streams, she put a portable DVD player and a collection of her favorite DVDs in a protective case before placing them inside. Mariah looked at the opened travel bags in front of her, doing a mental checklist to be sure she had everything. *All I need is my snow gear and purse,* she thought. Mariah was about to close her travel bag when a thought came to her. She stood still, dwelling on it. She returned to the bathroom and grabbed a small bag of medication tucked away in the back of her bathroom cabinet. She was about to bury the medication deep inside the travel bag when she stopped. *You haven't had a serious schizophrenic episode in a year and a half.* Mariah thought, holding the bottle in front of her. The custom ringtone on her cell phone caught her attention. She put the bottle on her dresser and hit accept call.

"Hey, Kylee, what's up?"

"Hi Mariah, you probably already know this, but the roads are bad from all the snow last night."

"Wait, it snowed?" Mariah asked sarcastically. She heard Kylee Campbell snicker on the other end.

"Yes, it snowed in Alaska; go figure. Anyway, I'm going to be about twenty minutes to half an hour late getting to your place. You still OK giving me a lift?"

"Nope, I'm afraid you have to find your own way." Mariah replied, trying to sound serious.

"Some friend you are." Kylee replied, trying to match the seriousness in Mariah's voice. *I can still tell when you're acting*, Mariah thought, proud she was still the better actress. Cutting the act, Mariah continued.

"Yeah, it's no problem; get here when you can."

"OK, see you soon."

"Bye, and hurry up!" Mariah said before ending the call. She put on her matching blue coat, gloves, hat, and snow boots, then took her three travel bags out to the gray SUV. She laid the bags at the back of it and opened the trunk. As she started to put the travel bags in Blaze leaped into the trunk.

"Blaze, not yet. Out." She dropped her bags, grabbed Blaze's collar, and gently pulled her out. Blaze walked around her a few times, then sat next to her.

"You always make more work for me. You know that?" Mariah asked, forming a snowball and tossing it at Blaze. She leaped into the air, the snowball dissolving in her mouth. Blaze started searching the ground in confusion, wondering where the ball had gone. Mariah put her bags in the trunk, put Blaze back inside the house, then went to work unburying the SUV from its snowy tomb. In around fifteen minutes, the task was completed. She went back inside, kicking her snow-covered boots on the door frame before she entered. Blaze gave a happy bark and jumped around her.

"Yes, I know I was gone for so long." Mariah said she was getting out of her snow gear. She played with her phone until she saw a red car pull into her driveway. "Well, there's Kylee time to go," Mariah said, looking down at Blaze. As she was turning off the lights, Blaze walked up to her, again with a leash in her mouth. "We're not going for a walk; we're going for a car ride." She said in baby talk as she rubbed Blaze's head and ears. They both walked over to the front door. Mariah slipped her boots back on and clipped the leash to Blaze's collar. When Mariah opened the door, Blaze almost pulled her off her feet as she excitedly jumped into the snow. "Hold on!" Mariah yelled, pulling Blaze back enough to lock the door. Kylee Campbell laughed as she got out of her car. She was a light-skinned young Hispanic girl in her early twenties of average height, weight, and beauty.

"Blaze sure loves the snow," Kylee said, grabbing her four suitcases.

"She sure does," Mariah replied, quickly making a snowball and throwing it at Kylee. The snow ball hit her left shoulder.

"Hey, no fair, my hands are full." Kylee said, kicking some snow at Mariah. "Sorry, I'm late. Most of the roads are still bad, and I'd rather get here late than not at all." Mariah opened the trunk.

"It's OK." Mariah said as Kylee put her bags inside. "You ready to go?" Mariah asked, putting out her index finger. Kylee did the same and twisted it around Mariah's.

"Ready if you are," Kylee replied, releasing their best friend's greeting. "Are you excited for your first shift as supervisor?"

"Yes, I'll enjoy being able to boss you around." In reality, the closer she got to starting her new position, the more nervous she became. She opened the back door and placed a towel over the seats. "Blaze." She said, patting it. Blaze jumped in. "Blaze, you know the rules. No slobbering or going to the bathroom back there," she reminded as she removed her red leash.

"She never does anything like that," Kylee said, getting in the passenger seat.

"You're one hundred percent right," Mariah teased, giving her a look that said *you're crazy*.

"I know I am. Now hurry up and start the car; I want the heat on!" Kylee whined, pretending to act like a whiny child.

"Coming, child," Mariah said, getting in the driver seat and starting the car. "Happy?"

"Yes," Kylee replied, giving her friend puppy dog eyes. Mariah backed up and started down the driveway.

"Thanks again for giving me a lift," Kylee said, taking off her black snow cap and shaking her long, curly brunette hair. "I'm not sure my little car would have made it."

"No trouble. What are friends for?" Mariah replied, turning onto the road.

"To give you rides and free food," Kylee answered, grabbing a stick of gum from the glove compartment. "And to keep you company during another two-week shift at Snowy Hills Kennels. Conveniently located in the mountains, miles away from civilization."

"But who else gets to spend two weeks looking at the beautiful Alaskan landscape with hundreds of furry friends?" Mariah patted Blaze's head as she passed the Snowy Hills town sign, which read: *Welcome to Snowy Hills. Population one hundred and forty people.* Snowy Hills was a quiet little town located just above the Goldstream Public Use Area and twenty-three miles north of Fairbanks, Alaska.

"From what Carmen says, we're not going to have time to enjoy it. Everyone's heading to Chena Hot Springs or fleeing to warmer climates to get away from the cold." Kylee's face got a dreamy stare. "Oh, how I wish I could join them."

"Well, you're stuck with me, Blaze, and the gang for two weeks." As she drove through town. Mariah glanced at the Snowy Hills Tavern, one of her favorite places to eat. "Don't worry, we'll find time to enjoy the landscape and dream about hot springs." Mariah stopped at a red light in the middle of town.

"How many sled dog teams were rented this week?"

"I have no idea," Mariah replied, putting her foot on the gas.

"Aren't you the team's supervisor? You don't know?" Kylee said, giving her a sarcastic, shocked look.

"I'll find out when I get there. I don't worry about work on my days off."

"Hold on," Kylee said, turning on the radio. "As much as I love talking to you, we need some music."

"Why are you listening to the radio?" Mariah asked, surprised. "Grab my phone and start one of my playlists."

"I like listening to the radio. You have a DJ and don't know what songs they'll play. Sometimes you find new music." Kylee moved the dial and wondered why the normal stations weren't coming through.

"I honestly haven't listened to the radio in forever. Your taste in music has improved," Mariah teased. Listening to the static Kylee was finding as she moved through the radio channels. Instead of responding to her tease, Kylee had a puzzled look on her face.

"Wonder what's going on with K572?"

"Who knows?" Mariah said, shrugging. "Maybe Reggie finally got sick of them and shut them down?" Kylee giggled.

"When we pass the radio station, stop, and I'll ask them." Kylee played with the radio for a few more seconds, finding only stations she didn't like or static. "I give up," Kylee conceded. She grabbed her own phone and plugged it in. Seconds later, rock music was playing. She looked at Mariah and said, "OK, so I wanted to ask you this since I saw you this morning. What made you dye your hair red?"

"I don't know," Mariah answered. "I was just in the mood for a color change."

"Wait a second." Kylee's face became serious. "Didn't I hear Zander mention something last shift about red being his favorite color?"

"I don't remember that at all." Mariah said, with a hint of anxiety in her voice. Kylee was her best friend; however, Mariah had learned that she had a bad habit of letting secrets slip when she was excited.

"So, that is the reason you're trying to impress Zander?" Kylee questioned in a lower tone.

"No, that's not the reason!" Mariah answered back as her face started to get red with embarrassment, expecting Kylee to come back with something like. *My best friend has a bit of a crush, huh?* Instead, she kept her face turned toward the window, away from Mariah's gaze. "Just let me drive." Mariah continued in an embarrassed voice. "The roads are probably icy."

"The roads are clear on the highway," Kylee replied, pointing out the window with no hint of returning to the previous subject.

"That's good. We should be there in about half an hour then." Mariah said as she merged onto the highway.

"Yep, half an hour." Kylee replied, playing with her phone. Since Kylee had teased her about Zander, Mariah decided to have some fun of her own.

"Half an hour until you see Shawn, right? Everyone knows you have a crush on him." Kylee opened her mouth with disgust.

"I would never get with that pothead! Let's stop talking about it, OK?" Mariah wondered why she heard irritation in her voice but didn't say anything. For the next twenty-five minutes, Kylee and Mariah made small talk. Snow and ice patches started appearing once they got off Alaska Route 2, causing Mariah to slow down and adding fifteen minutes to their trip. Mariah gently pumped the brakes, then turned onto the snow-covered Snowy Hill Road.

"Salt trucks must not have come through yet," Mariah said, putting her SUV into four-wheel drive.

"We still should make it on time," Kylee commented. Mariah looked at the clock, which showed twelve-fifty. As they drove, Mariah looked at the forest on either side of them, imagining it during the summer when it was alive and green. Now only the pine trees kept their leaves. Mariah slowed down as they approached a fork in the road. In front of her, a snow-covered sign read Snowy Hills Kennel left, K572 Radio Alaska right.

"Want to go see why your radio station is offline?" Mariah joked. Kylee opened her window. "Kylee, what are you doing?" Blaze sat up and started sniffing the air.

"Do you smell that?" Mariah sniffed.

"I don't smell anything."

"I do. I smell smoke, and I see it. Look just above the trees." Mariah leaned over Kylee, looking out the passenger-side window. She was right. A steady stream of white smoke was coming from the direction of the radio station, and the unmistakable smell of burning wood filled her nose.

"OK, there was a fire at the radio station," Mariah said, not giving it much thought. "Can we go now?" she asked, looking at the clock.

"Let's go see what happened," Kylee said in a serious voice. Mariah pointed to the clock, hoping Kylee would get the point. "Mariah, we're out in the middle of nowhere.   What if no one knows about this and someone's hurt?" Mariah tapped the steering wheel, thinking.

"Fine," she said, turning right. "But when I get yelled at for being late, I'm blaming it all on you." Mariah drove as fast as she safely could when the radio station came into view. Kylee gasped.

"My God, what happened?" Small streams of white smoke still sprung from the soaked remains of the smothering building. Two fire trucks, four police cars, a news van, and an ambulance were parked around it.

"I hope no one was hurt." Mariah added shocked by what she was seeing. She rolled down her window as a Fairbanks police officer approached the SUV.

"Are you young ladies lost?" the officer asked.

"No, we saw the smoke and wanted to see if someone needed help." Kylee replied.

"Everything is under control; we were guessing the fire happened late last night."

"Do you know what caused it?" Kylee asked.

"Are the two of you reporters?"

"No, we're late kennel workers on a side trip." Mariah said, recognizing the man. He snapped his finger. "The two of you work at Snowy Hills? Now I recognize you. Melina. Right?"

"No, it's Mariah, Mr. Jackson. How's Ruger?" She asked, thinking of his large German shepherd.

"Oh, your Ruger's owner? I love him." Kylee said sweetly.

"He's fine. Eating and sleeping. All a dog can ask for in life." Blaze barked. "Your dog agrees with me." He said with a smile.

"You done?" Mariah asked, looking at Kylee. "Do you know what caused the fire?" Kylee again asked.

"At the moment, we don't know what caused it; now, if you could please move along, this area is still under investigation."

"OK, thank you." Mariah said.

"Thank you. We should be dropping Ruger off in a few weeks." He looked at Kylee and pointed at Mariah. "Keep your friend out of trouble."

"Impossible." Kylee joked as Mariah drove off. The forest started too thin and soon became a barren, snow-covered landscape with only a few trees scattered about.

"And we're five minutes late and still have several to go," Mariah said, slightly frustrated.

"What's my punishment going to be, boss?"

"After work, you're to be locked in a kennel for the entire shift." Mariah said in an old English accent.

"Well, we were speaking to a client. So, we were working." Kylee countered.

"Nice comeback." Mariah complimented, enjoying Kylee's craftiness. Kylee leaned against the car door.

"I still can't believe the radio station burned down. I hope no one was killed."

"We can't do anything about it either way," Mariah replied. She saw the kennel driveway on their right. She slammed on the brakes, and the SUV slid past it with a screech. Blaze gave a grunt as she lost balance and fell against the back seat.

"Way to go," Kaylee said dryly.

"Shut up," Mariah countered. "That's what you get for making me laugh. Blaze, are you OK?" Mariah asked, looking through the rear-view mirror. Blaze had gotten up and was looking out the window, eager to be let out. Mariah backed up, turning into the snow speckled driveway.

"Well, we made it in one piece." Kylee commented as they drove in the tracks that other vehicles had left.

"With me driving, did you ever doubt we would?" Mariah asked jokingly.

"Many times," Kylee teased, putting her hat back on. Mariah pulled into one of the employee parking spaces, which were located farther away from the building than the client parking area.

"It looks like we're the last ones here," Mariah said, staring at the six other vehicles, then giving Kylee a fake glare.

"The other team must have left already," Kylee commented. Snowy Hills had two teams of eight employees. Because of the frequent below-zero temperatures and snowstorms, staff members needed to spend the night; that way, the dogs had twenty-four-seven care available. Each team stayed for two weeks, then had two weeks off. Each team had a supervisor, an assistant supervisor, four animal caretakers, a janitor who also acted as a cook, and a maintenance person. Mariah found her eyes shifting towards Zander's silver truck.

"Zander made it." Kylee said, a slight smile forming on her face. *Darn, she must have noticed.* Mariah thought.

"I hope so; we're going to need him this week."

"That's not what you're thinking about," Kylee said in a low voice.

"Shut up, Kylee," Mariah said playfully. Kylee looked at her, startled. "What, did you not want me to hear that?" Mariah asked. Kylee said nothing and got out of the SUV. Mariah soon followed, and immediately felt the freezing wind nipping at her. "Blaze, stay," she said before opening the back door and clipping Blaze's leash.

"I can take Blaze for a bathroom break." Kylee offered. "You should get in there, being in charge in all."

"Thanks," Mariah replied, handing the leash to her. "If you ever want to take over, all you need to do is find me a warmer place to work."

"No way." Kylee replied, waving her off. "I don't want anything to do with ordering people around. I'm good working with the dogs." Mariah watched as Kylee and Blaze disappeared around the lobby building. She grabbed her bags from the SUV, then detoured to open the large gate of the fence that surrounded the front portion of the garage. She noticed several large ice patches spread along the asphalt. *That needs to be taken care of before Carmen gets here,* she thought, making a mental note to herself. Before going inside, she looked at the row of decorative pine trees on her left. Her gaze shifted to the triple-stone retaining wall on the hillside across the parking lot. She imagined it being summer, with the layered flower gardens in full bloom. Her eyes moved to the sky above. At the moment, it was blue and clear. On the horizon, she saw nothing but gray clouds.

"Great, more snow," Mariah commented to herself. Knowing it would mean cancellations or people coming in at the last minute. She looked away from the clouds to the snow-covered pine forest that was directly behind the kennel. A light coating of snow powdered the green needles. Beyond them was the White Mountains National Recreation Area. She couldn't help but smile every time she saw it. *It may be cold, but the scenery makes it worth it.* Her thoughts moved to the coming Alaskan nights. How the Northern Lights would become visible. Mariah's daydreaming was interrupted by the crackling sound of a gunshot. She gasped and turned in the direction the sound came from. To her surprise, it didn't come from the woods, but from the barren, rocky landscape in front of the kennel that led to the main road. *What's a hunter doing over there?* She thought. Gunshots were not uncommon in the area, but they always came from the forest and normally sounded more distant. Mariah didn't know why, but an uneasy feeling was forming in her stomach. Kylee and Blaze entered her mind.

"Kylee!" she yelled, fearing the worst. In alarm, she rushed around the kennel. Several yards ahead of her, Kylee and Blaze were standing, looking in the direction that the shot came from.

"Kylee, you OK?" Mariah asked, rushing over to her. She could tell Blaze was on high alert. She growled softly. The hair on her back was standing up.

"I'm fine," Kylee replied, turning to her. "Blaze got freaked out by the gunshot, that's all." Mariah gasped again as a second shot rang out from the same direction.

"What's the matter with you? It's probably just a hunter," Kylee casually suggested. Relieved everything was OK. Mariah quickly blew the gunshots off. She wondered why she assumed something bad had happened.

"Nothing's wrong. Come on, we'd better get inside for the team meeting."

"Come on, Blaze," Kylee said, giving the leash a small tug. Blaze refused to move. Her fur stood up, like she was smelling or hearing something they couldn't.

"Blaze, what's wrong?" Mariah asked, crouching down next to her. Blaze didn't acknowledge her, her blue eyes fixed on the landscape in front of them. "Blaze," Mariah asked in a worried tone, wondering what her dog was looking at. Suddenly, a loud, piercing howl filled their ears. Blaze whimpered and leaped backwards, causing Kylee to lose her balance. She stumbled but managed to keep ahold of

Blaze's leash. The howl continued for a few seconds. It sounded far off and was coming from the direction Blaze had been staring at.

"What was that?" Kylee asked, now sounding freaked out. "A bear?" she suggested, hopefully.

"I don't think so; it sounded more like a…" Mariah stopped, not believing what she was about to say.

"Like a what?" Kylee asked. Mariah looked down at Blaze, who was shivering, trying to hide between her legs. "Like a what?" Kylee repeated, nervously looking around.

"Like a baboon or some type of primate," Mariah replied. Kylee's face seemed to relax a little.

"Please don't tell me we have a Bigfoot on the property." Kylee said, trying to lighten the mood. Mariah tried to laugh, but Kylee's words worried her. She reached out for Blaze's leash.

"It's OK," she whispered, gently stroking Blaze. "Kylee, don't mention anything, but keep an eye out for anything strange." Kylee gave her a weird look.

"What do you mean by strange? You're not seriously thinking Bigfoot? I was kidding."

"No, of course not," Mariah replied, sounding like she was trying to convince herself. "Just keep an eye out for signs of a bear roaming around the area."

"Got it," Kylee said, hugging herself to keep warm.

"Let's get inside," Mariah suggested, giving one last look in the direction of the sound.

CHAPTER 2

Minutes later, the two girls approached the building entrance. Blaze ran ahead, all too eager to get indoors. The lobby and staff living area were in a separate building from the kennels, which were located about twelve feet away. An eight-foot-tall, six-foot-wide fence created a hall connecting the two buildings. Mariah noticed Benjamin Jarvis walking inside the fencing, hunched over pushing a snow shovel down the concrete path. Benjamin had been born with Down syndrome. He was short with a flattened face with brown, almond-shaped eyes that angled upward. A large black wool hat covered his brown hair. Despite normally having to explain her instructions several times to him, Mariah admired his soft heart and willingness to listen.

"Hello, Mariah. Hello, Kylee," he said in a slow voice.

"Hi Benjamin," both girls said seconds after one another.

"Already hard at work, I see! It's pretty cold out here, huh?" Mariah continued as she tried to pull back Blaze, who was running for the door.

"Yes, my face is red and cold, but I'll get the walkways clear for everyone. It looks like Blaze is cold too," he pointed out.

"I'm looking forward to dinner. Your meals are always good," Kylee continued before going inside.

"Nice job on the walkways," Mariah complimented, walking towards Blaze, who was still tugging at the leash whimpering to go in. "If you get too cold, don't be afraid to take a break."

"After I finish this, is it OK if I go inside and have some hot chocolate?"

"That's fine," Mariah confirmed, walking quickly towards Blaze. "I'd better get inside; talk to you later." Both said goodbye, then Mariah opened the door to the waiting area. Right away, she enjoyed the pleasant feeling the warmth brought. "OK, we're inside!" Mariah told Blaze, who was happily jumping onto the white wicker couch. "Down," Mariah added, pulling Blaze off it. She saw Kelly Linn wave to her through the set of double doors that separated the waiting room from the main lobby. Blaze jumped up and down, her claws making a slight tapping sound on the light brown wooden floors. Mariah entered the lobby, which had a warm log cabin feel to it. She walked over to the large pine-wood receptionist desk, dropping her bags and hanging her coat on the office chair. In front of her, a fireplace crackled behind a gold barrier. Chairs were arranged in a circle in front of the reception desk. Ethan Frederick and Kelly Linn stood near the fire, making small talk. Mariah always found herself wondering how they got along. Their tastes in just about everything were completely different. Ethan had curly, messed-up brown hair, a wrinkled gray t-shirt, and old jeans. Several pimples broke out on his fair-skinned face. This was in complete contrast with Kelly's clear, fair skin, sleek brunette hair, and stylish brown dress skirt she was wearing. Kelly always wore business attire during team meetings. Mariah figured she was trying to impress their owner, Reggie Donald, into giving her a promotion. One of the many reasons Mariah was shocked when Reggie offered it to her instead. She looked at Kelly, wondering if she was resenting her for it. *In a few years, you'll probably get the job anyway. All I need is a few years of management experience, and I can transfer to a large kennel or pet store with a management job that doesn't involve snowstorms below freezing temperatures.*

"Mariah, I'll run Blaze back." Kylee offered, standing to her right in the doorway that led to the staff kennels.

"Thanks. Here," Mariah handed Blaze off to her. She then turned to her teammates. "Sorry, I'm a few minutes late, everyone. Where's everyone else?"

"Zander is putting his gear in his room. Carmen took the bus out to meet clients. Who knows where Shawn is?" Kelly answered. *Probably either too high or too drunk to get out of bed,* Mariah thought. "Why are you late anyway?" Kelly asked in an authoritative voice.

"The roads were bad, then Blaze needed a bathroom break." *Not that I need to explain it to you,* Mariah thought before sitting down. "How many dogs is Carmen bringing back?" Kelly thought for a moment.

"Six, all from the same family. I believe all are going into the suites." Mariah gave her a surprised look. "Someone booked all the suites?" Before Kelly could answer, the side door opened. Zander Conri entered the room, followed closely by Kylee. Mariah's focus left what she and Kelly were talking about. She found her eyes floating towards him as he sat down. Admiring his tall muscular build, tanned fair skin, and blonde short taper haircut.

"OK, everyone get settled, and we'll get the meeting started shortly," Mariah said, leaving her chair. She cut in front of Kylee to sit next to Zander.

"Hi Zander," Mariah said, feeling butterflies moving through her stomach.

"Hey Mariah. Make it in OK?" He replied in a voice that said he was pleased to see her.

"Yeah, the roads were a little icy, but nothing I can't handle. We saw a burned-down radio station, but Blaze is safe."

"Mariah. The meeting," Kylee said softly, sitting next to her. *Kylee, be quiet,* Mariah thought. The nervous knot in her stomach growing.

"When did you dye your hair anyway?" he asked. Mariah tried not to look overly thrilled, but inside she was jumping for joy. *He noticed!* Mariah thought, feeling over the moon.

"I wanted to change it for the winter season."

"Mariah, it's fifteen minutes past one. Are you going to start the meeting?" Kelly asked. Mariah looked at the clock and knew Kelly was right.

"Sorry, everyone. Let's start the meeting," Mariah said, getting up to look at any notes. Reggie left her on the desk. Ethan and Kelly took their seats. Kelly sat in the seat closest to Mariah. "Christmas and winter break may be over, but the winter season is still going strong. We are booked to capacity these next few weeks. Four sled dog teams were rented out and are off the property. We have fifty-seven sled dogs in the building, with one team returning later this week and three others going out early next week. Seventy-four dogs are boarding from the local towns, and we have six dogs coming in on the bus." The meeting was interrupted by the lobby door again opening. Shawn Fisher walked in. Mariah could smell the cigarette smoke on his worn brown coat. Shawn was the one person Mariah dreaded working with. He was always rude and disrespectful to her.

"Shawn, you're nearly half an hour late. Where were you?"

"The roads were covered in snow," Shawn replied, not caring that he was late.

"Everyone else had to drive on snow-covered roads, and we made it on time," Kelly added.

"It's a two-week shift, and I'm half an hour late. Sorry, sue me." *Why does he have to be on my team?* Mariah thought.

"That's what you said the last shift," Mariah said, feeling she needed to speak up. She planned on reprimanding him, but not in front of everyone else.

"And the shift before that," Zander reminded her.

"Smoke your five packs already, or is that something else?" Kylee added as she fanned the air to blow the smell of smoke away from her.

"Screw you," Shawn said.

"Leave her alone," Zander cut in with a serious voice.

"Why don't you come over here and do something about it then?" Shawn challenged, crossing his arms and glaring at Zander.

"Enough, you two!" Mariah yelled in a voice that made everyone look. "Shawn, you're late again. This cannot keep happening! Now sit down so we can continue the meeting!" Shawn gave a final glare to Kylee and Zander before sitting down. Mariah sat back down, hoping things would go smoothly from now on. She talked about various kennel topics, including the six dogs coming in on the bus and how Reggie wanted them to go back home looking extra clean because they were owned by a wealthy client. "Does anyone have any questions before we end?" Ethan raised his hand. Mariah motioned for him to go ahead.

"I'm sure everyone knows this, but I just wanted to mention that we were supposed to get a couple snowstorms during the shift."

"Did you have to remind me of that, Ethan?" Mariah teased. "Regarding that, I know all of you know this, but I'm going to say it anyway. Make sure you and the dogs are staying warm, and watch out for signs of hypothermia for yourselves and the dogs. If no one has anything else, I'll give out assignments for the week."

"Is the maintenance list ready?" Shawn asked in a tired, annoyed voice.

"I'll have it printed out in a minute." Mariah replied. Her voice remaining professional.

"In the meantime, I'm taking my bags to my room." Shawn grabbed them and walked off. Mariah wanted him gone, so she didn't stop him. She started to fill out the crew placement sheet while everyone else gathered around the desk. She looked up to see her four crew members standing around the desk.

"You guys waiting for something?" Mariah teased.

"We're waiting for you to start bossing us around," Kylee replied.

"Go clean the toilets." Mariah pointed to the bathroom.

"That's the pothead's job," Kylee added.

"Kylee, professionalism," Kelly said. "Even if it's true, watch what you say."

"Whatever," Kylee replied sarcastically.

"OK," Mariah added, motioning for everyone to stop. She laid the crew placement sheet in front of everyone. "For the first week, I have Kylee and Kelly in the sled dog section, Zander and Ethan taking care of client dogs. On the second week, Kylee and Zander will take sled dogs, and Kelly and Ethan will do client dogs. Carmen and I will jump in to help when we can. I'll make the dog's food and hand out meds. Carmen will take suites and baths. Shawn has maintenance and snow removal. Benjamin's doing cooking, snow removal, and janitorial work."

"Sounds like a plan," Zander agreed. "Though if I may suggest keep the same people working together, that way we can work out a system." Mariah looked at her paper and said.

"OK, if that's what you want." She looked at her teammates for objections. Seeing none, she continued. "You and Kylee will be a team. Kylee smiled and raised her eyebrows at Zander. And Ethan and Kelly will be a team."

"Works for me," Ethan agreed.

"OK, then. Everyone take half an hour to get settled, then get to work." As everyone exited the room, Mariah went to the other end of the lobby, where a second door opened to a small hall. Straight ahead was the staff recreation room. To her left was a set of wooden stairs going upward to the staff rooms. Between the stairs and the recreation room were two more doors. The door closer to the recreation room led to the kitchen and dining area; the other door led to Reggie's or the acting supervisor's office. Mariah passed the stairs and poked her head inside the dining area, which was an average-sized room with two folding tables. As she guessed, Benjamin was sitting at one of them, sipping on a cup of hot chocolate.

"Hey, Benjamin." He looked up at her, trying to wipe the dark brown stains from his shirt.

"Sorry, some of the cocoa spilled while I was drinking it."

"Don't worry about that," Mariah replied, giving a gentle smile. "When I was outside, I noticed some ice in the area where the bus parks. Can you lay some salt down for me, please?"

"Yes, I can do that, Ms. Mariah."

"You don't need to call me Ms. Mariah. We're friends, so you can call me by my first name."

"We're friends!" Benjamin said happily, as if he were realizing it for the first time.

"Of course we are," Mariah confirmed. "Also, I know you've been wanting to work with the dogs more, so tomorrow I'll have someone work with you." Benjamin's face lit up.

"Yaa," he said happily. "Do you want to join me for some hot chocolate?"

"I'd love to too, but I need to get settled and make sure things are in order," Mariah replied, appreciating the offer.

"When is Carmen getting back with the new dogs?" Benjamin asked with a strangely interested look.

"She should be back in about an hour. I'll see you later." Benjamin waved bye before she left. Mariah returned to her office chair. She looked around the empty room, taking it in. This was it; she was in charge of the kennel. This was a massive step in her career. She let out a happy yelp before spinning the chair around.

"Mariah, what are you doing?" She heard Zander ask.

"Zander!" she said, startled, stopping the chair. Her face turned slightly red with embarrassment. "I thought you were getting settled in?" She said with a hint of excited nervousness.

"I get it; you were having fun." Zander came up to the desk. "I need to talk to you if you have a minute."

"Su...sure." She said trying to hide the excitement in her voice. *Wonder why he wants to talk to me?* "What did you need?" He didn't answer right away, as if thinking how to form his thoughts.

"Um." He laughed under his breath before continuing, like he was still trying to form the words in his head. *This is it; he's going to ask me out!* Mariah thought, feeling the excitement building inside her. To her disappointment, Zander said.

"Uh, follow me upstairs, please."

"OK," Mariah said, slightly confused. Mariah and Zander went up the stairs to a long hallway. The women's rooms were on the left side of the hall, and the men's rooms were on the right side. Each section had a bathroom at the end of the hall.

"Hey guys, what's going on?" Kylee playfully asked, poking her head out of her room door.

"Kylee, you should come along; you're going to get a kick out of this," Zander suggested.

"Sure, where are we going?" Kylee asked, placing the folded shirt she was holding on her bed, then skipped over to Mariah's side. *Why does he always want her around?* Mariah thought feeling a wave of jealousy come over her. *Don't be jealous; Kylee's his friend, that's all.* That thought left her when they got to the boy's end of the room. The smell of smoke filled her nostrils.

"I already told him he couldn't smoke in the room, and he told me to F off," Zander said, annoyed, motioning to Shawn's room.

"OK, I'll handle it," Mariah promised in a frustrated voice. Zander stepped back with Kylee. Instead of knocking, Mariah slammed the door open. Shawn, who was sitting on the bed with a cigarette in his mouth, fell back in surprise.

"Shawn, what are you doing?" Mariah asked in an angry, serious voice with an equally serious look on her face. "You know we can't smoke in these rooms!"

"Who do you think you are barging in here like this?" He demanded. As much as he tried to sound tough, Mariah could hear the fear and shock in his voice.

"I'm the one who's in charge; that's who, and you're going to be following the rules from now on, or else you'll be gone," Mariah replied, taking a few steps back to stop the burning in her eyes. Shawn stood up but was visibly shaken.

"You can't fire me," Shawn countered. Unfazed, Mariah tilted her head slightly and yelled.

"Oh, I can't. One call to Reggie and you're gone," Mariah assured, brushing past him and grabbing the pack of cigarettes.

"What do you think you're doing? Those are mine!" Mariah walked into the bathroom, put the cigarettes in the toilet, and flushed.

"You'll pay for that!" Shawn yelled, charging towards her. "I'll..."

"You'll do what?" Zander asked, getting between them. By this point, Kelly and Ethan had come out of their rooms to see what the commotion was about. *Please don't come to blows.* Mariah thought, not wanting to have to explain to Reggie why a fist fight broke out on her first day. She glanced at Kelly, knowing she was probably hoping it would happen. To her relief, with Zander and Kylee in his way,

Shawn put his hands up and backed down. With the situation defused, Mariah addressed Shawn again.

"Shawn I'm only going to say this once. People on the other team use those rooms too, people who don't want the smell of smoke inside them. If you want to smoke, do it outside; otherwise, all your packs will go down the drain. "Mariah held her stare, daring him to speak. With his tail between his legs, Shawn retreated back into his room. With the show over, Ethan did the same. Mariah gave a heavy sigh and turned to her friends.

"Too much?" she asked Kylee and Zander in a calm voice.

"No, you did great; way to go, boss," Kylee praised, putting her arm up for a high five.

"I honestly didn't expect that," Zander added.

"Thank you for stepping in," Mariah said with gratitude, giving him a gentle slap on the shoulder.

"No problem, anytime," Zander acknowledged.

"The look on his face was priceless," Kylee added. "Well, I'm going to finish unpacking."

"Same," Zander agreed. As she went back to her room, Mariah noticed Kelly still standing in the hallway.

"Need something?" She had no doubt Kelly was going to tell Reggie all about the incident. It didn't matter to her, though; she was reprimanding an out-of-line employee and was proud of how she handled it.

"No, nothing at all," Kelly replied.

"Cool, get settled, then regroup with Ethan and check on your dogs. Same goes for you two." Mariah said, pointing to Zander and Kylee, who were still in the hallway. "Oh, and when Carmen gets here, can you help her unload? I don't want her to have to make six trips back and forth." Both Zander and Kylee said.

"Sure." Then Mariah went into her room, closed her door, and started unpacking. *I dealt with the Shawn problem; let's hope the rest of the week goes smoothly.*

CHAPTER 3

Around half an hour later, Zander exited his room. He held his coat and snow gear under his arm. He never liked the extra heat that layers of extra clothes brought to his body while walking around indoors. When he went down to the lobby, Mariah was already seated at her desk, working on the computer. He thought back to when he had first met Mariah while taking animal training and behavioral courses at the University of Fairbanks. She was in one of his classes for a semester. The two talked a few times and friended each other on social media, but never hung out outside of the college campus. Since she left college, he had not seen her in person until the two met again at Snowy Hills. *She sure has come a long way,* he thought proudly, knowing how much she had overcome to get here. He was glad to see her sitting in the leader's chair; having a friend in charge was going to make things much more pleasant during work shifts. He thought about the last team supervisor, a large woman named Tiffany; he'd never bothered to learn her last name. Tiffany quickly gained a reputation for being an office worker who knew nothing about dogs or how to handle them and would often interrupt his or other people's tasks to get dogs from clients. She remained the supervisor for a year until Zander and Mariah had had enough of her. They manipulated a situation where two extremely hyper huskies got lost in the lobby, and with no working walkie-talkie around, Tiffany was forced to handle them. While she was trying to corral them into the client waiting room, Zander opened the outside door to bring in a client's dogs. The two rambunctious huskies ran for the opened door, and in seconds they were heading for the Alaskan wilderness. He and Mariah, of course, were the ones to recapture them a day later. The moment Reggie Donald saw what happened on the security camera's Tiffany, was let go. Due to Mariah's leadership in recapturing the dogs, she was promoted to supervisor. A move Zander knew irked Kelly Linn, who had been Tiffany's supervisor's assistant, the eyes and ears of the kennel. Zander had been sure to put her down when talking to Reggie, while at the same time saying how good of a leader Mariah would be. The moment Mariah was told she was promoted to supervisor, he suggested she make Carmen Kramer the supervisor's assistant. She had a similar personality to Mariah and was on good terms with him. With a friend in charge, he could now act as a shadow leader. He could advise Mariah and get his ideas implemented without any of the responsibilities of being an official leader.

"Hey, what's up?" Mariah asked, turning her attention away from the computer. Zander placed his elbows on the counter.

"Can I have the dog list, please?" He always wanted to know what the kennel situation was like so he could prepare a plan for the two weeks of work ahead of him.

"It's laying on the shelf," Mariah replied, pointing to it. Zander went over to the desk organizer between the two computers and picked up a small stack of papers.

"The walk list is there too; if you could hang it up for me, I'd greatly appreciate it." Mariah said, relaxing in her chair.

"No problem," Zander said, looking at the list of dogs currently staying at the kennels. The sled dog section had twenty-four Siberian huskies, sixteen Alaskan malamutes, ten samoyeds, and seven chinooks. The main kennel area had forty-two mixed breeds: ten Siberian huskies, six German shepherds, a chihuahua, a yorkie-poo, a toy poodle, five Labradors, including a family of yellow, black, and chocolate Labradors, a rottweiler, and seven pit bulls. "Alright then, I'm going to get started." Mariah gave an unsure smile. Zander knew she was about to say something he wasn't going to like.

"You're not going to like this, but last shift Benjamin talked to me about wanting to handle dogs, so I thought I'd give him a chance to rotate some of the calmer dogs. Will you be willing to help him with that?"

"I don't mean to talk bad about Benjamin, but are you sure it's a good idea to have someone with his disability handling people's pets?" Zander responded, not at all thrilled with the idea.

"That's why I want my most trusted team members watching him," Mariah said with confidence.

"Glad you think so highly of me," Zander replied. He hesitated for a moment, then conceited, "Sure, I'll do it."

"Thanks, knew I could count on you," Mariah said sweetly. Zander heard her phone ping. Mariah looked at it. "Carmen should be here any minute. Can you grab someone and help her unload the dogs?"

"On it." Zander put his snow gear on and left the office building. He opened a gate on his left, entering the fenced-in walkway. Moments later, he was inside the main kennel lobby. He placed his coat and snow gear on the coat rack. Directly in front of him, two doors were at each end of the wall. The door on the right side led to the sled dog kennels. The other led to the client dog kennels. A bathroom was to his left. Next to that was a large storage closet. To his right was another door that led to the batheing and grooming room. Directly behind that was a laundry room where a large industrial washer and dryer were kept, along with clean bedding and dog toys. Between the entrances to the dog kennels was a desk where brushes and dog cologne sat. He picked up a bottle. The label read cookie dough cologne. *Who would waste money on this?* It wasn't his first time seeing the dog cologne, but it always baffled him why people spent money on it. He put it down, then entered the client dog room. To his right was a small hall that led to the kennel kitchen. In front of him was a long hall with thirty-seven cages on each side. Each kennel was six feet by eight feet and had a heated outdoor area. Excited barks filled the room. Some dogs stood at the gate barking, while others jumped up and down. Some only wagged their tails, looking through the gate. Those types were Zander's favorites to work with: polite and calm.

"Hey everyone, you miss me?" he asked as he walked, glancing at each cage. He knew most of the dogs. Duncan, a black Labrador mix with a curly coat, gave a happy bark as he passed. Across from Duncan was a family of three Labs.

Since each dog was a different color, Zander always called them the Neapolitan family. He gave Goose, a pit bull, a gentle tap on the nose. He noticed a German shepherd had made a giant mess of freshly deposited crap. *Kylee can clean that up.* He thought, snickering. When he reached the end of the hall, a door to the outside play yards was in front of him. To his left was a door leading to the sled dog housing and training section of the kennel. To his right was another hall with cages for twenty-six more client dogs, where many of the smaller dogs were kept. Zander had named it Small Dog Heaven. He reached into his pocket to hang the walk list on a clipboard hanging on the wall and felt nothing. *I must have left it in my coat pocket.* Zander returned to his coat and started going through the pockets. He soon felt the walk list. While he unfolded it, he heard a click, then felt a spray hit the back of his neck and hair. Soon, he could smell gingerbread. He turned around to see Kylee with a bottle of cologne.

"Knock it off," he said, taking the bottle and giving her a few squirts with it. Kylee started flipping her hair around.

"You missed a spot," she said, holding a section of hair out. *Only you, Kylee,* Zander thought. Loving her playful and fun attitude. He gave the section a spray.

"Carmen's going to be here any minute, so let's head to the garage; we'll have plenty of time to fool around later."

"If you insist," Kylee replied, putting the cologne back.

"Gingerbread smells better on you than it does on me," Zander complimented as they walked.

"Thanks, I feel just the opposite," Kylee said, returning the compliment before skipping ahead of him.

"I love her," Zander said to himself, watching Kylee skip, her fun-loving, carefree attitude in full swing. Zander hung the walk list up before going to small dog heaven. At the end of the hall were two doors, one in front and one on the right. The door at the front led to the garage, where the minibus was kept. The door on the right had a flight of stairs leading down to the kennel suites. Zander went inside the garage. Right away, the musty smell hit him. Locked cabinets held propane and gasoline cans. Along the back wall was a large pegboard that held the tools. A large tool box and bags of rock salt sat on either side of the pegboard. Kylee was sitting on a work bench. Her moving legs made a tapping sound when they hit the wood.

"Do you want to wait in here or go outside?" Zander asked, already knowing what Kylee would say, but asked anyway for his own amusement.

"It's warm in here," Kylee replied, giving him a look that said that's one of the dumbest questions I ever heard. "These are the dogs coming from that rich owner. I can't wait to see what breeds he has." Kylee continued in an excited voice.

"Just because the owner's rich doesn't mean he has rare breeds," Zander commented.

"True." Kylee agreed. "But I hope he has a bunch of rare dogs we've never seen. Speaking of rich owners, why would anyone want to vacation in Alaska?"

"Northern Lights, king crab, skiing..."

"Good point," Kylee agreed. Kylee and Zander waited for several minutes until they heard the low rumble of the bus's engine. "I'll go open the gate," Zander offered.

"And I'll stay in here where it's warm," Kylee said, giving him a smile.

"It's twenty degrees out; it's a warm day." Kylee stuck out her tongue. Before he went out the door, Zander saw the minibus coming down the driveway. The large pile of shoveled snow caught his eye and gave him an idea. He rolled himself a snowball and went back inside.

"What's up?" Kylee asked.

"I have something for you," Zander said with an evil grin, keeping both hands behind his back.

"No!" Kylee yelled and started to back away. Zander tossed the snowball at her, hitting her in the back.

"You're cruel and inhuman," Kylee said, trying to create a mean face. "I challenge you to a snowball fight." Zander could tell the bus was near the gate.

"I have to open the gate; we'll have our snowball fight later." Zander went outside. The red minibus was coming to a stop in front of the gate. Zander had named it the Snow Beast due to it being modified to handle the harsh Alaskan winters with large snow tires and a plow in front. Zander unlatched the gate, giving it a strong pull to break the ice under the wheel. As he pushed it open, he kept one eye on the door to his side, in case Kylee decided to get her revenge. The bus drove through the gate. Zander could hear the bits of ice crunching under the tire chains. Zander closed and latched the gate behind him when he came around the side of the bus. Kylee tossed a snowball at him, striking him in the chest. He saw she was getting ready to toss another one; he ducked when she threw it, and he heard the thud when the snowball broke on the bus's side. "Alright, want to go, Kylee?" Zander said making a ball of his own. Kylee responded with more shots of her own. He returned fire. He couldn't see her, but he guessed Carmen was enjoying the situation. The snowball fight came to a stop when Mariah's voice came over the radio.

"I'm coming to help you guys unload." Zander dropped his snowballs.

"Truce?"

"Only if you're thinking what I'm thinking," Kylee said, handing him a snowball. Minutes later, Mariah opened the gate. When she got in striking range, Zander and Kylee tossed their snowballs, hitting her in the chest and stomach. Mariah screamed in surprise, making them both laugh.

"I don't even want to ask what's going on," Carmen said, amused, casually stepping out of the bus's side door, holding the leash of a reddish Rhodesian Ridgeback.

"Two people are about to get fired," Mariah said in a joking voice as she brushed herself off.

"Who's going to unload the bus then?" Zander countered.

"Yeah, can you at least wait until the dogs are unloaded to fire them?" Carmen asked, joining in on the joke. She was a tall, pretty girl with clear, fair skin and dirty blonde hair, which she kept in a ponytail. Kylee started petting the Ridgeback, who licked her face in return.

"Did it give you any trouble?" Zander asked, recalling the breakdowns that occurred twice last shift.

"No, shockingly, Reggie finally listened and got it fixed. It drove fine," Carmen then smartly said. "At least for today."

"Reggie actually got everything fixed." Zander asked skeptically as he joined Kylee, petting the dog. Carmen gave a look of annoyance and moved some wires that were coming up from inside the bus floor. The exposed wires were duck taped to the wall every few feet, ending at the roof, where the radio antenna was attached.

"It's drivable. Shawn's going to have to get this repaired. I seriously thought the tape would come loose every time I hit a bump."

"It looks sturdy to me," Zander commented, giving the wires a tug of his own. The tape flexed slightly, but he could see where it would make Carmen nervous. "Anyway, Shawn might be in his room for a while; he's still getting over the humiliation from this afternoon."

"What happened?" Carmen asked, giving Zander an interested look.

"We can talk about it later." Mariah cut in. "If you want to get the dogs' paper work and food together, Zander and I can put the dogs away."

"Works for me." Carmen replied.

"I'll take the ridgeback." Kylee said, taking the leash. Zander followed Mariah inside the minibus. It was a cramped space, only three feet wide and six feet high. Rows of crates were double-stacked from the front of the bus to the back door. It smelled like dog and old machinery. He moved sideways past Mariah, who was opening the first crate.

"Zander, look at this," she said excitedly, bringing out a grey cane corso. The large gray dog's stubby tail wagged excitedly. Her large head moved to sniff Zander's arm.

"Cool," Zander replied before he looked in his own crate. "Wow."

"What's in there?"

"Something cooler than yours," Zander bragged as he opened the crate.

"What do you have, a great dane, St. Bernard?" Mariah asked.

"Neither," Zander continued, as a large Tibetan mastiff came rushing out. Zander quickly got control of him, placing the slip lead around him.

"No way!" Mariah said, her eyes wide with delight. The mastiff pulled, causing Zander to slightly lose balance. He went up to the cane corso. The two happily sniffed each other.

"I know you're happy to see your sister," Mariah said, rubbing the Tibetan mastiff's thick gold fur. The two excited dogs got on their hind legs, trying to wrestle the other dog to the ground.

"Wo," Mariah said, holding on to the bus seat to keep her balance. "I'm taking her back before I get knocked down," she added with a grin. Zander held the Tibetan mastiff back until Mariah got inside.

"Alright, let's go, boy," Zander said. To his delight, the large mastiff walked well. He went inside, opened the door to his left, and started down a flight of wooden stairs.

"What'd you guys get?" he heard Kylee ask.

"A cane corso," Mariah replied. "Wait till you see what Zander is bringing down." He came to the end of the stairs and stepped into a large room with white-painted walls adorned with several dog pictures. On the ceiling was a large, hand-painted dog mural, the suite's claim to fame. A side entrance was to his left; this was the original basement door. Three dog enclosures were to the right and left of it. Since the kennel was built on a hillside, the basement was above ground, which allowed each enclosure to have a fenced-in outdoor area for the dogs to use.

"Oh my God, he's beautiful!" Kylee said, rushing over and rubbing the dog's long hair.

"Say hello to your new teddy bear," Zander said.

"Are you a great big teddy bear? Are you a great big teddy bear?" Kylee asked in baby talk. "What kind of dog is this anyway?"

"It's a type of bear, actually." Kylee gave Zander a look that said, *I'm not buying it.*

"I knew that," Kylee replied sarcastically, still hugging the dog.

"It's a Tibetan mastiff. First one I've ever seen." The mastiff's big tongue moved across Kylee's face.

"*Eeeww*," Kylee cried, trying to wipe the drool off her face. Zander and Mariah shared a laugh. Excited by the laughter, the two dogs started playing again.

"Let's get these guys inside. Before they pull us down," Mariah suggested, trying to control the large, happy dog as she and Zander put both dogs in the suites.

"Do you guys need help unloading?" Kylee offered.

"We have three dogs left, so sure." Zander accepted. Mariah gave a look of agreement.

"We've had a cane corso and a Tibetan mastiff. Wonder what else is in there?" Kylee said giddily as the three walked up the stairs.

"We probably got the exciting ones first; the others will probably be two labs and a cocker spaniel," Zander said, hoping it wasn't true but not wanting to get his hopes up.

"Is that your final guess?" Mariah asked.

"Yep, what are your girl's picks?"

"What do I get if I win?" Kaylee replied.

"A night with me," Mariah abruptly gave Zander a shocked look. Kylee playfully punched his shoulder.

"Pig," she said as Zander pushed the outside door open.

"OK, in all seriousness. The winner doesn't have to pick up any crap tonight."

"How does that prize include me?" Mariah asked.

Zander thought for a moment. "If you win, me and Kylee will pick up Blaze's poop and feed her for a day."

"I don't want that," Mariah said, crossing her arms.

"What do you want?" Zander asked.

"A night with you," Mariah said in a joking voice.

Zander snickered, then turned to Kylee and said, "See, she's worse than me."

"You're both pigs." Kylee added.

"OK, all jokes aside, what do you want, Mariah?" Zander asked.

"In all seriousness, for one night, I want each of you to wake up at four a.m. to take Blaze outside so I can sleep without interruption."

"Want to take the chance?" Zander asked Kylee.

"Mariah's not winning anyway, so deal!" Kylee agreed.

"Great, my picks are three mutts," Mariah replied.

"That's too vague," Kylee argued.

"No rule against it," Mariah countered.

"We just made one," Zander added. "You can pick mutts, but give me details."

"Fair enough," Mariah conceded. "All three will be large dogs, two with short-haired coats and one with long hair. Now hurry up and pick yours," Kylee thought out loud.

"They've all been big dogs." She snapped her fingers. "A German shepherd, great dane, and rottweiler."

"Let's see who wins," Mariah said, entering the bus. Zander followed behind her. He could hear the sound of dogs moving and excited tails thumping against the crates.

"So the person who gets the most picks right wins, right?"

"Sounds good to me," Mariah replied, slightly turning to look at him.

"What happens if no one gets any right?"

"Nothing; no one wins," Zander answered. Mariah went to the crate at the end of the bus.

"Everyone, close your eyes until it's your turn to look," Kylee quickly said before Mariah reached her crate. Zander went to the crate next to Mariah and closed his eyes. He heard a bark that came from a larger dog.

"OK, Mariah, you first," Zander said.

"Oh, my gosh!" he heard her say.

"What?" Zander opened his eyes but kept his gaze away from the dog in front of him.

"It's an Irish Wolf Hound," Mariah said excitedly, putting her fingers through the grate to let the dog sniff.

"My turn," Zander said.

"Nope, ladies first," Kylee said, looking down at her cage. "Um." Kylee sounded confused. She looked at the dog for a few moments, then stood up and said, "OK, I don't know what this is. It looks like a dingo."

"I hope not," Mariah responded with slight concern. Kylee again looked at the dog.

"A basenji, maybe?" she continued in a confused voice.

"If it's a mutt, point for me," Mariah reminded. Zander bent down next to Kylee, finding himself just as confused. She wasn't exaggerating. The small cropped ears and light orange coat did remind him of a small dingo.

"This might be a dingo." Zander confirmed, finding himself excited by the possibility. Mariah came over and looked.

"It's a Shiba Inu,"

"Really? Looks too big," Kylee countered.

"She's right, it's not a Shiba Inu. It's too big, and the body's too long," Zander agreed. The dog moved its head back and let out a long, ghostly cry. Zander thought it sounded like a cross between a wolf's howl and a whale song.

"I take it back," Mariah said, now looking as confused as the others. She opened the crate, and the dog came out, taking the time to sniff each of them.

"Let's look at the paperwork." Kylee suggested.

"Carmen already took it downstairs." Mariah reminded her. "It's probably a mutt."

"We don't know that yet," Zander stated. Mariah pulled out her phone.

"I'm asking the Internet." Mariah held the phone a few inches from her face and said, "Dog breeds that look like Dingos and make howling sounds." She looked at the dog while waiting for the results to load. "It's saying this is a New Guinea singing dog." Mariah showed Zander and Kylee the photo. Zander looked at it. The photo made him recall some online videos he had seen.

"Yep, it's a New Guinea singing dog. I can't believe one's actually here."

"I've never heard of that breed," Kylee said.

"Because it's a fancy name for a mutt," Mariah stated.

"No, it's a pure breed, related to Dingos. It's a very rare breed; if I'm not mistaken, I believe it can climb trees."

"You're making that up," Kylee argued.

"We'll have to test it out," Zander said confidently. He looked at Mariah, who was scrolling through her phone.

"OK, you win," she conceded. "Your turn, Zander." Zander went over to the final cage and crouched down. He sighed. "It's a rottweiler."

"Ha! I win!" Kylee said, doing a quick victory dance. Zander opened the crate door. Instead of bolting out or staying still like most dogs did, the rottweiler put his head through the loop leash and calmly walked out.

"That's a good boy," Zander complimented. He left the bus while Mariah grabbed her dog. The rottweiler stopped momentarily to look around. When they got to the garage, he again stopped. Zander watched in amusement as the rottweiler's head looked around the room. He could hear the sound of his nose sniffing. "I know, gasoline smells bad." Zander commented, giving a slight pull to get the dog moving.

He started to open the door to the suite room when he felt the lead slip from his hand. The kennel erupted in excitement, and Zander chased after him as the rottweiler ran down the halls. *Please don't get outside.* He thought seeing him get on his hind legs pushing at the door that led to the batheing room and exit. "Hey boy, come back here." The rottweiler ran back down the hall towards him. Zander tried to grab him, but he tilted his head, causing him to miss the leash. Zander cursed as the rottweiler ran to the sled dog door and again got on his hind legs to look through the glass. He heard Kylee give a surprised gasp, followed by an amused laugh. "I got him." Zander yelled to Kylee and Mariah, whose dogs were barking in excitement. "Yes, that's the sled dog room. Come on, let's go," he said, feeling a little embarrassed that the dog had gotten away from him in front of Kylee and Mariah. Moments later, the three were in the suite room.

"Let's see where these guys go," Mariah said, looking at the dog charts. She pointed toward the door she was standing by. "The wolfhound goes here," Mariah said to herself, putting the dogs in the suite. He walked around the room, then lifted his leg. "Great," Mariah said dryly.

"What's his name?" Kylee asked.

"Neit?" Mariah read. "I have no idea what it means."

"Neit is right. It's the Irish God of War," Zander confirmed.

"Make love, not war," Kylee joked, bonking the dog on the nose. She walked over to the door next to Mariah.

"Zander, your dog goes here," she said, leading her dog to the next door. The rottweiler started to pull in the direction of the room. Zander tightened his grip on the leash as the dog led him to the room. The rottweiler went inside and sat down.

"This guy's smart." Zander looked at the chart and saw that the dog's name was Matrix. "Good boy, Matrix," Zander said, rubbing his head. "You're smart, smarter than those two at least."

"If that's the case, how dumb are you?" Mariah retaliated.

"Smarter than the three of you," Zander countered.

"You wish," Mariah replied, throwing a stuffed dog toy at him.

"Alright Echo I'll see you in a bit. You can sing for me later. Let's see what the other dogs' names are," Kylee suggested, walking over to the other charts. "The Ridgeback is Hexum, the cane corso is Athena, and the mastiff is Goliath. How appropriate." Athena was sniffing around her new enclosure. Goliath was relaxing on his cot. Echo and Neit were on their hind legs, their tails wagging and barking every once in a while. Matrix sat in front of the chain-link fence door, his face slowly moving in a circle around it.

"What is he doing?" Kylee asked.

"Maybe he sees a ghost?" Zander teased.

"OK, we can play with these guys later. We have things to do," Mariah said, walking towards the stairs.

"Yeah, Kylee, let's get our play group started," Zander said, lightly smacking her on the back.

"I was waiting for you," Kylee replied, following him. As the door closed, Zander heard a snapping sound. He held it open a crack to listen.

"You OK, Zander?" He heard Kylee ask.

"Yeah, did you hear anything a few seconds ago?"

"No." Kylee replied. "What did you hear?"

"It sounded like metal snapping." Zander reentered the suite. He looked around the room and saw nothing out of the ordinary.

"Everything looks alright to me." Kylee said, standing beside him. "Maybe it came from upstairs?" Zander checked several of the gate latches and double-checked the room while Kylee talked to the dogs.

"I guess you're right." Zander said still feeling unsettled by the sound, but everything was fine. "Let's get the play group started." After they exited, he glanced at the room again. Matrix met his gaze, not having moved the entire time. *Weird dog.* He thought before closing the door.

Chapter 4

For the rest of the day, it was business as usual at Snowy Hills Kennels. Ethan and Kelly spent the day exercising and training sled dogs, while Zander and Kylee did play groups and walked dogs on shoveled paths. When the walks were finished, the staff started cleaning any messes and made sure the dogs would be settled in for the night. Kylee enjoyed her winnings and was sure to supervise Zander's cleaning of the kennels in her section. Mariah and Carmen had spent the day answering phone calls, admitting, and checking out dogs. When four o'clock came around, Carmen remained in the lobby to finish the day's paperwork. Mariah went upstairs to the dog kitchen, pulled a large amount of stainless-steel dog bowls from the drying rack, and started to prepare the evening meals. She went down the client dog feeding list, creating a stack for the left side, then a stack for the dogs on the right side. Mariah paused when she got to a Labrador mix named Duncan. His feeding instructions read. *Cooked prime rib in the fridge. Please give half the container along with a baked potato.*

"This dog eats better than me," Mariah muttered to herself as she put the potato and steak in the microwave. Duncan's owner, Arthur Lawrence, was wealthy and probably fed Duncan like this every day. Duncan normally stayed in the suites, but they were reserved by the new client before Duncan's appointment was booked, which made Mariah very glad she wasn't working when Arthur made the appointment. Arthur was known to get fussy when things didn't go his way. The smell and sound of sizzling steak made her want to eat it herself as she placed the food in a bowl. When she finished, Mariah put the food bowls on a cart, then went into Kylee and Zander's section. Zander was scooping dog poop from a cage floor, while Kylee went behind him, spraying disinfectant.

"Food's on top," Mariah said before returning to the kitchen. She made the food for the sled dogs. This took a lot less time because each dog got a mix of two different dog foods. One helped build muscle, and the other improved the dog's skin and gave them a shiny coat. After handing it out, Mariah made up meals for the suite dogs. Mariah looked at the feeding instructions, wondering how crazy the list was going to be; if someone was going to book their dogs in the suites, she was sure they would be fed like kings. To her surprise, all the dogs were scheduled to get the type of dog food the kennel offered. She defrosted some hamburger and rolled it into small balls, placing a calming and anxiety-relieving tablet in each one. It was kennel policy to give each new dog these pills to help them adjust on their first night. Mariah entered the suite area, placed all the bowls at the doors, and started handing them out. Athena jumped up and down, quickly eating her food. Hexum sniffed at the food, then slowly started to eat. Goliath barked in excitement when Mariah opened the door. Due to his size, he had a larger bowl than the others; despite this, his face nearly covered the bowl when he ate. Neit was sleeping, but quickly got up when he smelled the food. When Mariah opened Echo's door, she jumped at her, placing her paws on her stomach, and licked her arm.

"Thank you," Mariah said, rubbing her head. When she got to Matrix's suite, he was sitting on his cot with his front paws crossed. "Matrix, time to eat," she said, shaking the bowl. He got up and sniffed the food. Mariah closed the door. He looked up at her with half-mooned eyes. *OK, he's food aggressive,* Mariah thought, backing away. She snapped her finger and gave him a wink. "I'll leave you to it." Matrix barked. "Sorry," she said with a smile, knowing the finger snapping was a dumb idea. Matrix bit down on the ball of hamburger. He looked right at Mariah and flicked his tongue, sending the ball of hamburger onto the floor in front of her. "Smarty, you smelled the pills, didn't you?" Matrix tilted his head slightly and winked at her. Shocked, Mariah took several steps back. A nervous feeling came over her. *Did he just wink at me to let me know he knew about the pill?* She looked at Matrix. The way he was standing made all his muscles stand out. For the first time, she noticed he looked several inches taller than a normal rottweiler and was more muscular. The way he was looking at her worried her. It was like he was saying. "Yeah, I knew. Don't try that again." Mariah tossed the meatball inside the suite again. It hit the floor a few feet from where Matrix was sitting. He got up, went over to it, and used his paw to bat it in the drain. Mariah picked it up again.

"You aren't going to eat this, are you?" Mariah asked, holding it in front of him. Matrix sat back down and looked at her. Deciding to have some fun,

Mariah got ready to toss it again. Matrix gave a low growl, then slammed into the door, barking viciously. The gate shook from the impact. The chain link in the middle pushed forward, nearly striking Mariah in the face. She quickly backed up, nearly tripping over her own feet. *So much for shoving it down his throat.* She took a moment to stare at the snarling rottweiler biting at the fencing before leaving. *This dog has issues,* she thought. Moments later, she was back in the lobby. Carmen was typing away on the computer.

"You OK?" Carmen asked as Mariah sat down.

"I think that dog Matrix has issues," she replied.

"The rottweiler?" Carmen asked. She stopped her work and looked at Mariah. "Is that why you look freaked out?" Mariah was hesitant to tell Carmen what happened, but then decided there was no harm in doing so.

"Yeah, I was giving him his anxiety meds and he spit the hamburger out. He didn't even try to chew it. He sniffed it for a moment, then spit it out."

"What? That's what you're worried about." Carmen laughed.

"That's not what worried me. It's the way he was looking at me, like he knew the whole time."

"Did you try shoving it?"

"No! He growled and tried to attack me." Mariah threw her hands up. "That was it for me." Carmen got up.

"I'll go give it a try."

"Carmen, I don't know if that's a good idea."

"What harm is looking at the dog going to do?" Mariah realized how she was sounding; she had been snapped at and even bitten before. She couldn't figure out why this was bothering her so much.

"You're right I'll come with you. We're not expecting any clients, right?"

"Nope, we're done for the day." Moments later, Mariah and Carmen were back in the suite room. Carmen was holding a fresh ball of hamburger. Matrix's meal was finished; he was sleeping on his cot on his side.

"Matrix, buddy, you want a treat?" Carmen asked in baby talk. Matrix got up and wagged his tail. Mariah felt her body tense as Carmen opened the suite door.

"Carmen, be careful," Mariah said, readying her small bottle of pepper spray. Matrix went up to Carmen, greeting her like any friendly dog would do. Carmen rubbed his back.

"That's a good boy. Here, you want a treat?" She held the newly prepared medicated hamburger ball in her hand. Matrix sniffed. Mariah put her finger on the bottle's trigger. Matrix gave the hamburger meat a lick, then quickly ate it. Afterwards, he licked Carmen on the cheek. Carmen turned to Mariah, still petting him.

"OK, maybe I'm crazy," Mariah said, embarrassed. "Carmen, step away from him a second. I want to see if he has a problem with me."

"Could be. Maybe you look like someone who mistreated him." Carmen stepped back, and Mariah approached the suite. To her surprise, Matrix behaved the same; the look of malice was gone. Only a happy dog stared back at her.

"Matrix, why were you good for her and bad for me?" Matrix continued to wag his tail and dance around happily. Mariah cautiously opened the suite gate.

Matrix went up to her and licked her hand. She petted him on the head. "I don't know why he acted that way before." Mariah admitted.

"Could have been a lot of things. The other dogs barking, the way you were standing."

"I'm still going to write 'use caution' on his chart," Mariah said, closing the gate.

"Fair enough. You all done in here?"

"Yeah, I've got to do meds," Mariah replied as she wrote on Matrix's chart.

"I'm almost done with check-ins. I'll help you after that."

"I'll probably be done before you; the list isn't that long," Mariah replied. As Carmen walked up the stairs, Mariah again looked at Matrix. He was sitting down, giving her the same look he had before, and this time she was sure she saw a wicked smile on his face. A disturbing thought entered her mind. *Did he fake all that just to make me look crazy? Or is my illness returning?* That frightened her more. Concerned, she took two steps toward him. Matrix locked eyes with hers; his mouth wrinkled as he bared his teeth at her.

"Carmen!" Mariah shouted. When Carmen started coming down the steps, Matrix started panting and wagging his tail. For a moment, Mariah felt her breath leave her. She had to be going crazy; there was no way this dog was toying with her like this.

"What's up?" Carmen asked, snapping Mariah out of her thoughts.

"Sorry, I didn't mean for you to come down." Mariah said as they started up the stairs again. "I was curious if the owner mentioned any behavior problems with him."

"He didn't say anything to me. He was in a hurry, something about a business trip. He pretty much handed the dogs to me and left."

"What was he like?"

"He was friendly enough, a middle-aged guy. I'd say in his early 40s or late thirties. Why do you ask?"

"I was just curious why he owned so many rare breeds."

"Like I said, he was in a hurry, so I really didn't get a chance to talk to him; he handed me the dogs, filled out the paperwork, and left." Not wanting to get the issue stuck in her mind, Mariah didn't speak of it anymore and went on with her duties.

***

By six, everything for the day was done. Everyone went to the kitchen for dinner, which was grilled barbecued chicken with mashed potatoes and a fruit basket. After dinner, Shawn went to his room, and Carmen took a hot essential oils bath. Kylee and Mariah relaxed on a couch while Ethan and Zander played a round of pool and Benjamin and Kelly played a board game. Zander could already hear Kelly correcting Benjamin on some minor game rule he had broken, then saw Mariah shaking her head at Kylee. He smiled, noticing Kylee making a talking motion with her hand, before going back to reading her book.

"What's so funny?" Ethan asked, hitting and missing the pocket.

"Kylee was just making faces," he replied, not wanting to say she was making fun of Kelly with her in the room. "So, when are you leaving for vet school?" Zander asked as he put the 13-striped ball into the left pocket.

"I'm starting in the fall semester, so my last day will be the end of August.

"We'll need someone new to crack jokes," Zander said as he put the eight ball in the right corner pocket.

"I'll be around for a while yet. Good game," Ethan said, putting up his hand for a high five.

"Same to you," Zander replied. "Want to go another round?"

"Sorry, no, I'm going to head upstairs to watch some videos."

"Alright, see you tomorrow." The two slapped hands again. Ethan went upstairs, knowing Kylee and Mariah had no interest in playing, Zander put his pool stick away, then walked over to the couch.

"What are you two up to?" he asked.

"I'm watching a show. Care to join me?" Mariah replied, patting the seat next to her.

"What are you watching?" Zander asked with interest.

"Chef Architect. It's a show where four teams of two have to make themed buildings or statues out of food."

"Life size?" Zander asked in a joking manner.

"Come over and see," Mariah replied, smiling in a cute way.

"Nah," Zander replied. "Cooking shows never interested me. What are you doing, Kylee?"

"I'm reading *The Cross and the Pentagram*," Kylee replied briefly, looking up at him.

"Is it any good?" She nodded her head, yes. He could tell she wanted to keep reading, so he sat down, pulled out his tablet, and started looking over sports articles. Around half an hour went by, with no one saying much. Benjamin and Kelly finished their game and went upstairs. Mariah was enjoying the ending of her show when Zander said. "Well, that's a disturbing article."

"What is?" Mariah asked as she and Kylee looked with interest.

"You know that radio station a few miles from here that burned down earlier today?"

"We saw it, remember?" Kylee reminded.

"I know that," Zander replied. "It looks like one of the hosts committed a murder suicide."

"You're kidding." Kylee said, her face showing she was sure he was joking. Mariah, on the other hand, looked concerned.

"No seriously, Kylee." Zander turned the tablet around. The article read: LOCAL RADIO HOSTS MURDERED IN MURDER SUICIDE.

"What happened?" Mariah asked. Her voice having a slight tremble in it.

"At the station, they found Michelle Lee shot in the head outside the radio station, and Kyle Nottingham mangled near his truck, which had been disabled."

"What do you mean, mangled?" Kylee asked. She started to fidget nervously. Zander found himself enjoying making his two friends nervous. *Nothing like giving them something to think about tonight.* Zander thought as he continued to read the news article.

"Kyle Nottingham was found with deep lacerations all over his body." Zander shot a glance at Kylee and Mariah to see if that had shaken them. Both were looking at him intently. "The other DJ, Brian Clint, was found a mile away from the station with a shotgun and suicide note that confessed to the murders."

"I listened to them on the radio all the time; they always seemed like such good friends. Why would he do that?" Kylee asked sadly. Zander searched the article again.

"The note said something about a love triangle. I guess Michelle chose Kyle, so Brian killed them both for revenge, then committed suicide late last night or early this morning." Mariah let out a quick gasp. Kylee and Mariah both looked at each other. Fright forming in both girls eyes.

"No, that couldn't have been what we heard." Kylee said, shaking her head like she was trying to convince herself.

"What are you talking about?" Zander asked, realizing they knew something he didn't. Mariah's face turned serious. Zander knew the look; it was the look she gave when she was about to say something important.

"Zander, I need you to promise me to keep what I'm about to tell you between the three of us." Mariah moved her index finger to each of them.

"OK." He put the tablet down, wondering what Mariah was about to say.

"When Kylee and I got here, Kylee was walking Blaze, and we heard two gunshots... We thought it was a hunter, but now I'm not so sure." Zander looked at both girls, wondering if they were trying to turn the tables and scare him. Mariah maybe, but he knew Kylee couldn't keep a straight face if she were in on it. She looked nervous, as if she were trying to figure the situation out herself.

"It probably was a hunter; this happened last night. If you did hear him blowing his brains out, he probably wouldn't have fired twice." Zander checked the article to see if he could find the exact time of death. He noticed another new story on the sidebar. "Turns out a local hunter didn't come home this morning."

"What do you mean?" Mariah asked.

"There's not much information on it; only a local hunter, Bret Stoffel, went hunting this morning and never came home. Police are investigating the possibility of a missing person's case."

"What about the other sound?" Kylee mentioned. Mariah glared at her.

"What sound?" Zander asked. His curiosity and confusion growing.

"It was nothing," Mariah quickly shot back.

"It was odd," Kylee stressed, sounding very uneasy. Zander saw her look toward the window. He looked, seeing nothing but a snow-covered field with the outline of trees in the distance.

"Think it's out there?" He asked. "Could be watching us right now." Kylee groaned and looked away from the window. Zander reached over and closed the blind. Kylee smiled in appreciation.

"OK, seriously, drop it, Kylee; I don't want rumors starting around here." Mariah said in a serious tone.

"What are you talking about?" Zander asked again. "I won't say anything to anyone." Mariah remained silent for a moment.

"After the shots, we heard a loud call we couldn't identify; that's all."

"What did it sound like?" Zander pressed, finding himself interested.

"Like a large primate, that's the best way I can describe it," Kylee replied. She glanced at Mariah, who huffed and gave her an annoyed look.

"You heard Bigfoot?" Zander asked skeptically. Mariah lightly smacked the couch arm.

"No one said that; we only heard a sound, and we didn't know what made it."

"Hold on a second," Zander said with a grin, picking his tablet back up.

"What are you doing?" Kylee asked.

"I'm playing a supposed Bigfoot call."

"Seriously?" Mariah said in a dry tone.

"Yes, we need to find out what you heard," Zander replied, still grinning. "The first video's starting." Mariah and Kylee listen. The video started with the sound of trees moving in the wind, then a series of loud howls and woops occurred.

"Did it sound like that?" Zander asked when the video ended.

"Kind of. From what I remember, it was a little deeper and more blood-curdling." The two looked at Mariah, who had beads of sweat forming on her forehead.

"Oh, Mariah thinks that's what she heard." Zander said in a teasing voice, not taking the situation too seriously. Mariah stood up.

"OK, you two, stop thinking about this! There's no such thing as Bigfoot or the kennel ghost; it's all imagined!" She briefly motioned to the tablet. "Yes, it sounds a little similar, but we all know it wasn't Bigfoot."

"What was it, then?" Kylee asked, giving Zander a light nudge with her elbow. Mariah slammed both arms to her side and quickly replied.

"I don't know a bear, a moose, a psychopath using a recording!"

"Sorry, we were just having fun," Zander said, realizing Mariah was getting upset. The look of irritation on Mariah's face faded.

"No, I'm sorry. I shouldn't have snapped." She sat back down and continued. "If we want to scare each other, that's fine, but please don't go spreading this type of stuff around to the other staff. It will only cause drama we don't need."

"I'm not saying its Bigfoot, but if there's a chance a dangerous animal is roaming around the woods, we might want to let the others know." Zander suggested. Mariah gave a slight huff of frustration. She sat back down and put a hand on her head, then looked at Zander.

"What do you want me to say, Zander?" Sarcasm formed in her voice. "Hey, everyone, we have a giant man eating bear on the loose, or maybe it's a Bigfoot? If you happen to see it around the kennel, let me or Carmen know."

"How about saying people have been seeing a bear in the area, so let someone know if you happen to see it?" Zander suggested. Hoping that would calm Mariah, who he could tell was getting more stressed about the situation.

"That sounds like a good thing to say," Kylee agreed.

"Ok fine." Mariah said more relaxed. "I'll mention something about a bear. But if either of you say anything about a Bigfoot or a man eating bear, even as a joke, I'm going to be pissed."

"OK," Zander and Kylee said at the same time. The three sat and talked for about half an hour. They had finished a conversation about going to an upcoming winter light show when Kylee yawned.

"Well, I'm going to bed. Goodnight," Kylee said as she got up.

"I'll clean out your mug," Zander offered.

"Thanks," Kylee replied, drinking the last of her tea. After Kylee left, Mariah asked.

"You staying up for a while, Zander?"

"I was going to go upstairs and watch some TV for a while, but if you want to talk some more, I can stay."

"I was planning to stay down here a bit before I take Blaze out for the last time tonight. If you wanted to keep me company, that would be great." Mariah again patted the cushion next to her.

"What are friends for?" Zander said, sitting next to her.

"You did a great job on your first day in charge," he complimented.

"It was a little hectic, but I knew I could do it."

"You glad you made Carmen your assistant?" Zander asked. Knowing Mariah, she was unsure about how the two of them would work together. Personally, he thought she made the right choice. She was more experienced than Mariah. During Tiffany's time as supervisor, when Tiffany or Kelly would call out or were on vacation, Carmen would act as second in command.

"Yeah, Carmen's great. She helped me out a lot today." Mariah leaned in a little closer to him. "I also learned she hated Tiffany as much as we did."

"Maybe one day we can let her in on our secret?" Zander suggested.

"No, not even Kylee knows about that; let's keep it that way," Mariah said seriously.

"Wonder what Kylee would do if she did find out?" Zander commented, honestly not having any idea how she would react to it.

"She would probably say something like. *That's horrible. I can't believe you did that*, then forget about it a few minutes later. She had no love for Tiffany either." Both remained silent for a moment until Mariah asked.

"So you still thinking of staying here and training sled dogs, or are you eventually planning on moving to the lower forty-eight states?"

"For now, I'm planning on staying right here, maybe eventually taking over the sled dog training program. Eventually I might move to another state, but for now this is home, and I'm in no hurry to leave." Mariah looked out the window.

"Don't you ever get tired of the cold and snow?"

"No, it may be cold here, but it's all I ever knew. If I moved to a place like Florida or a warmer state, I'd probably roast and be miserable in the heat." Zander looked out the window himself, admiring the beauty of the snow-covered field, the green glow of the northern lights above, and the snow-covered pine trees in the forest. He pointed to the sky. "At times, the cold can be just as beautiful as any beach."

"Not true. Nothing beats a warm day on the beach, which is why I'm moving to Florida as soon as I can." *Have fun.* Zander thought having no desire to go to a tropical state. For the next hour, the two had small conversations about life events, interests, and work. At fifteen minutes to eleven, Zander got up and said.

"Well, I'm going to be turning in for the night. Good night; see you tomorrow."

"Night," Mariah replied, getting up herself to let Blaze out. Zander took another moment to stare at the snow-covered field, then went to his room. The room was the size of a small hotel room with a bed, dresser, and nightstand. A person from each shift shared a room, so no one had any personal furniture. From his window, he saw Mariah walking with Blaze a few feet from the building. She looked up at him, giving him a wave. He returned it. He could hear the distant barking of dogs from the kennel. A feeling of dread and worry began to come over him. For some reason, he wanted Mariah back inside, behind locked doors.

"I can't believe you're letting that story get to you." He said to himself, seeing nothing but the forest and snow illuminated by the moonlight. Mariah walked back inside; he heard the door shut under him, and yet the feelings of dread and terror remained. Zander realized it wasn't the outside world causing them but the dogs barking. A sound he had heard hundreds of times. *What's going on?* He thought, wondering why the barking was making him nervous. He heard Mariah's footsteps coming up the stairs and quickly shook the feeling off as nerves. He turned off the lights and laid down for the night.

CHAPTER 5

Mariah woke up to Blaze licking her face. An unfortunate morning wakeup call that came included with the dog. Mariah looked at her clock, which read four-eleven.

"Blaze, it's too early. Go back to sleep," she said groggily, pulling the covers over her head. Undeterred, Blaze started barking, wedging her nose under the covers to lick her face. Giving up the fight, Mariah threw the covers off and got up. She walked Blaze to her kennel and put her inside. *One of the perks of working here is that I don't have to go outside in five-degree weather for Blaze's potty breaks.* Blaze ran outside to do her business. Mariah could see snow getting kicked up as Blaze rolled in it. Mariah had thought about leaving Blaze in the kennel all night, but she knew she'd miss her best friend, even if she was a pain sometimes. She noticed Kelly's dog Bee's kennel was still empty. *Probably sound asleep upstairs,* Mariah thought. "Why can't you be more like that?" she asked Blaze, who had come back inside. Mariah grabbed a pre-measured bag of Blaze's food and put it in Blaze's bowl, then went back to her room and went back to sleep.

Mariah's alarm went off at seven. She stretched, got up, and went to the bathroom. Kelly had worked out a morning bathroom system. She would use it from six thirty to seven, then Mariah from seven to seven thirty, Carmen after her, then Kylee, who liked to sleep in as long as possible. Mariah loved the idea. To her, nothing was worse than wanting to get ready in the morning and having to wait for the bathroom. She showered and brushed her hair and teeth. She'd put her makeup on in her room. She opened the door to see Carmen waiting.

"Morning," Carmen said in a tired voice. Mariah repeated the greeting and went downstairs to breakfast. After eating bacon and eggs, she returned to her room to change into her work clothes, which were blue jeans and a dark green t-shirt with the kennel's name on it, then went to her desk. She looked out the large window that overlooked the front lawn and driveway. Snow drifts had made their way onto the driveway and sidewalks. She found herself staring at the newly fallen snow, looking for any types of large tracks around the kennel building. *What if whatever you heard yesterday got into the kennels and killed all the dogs?* Mariah quickly removed the thought from her head. Don't be silly; bears don't act like that.

"Ready for the day?" Carmen asked, sitting next to her. Mariah jumped slightly, not hearing her come into the room.

"Should be just like any other; I don't even know why we bother with these meetings." Mariah grumbled. Carmen snickered in amusement. "I mean, everything is always the same, and if there is a problem, it was addressed when it happened. I feel like saying the subject of today's meeting is there will be no more meetings." That made Carmen burst into laughter. *Oh, the look on Kelly's face,* Mariah thought with a grin. While waiting for everyone, Mariah printed out the walk and bath list for the day. Soon, everyone began entering the lobby. She glanced at Shawn, who refused to make eye contact with her, then clapped her hands to end the low chatter coming from everyone.

"Alright, the only big announcement for the day is a sled dog team is coming back on Friday, and two are going out this coming Monday. So, Carmen," she said, turning to her. "Either today or tomorrow, be sure the dogs are bathed and looking nice for the customers." She turned her attention to Benjamin and Shawn. "Keep up on snow and ice removal as needed throughout the day, and Shawn, at some point today, check all the heaters to make sure they are working and we have replacement parts on site. I want heater checks done every other day from now on."

"I'll get to it," Shawn said, keeping his head down. *Looks like he learned his lesson.* Mariah thought pleased with the outcome. "The rest of you know what to do; let me know if you run into any problems. Meeting adjourned." Mariah playfully relaxed in her chair. Ethan walked up and grabbed the sled dog walk and training list. Zander grunted softly and gave Mariah a look that said, *aren't you forgetting something?* Mariah felt a wave of frustration forming inside her. She knew Zander was right, but at the same time, mentioning what he was thinking would undoubtedly cause problems. Mariah shook her head no to Zander.

"Mariah, it's the right thing to do," Zander said seriously.

"I agree," Kylee added.

"What are you two talking about?" Carmen asked. Knowing her friends were right, Mariah said.

"Hey everyone, one more thing." She paused to gather her thoughts. "During your walks today, keep an eye out for a bear."

"What?" Ethan replied in a surprised voice.

"When we were driving here yesterday, Kylee and I think we saw one," Mariah said quickly, hoping no one else would ask about it.

"Should we call the wildlife department?" Kelly asked with a nervous tone in her voice.

"Why? It's not like bears are uncommon around here," Zander countered.

"A bear around a kennel should be reported," Kelly said seriously. "What if it breaks down a fence or attacks someone?"

"I agree with Kelly," Shawn added.

"A bear's not going to come around here with all the dogs," Ethan stated confidently. *Great, I knew this would happen.* Mariah thought. Regretting she said anything. Benjamin walked up to the desk.

"Ms. Mariah, if I see the bear, will it try to eat me?"

"No, Benjamin, as long as you leave the bear alone, you will be fine. If you see one, come inside and tell someone." Mariah then spoke up before an argument started. "Everyone. I want to reword what I said. No one has seen a bear around here. Kylee and I didn't see a bear. We only heard what sounded like a bear." She looked at Kylee, who agreed with her statement, then looked at Kelly and said, "Being a responsible leader, I wanted to tell everyone to keep an eye out just in case one is roaming around the area." Kelly returned an aggravated look.

"Come on, let's get started." Ethan said, giving Kelly a friendly pat on the back to break the tension.

"Thanks for the warning." Kelly replied politely and left with Ethan. Shawn and Benjamin left with them.

"Let's get started, Kylee," Zander said, grabbing the client's walk list.

"Right behind you," she said playfully. Kylee and Zander left. Carmen spun her chair around to face Mariah.

"Remember last year when a grizzly bear was seen near town?"

"Of course I do. Are you saying it's the same bear?"

"No, I just don't remember you being that freaked out about it; in fact, you thought it would be fun to see it walking around."

"Ok, what's your point?" Mariah asked, hoping the subject would be over soon.

"I'm just saying I know you, and a bear wouldn't freak you out that much."

"I never said I was freaked out. Being the supervisor, I wanted to let everyone know what I heard to cover myself in case something does happen," Mariah replied, hoping that would satisfy Carmen, which it appeared to because she dropped the subject or she knew Mariah didn't want to tell her the truth. After Mariah finished looking over the incoming dog list, she dangled two lists in front of Carmen. "Do you want feed or meds today?" Carmen looked at both lists for a moment, then said.

"I'll take meds; it's easier than making up meals for a hundred dogs."

"Exactly what you'll be doing tomorrow."

"Really?" Carmen replied. "What if I say no, thank you?"

"I can make you do it every day if I want. I'm in charge, remember?" The two shared a quick laugh, then went to work. Mariah made the sled dogs food and handed it out; after that, she checked on the snow removal progress. Benjamin had cleared most of the outdoor steps and was working on the walkway between the kennel and office building.

"You're doing a great job, Benjamin," Mariah complimented. Looking at the half-cleared walkway.

"Thank you," he replied in a slightly tired voice. "Once I finish, I'll start cooking lunch."

"Looking forward to it. I'm going to go in and finish making the doggy's breakfast."

"I saw someone come out of the woods."

"Was it a hunter or a hiker?" Mariah asked, thinking nothing of it.

"I don't know. He had a white deer head; his ribs were sticking out, with blood around the edges. It looked like brown and black animals' skins covered his body."

"What?" Mariah asked. Shocked by Benjamin's horrifically detailed description. Benjamin didn't respond; he only put his head down.

"I'm sorry; I didn't mean to make you upset."

"Just don't bring that up again," Mariah replied, walking back to the kennel. She looked toward the forest and froze in her tracks. Standing right outside the tree line was the being Benjamin had described. The eye sockets in the deer skull glowed a reddish orange. His long, boney arms outstretched towards her. The deer's mouth opened, making an unearthly cry. *No, not now.* Mariah thought. She was scared out of her mind. Her breathing rapidly increased. She closed her eyes and repeated. "It's not real. It's not real." She felt someone touch her shoulder. She let out a scream of fright. Shawn stepped back in alarm.

"Mariah, are you OK?" he asked. "You're standing still, chanting to yourself."

"I'm fine," Mariah replied, lying through her teeth. "I'm going back inside; nice job on the walkways," she said quickly before rushing off. When she got to the kennel kitchen, she focused on preparing the client's dog food. *I wonder what Duncan's getting this time.* She was trying to keep her mind off the situation. Duncan was scheduled to get two eggs and three strips of bacon; under the meal was a highlighted note: *please have a chicken pizza ordered to the kennel for Duncan's dinner. Are you serious?* Mariah thought. Once the meals were made, she went to the client wing and started putting the bowls on top of the cages. Zander was opening the sliders to let dogs back into clean enclosures. Kylee was kicking dirty bedding into a pile.

"Hey, food's on top!" Mariah yelled over the barking dogs.

"Thanks." Zander acknowledged opening another slider. When she reached where Zander was working, she said in a cute, flirty voice.

"You won't believe what Duncan's getting for dinner."

"Filet mignon with a side of caviar?" Zander guessed. Mariah snickered and shook her head.

"No, today I have to order him a pizza for dinner," Mariah rolled her eyes.

"Duncan's owner has mental issues." Mariah cringed as the thoughts of what happened outside came flooding back to her. "What?" Zander asked as he started handing out the feed.

"All nothing. By the way, I was thinking, since I'm getting pizza anyway, why don't I order some for the team? Let's have a pizza party night."

"Sounds good to me," Zander agreed.

"I was thinking of getting three; what would you like?"

"Kylee, we're having pizza night; what kind do you want?" Zander shouted.

"I like it simple, plain cheese," Kylee said, looking grossed out as a mixture of pee and water dripped from the bedding she was holding.

"I'll have meat lovers," Zander requested.

"I'll keep those requests in mind," Mariah promised. "Well, I'd better get down to the office." Mariah made a quick detour to see what type of pizza Ethan and Kelly wanted, then returned to the front desk. Carmen was already there. Before sitting down, Mariah saw she had a weather website open.

"How much snow are we getting?" Mariah asked, knowing more snow was coming.

"Tomorrow and Thursday are sunny; Friday, a snow storm is supposed to come through with eight to ten inches expected."

"Good amount," Mariah said, annoyed by the news but not surprised. She looked at the clock on the computer; it was a little over a quarter past eight, around half an hour before she needed to open. "We never got the weight on the new dogs in the suites. Want to do it before we open up?"

"Might as well. I'll go grab one," Carmen offered. She grabbed a slip leash and headed to the kennels. While she waited, Mariah looked at the client pick-up and drop-off list again. It would be a slower day, which was normal on weekdays. She heard the outside door open. She got out of her seat and turned on the pet scale. It made a beep as Carmen returned with the cane corso.

"Alright, Athena, hop on the scale," Mariah said. Patting it. Carmen walked Athena on the scale, who was happily wagging her tail. She jumped slightly to give Mariah a lick.

"Athena, you need to stay still, buddy," Carmen said happily. Mariah grabbed a dog biscuit, which got Athena's attention.

"Athena, sit." Athena sat down. She remained still long enough for Mariah to read her weight, which was ninety-eight pounds. "Good girl," Mariah said, handing her the treat. Athena took it and ate it in one bite. Mariah recorded the weight, while Carmen took Athena back to her suite and returned with Echo. Echo jumped around at first; being a smaller dog, Carmen lifted her on the scale and gently held her still. Mariah got the weight, which was twenty-seven pounds.

"I really want to see this girl climb a tree," Carmen commented.

"We can take her outside later," Mariah promised. "Have you heard her sing?"

"No, she stayed quiet on the bus ride."

"Echo, sing," Mariah said, doing her best to imitate the howl. Echo got excited and started jumping around, knocking over one of the kennel's artificial trees. Mariah gave a playful huff.

"Echo," Carmen said, giving Echo's leash a slight tug. "Come, time to go." Mariah picked up the tree and reset the scale. A few moments later, she could hear Carmen talking, but didn't hear a dog with her. "Mariah giving you a heads up; I'm bringing in Matrix." Mariah felt a feeling of uneasiness come over her.

"OK, bring him in." The lobby door opened, Carmen walked in. Matrix sat down in front of her. Seeing him caused Mariah's feeling of uneasiness to turn to fear.

"This guy's unusually calm and smart," she said. He basically put himself on the leash. Knowing dogs could sense feelings of fear and uneasiness, Mariah tried to calm herself. *Why does he bother you so much? He's a dog with behavioral issues; you've dealt with dozens of these before. Just treat him like a normal dog, because that's what he is.*

"Are you a smart boy?" Mariah asked in baby talk. She retreated behind the desk when Matrix started to walk forward.

"Matrix, hop on the scale," Carmen said, patting it. Matrix climbed onto the scale and sat down. "Well, that was easy," Carmen acknowledged, impressed.

"He sure is smart," Mariah agreed, holding onto her can of pepper spray.

"I wish all dogs were this easy." Carmen let go of the leash to get a more accurate weight reading.

"You sure that's a good idea?" Mariah quickly asked.

"Where's he going to go?" Mariah felt her uneasiness come back. "One hundred and thirty-seven pounds."

"OK, Matrix You can get off now," Carmen said. Matrix climbed off the scale and sat next to her. Carmen grinned in amusement. Figuring now was a good time for a peace offering Mariah reached into the jar of dog treats and handed him one. Matrix ate it, then walked behind the desk. Mariah's first instinct was to run, but she remained still, knowing running might trigger Matrix's prey drive. "No, you can't go back there," Carmen said, grabbing the leash. Matrix wagged his tail, only standing a few feet from Mariah. She noticed his eyes seemed focused on the computers. He walked into the desk leg space and started sniffing at the wires.

"Matrix, don't mess with those," Mariah said, grabbing at his collar on instinct. Matrix gave a loud bark and turned his head. Mariah quickly moved back. She raised the pepper spray, getting ready for the attack she knew was coming. Matrix locked eyes with her. He huffed and gave her a look like he was daring her to spray him. His gaze moved over to Carmen, who was reaching for the leash she had dropped. Before she could grab it, Matrix casually walked towards Mariah, who fired a small blast of spray. Matrix's head quickly went down. The trail of spray hit the wall. Mariah was about to fire again when Matrix rushed by her. His full weight slammed into her leg, knocking her against the wall. Mariah and Carmen both screamed in concern. Mariah covered her face, waiting for him to charge again. Instead, he went over to the large window and looked through it.

"Mariah, are you OK?" Carmen asked, concerned.

"I'm fine," Mariah confirmed, still worried about what he was going to do.

"Matrix, it's OK? Do you want another treat?" Carmen asked, tossing one to him. Matrix ignored the treat; he didn't even look at it or her. He remained on his hind legs, looking out the window.

"That's the kennel where you and the other doggies are kept." Carmen said daring to move closer. Mariah moved back, not wanting to agitate him anymore. "May I look out the window with you?" Carmen asked, standing next to him. Matrix huffed. He got back on all fours, put the slip lead in his mouth, and sat down in front of Carmen. He flicked his tongue, dropping the leash in front of her. Carmen cautiously picked it up. Matrix licked her hand and wagged his tail. Carmen started petting him. "I see what you mean; what was that about?"

"I don't know. Maybe he doesn't like his collar touched, or maybe he just hates me," Mariah replied, looking for a reasonable explanation.

"Maybe a girl with red hair abused him in the past." Carmen suggested. "He seems happy now."

"Write do not touch his collar on his chart." Mariah squatted down. "Matrix," she said in baby talk, tossing another treat to him. Matrix responded with a low growl. "OK, he hates me." Mariah conceded.

She found herself feeling relieved that he was acting consistent.

"Well, I'm going to take him back now." Mariah watched Carmen lead him away. *The sooner you're gone, the better.* She thought. Carmen briefly stopped to open the door. When she did, Matrix turned, looked right at Mariah, and she swore he winked at her. Mariah felt a lump in her throat. *Am I seeing things, or did he really do that?* She questioned. She used the several minutes Carmen was gone to calm herself. Later, when she was weighing the other dogs, Mariah couldn't help but keep thinking about how Matrix had acted yesterday, and she swore he winked at her a few minutes ago. Like he was taunting her.

"That's the last one," Carmen said, holding onto Neit. Mariah looked at the clock, which read ten minutes to nine.

"Not bad timing." Mariah complemented. "I'm going to grab some more coffee before we open. Want some?"

"Sure," Carmen accepted. Before going to the kitchen, she took a detour to visit Blaze. Blaze was outside, trying to eat the small flakes that blew in the wind. Mariah called her and handed her a treat. She looked up, hearing the door open. Kelly came in holding her small Yorkie terrier, Bee. Mariah felt her guard go up, figuring she was about to get a lecture on why she was having problems with Matrix.

"Hey, Carmen told me that dog Matrix was showing aggression towards you, gave you a little bit of a fright. You OK?" She kissed Bee on the head before putting her in an enclosure two down from Blaze's.

"Yeah, I'm fine. He seems to hate me for some reason." Mariah gave a shrug. "Just one of those dogs."

"We all have that one dog that hates us. Remember how Coco was with me?" Kelly reminded.

"Yeah." Mariah said she felt her guard going down. Coco was a small black and white pit bull who loved everyone at the kennel but would become aggressive when he saw Kelly.

"Speaking of the suite dogs, are they getting walked?"

"You don't know?" Mariah teased.

"Strangely enough, I forgot to check; I was busy with the sled dogs yesterday." *Kelly's not bad all the time.* Mariah thought, finding herself enjoying the talk.

"Yes, the client did want walks for the suite dogs." *Which unfortunately includes Matrix.* "I'm going to make it that only Carmen can handle Matrix. When we have some free time today or tomorrow, we'll see how he does with you and Zander."

"If I may suggest, since he's OK with Carmen, have her introduce him to me and Zander."

"That's exactly what I was thinking," Mariah replied, feeling the choice was obvious. "Well, I'm going to get some coffee before we open up."

"Alright, see you at lunch," Kelly replied as they left the room. Kelly went to the main kennel, while Mariah walked to the kitchen. She was still feeling tired and could smell the aroma of freshly brewed coffee. She reached for the pot when she noticed Benjamin was by the stove, holding his hands over one of the lit burners.

"Benjamin, what are you doing?" Mariah asked, alarmed.

"I was outside shoveling, and my hands got cold, so I came inside to warm them up," he replied.

"Well, be careful; don't burn yourself." Mariah grabbed the coffee pot. It made a hiss as she lifted it from the maker.

"I'll make you some more when it's empty. I know you and Carmen like to drink it," Benjamin said.

"Please do," Mariah said, taking a sip and enjoying the feeling of the warm liquid going down her throat. "By the way, Benjamin, I have some good news," she said as she walked over to him. Benjamin looked at her, seemingly eager to hear it.

"After lunch, I'm going to have Zander work with you on dog walking. You can take some of the sled dogs out." Benjamin's face lit up with excitement.

"Really? Thank you, but...well, never mind," Benjamin said bashfully.

"What is it? You can tell me." Benjamin looked right at her, which Mariah found odd because normally he looked down or shifted from side to side when people spoke to him.

"Well, I don't really like that area; there's too many dogs, and all the barking hurts my ears. What about the suite area? It's smaller and quieter." Mariah nearly said no, thinking of Matrix, then remembered the other dogs there. She didn't know why, but she went along with his request.

"OK, I'll let you work in the suites." Mariah's face went from friendly to serious. "But Benjamin, do whatever Zander says, and don't touch any dogs unless Zander says you can."

"I'll do whatever he says, I promise. Thank you so much for letting me work with dogs, Ms. Mariah."

"Please let everything go well." Mariah said to herself. Thoughts of Matrix getting out and attacking Benjamin nearly caused her to run to him and tell him she changed her mind. "No, Zander knows what he's doing; he'll handle it." Mentally satisfied, Mariah went back to her desk work.

CHAPTER 6

Zander put Runway, a brown cocker spaniel, inside her cage. He rubbed his hand across Runway's fur, rubbing off the snowflakes that coated it. He checked his watch; it was nearly twelve-thirty. *Time for lunch.* He thought. A short time later, Zander walked into the office.

"Hey," he said to Mariah.

"Hey," Mariah replied. A bright smile formed on her face. "What are you up to?"

"I'm heading to lunch. Carmen told me what happened with that dog, Matrix. Are you OK?"

"That incident is now famous," Mariah teased. "I'm fine," she assured. "It was scary, but no one was hurt."

"Any idea what set him off?" He asked as he put his lunch start time on the crew sheet.

"I don't understand what's wrong with that dog. It's like he's bipolar; one moment he's completely fine, the next he acts like he's going to bite you." Mariah grumbled, leaning back in her chair. "That dog makes me feel so uneasy. I'll be happy when he's gone."

"When's he leaving?"

"That's a good question," Mariah said, typing Matrix's name into the computer. "Eight-teen days."

"That's not long."

"Not soon enough." *This dog does have her freaked out.* Zander thought never hearing her talk about a dog in this way. "It's like when he watches you, he knows everything you're doing. And that look he gives you, it's like..." For a moment, Zander noticed a frightened look on Mariah's face. "Never mind." Her smile came back. "What are you having for lunch?"

"Like what? You can tell me," Zander replied, knowing something serious was on her mind if she was hesitant to tell him about it. Mariah's fingers tapped the counter, her tongue briefly touched the roof of her mouth.

"It's like he's smarter than a normal dog; in a way, he seems manipulative, and I swear he winked at me today after he was acting aggressive." As much as he tried to control it, he snickered at the comment. "You don't believe me, do you?" Mariah replied with a look of disappointment. Zander took a moment to think of a response.

"I believe you think it's real, but I also think you're looking into it too much."

"Maybe you're right," Mariah agreed, rubbing her head slightly.

"Sorry if this is none of my business, but are you OK? Like in your personal life?"

"Yeah, everything's fine," Mariah replied with a hint of defensiveness in her voice.

"No, what I was asking is, do you think your condition's flaring up again?" Mariah became visibly uneasy. She looked around the room as if double-checking to see if anyone was around, then answered in a whisper.

"No, it's not. I haven't had a serious schizophrenia episode for several years. You know that. Why would you even ask that?" Zander didn't want to push the issue, but he was growing concerned about her. He had researched schizophrenia after Mariah told him she had been struggling with it since she was a child and knew people suffering from schizophrenia could have delusions and hallucinations.

"Mariah, first you're worried about hearing Bigfoot; now you think a dog is evil and plotting against you." An agitated look formed on her face. "I'm saying this as your friend." Zander stressed, hoping he hadn't gone too far. "Just saying it sounds like a schizophrenia episode to me." Mariah leaned back in her chair and threw her hands up.

"Admittedly, I have had hallucinations in the past, but this was different; I never had a hallucination occur on something that was already there, and Kylee heard the strange animal sounds too." Zander watched her as she spoke; she didn't appear to be trying to make stuff up on the spot.

"I believe you," he said sincerely. "I wasn't judging, just making sure you were OK."

"Thanks for asking, but I'm fine." Mariah confirmed her body language, showing she was beginning to relax.

"Hey, amigos," Kylee said, entering the room. "What are you up to?"

"Going to lunch," Zander answered.

"We don't have any clients right now, so I'll join you," Mariah added, leaving her chair.

"Won't be a party without you. You coming, Kylee?"

"Yeah, join us," Mariah said.

"You leave me no choice," Kylee playfully shrugged.

"All Zander. I want to get this out of the way before the fun starts." *You're going to ask me to train Benjamin?* Zander thought, knowing what she was going to say. As he guessed, Mariah's next words were.

"Zander, after lunch, can you take Benjamin to the suite area? I want you to train him on how to clean the suites and take a dog for a walk after that."

"You sure he wouldn't be better off walking a sled dog and someone like Kelly training him?" Zander asked as a last-ditch attempt to get out of it. He had no desire to explain the same thing one hundred times.

"I trust you more than Kelly, and Benjamin admires you."

"A great honor," Kylee teased. Mariah playfully pushed her and continued.

"A small client dog will be better than a husky. Have him walk Echo? She seems like a calm, friendly dog," Mariah suggested. *I'm not getting out of this, am I?* Zander realized. Mariah must have noticed his look of annoyance. "Please. For me?" Mariah asked, giving a cute look.

"Sure," Zander finally conceded.

"Thanks, Zander. You're the best," Mariah said with a grateful smile.

After lunch, Zander pulled out his walkie-talkie. "Benjamin? Benjamin, can you hear me?" He repeated it several times with no answer. *These walkies nev-*

er work. He thought wondering why the kennel didn't spend the money on good-quality walkie-talkies. He put the walkie-talkie back on his belt and went looking for Benjamin, wanting to get this over with. Since employees were responsible for their own lunches, he knew Benjamin would not be in the kitchen; he didn't normally start dinner until three-thirty. He put his winter gear on and went outside, spotting Benjamin spreading salt along the walkways. He walked up to him, avoiding the shovels full of snow Benjamin was tossing. Benjamin looked up and put his shovel to the side.

"Hey, Mariah wanted me to train you on dog walking. Is now a good time to start?" Zander asked in a neutral voice.

"Yes!" Benjamin said eagerly. He turned to the mostly finished sidewalk. "Let me finish this sidewalk, and I'll meet you downstairs."

"OK," Zander agreed. "I'll meet you in the suite area." Fifteen minutes later, Zander was standing inside the suite area, still waiting on Benjamin. *What's taking him so long?* He thought as he headed up the steps to look for him again. Zander returned to the now-finished sidewalk. Benjamin was nowhere to be seen. Discouraged, he went back to the quarters and went into the kitchen. To his annoyance, Benjamin was there, laying out ingredients for dinner. Zander saw unopened taco shells, lettuce, and chips laying on the counter, and a pack of ground beef was laying in the sink.

"Benjamin, what happened?" Zander asked, frustrated. "I thought you were going to meet me in the suite."

"I am, but I wanted to get the dinner ingredients ready first," Benjamin replied nonchalantly.

"Well, do you want to do that or work with dogs?" Zander asked, hoping Benjamin would forget about the dogs.

"No, I'm ready to go." Benjamin replied, going over to the sink to wash his hands. "Sorry to keep you waiting." Too late. Zander thought but didn't say anything. Knowing it was his own fault, he lacked patience.

"Let's go!" Benjamin said excited. He began walking ahead of him at a quick pace. I didn't know you could move that fast. Zander thought. Only ever seeing Benjamin move at a slow, waddle-like pace.

"Zander, you're the best. I'm so glad you're the one training me."

"That's good to know," Zander replied in a dry voice. When they returned to the suite area, Benjamin ran up to Hexum's cage.

"Am I going to walk this dog?" He asked, pointing to him.

"No, you're going to be working with Echo," Zander said, standing near her suite. Echo got up and started wagging her tail. Zander's voice became more serious when he said. "Benjamin, don't touch any of the other dogs, and stay away from the rottweiler." Matrix looked up, like he knew the word rottweiler. Zander looked back at him, trying to see the look Mariah was describing. Matrix drank some water, then went outside. Seems like a normal dog to me. He looked at all the dogs' suites. He was pleased to see there were no messes, which meant less time teaching.

"This is the dog that sings, right?" Benjamin asked, walking up to Echo's cage with a leash.

"Yes. Before we go on a walk, Mariah wanted me to show you how to clean a cage, so we're going to do that first."

"OK," Benjamin agreed, dropping the leash on the ground. The sound of the steel clip hitting the ground made all the dogs, except Matrix, bark with excitement.

"First thing we need to do is get the dogs to the outside portion of the cage. Some dogs go by themselves; others, you need to put a slip lead on them and walk them to the other side." Zander whistled, getting Echo's attention. "Echo, go outside," Zander said in baby talk, pointing to the outside portion of the cage. To his surprise, she listened the first time. "Alright, Benjamin, it's cold outside, so you need to get the work done quickly," Zander said, closing the slider. He went inside, spilled the water in the water bowl in the drain, then lifted the cot. "Do you see a mess anywhere?"

"No, it looks clean." Benjamin replied.

"You're right, if it was dirty, you'd pick up the poop or wash down the pee, then use the disinfectant hose to clean it. After that, you get the squeegee and wipe the water in the drain. Since there's no mess, we don't have to clean anything; only refill the water." Zander grabbed the water hose, refilled Echo's water, and then let Echo back inside. Echo walked in and let out a howl, which made Benjamin squeal in delight. "Any questions about what we just went over?" Benjamin shook his head no. Zander repeated the process with the other dogs.

"Now we'll move on to walking the dog." Zander picked up the leash and saw Benjamin standing near Matrix's cage.

"Zander, could you come help me with something?" Benjamin asked.

"Benjamin, come over here. I want to show you how to hook up a leash." Zander said, ignoring his question.

"But Zander, I need your help; this dog peed; you said we needed to clean it." Zander gave him an irritated look. Matrix let out a low growl.

"Zander, this dog is growling," Benjamin said fearfully.

"Benjamin, this is not the dog you're working with. I told you to stay away from him, remember?" Benjamin moved away from Matrix's suite. Zander saw his tail start to wag. "You don't like him either, ha, boy?" Zander whispered. He noticed the mess on Matrix's blanket Benjamin was talking about. "Hold on, I need to clean this quick," Zander continued, not thinking about where the sudden urge to clean the mess came from. He pushed the latch up and slightly opened the suite. "Hey, Matrix, you know me." Matrix sat down. Zander watched and saw no signs of aggression. He could hear the thumping of Matrix's wagging tail on the floor. Zander reached forward to put the slip lead around his neck. As the leash went around his head, Matrix bit down on Zander's right hand, then backed away towards the sidewall.

"Shit!" Zander cursed, feeling like an idiot. Matrix laid down as he relatched the gate. Zander swore the rottweiler had a slight grin on his face. Mariah was right about this. He looked down at his hand. A small trickle of blood was coming from the shallow tooth marks that circled the middle of his hand. Small droplets fell to the floor.

"Zander, are you OK?" Benjamin cried in alarm. "Bad dog!" He scolded. "Bad dog."

"I'm going to get this taken care of!" Zander said, in no mood to deal with Benjamin. He pointed to the red spots that dotted the floor. "Can you mop the blood off the floor?"

"What about the scary dog?" Benjamin protested.

"He can't get out, and he's lying down; you'll be fine. Please do as I say." Zander stressed as he headed up the stairs. He heard Benjamin opening the closet to get the mop as he left the suite. "At least he listened," Zander said, holding his wound. He glanced at it again, pleased to see it wasn't that bad; his pride was hurt more than anything. He spotted Kylee at the walk list. She turned, looking confused.

"I thought you were helping Benjamin walk dogs."

"We had a slight complication," Zander answered, holding up his wounded arm. Lines of blood started seeping down it.

"My God, what happened?" Kylee asked, shocked. She dropped her highlighter and rushed over to him.

"I got bit; what do you think happened?" He snapped, annoyed by her dumb question. *Don't take it out on Kylee.* He mentally corrected himself. She didn't seem to notice.

"I'll get the first aid kit," she said in a concerned voice. Zander followed her to the bathroom, where a small medical kit was kept under the sink. Kylee grabbed it and laid it on the sink.

"Sit," Kylee ordered, pointing to the toilet. Zander sat down. She turned on the water and ran a light blue washcloth under it. "Here, use this to clean the cut."

"Thanks, doc," Zander replied, wiping it across the wound. He tried to see how deep the wound was; from the looks of it, most of the marks barely broke the skin. Only a few appeared to be deep. Kylee was going through the medical kit, pulling out gauze and medical tape. She held a bottle of bactine over Zander's hand. "Ready?"

"Go for it." Zander closed his eyes in pain, gritting his teeth as the bactine entered the wound. Kylee wiped it with the now-red-spotted washcloth. She placed gauze strips on the wound and used the medical tape to hold them in place.

"Does Mariah know this happened?"

"No, I haven't told her yet." Zander reached for his walkie-talkie. Nothing happened when he hit the talk button. "My walkie's dead."

"What's new?" Kylee replied with sarcasm. "Mine's probably dead too." She pulled out her walkie-talkie. "Mariah, are you able to talk?" *Are you able to talk* was the code for something bad has happened.

"Yeah, what's wrong?" Mariah replied in a concerned tone.

"Nothing serious," Kylee assured.

"Easy for you to say." Zander commented in a playful tone.

"Zander got bit; he's bleeding."

"Where are you? How bad is it?" Mariah asked, her voice turning frantic.

"We're in the kennel bathroom; the wound doesn't look too bad. Right?" Kylee asked, looking at Zander.

"I'll live," Zander agreed.

"I'll... I'll be right there." Mariah replied.

"Who bit you anyway?" Kylee asked.

"That dog, Matrix. It was weird; one second he was calm, then he bit me, then he was calm again."

"Mariah said the same thing about him." Kylee agreed.

"I know, I thought Carmen and Mariah were exaggerating the situation, but that dog does seem to have behavioral problems."

"Maybe he doesn't like leads?" Kylee suggested.

"Carmen had no issue with him, and when he arrived, he was fine with me." Zander heard the outside door open. Mariah entered the room, her eyes wide with worry.

"Zander, OK, you?" Mariah asked, her voice filled with concern. *Great.* Zander thought, noticing her messed-up word usage. Kylee momentarily looked confused.

"I was bleeding to death, but Kylee stopped it," Zander replied, motioning to her, making light of the situation to calm Mariah.

"Funny," Mariah muttered clearly, not in the mood for humor. Zander held out his arm to show her the wound. The gauze now had a red tint to it. "Do you think you need to see a doctor?"

"No, I'll be fine." Zander assured.

"You had a tetanus shot, right?" Zander thought for a moment.

"I believe I got one a few years ago."

"I want to look at the wound and get a photo for the dog warden, and I'll need to write down what happened. You know fun paper work." Mariah faced Kylee and pointed to the kennel door.

"You back to work."

"Yes ma'am. I'm going to write no-touch on Matrix's chart."

"I should have known it was him," Mariah said. "Yes, please do that." Mariah's eyes moved around the room. "Wait, where's Benjamin?" Mariah asked. *Damn, I forgot all about him.* Zander thought.

"He's in the suite, cleaning up the blood on the floor," Zander admitted. Mariah told Kylee to check on him, then motioned to Zander to shut the door. The moment he did, Mariah angrily said.

"Zander, you, Benjamin helping were supposed walk dogs; Matrix, are you handling?" *Shit,* Zander mentally cursed.

"Mariah, you're having a word salad episode. You need to calm down." Zander said in a soft, gentle tone. A look of horror formed on her face.

"No! No! Please no!" Mariah pressed her head against the side of the wall.

"Mariah, it's ok; everything's fine. Calm down." Mariah breathed in and out heavily a few times.

"Am I talking, right?"

"Yes." Zander confirmed. Sorry about the Matrix incident. He peed in his suite and wouldn't go outside. I tried to get him out so we could clean it, then he bit me. I didn't know it would happen."

"Well, it did!" Mariah snapped. "I wish you would have listened to me."

"Sorry, I made a mistake." Zander admitted not knowing what else to say and being more concerned about her schizophrenia flaring up.

"When Matrix is done with quarantine, no one is to touch him. He's just acting too weird." Mariah's tone had gone flat. Another sign she was seriously upset.

"I agree with that," Zander said. The two remained where they were for several minutes. Zander continued to calm Mariah until she was able to continually speak and think clearly. Listening to Zander's advice, she left a message with her psychotherapist, and then the two slowly walked to the lobby.

"I heard you got bit. You OK, Zander?" Carmen asked.

"I'm fine. As you might have heard, it was Matrix," he replied, showing the bandage to her. Carmen looked at Mariah, shaking her head.

"Ouch, at least it doesn't look that bad."

"Yeah, at least it was just a warning bite; if it was an aggressive attack, I'd be screwed." Carmen looked at the bandage again.

"How was he acting after the bite?"

"It was weird; after the bite, he got calm again and laid down." Mariah opened a file cabinet drawer and handed Zander an incident report.

"Carmen, can you please print and fill out the quarantine papers?" Carmen did as Mariah asked. Zander began filling out the incident report with the details of what happened. He thought about joking with Mariah about how, thanks to him, she didn't need to deal with Matrix, but he decided against it. "Finished." He said handing it back to her. Mariah opened the filing cabinet and placed it inside.

"You want to go relax for the rest of the day?" Mariah asked, still using the same dry tone.

"No, the bite wasn't that bad. I'll be fine."

"Alright, be sure to keep an eye on it."

"I will. If you need anything, let me know." Mariah gave a faint smile. Zander left the lobby. He looked at his arm again. The bite felt like it was pulsing, and the pain seemed to be moving up his arm. He hadn't mentioned it to Mariah because he didn't know if he was imagining it and didn't want to upset her more. *I hope this isn't nerve damage.* He figured he'd wait to see what it felt like tomorrow. He shrugged the thoughts off and went back to the dog walks.

***

Mariah Forester held the kennel phone to her ear. Dreading the fact she was going to have to tell the client his dog was going to be quarantined for biting someone. *First week as supervisor and someone gets bit, I'm doing great,* Mariah thought as she listened to the ringing. *Just speak clearly and stay calm.* She was scared to death; she was going to have another word salad episode. At least in this case, the dog was scheduled to be here for another eighteen days, so the client wouldn't have to pay any more money for the quarantine time. As the phone rang, Mariah remembered the last dog bite. A former new staff member had accidentally taken an aggressive St. Bernard for a walk. It ended with several stiches and the dog getting quarantined one day before the owner picked him up. To no one's surprise, the owner was furious. That was one time Mariah was happy she was not in charge. The phone went to a standard voice mail message.

"Hello, Mr. Ransier, this is Mariah calling from Snowy Hills Kennels. I'm afraid I have some bad news about your dog, Matrix. He's fine and in good health; however, he unfortunately bit one of our staff members and has to be quarantined for ten days. Please give me a call back. Mariah gave the kennel number and hung up. She turned to Carmen, hoping everything would turn out okay. "Was that good?"

"You did fine," Carmen replied, showing no signs that anything was wrong. "I reported the incident to the dog warden; he'll be here to start the quarantine tomorrow." Carmen opened the filing cabinet and pulled the rabies vaccination records.

"I hope he doesn't have rabies," Mariah muttered. Finding herself worrying about Zander.

"What made you say that?"

"You heard that?" Mariah asked, thinking she had spoken softer. Carmen gave a small laugh.

"You're fine. Don't worry about rabies; he's not showing any symptoms and looked very healthy, plus we have proof of vaccination." Carmen replied, holding the paper up.

"You're right," Mariah agreed. "I'm just upset Zander got bit and worried about what's going to happen to me."

"You're doing a great job. I see that, and so does everyone else."

"I'm glad you think so," Mariah replied, relieved. She grabbed a dog behavior book from the shelf behind them. "I wonder if anything in here explains his behavior."

"Like we said before, some dogs are wired wrong." The conversation was stopped by the phone ringing.

"That's most likely the client," Mariah said out loud. Again, feelings of dread crept into her. She reached for the phone before realizing the ring tone was wrong. "It's my phone," Mariah said, picking it up. Her face grew pale when she saw the number. She looked at the clock. *With everything going on, I forgot.* "Carmen, this is personal; it might take around an hour, so can you handle things?" she asked, hoping Carmen wouldn't ask too many questions.

"Sure," Carmen replied.

"Thanks," Mariah said as she walked to her room. "Hello."

"Hi, Ms. Forester. This is Karen with Rochester Psychotherapy; how are you?" Mariah shut her room door.

"I'm doing OK." *I'm worried I'm losing my mind. Why do you think I scheduled our call?* Mariah sat on her bed, nervously grasping at her sheets.

"Before I transfer you to Doctor Rochester, I wanted to let you know your insurance information went through; however, there is a twenty-dollar copay." *As usual.* Mariah thought, annoyed.

"I can take care of that now," Mariah said, taking her credit card from her purse. *Please just transfer me to the shrink.* She thought as she read off the card numbers.

"The payment went through; I'll transfer you to Ms. Rochester." The receptionist said in a robotic voice.

"Thank you," Mariah responded, hoping she hid the frustration in her voice. The phone rang twice.

"Hi, Mariah, this is Amanda Rochester from Rochester Psychotherapy."

"Hello, thanks for talking with me."

"No trouble; what can I help you with?" She asked in a calm, caring voice, though Mariah could tell it was the same scripted voice she had used hundreds of times.

"I think... I think my condition might be returning," Mariah said slowly. Those were words she never wanted to hear again.

"Why do you say that?"

"I think I'm starting to see and hear things that aren't there. You know, hallucinations, and I'm having word salad episodes." Mariah tried to keep the thoughts of her previous episodes in the back of her mind.

"Alright, Mariah, I have your file in front of me. Before we begin, does your phone have FaceTime? I like to see people's faces during these sessions."

"Sure, one moment." Mariah replied as she opened FaceTime. Amanda Rochester was an older woman with whitening blond hair. A bookshelf filled with large hardcover books covered the wall behind her. Mariah remembered, as a kid, asking another therapist when he had time to read all those books.

"You look well; that's good to see." She continued, complimenting Mariah.

"Thank you. Is my lighting okay? I can turn more on if you need me to," Mariah asked, noticing she only had her small desk lamp on.

"The lightings fine for me. Now, can you tell me why you feel your condition is returning?" Mariah gave a nervous laugh, then went on to explain the situation that was going on with Matrix, the word salads, and the creature she saw while outside with Benjamin. She didn't bother saying anything about the sounds. Like she told Zander, Kylee had heard them too. Mariah watched as Rochester typed on her computer.

"Has anything changed in your personal life? Are you going through stressful situations or feeling depressed?" Mariah casually shook her head no.

"Nothing I can think of off the top of my head. I recently got promoted at my job, but I'm very happy with it. Some of the decisions I have to make can be stressful, but nothing too serious." Rochester made another note. Mariah was tempted to ask what she was writing but didn't.

"Have you seen anything traumatic recently?" Mariah was about to reply no, then remembered the radio station and possibly hearing those gunshots. She explained what had happened at the station.

"I doubt that has anything to do with it, though," she said at the end. "It's not like I knew any of those people."

"That might be your trigger," Rochester quickly added. "Your conscious mind might not realize it, but it might be affecting your subconscious, which, along with the stress this dog is giving you, is probably why your schizophrenia is resurfacing."

"Do you think I need to go back on my medication?" Mariah asked, dreading the answer. She had been off her medication for a year, and she wasn't looking forward to the possibility of going back on them.

"Yes, I would strongly advise you to go back on your medication."

"Damn it!" Mariah sighed. *I didn't come this far just to relapse.* She knew the medicine often made her feel tired and dizzy. *How can I do my job feeling like that?*

"OK, Mariah, there's no need to get upset."

"Sorry," Mariah replied sincerely. "I've come so far in my recovery, and I'm worried about how the medication might affect my job."

"In that case, I would suggest trying to relax and remove yourself from stressful situations for a few days, and, if you feel comfortable with it, talk about what you're going through with a close friend. It should release any pent-up emotions." Kylee and Zander came to mind. "However, if your symptoms get worse, I strongly suggest you start taking your prescription again."

"I'll consider that. I guess I'm worried if I talk about it with friends; they'd doubt my leadership."

"I'm sure they'd respect you more; it takes a strong person to talk about their feelings." Mariah wondered if she really believed that or if it was just a doctor trying to make her feel better.

"Thank you for everything, Doc; you've been truly helpful. I'd better get back to work now."

"OK, Mariah, anytime you need anything, I'm here to talk." *Just be sure to schedule an appointment and give me my damn money,* Mariah thought.

"Thank you; I'll definitely do that." Mariah replied. She ended the call and looked in her mirror to make sure she didn't look upset or worried, then exited the room. Shawn was leaning against the wall near her door. She let out a gasp of surprise.

"What the hell are you doing?" she asked, trying to not sound as upset as she was. *Did he hear all that?* Mariah thought feeling anger and worry building inside her.

"I'm on break," he said with a sly smile. He lit a cigarette in front of her. "Funny, I could have sworn I accidentally overheard you talking to a shrink. He blew some smoke above her head. "But I doubt it. What kind of place has a mentally ill person as a leader?" A sense of panic gripped her. She doubted it would affect her career, but the thought that her secret was out frightened her.

"I have no idea. You'd probably know more about mental illness than I would," Mariah shot back, keeping a neutral face. Shawn's sly smile returned as he put the cigarette in his mouth.

"Do that outside, please," Mariah ordered, adopting a nonchalant tone. Shawn didn't reply; he grabbed his coat and walked downstairs. Mariah went back to her room, closed the door, and leaned against the wall, gripped by panic. She grabbed her blankets and tossed them across the room. She punched the mattress, slammed a fist into her pillow, and tossed it across the room, knocking her purse off the dresser. She thought she heard what sounded like a dozen voices outside her room door. Each using different words to mock her mental illness. *What, did he go get everyone and bring them up to look at me, like I'm some kind of circus act?* That was it for her. In a blind rage, she yelled. "Shawn said lost!" She pulled the door open. No one was there, and the voices had stopped. She looked down both halls and saw nothing. She started to breathe heavily and fell back on her bed. *This can't be happening.* She didn't know how much time had passed; she lay there until another knock at the door caught her attention. "Who is it?" she asked, fearing her mind was playing tricks on her again.

"Mariah, it's Carmen; are you OK?" Mariah got up, about to open the door, when she saw the condition of her room. "Yes, I'm fine." She quickly threw her blankets and pillow back on the bed, then opened the door. Carmen stood there with a concerned look on her face.

"You've been in here for about two hours. Are you sure you're OK?" Was it really that long? Mariah mentally questioned.

"Carmen, I'm so sorry; I must have lost track of time," Mariah said in an apologetic voice.

"You look kind of pale; are you sure you're OK?" Carmen again asked.

"Yes, I'm fine; I'll be right down, and thanks for checking in on me," Mariah replied, lightly smacking her on the shoulder. OK, you're real. After Carmen left, Mariah took several minutes to get herself back into a mental state so she could properly do her job, then returned to the lobby. To her relief, the rest of the day went without a hitch. After work hours, she played some board games with Kylee and Zander. At a little past ten, she grabbed Blaze, went to her room, and laid in her bed. With nothing to occupy her mind, the thought and fear that Shawn might know something about her past or that she might be having another episode of schizophrenia came back to her. Don't think about it; it will only make it worse. As much as she tried, her thoughts kept returning to Shawn and Kelly in a locked room, plotting to get her fired or sent to a mental hospital. Don't be ridiculous; that's not happening. Kelly hates Shawn as much as the rest of us. Of course paranoia is a symptom of schizophrenia, she thought, feeling her heart race. She reached into her bag, looking for her medication, then remembered she had left it at home. Of course. She cursed herself. She tried to fill her mind with happy thoughts, like how much she enjoyed working with Kylee and Zander. She turned her attention to Blaze, who was lying on her back on the bed. She laughed at the goofy look on her dog's face. She sat up and started to gently stroke Blaze on the chest. Blaze licked her hand. The comfort and joy the simple act of petting a dog brought helped relax her. Soon, tiredness came upon her. "Goodnight Blaze." Mariah said before pulling the covers up to her face and drifted off to sleep.

Mariah slowly awoke. Through the haze of sleep, she could hear Blaze barking furiously. She looked at the clock, which read one-fifteen a.m.

"Blaze, shut up," she said in a drowsy voice. She pulled the pillow over her ears before closing them. Seconds later, she thought she heard a low yelp before Blaze's barking fell silent. "Blaze," Mariah said, beginning to worry why she wasn't hearing anything. She started to pull the covers off her body when Blaze jumped on the bed, spun in circles a few times, then laid down. "Did you scare off the ghost?" Mariah said jokingly. She glanced across the room. A small beam of light from the hall shone under the door. The light seemed to reveal a shape sitting in the darkness in the corner of the room. She couldn't make out what it was, but knew nothing should have been there. She looked at Blaze, who was sound asleep at the other end of the bed. "Ugg." Mariah moaned, thinking she was seeing things, not wanting to spend the rest of the night worrying about it. She laid back down, closing her eyes. She felt the moist air from two nostrils hit her face. "Blaze, go back to sleep," Mariah said, reaching out, stroking the muscular square face in front of her. Her hand soon dropped to the side of the bed as she drifted off to sleep.

CHAPTER 7

The next morning, Mariah woke up feeling oddly awake and refreshed. Blaze jumped off the bed, wagging her tail. She barked in excitement as she pawed at the door.

"OK, Blaze Let me get dressed, then I'll take you out." Mariah grabbed a light blue morning robe from her dresser and pulled it over her shoulders. Blaze dropped a shoe in front of her. "I'm getting there. It's four in the morning; give me some time." *Only it's not four in the morning,* Mariah realized, looking at the clock on her nightstand, which showed ten minutes to six. Knowing her alarm was about to go off, she shut it off. "You let me sleep in!" Mariah said stunned and feeling very lucky. She smiled and rubbed Blaze's head. "Thank you! I hope you make this a habit." Mariah took Blaze to her kennel and dropped her food bowl in the suite with a few extra treats. Mariah returned to her room to shower and dress. Before heading down to breakfast, she walked to her nightstand to grab her phone, only to find it gone. *What the hell?* She looked around the nightstand. "Where is that thing?" She said annoyed, searching under the bed. *Blaze if you chewed it up, I swear.* Mariah grabbed her blanket and started shaking it. Nothing. She went to her closet and started going through her coat pockets. "It's not here." Her thoughts went to Shawn, and the memory of seeing something in her room last night. *Had he taken it for revenge? Was he hoping to find something about my condition on it?* Mariah knew Doctor Rochester's office number would be on top of the call list. *Don't freak out; you can't prove he did it; even if he did, he doesn't have your passcode.* Mariah reminded herself. Annoyed, she headed down to the kitchen; if Shawn was there, she planned on questioning him about it. When she arrived, only Zander and Kylee were sitting at a table. Benjamin was busy preparing food. *Had one of them taken it as a practical joke?* She doubted it, but at this point, she hoped it was just a prank by her friends. Mariah approached the table.

"Hey, my phone is missing. Did one of you take it as a joke or something?"

"I was about to ask you the same thing," Zander added, stirring his coffee with a spoon.

"What?" Mariah asked, surprised.

"Both our phones seemed to have disappeared last night," Zander continued. "Kylee and I were hoping you did it as a joke."

"Kelly also complained about her phone missing. She's telling Carmen about it. I heard Carmen say something about filing a police report." Kylee added.

"What is going on?" Mariah asked, sitting down next to Zander.

"We have a phone thief."

"Way to point out the obvious, Kylee." Zander complimented sarcastically.

"What about Ethan? Has he complained about a missing phone?" Mariah asked, feeling more and more nervous.

"Hasn't come down yet. He's probably upstairs looking for it," Zander replied.

"Do you think Shawn took them?" Mariah asked with suspicion in her voice. Kylee nodded her head, yes.

"We haven't seen him yet either," Zander added. "It won't surprise me if he did, but I think he'd wait until the end of the shift to take them. Unless he's handing them off to one of his stoner friends in the middle of the night." Mariah's eyes widened slightly, her thoughts returning to the presence in her room.

"Last night, Blaze was barking at something in my room." The look on her friend's face showed both interest and confusion.

"What are you talking about?" Kylee asked.

"Are you sure Blaze wasn't barking at a mouse or someone walking down the halls?" Zander added.

"I don't know. She barked for a couple seconds, then came back to bed, and then I saw the shape in the room. It could have been a hallucination." Mariah stopped herself, realizing what she had let slip. *Please forget you heard that,* Mariah thought, feeling her palms becoming sweaty.

"Why do you think that?" Kylee asked.

"I was just brainstorming," Mariah replied quickly. "I know someone was in my room last night, and now my phone's missing." She looked at Zander, who was staying quiet. *Your secret's safe,* his look said. That made her feel much better.

"Well, did you see who it was?" Mariah rolled her eyes. *Kylee and her dumb questions.* Mariah chose her next words carefully; she didn't want to snap at Kylee or accidentally let information about her condition slip. She was also hungry. The strong smell of eggs and sizzling meat was making her stomach growl.

"I only saw a shape sitting or standing near the door. I was still half asleep, and have no idea who it was."

"Do you remember any details about the outline: muscular, slim?" Kylee continued.

"I honestly can't remember," Mariah said truthfully. Hoping that would end Kylee's questions. Everyone's attention shifted when Ethan came into the room. By the look on his face, Mariah knew what was wrong.

"Hey guys, weird question, but..."

"Yes, our phones are missing too," Zander interrupted.

"Really? I thought it was one of you guys messing around." He said, now looking as confused as they were.

"We thought the same thing; Kelly and Carmen are up front filling out a police report," Zander continued.

"Wait, Kelly and Carmen's phones are missing too?" Ethan asked with a surprised tone.

"Yes, my phone is missing, and I'm pissed off about it." Carmen replied just entering the room. "I'm asking for the police report. Everyone is missing their phone, correct?"

"Looks like it," Mariah answered in an angry voice. She noticed Benjamin was walking over to the table with a tray of eggs and sausage. A small silver lining.

"Morning, everyone." Benjamin said, placing the plates in the center of the table.

"Thank you," Mariah said, piling some eggs on her plate.

"Benjamin, is your cell phone missing?" Kylee asked. Before Benjamin could answer, Shawn stormed into the room.

"My phone is missing; which one of you stole it?" he demanded. Mariah put her fork down, knowing an argument was about to happen.

"Shawn, we were just talking about you." Zander acknowledged. "Our phones are missing too; you wouldn't happen to know what happened to them, would you?"

"No, I don't know where your phones are. I want to know where mine is; I just dropped a grand on that thing." *Please don't let this turn into a fist fight.* Mariah thought. Shawn gave her a cold look.

"If I don't get my phone back today, I'm suing you and the company."

"Go ahead and try," Mariah replied, in no mood to take his crap. "Tell it to the police when they question you."

"You called the police on me?" Shawn said with a slight hint of fear in his voice.

"We called the police because everyone's phones are missing," Carmen corrected.

"Well, it's not like some stranger walked in here and took them; it had to be someone here," he yelled. Mariah found herself doubting Shawn was the one who took the phones. The anger and confusion in his voice were real, and she knew he was a bad actor. "You seriously think I took them?" Shawn continued. A hurt look briefly showed on his face. Kylee gave a sarcastic smile and shook her head. "Well, I didn't; maybe we should ask our mentally ill leader here what happened."

Mariah gasped. Nervousness and fright overwhelmed her. She tried to hide it but couldn't keep the concern off her face.

"Shut up!" She shouted.

"What, did I touch a nerve?" Shawn taunted. "Yeah, that's right, I heard her talking to a doctor yesterday about having schizophrenia." Mariah squeezed her hands together; they were wet with sweat. She heard Zander's chair pull out.

"You should go," he said, getting in his face.

"Yeah, what are you going to do about it?" Shawn countered. Mariah wanted to shout at them, but her throat muscles seemed paralyzed. She could hear Kylee and Carmen yelling at them to stop. Ethan was between them, trying to break up the fight. Mariah heard a smack. She looked up to see Benjamin bringing his serving spoon forward for another strike that hit Shawn in the back of the head.

"Stop! Stop fighting!" Benjamin commanded.

"What did you say, retard?" Shawn asked, holding the back of his head.

"You're an angry coward. Now go!" Benjamin said, lifting his spoon again.

"I dare you to hit me with that again." Shawn shouted, walking towards him. Zander grabbed the back of his shoulder, and Benjamin delivered a kick to the groin. Shawn let out a scream of pain and fell to his knees. Mariah felt her mouth drop. *Where did that come from?* Normally, a fight would cause Benjamin to break down into tears. The room erupted with laughter as Shawn moaned in pain, cursing. Soon, Mariah found herself joining them.

"OK, that's enough," Kelly said, entering the room. "I don't know what is going on, but it stops now. Shawn, are you OK?" She asked, looking down at him. Shawn got up, trying to keep what was left of his dignity. *I'll never forget what you did to me.* Mariah thought. She grew concerned when he passed Benjamin, but to her surprise, he patted him on the shoulder and said,

"Good kick." Shawn exited the room, and Kelly continued her speech.

"Everyone, if your phone is missing, I need you to come to the office and fill out a report. That OK with you, Mariah?" Mariah quickly made eye contact with her, getting her mind back into its leadership role.

"Yes, that's fine," Mariah replied confidently. "Everyone do that, then get to work." As everyone headed to the lobby, Mariah's thoughts went back to Shawn's outburst. All of her co-workers had heard what he said. She dreaded the fact that each of them would probably ask her about it. *Calm down. Don't get stressed or anxious,* Mariah told herself, knowing it would only make her schizophrenia worse.

"Mariah, are you alright?" she heard Kylee ask.

"Be right there." Mariah replied.

***

A few minutes later, Kylee handed the finished police report to Mariah. The thought of someone coming into her room while she slept and going through her things gave her goosebumps.

"What will happen now?" Kylee asked.

"The officer I talked to said he would contact our phone companies to trace them if they're being used. Since no one saw anything, they can't do much at the moment."

"I hope they get some information soon. I miss my phone," she said, making a sad face.

"Me too," Mariah replied, leaning back in her chair.

"Things sure are exciting with you in charge," Kylee teased, pleased to see Mariah was back to her old self. She wondered why she seemed so upset when Shawn called her mentally ill and claimed she had schizophrenia, but decided not to ask.

"Glad you think so," Mariah complimented, returning to a normal position. "So, Kylee, would you be OK training Benjamin on how to walk dogs? As you know, things didn't go well the last time, and he feels pretty bad about it."

"I can train him, no problem." Kylee replied with a genuine smile. She had no issues with Benjamin, and was looking forward to the challenge of training him. Straight out of high school, Kylee Campbell had gone to tech school, earning two associate's degrees in veterinary technology and business management. She worked at Snowy Hills during her holidays and summer breaks. Mariah trained her during her first week, during which they became best friends. After graduating, she decided to come on full-time for a year or two while she decided whether to go back to school to become a veterinarian.

"Perfect. Don't need to tell you this, but don't touch Matrix. I don't need another bite on my hands."

"I won't, promise," Kylee replied, then left the room to find Benjamin. Moments later, she approached him, who was near the bus, putting a bag of salt in a spreader. The smell of newly opened rock salt was in the air.

"Hi Kylee." He waved to her.

"Hey, Benjamin, ready to walk some dogs?" Kylee asked in an excited voice.

"Yes!" Benjamin said, laying the snow shovel and salt spreader against the wall. "I was really worried that when Matrix bit Zander, I would get blamed, and Mariah wouldn't let me learn how to handle dogs anymore." Kylee put a hand on his shoulder.

"What happened with Zander wasn't your fault."

"Was it Zander's fault?" Benjamin asked. Kylee removed her hand, shocked by his unexpected suggestion.

"No, Benjamin, it wasn't Zander's fault either." Kylee replied, agitated. "Sometimes these things just happen."

"When is Zander going to become sick?" Benjamin asked, his tone turning to concern.

"What are you talking about?" Kylee asked. *Where is he getting these ideas?*

"I heard Kelly say something about rabies, and Zander might have it." *This is how rumors get out of control,* Kylee thought. Her agitation turning to an unexpected wave of anger.

"No, Benjamin, Zander doesn't have rabies. Kelly was probably talking about something else, and you misunderstood what she said."

"If he does have rabies..." Kylee cut him off before he could finish.

"Enough about rabies. I don't want to talk about it anymore." The thought that one of her friends might be sick caused her to worry. Even if she knew it wasn't true.

"You OK, Kylee?" Benjamin asked, "You look angry." Kylee smiled again.

"I'm fine; let's stop talking about people getting sick and go walk some dogs!" Kylee said, trying to get them both psyched up.

"Yes, I want to walk one," Benjamin agreed. The two made small talk until they reached the suite area. All the dogs except Matrix were sleeping on cots. He sat near the gate, watching them. To Kylee's surprise, not a single one barked or got up to greet them.

"I think we're interrupting nap time," Kylee said, trying to make light of the situation, but inside she knew something was wrong.

"Thanks for helping me, Kylee. I thought since it was my fault Zander got bit, no one would want to work with me again," Benjamin repeated, which told Kylee it had been on his mind for a while.

"No problem." Kylee replied, "Everyone makes mistakes now and then, and it wasn't your fault Zander got bit; it was that mean dog over there." Matrix raised his head and barked.

"OK, that was creepy," Kylee said softly.

"Which dog am I walking?" Benjamin asked. He put his slip lead in his pocket and grabbed a leash and choker from the wall. Kylee found herself not knowing what to do. She could tell none of the dogs were dead, but they weren't getting up. *What's going on?* Kylee tried to remember if she'd ever read or seen a situation like this before. She reached for her walkie-talkie, then decided Mariah had enough on her mind at the moment, plus she wasn't even sure anything was wrong. Maybe these dogs did this at home, and they had gotten used to their surroundings.

"Alright, Benjamin, you're going to be walking Echo. Do you know who that is?"

"Yes," Benjamin replied, walking over to Echo's suite. He started to unlock the gate when Kylee put her hand on it.

"So, what do we do before we take a dog out?" Benjamin thought for a moment. Kylee pointed to the chart.

"I look at the chart to make sure the dog doesn't have notes."

"Good job." Kylee complimented picking up the chart; she held it so both of them could see it. "See, this dog doesn't have any notes, which means it's a safe dog to walk. If it did have notes, one second." She grabbed Matrix's chart. She briefly looked at him. The way his eyes were lowered and, sides of his mouth were moved upward made it look like he was giving an evil grin, which made Kylee feel uneasy. "I see why you freak people out." Kylee said softly. Matrix rushed the suite door, stopping right in front of it and barking. Startled, Kylee stepped back. "You'll never make any friends if you keep acting like that," Kylee said smartly. She quickly shook off the nerves and showed Benjamin the chart. "Now, if you see Sharpie written on a chart, what does it mean?"

"It means the dog may bite, and I shouldn't touch it."

"Yes," Kylee said, pleased. "Now get your leash and take Echo out. She likes to jump on you, so be careful." *Please get up, Echo.* Kylee thought as Benjamin opened the door.

"Hello, nice doggy." Benjamin said as he happily petted her. He placed the leash around her neck and gave a little pull. Echo remained still. Benjamin pulled a little harder.

"Kylee, this dog doesn't want to move," Benjamin said, confused. *What is going on here?* Kylee thought. The last time she walked Echo, she was running and jumping all over the place.

"May I have the leash?" she asked Benjamin, who handed it to her. "Echo want to go for a walk?" She asked in baby talk. Echo moved her head slightly, but remained still. *What is going on?* Kylee again wondered. She looked at the other dogs; none had moved except Matrix, who was still staring her down. Normally, the site of a leash would cause every dog to be jumping around and barking in excitement. Now none of them seemed to care.

"Echo, are you feeling OK?" Kylee asked, rubbing her head then feeling her nose. It was cool to the touch. That's good. She thought.

"Is everything alright, Kylee?"

"I don't know," Kylee replied with slight concern in her voice. "I hope they're not sick."

"What if they are?" Benjamin asked, rubbing Echo again.

"Carmen will have to take them to the vet," Kylee said in a calm voice. Benjamin glanced at Matrix, who sat down and barked twice.

"At least somebody feels good." Kylee said out loud. Echo gave an excited bark and rushed out the gate, and Kylee felt the leash slip from her hand. The other dogs started barking in excitement. Kylee rushed to the door and grabbed the leash.

"Kylee, let's go for a walk." Benjamin said as Echo jumped up and down at the door. She handed him the leash.

"One second." Kylee said, looking at the dogs in confusion. *Two seconds ago, you were acting sick; now you're fine.* Kylee thought as she tried to make sense of the situation. She walked up to Hexum, who was wagging his tail in excitement, then heard the door above close. "Benjamin!" She yelled, heading up the stairs. When she was a quarter of the way up, Matrix slammed against his suite wall. Surprised by the noise, Kylee turned her head and lost her footing. She felt her shoulder slamming into the steps, then her body rolled down to the floor.

"Ow," Kylee moaned in pain, holding her head and shoulder. She slowly moved her arms and legs, making sure nothing was broken, then got up and ran outside. "Benjamin!" She yelled. She heard dogs barking near the yards used for training the sled dogs. *Please don't let Echo loose, Benjamin; please don't let her go!* Kylee thought as she ran down the path. She saw Kelly inside the yard with two huskies, Thunder and Sage. Kelly was trying to get a leash on them. She rushed faster, seeing Benjamin struggling to hold onto the leash, then her fears came true. Echo pulled the leash from his hands.

"Benjamin, come get Echo!" Kelly yelled, getting the leashes on Thunder and Sage. "Echo, Echo." She called, trying to keep Echo near the fence. Kylee breathed in relief when Benjamin grabbed the leash. "Benjamin, wrap the leash around your arm." Kelly ordered. He did as he was instructed. "Benjamin, why are you walking dogs by yourself?"

"I thought Kylee was behind me. She said we were going outside."

"I said to wait!" Kylee said finally catching up to them. *Great.* She thought seeing Kelly was clearly pissed.

"Kylee, why weren't you supervising him? You should know better than to let him walk around with a client's dog. Benjamin dropped the leash, and Echo was loose. Do you know what could have happened?" Kylee felt like arguing against the verbal beating, but she knew she deserved it.

"Sorry, I fell down the stairs while I was following him. I guess Benjamin didn't realize." Kylee said, looking at the snow, ashamed of her careless actions.

"Kylee, are you OK?" Kelly asked, her face gaining a look of concern.

"Yeah, yeah, I'm fine." Kylee looked up at all three dogs. "Well, Benjamin got the dog back; everything's OK." Kylee replied, being her usual upbeat self.

"I didn't know you fell, Kylee." Benjamin added. "Sorry, the dog slipped away from me. I didn't mean for it to happen."

"It's OK; accidents happen. But next time, don't go outside with a dog unless someone is with you," Kylee said in a stern tone.

"Yeah, this time Echo ran towards the gate to play with the other dogs, but next time she could run into the woods and get lost." Kelly added. Kylee shook her head in agreement. The friendly look on Kelly's face suddenly turned to concern. "What the hell is he doing out?" she shouted, worried. Kylee turned around and felt her mouth drop. Matrix was walking down the trail several feet from them. Kylee and his eyes briefly met. Kylee looked away, not wanting him to perceive the stare as a challenge. *How did he get out? How did he get out?* Kylee thought in a panic. Thinking quickly, she whispered the only thing that came to mind.

"Benjamin, walk slowly to the gate." She said raising a finger at the gate that led into the play yard. She saw Kelly pulling her walky-talky out of her pocket. Before anyone could act, Matrix barked loudly and charged the fence. Kylee stopped moving as he showed his teeth and started biting at the fencing. Kelly tried to hold Thunder and Sage back but lost her footing on an ice patch. Thunder growled, Sage cried in pain, and stepped back, a small patch of red forming under Sage's toe. Thunder and Matrix continued to try to bite each other through the holes in the fencing. Kylee tried to move or think of what to do but was frozen in place. A dog fight had never happened in front of her. The sounds of snapping and snarling were only feet away; Kelly's screams for her to get the dogs only made it worse. Kelly was firing the pepper spray at Matrix, which seemed to have no effect. Kylee reached for hers, only to find her pocket empty. She grabbed her walkie-talkie to call for help. She hit the talk button. Her screams for help were followed by a curse when the walkie-talkie went dead.

"Matrix, stop!" Benjamin said, letting Echo walk towards him. Kylee saw what was happening, but her mind wasn't registering how serious it was. The panic she was feeling scrambled her thoughts. Matrix's focus turned to the two of them, giving Kelly enough time to grab Sage and Thunder. Matrix sniffed Echo and started to wag his tail. Benjamin placed his slip leash around Matrix's face, inches apart. Kylee felt her body shaking; small spots of red covered the play yard, and more blood was coming from Thunder and Sage.

"Let's get you back inside." Benjamin said, leading Matrix away.

"Kylee, get Benjamin!" Kelly screamed, pointing to him. Kylee snapped out of her shock and fully comprehended what was going on. By then, Benjamin was going inside the kennel.

"Benjamin, wait!" She yelled, rushing after him. *Way to go, Kylee.* She thought, fearing any second, she was going to hear Matrix's snarls and Benjamin's cries of pain. When Kylee reached the suite, Benjamin was putting Echo away; Matrix was already in his suite, laying down like nothing had happened.

"The gate was opened when I came in, Benjamin said, pointing to it." Kylee put both hands on Benjamin's shoulders.

"Benjamin, you can't walk off like that! You know how lucky we are; no one got bit?" Kylee said, exasperated.

"Why are you upset? What did I do wrong?" Kylee felt like screaming. *You walked off without me, then walked off with two dogs, and one of them was no-touch!* Kylee managed to calm herself. She didn't want to take out her frustrations on Benjamin.

"Benjamin, I know you want to walk dogs, but what you did was dangerous and careless. Not every dog is nice or easy to walk. You need to wait and let us train you on how to walk them. OK?"

"Kylee!" Kelly yelled, storming into the suite. All the dogs started barking. *Here we go.* Kylee thought, readying herself for the scolding she knew was coming.

"Benjamin, can you give us a minute?" She asked when she got to the bottom of the stairs.

"OK, thanks for teaching me, Kylee." He said. Kylee tried to reply but couldn't make a sound. She glanced at Matrix, who was biting at the chain link. *I'm done for.* She tried to look Kelly in the eye, but she looked at the floor when she saw her glare. Once Benjamin left the suite, Kelly unloaded on her.

"Kylee, could you have been any more irresponsible? How did an aggressive, no-touch dog get out of his cage and end up outside?" Kelly pointed to Matrix. His lips curled, showing his teeth. "That dog is in quarantine! Do you know what would have happened if he bit someone?" Kylee felt tears building in her eyes. She nodded her head, yes. "The dog warden would have shut this place down! He still might after the bite incident.

"Kelly, I know," Kylee said in a teary voice. "I have no idea how it happened, I swear. When we left, Matrix was in his cage. Someone must have opened it after I left," Kylee insisted. She knew she had nothing to do with it, but also knew convincing everyone else was going to be next to impossible.

"You weren't around his suite at all?" Kelly asked skeptically.

"I only took his chart off to show Benjamin what a no-touch or aggressive-dog chart looked like, but I didn't touch the cage latch, I swear." Kylee quickly replied, trying to convince herself there was no way she could have accidentally pushed it open.

"That must have been when it happened, Kylee; who else could have done it? Was the clip on the latch?" Kelly asked, pointing to the clip hanging from the suite door fencing.

"I... I don't know. I think so." Kylee said now beginning to wonder if the door was clipped or not. "Benjamin must have forgotten to put it back on when he took Matrix in," Kylee replied, taking the clamp from the fencing and putting it in the gate hatch hole.

"You mean you didn't catch up to Benjamin until he was in the suite?" Kylee moaned, knowing she was digging herself into a bigger hole. "Kylee, on your watch, a dangerous dog got out and bit one of our sled dogs. Do you know how lucky we are that wasn't a client dog, or that he didn't bite Benjamin or someone else?" Kelly snapped in a lecturous voice. Kylee used all her strength not to burst into tears.

"Thunder and Sage didn't get bit badly, at least." Kylee said softly, knowing how badly she had messed up. Her only source of comfort was her boss, who was also her best friend. *She wondered if that would even matter.*

"Kylee, that's not the point. The point is a dangerous dog got loose on your watch and could have gotten lost or seriously injured someone." *Do you have to keep repeating it happened on my watch?* Kylee thought, becoming increasingly upset.

"Well, none of that happened, and everything's fine now!" Kylee snapped sick of the berating. Kelly looked momentarily stunned by the outburst. She put her hands up and said.

"Kylee, I'm not going to argue with you," then turned around and walked upstairs. Kylee knew where she was going: down to the office to talk to Mariah.

CHAPTER 8

Mariah sat at her desk, going through the newly boarded dog's files on the computer. She glanced at the fireplace, listening to the crackle of the wood as it burned. She looked into the flames, picturing herself in her own house with her own fireplace, on a couch enjoying a TV show with her husband, Zander, while Blaze laid on the floor at their feet. She looked up when she heard the waiting room door open. Moments later, Kelly rushed into the lobby. Mariah could tell by her posture that something was wrong.

"Mariah, there's been an incident. I need to talk to you now!"

"OK," Mariah replied. *Who was five minutes over a walk?* She thought, but gave Kelly her full attention.

"In the office." Kelly added. Instead of asking for an explanation, Mariah knew doing as she requested would get her out of her hair a lot sooner than arguing the point would. Mariah reached under the desk, where a small lock box was screwed to the wall. She turned the numbers to three, one, four and removed the office key. After a short walk down the hall, Mariah unlocked the office door and sat down. Kelly did the same.

"Now what's the problem?" Mariah asked in a neutral tone.

"Somehow Matrix got outside the fenced-in area! He attacked Thunder and Sage!" Mariah felt her body tense.

"What?" She yelled, hoping she heard her wrong. Kelly explained the full situation in detail. Mariah didn't believe what she was hearing. There was no way Kylee would have been careless enough to let Benjamin walk a dog alone.

"Where was Kylee when this was happening?"

"She claims she fell down the stairs," Kelly replied.

"Is she OK?" Mariah cut in, in a worried tone.

"Yes, fortunately, she's fine."

"OK...OK. I'm assuming all the dogs are back in their kennels." Mariah asked, swallowing.

"Yes. correct." Kelly confirmed. Mariah felt the tension leave her body.

"Were the bites serious?"

"Ethan looked over Sage and Thunder; they both have small cuts on their front paws and legs."

"Do we need to schedule a vet trip?" Mariah asked, knowing that if they did, it would need to be done before the storm hit.

"Ethan's cleaning the wounds now. I'll take a better look at them when we're done here and get back to you."

"I'll take a look at them too." Images of Matrix started filling her mind; the thought of him walking around loose made her skin crawl.

"Is that all you're going to do?" Kelly asked. Mariah scowled, knowing what she was talking about.

"Let's go back to the beginning. Matrix is on quarantine; everyone knows not to touch him. How did he get out?"

"I have no idea. All I know is Matrix's gate was unclipped, and Benjamin walked him back to his suite with Echo."

"And Kylee was laying on the stairs while this was happening?" Mariah asked, wondering how badly her friend was injured.

"No, she arrived a few seconds later, and froze up while the attack was occurring." *That sounds like Kylee,* Mariah mentally admitted.

"I'll talk to Kylee and Benjamin and go from there." Kelly gave her a look that clearly said that's not good enough. "What?" Mariah asked, ready to tune her out.

"Mariah, Matrix got loose, breaking a quarantine under Kylee's watch. We got lucky this time, but he could have run off or seriously injured another dog or person." *Keep repeating the same points.* Mariah thought. "In addition to all of that, she let Benjamin walk off with Matrix and Echo." They locked eyes for a moment. Kelly must have known what she was thinking because she added. "This is a serious incident; you can't let this slide. When Animal Control finds out, you know as well as I do, we're going to be in trouble." Mariah put her hands on her head. The situation was bad, and, unfortunately, someone needed to be punished.

"Kylee knows better than to handle a no-touch dog; there is no way she let Matrix out," Mariah replied, coming to her friend's defense.

"I know that," Kelly admitted. "I never said the incident happened on purpose, but it still happened."

"I'll reprimand Kylee, then call animal control. Do I need to do anything else?" Mariah asked sincerely. This situation was more than she was prepared to handle, and despite Kelly's by-the-book attitude that drove her crazy, her experience was helpful. Kelly seemed to notice she was asking for advice; her angry look lifted slightly.

"Have everyone write down what happened; I'll grab written reports for Ethan and myself." An excited looked formed on Mariah's face.

"We can check the suite's camera to see what happened." *That should clear Kylee. Why didn't I think of that earlier?* Her excitement soon faded when Kelly reminded her the suite camera was broken.

"Shit," Mariah said under her breath. She got out of her chair, Kelly did the same. "Get the reports; I'll regroup with you in a bit."

"I'll get right on it. You want me to take Benjamin's report as well?" When they exited the office, Kylee was sitting in the hallway; her face was red, and her eyes were swollen from crying.

"Yes, if you could." Mariah added. Kelly walked toward the lobby. Mariah didn't say anything; she only motioned for Kylee to come inside. Kylee sat down and said in a teary voice.

"Mariah, I'm so sorry; I don't know what happened!"

"Kylee, I know." Mariah cut in. "Kelly said you fell down the stairs. "Are you ok?"

"Yes." Kylee replied, showing a light bruise on her shoulder. "It wasn't that bad of a fall. I only hit my shoulder."

"Hold on." Mariah got up and looked outside the office to make sure no one, like Shawn, was listening. She sat back down and said, "Kylee, when Reggie or someone else asks you about your injury, don't say it wasn't that bad." Kylee looked at her, puzzled. Mariah thought for a moment, then added. "Say something like I fell, and I don't know how long I was lying there."

"What. Do you mean lie?" Kylee asked with surprise in her voice.

"No, don't lie, but don't make it sound like it wasn't a big deal either, and just to make it look better, I'm going to have you visit a doctor."

"Mariah, I don't need a doctor." Kylee insisted. "It's not like I hit my head." Come on, Kylee, get with the program. Mariah thought.

"Kylee, I'm going to be honest with you; you're not in a good position right now. There's even a chance animal control is going to shut us down for a bit due to Matrix getting loose."

"I know." Kylee sniffled and wiped some tears from her eyes. "Am I going to get fired?" She continued with dread in her voice.

"I'll do all I can to make sure that doesn't happen." *Even if it means sacrificing Benjamin,* she said to herself.

"Kelly's going to throw me under the bus, and she's right. It was an accident, but it's my fault this happened." Kylee wiped the tears from her face.

"Your right, I doubt we've heard the last of this." Mariah said, knowing it was inevitable. Kelly was going to tell Reggie all about what happened, if she hadn't already. Mariah reached into a cabinet and pulled out a form.

"I need you to write down everything that happened; you know the drill." Mariah looked out the window as Kylee started writing. "Two dog bites in two days. I'm doing a great job as supervisor." Mariah said out loud.

"You're doing fine; both situations were beyond your control." Kylee sniffed. "This was all on me." *Kylee, you're in danger of losing your job, and you still want to encourage me,* Mariah thought. Feeling guilty, she put Kylee in that position.

"No, Kylee, in the end, it was my fault. As mean as it sounds, I should have listened to Zander and not let Benjamin walk dogs."

"Well, it's over now. All we can do is repair the damage that's already done. You need anything else?" Kylee asked, handing her the paper.

"No, you're good to go, all, and *if* your shoulder starts getting worse, let me know and go to the doctor." Mariah gave her a look that said *hint, hint.*

"I thought you were sending me to the doctor."

"Yes." Mariah remembered. "Why don't you go make the appointment now?" Both girls stood up, and Mariah gave Kylee the hug she knew she needed. Kylee started to leave the office, then turned around.

"Mariah, is everything going to be OK?" She asked, worried.

"If we play our cards right, yes, you'll be OK," Mariah confirmed. "Now go make a doctor's appointment and bring a doctor's note back." Mariah waited for Kylee to leave, then called Reggie. The phone only rang once before he picked up.

"Mariah, I was just about to call you. What in the hell happened?" He asked a voice in a frantic, thick Jamaican accent. "Do you know what kind of situation we're in?" *Kelly didn't waste any time, did she?* Mariah thought bitterly.

"I'm well aware of what happened." Mariah replied. "I have written reports on the incident from Kylee, Ethan, Benjamin, and Kelly."

"Scan and e-mail them to me later. Right now, I want to hear about what happened from the head horse's mouth."

"I didn't see anything," Mariah admitted. "I can tell you what I was told."

"Good enough." Reggie confirmed. Mariah explained what happened, making Kylee look as innocent as she could.

"How did Matrix get loose?" Reggie asked. Mariah could hear a pen writing when he stopped speaking.

"I have no idea; from what I can gather, someone left the clip off the latch; he must have smacked it while jumping and the cage opened."

"Why was Kylee messing with a no-touch dog during training?" Reggie questioned.

"She wasn't." Mariah replied with assurance. "It had to have happened last night or during the morning feeding."

"I assume you checked the security feed." Mariah reminded him the suite camera was broken, which made Reggie curse.

"Mariah, what do you think I should do about this situation because we're in deep shit?"

"I'll have a staff meeting and reinforce the need to clip the gates and give everyone a stern warning; this can't happen again."

"Someone needs to be punished." Reggie added. "An incident like this cannot go unpunished."

"Who?" Mariah asked. "I don't know who left Matrix's gate unlocked, and I won't accuse someone without evidence."

"It happened under Kylee's watch; she should be held accountable. Do you agree?" Mariah started to speak before Reggie continued. "Letting Benjamin, a mentally disabled employee, handle a dog that has bitten twice is a huge liability. We're lucky he wasn't bitten or killed."

"She told Benjamin not to touch the dog or go off without her repeatedly, plus she hit her shoulder and head pretty hard, so I doubt she was thinking clearly," Mariah added. She heard Reggie groan; she knew he was thinking hard, so she decided to keep the pressure up. "Kylee's one of our best employees; do we really want to fire her for something that wasn't even her fault and for getting injured?" After a few moments of tense silence, Reggie said, "Give Kylee a written warning and tell her if anything like this happens again, it will be the end of her employment."

"I will." Mariah replied. *Kylee's going to be OK.* After finishing the call with Reggie, she rushed back to the lobby.

"Did Kylee leave yet?" she asked Carmen.

"No, she made the doctor's appointment, then went to her room." Mariah walked to Kylee's room and knocked on the door.

"Come in," Kylee mumbled. Mariah opened the door. Kylee was sitting on her bed; a suitcase was next to her. She looked like a prisoner, ready for judgment.

"Do I still work here?" she asked with a sniffle.

"Of course you do," I told you, I'd take care of it." Kylee's face instantly lit up. "Really!"

"No, I just said that to get your hopes up before I crush them." Mariah teased with a smile.

"I thought for sure I was done for." Kylee breathed in relief. Mariah's face again turned serious.

"It was an accident, Kylee." She handed her a paper. "Though I need to give you this, it's a written warning about what happened."

"Fair enough."

"When's your appointment?"

"I had it already." Kylee answered. Mariah gave her a surprised look.

"I had a video call with my doctor. He said to put ice on it and go easy the next few days."

"Do you have a doctor's note?"

"Yes. I'll email it to you."

"Cool. You still work here, and dogs need walked so get off your butt and get back to it." Mariah replied, sticking her tongue out.

"I'll be ready in ten minutes." Kylee assured, cheering up.

CHAPTER 9

The next afternoon, Mariah saw a white Jeep coming up the driveway that had *Fairbanks Dog Warden* on the side. *Here we go,* she thought as the Jeep pulled into the parking lot and came to a stop. Alex Mackenzie stepped out, holding a large clipboard. He was a tall, middle-aged man with a long graying beard that covered most of his face. Mariah picked up her walkie-talkie.

"Zander," she said, then remembered he was feeling sick this morning and was taking the day off. "Ethan," she corrected. "The dog warden just showed up; please make sure everything looks nice up there."

"Will do." He replied. Mariah grabbed a folder containing Matrix's information and the incident reports on the bite. She breathed heavily, showing clear signs of nervousness.

"You'll do fine," Carmen encouraged. Mariah shot a nervous glance at her as Alex opened the lobby door.

"Hello." He said in a ruffled voice. "Were in for quite a storm over the weekend, aren't we." He sat the clipboard on the table, which looked to have nearly a dozen papers attached to it.

"Looks like it. Here's the information on what happened with the recent dog bite." Mariah said handing him the folder. He looked it over for a few minutes.

"I was also informed that this dog escaped and was running around the property yesterday."

"Yes," Mariah admitted. "We still don't know how it happened, but he's locked up now."

"Someone didn't get the memo he was under quarantine." Alex replied; his tone had a slight hint of humor in it.

"I guess so," Mariah replied, not knowing what to say.

"You understand it's unlawful to handle a dog that is under state quarantine for the time of the quarantine?" he asked in a sterner tone.

"Yes, I fully understand that. I was shocked when it happened; we managed to get him back in his cage without incident." Mariah quickly said hoping she hid her nervousness.

"No one's handled him since, correct?" Alex asked, tapping his pen on the counter.

"No. We get him to the outside portion of the cage, then closed the slider to clean it," Mariah answered, worried she was talking too much.

"We'll get the quarantine started then. While I'm here, I'm also going to do the yearly kennel inspection. Kill two birds with one stone."

"That would be great," Mariah replied, pleased she had told Ethan to tidy up the kennel.

"May I see your rabies vaccination records?" Alex requested.

"For my personal dog?" Mariah asked, concerned that she had left it at home.

"No, the rabies vaccination records for the dogs currently boarding with you." He replied with an amused smile.

"Right." *Get a grip, Mariah.* She told herself. She turned her chair around and grabbed a large red folder from the book shelf. While Alex was going through the records, Carmen went to the kennel area to make sure everything was in order. Mariah watched nervously as he wrote on his clipboard, wondering if she had done anything wrong.

"All the paperwork seems in order," Alex stated minutes later.

"That's good." Mariah saw Carmen returning. With Alex's back turned, she gave Mariah a quick thumbs up.

"Alright, let's get the inspection started." Alex said picking up his clipboard. "Yes, I'm old-fashioned." He held the clipboard out. "I never could get into those tablets."

"Some of us are." Mariah replied, realizing he must have noticed her eyeing the clipboard. Alex began walking out the door.

"Mariah, you're supposed to walk with him," Carmen whispered.

"Right," Mariah said, grabbing her winter gear from the coat rack. She went outside to be greeted by a cold gust of wind. She hid her face in the artificial fur that covered the hood.

"Last time I was here, Tiffany was in charge. So you're the new supervisor?" Alex said as they walked towards the kennel. Hearing you're the new supervisor caused a feeling of satisfaction to come over Mariah.

"Yes, I got promoted after she left."

"Is Kelly still around?"

"Yes, she got transferred to kennel staff; Reggie wanted someone with more experience in the back," Mariah replied, trying to sound as professional as possible. "That feels better," Mariah commented when they got inside, grateful for the heat.

"Now I've been walking and talking with you, but I never got your name," Alex reminded her.

"Oh, I'm Mariah," she replied, realizing she had never introduced herself. The two playfully shook hands. Mariah felt the nervousness slowly leave her. Alex Mackenzie seemed like a normal guy just doing his job. The two entered the client boarding area. Mariah walked with Alex, watching as he looked at every dog chart and enclosure. When he pointed out a few of the dogs made messes in their enclosures, Mariah assured she would have someone clean them right away. When they exited the client area, Alex stopped and started writing on his clipboard again.

"How'd we do in this section?" Mariah asked, hoping it was OK.

"You did fine," Alex replied. "As I mentioned in there, some of the cages needed cleaning, and I saw some food in the drains. I know you're aware of those problems, and they will be taken care of."

"Kylee's on it right now," Mariah confirmed. Next, they went through the sled dog section, which was nearly perfect. Mariah sniffed. A mix of gingerbread and cookie dough cologne filled her nostrils.

"Hello, Kelly, Ethan. Looks and, more importantly, smells great." Alex complimented. "I thought at first I walked into a bakery." Mariah gave a happy nod to Kelly and Ethan. Once they were finished, Alex said.

"So we only have the suite area left; that's where Matrix is, correct?"

"Yes." Mariah replied. *Let's get in and out of there.*

"Alright, I'll start the quarantine, then be out of your hair."

"So we passed?" Mariah asked, worry beginning to fill her again as she waited for a reply.

"Yes, ma'am, everything looks great." Mariah's feelings of nervousness turned to feelings of pleasure and accomplishment, her first inspection, and she passed.

"Yes!" Mariah yelled as she happily leaped into the air. Her face quickly gained a look of embarrassment. "Sorry."

"You're perfectly fine." Alex replied, giving her a friendly pat on the shoulder. He started going through his papers, then gave an embarrassed laugh of his own. "You know what I left the quarantine papers in the truck. I'll need to go grab them quick." Mariah walked with Alex, and after he found his papers, they walked towards the basement side entrance. Echo and Athena rushed to the outside portions of the suites, giving friendly barks.

"So do I have to do anything while he's on quarantine?" Mariah asked.

"You notified the owner about the situation already. Correct?"

"Yeah, I did that right after we reported the bite."

"Then no. You only need to wait until the quarantine is lifted. Oh, and I wanted to talk to..." He looked at the bite record. "Zander in person before I leave."

"Of course." Mariah replied. She didn't mention he was feeling sick. Figuring it would cause unnecessary problems. She stepped onto the first of four half-rounded stairs that connected to a stone supporting wall on either side. A stone pattern covered the floor, leading to a wooden door.

"After you," Mariah said, opening the suite door.

"Thank you," Alex said, heading in. Mariah glanced at the dogs. Neit looked up from his water bowl; drips of water fell from the long hair on his mouth; Goliath came inside and started giving an excited bark; Matrix was standing outside his suite to the left of the suite door. Mariah did a double take. Before she could say anything, Matrix charged, knocking Alex against the wall. He bit down on Alex's arm, shaking his head left to right. Alex cried out in pain, trying to keep his balance as Matrix tried to pull him to the ground.

"Matrix stop!" Mariah screamed out of instinct. She pulled out her pepper spray and fired. Matrix grunted in surprise and released Alex's arm. Mariah closed the suite door as Alex fell backwards. Matrix stood on two legs, looking at Mariah through the tiny squares of glass. She saw the same knowing grin she had seen before form on his face. He turned his head slightly and winked. Mariah felt her feet leave her. Alex held his arm, moaning and cursing.

"The main door to the suite is closed, right?" Alex asked in a pain-filled voice. Mariah sat on the ground, her eyes wide with shock, feeling the same type of fear and anxiety she was sure Kylee felt the day before. Mariah tried to speak, but no words would form. *How had he gotten out?* She knew she had checked his suite this morning, and it was locked. *Or was it?* Mariah thought, fearing she imagined the suite was closed when it was wide open. Alex took a bandanna from his pocket and wrapped it around the wound. "That was Matrix?" Alex asked in an angry tone. Mariah brought the walkie-talkie to her mouth.

"Carmen I need help area suite area! came to the side entrance." Mariah said.

"You need help in the suite area?" She heard Carmen say sounding confused.

"Yes!"

"I'll be right there."

"Is there a way we can get him back in the cage without anyone going inside?" Alex asked.

"Um, I...." Mariah tried to think but couldn't; all she could focus on was Matrix's barking.

"What happened?" Carmen asked, rushing down the half-rounded stairs. Mariah couldn't speak; she only pointed at the door.

"How did he?" Carmen said, stopping mid-sentence, then gasped when she saw Alex's arm. She walked up to the glass. "Matrix, down." He calmed down for a moment, then started barking again. Alex repeated his question about getting Matrix back in the suite.

"Mariah, if you can get him outside, I can run in and close the gate." Carmen offered.

"Are you sure that's safe?" Alex questioned.

"Yeah, the dog's been fine with me and seems to hate Mariah, so it should work." Carmen turned to Mariah. "Mariah, can you do it?" Mariah shook her head and grabbed for the suite door.

"Not a good idea." Carmen reminded placing a hand on it. Matrix jumped at the glass again. Mariah snapped herself out of her haze. By now, all the dogs were outside, excitedly barking and jumping at the fencing. Mariah crouched down in front of the outside portion of Matrix's suite and started calling him. The other dogs continued to bark in excitement. Soon, Mariah saw Matrix's head in the slider. He let out a vicious bark, then rushed at her, slamming into the fencing, snapping and growling. Alex backed away. *Please don't break,* Mariah thought, looking at the chain link. She saw Carmen rush inside.

"We're good." Carmen confirmed seconds later.

"OK," Mariah answered in relief, then felt her body shaking with nervousness as she walked into the suites. Matrix soon followed, continuing his snarls before laying down. *I'm dead.* She thought, knowing how serious this was. *Everything had been going so well. My entire career is going down the drain, thanks to that dog!*

"The door seems solid," Alex said, checking the latch. "I don't see how he could have opened it himself." Alex turned his attention to Mariah and Carmen. "Ladies, if you don't mind, can we finish this back in the lobby?"

"Sure," Carmen said, looking at Mariah for clarification. Mariah shook her head; it was OK. Back in the lobby, Mariah could still feel her body shaking. *How could this have happened?* Matrix was locked in the cage; she was sure of it. Had Shawn let him out for revenge, or had Carmen done it to take her spot? Mariah shot an untrusting glance at her.

"Mariah, this is unacceptable." Alex paused, like he was about to say something difficult. He didn't need to say anything; Mariah already knew what was going to happen. "I'm afraid I'm going to have to shut you down until that dog is gone and a full inspection of the staff and facility is conducted." He handed her and Carmen both a citation.

"No new dogs can be admitted; the only people allowed in the facility other than staff are owners of dogs who are already boarded."

"I understand," Mariah replied in a shaky voice.

"Can you call the owner? I would like to speak to him personally." Mariah grabbed the phone and started to dial. Her fingers stopped hitting the buttons. She felt her eyes swelling up.

"Hey, Mariah." Carmen said, giving her a hug, which did little to help. "Mariah, you're in no condition to work; why don't you go upstairs and rest? I can handle everything." Carmen offered.

"That will be fine," Alex agreed. Mariah put both hands over her face as she sprinted for the staff kennels. She grabbed Blaze, the source of comfort she desperately needed, then rushed upstairs, not wanting anyone to see her in this state; everything was falling apart around her. When she got upstairs, she saw Matrix standing in the hallway with that grin on his face. She went straight to her room, knowing it was a hallucination. She fell on her bed, put her hands around Blaze, and started to cry.

CHAPTER 10

Alex Mackenzie drove down Snowy Hill Road. The sky was dotted with clouds, and small snow flurries danced off the ground. He came to a stop at a stop sign. He looked down at his arm. He had always handled dog bite reports but never expected to get bitten himself. He didn't hold a grudge against Snowy Hills or Mariah, but policy was policy, and the place needed to be closed until they got a proper handle on things. He turned left, towards the highway. The frozen fields turned into thick forests on both sides. He slowed down to see if he could spot any wildlife. Suddenly, a large rock slammed into his window from the opposite side of the forest. The passenger side windshield shattered, leaving large cracks on the driver's side. Alex hit the brakes. He tried to maintain control as the jeep went off the road. He could hear the scraping sound of sticks underneath the Jeep before it came to a stop. Alex cursed, getting out of his Jeep. If the rock was someone's idea as a joke, it wasn't funny, and he was going to make sure they paid for it.

"I'm a dog warden, a government official!" he yelled. He listened, expecting to hear rustling in the bushes and see several teenagers making a break for it. After seeing or hearing, he looked at the rock standing upright on the passenger seat. *My God, the size of it.* He estimated the rock was two feet long. He grunted as he picked it up, guessing it was between fifty and a hundred pounds. He dropped it by the Jeep. He examined the surroundings again. Everything was flat; the rock couldn't have slid off, not at that speed or height. *Who could have thrown a rock that size that far?* Alex stepped back when a loud, high-pitched roar filled the air. He could feel the sound vibrating in his chest. *Must be the biggest bear in the county.* Feeling safe near his Jeep, he looked across the forest, hoping to catch a glimpse of the bear. The mostly barren trees and snow-covered ground would make the bear easy to spot. He focused in on a group of five large pine trees, four of which still had needles; the one on the end was completely brown. *Something must have ripped that tree up,* Alex thought, looking at the pieces of long moss that covered the tree. He looked between the trunks of each one, wanting to see if the bear was hiding in the tangle of green. He felt a thud on his jacket, and a minor pain went down his back. He turned around to see a small rock laying on the ground at his feet.

"Whoever's out there, there's a man eating bear in the woods. I'm sure you heard the howl. Come on out, and I'll give you a lift out of here," he shouted. *A ride to the police station too,* he thought. After no one came out, he again turned to the pine trees. He did a double take when he saw only four. The brown one on the end was missing.

"What the hell is going on?" He said out loud. Feeling a wave of fear come through him as a frigid wind started to blow, he walked towards his Jeep. He could still drive it and would figure out what had happened back at the office.

He opened the door and felt warm air strike the back of his neck, and felt the presence of something large behind him. He started to turn around when he was thrown into the car window. Barely conscious, Alex felt his body getting lifted into the air; he couldn't see his attacker, only the foul smell coming from it. He felt the hands holding him up release him. The black asphalt was getting closer, then everything went black.

***

Zander Conri sat up, gasping. "Damn, what a dream," he said as he rubbed the sleep from his eyes. Recalling the realistic dream he had about a samurai and some woman with horns and dragon wings fighting the Wendigo in a destroyed Native American village. It had been so lucid at the time; now that he was awake, he laughed at it. He looked out the window. It was bright out. The sun was near the tree line. His head was pounding. He grabbed his water bottle and took a drink to remove the dry feeling from his throat. He removed the covers to feel the cold chill that came with a fever. He grabbed his coat, putting it over the red exercise pants and shirt he wore to bed. He went to the bathroom, still feeling weak and miserable. While washing his hands, he looked in the mirror. He noticed his green eyes had a slight yellow tint to them. "What's happening?" He said softly. He removed the bandage from his hand, fearing how the wound would look. To his relief, other than itching, it looked healthy; the bite marks were starting to scab. *Maybe the dog does have rabies?* He thought. *No, the symptoms are too soon, plus Mariah and Carmen both saw the dog's vaccination records.* It was just an odd coincidence that he got sick right after the dog bite. He'd see a doctor in a few days if he wasn't feeling better. If it was rabies, he knew once the signs appeared he was as good as dead anyway. He exited the bathroom and thought about going back to sleep before deciding to go downstairs to get something to eat.

"Feeling alright, bro?" Ethan asked from his room.

"Still feel sick, but I'm alright. How'd the inspection go anyway?"

"We got shut down." Ethan said in a concerned tone. *What?* Zander wondered if he had heard him correctly. *No, Ethan's just messing with me. It wouldn't be the first time Ethan pranked someone.*

"Very funny." Zander replied, not taking it seriously.

"No, I'm serious; the dog warden got bit, and we failed the inspection. He shut us down until further notice." Despite not being there, he knew that dog Matrix was somehow involved. He'd heard all about his strange escape from the day before. He had been doing a small dog play group when it happened, and due to his walkie-talkie battery dying, he had no idea the incident occurred until later that day. It still irked him he hadn't been around to help Kylee.

"Where's Mariah?" he asked, concerned.

"She went to her room after it happened. No one's seen her since. Kylee and I were thinking of checking up on her, but decided to leave her alone until tomorrow."

"I'll check on her."

"All right, bro. I'm going to go eat. Let us know if she needs anything," Ethan said, passing him. Zander knocked on Mariah's door. He heard the rustling of covers inside. He knocked again. "Mariah, you OK?" He heard Blaze clawing at the door, giving a cheerful bark.

"Blaze, come." She heard Mariah say softly, followed by "Come in." He opened the door. The room was dimly lit. She was lying on the bed on top of the covers. Her makeup was running and her hair was a mess; he could smell sweat. It smelled like she hadn't taken a bath in a few days; that was unusual.

"Hey, how are you feeling?" Zander asked, not knowing what else to say. He gave Blaze a rub between the ears.

"How do you think I'm feeling?" Mariah snapped. *Alright, she's in no mood to talk,* he thought, backing away.

"OK, I'll leave you alone."

"No, please stay!" Mariah begged. "Sorry, I yelled at you."

"I get it." Mariah pointed at the opened door. He closed it, turned on the room light, and stood near the bed.

"You feeling OK?" Mariah asked, moving to a sitting position.

"I still have a low-grade fever, but other than that, I'm good," Zander assured. He knew Mariah had enough on her mind without worrying about him.

"Zander, if you're still feeling bad, you don't need to stay with me; go rest."

"No, I've slept enough. I heard the dog warden got bit, and we got shut down. I know this might be a dumb question, but how are you holding up?" Mariah's hands brushed her face. Blaze jumped on the bed and licked her arm. Mariah gently rubbed her.

"Zander, I don't know what to do. The kennels getting shut down; everyone's probably freaking out." Her face twisted into a look of hate. "If only that damn

Matrix hadn't come. Two bites in two days." *I knew Matrix was involved.* He could tell Mariah was on the verge of tears. To comfort his friend, Zander sat next to her and placed a brotherly arm around her shoulder.

"You're doing fine, buddy. It was my fault I got bit."

"And it's my fault the dog warden got bit." Mariah added, leaning closer to him. "Do you even know what happened?"

"Only a little." Zander admitted. He was shocked when Mariah explained in detail what happened. She was right; something was seriously wrong with that dog. *How had he gotten out of a locked kennel twice?* He thought, then asked.

"Did anyone figure out how he got out in the first place?"

"No," Mariah replied. "After what happened with Kylee and Benjamin, the gate should have been locked; it must have happened during morning cleaning."

"Carmen did the suites, right?" Mariah shook her head, yes. "She wouldn't have left it opened." Zander said out loud.

"And Kylee was down there half an hour before the dog warden came and didn't see anything." Mariah added.

"Well, we know she didn't do it." Zander stood back up, thinking about whether he should say what he was thinking. He looked at Mariah, avoiding looking at her straight in the eyes. "Do you think Shawn did it? You know, as revenge for your lecture?"

"That could have happened," Mariah confirmed. He could tell by her tone she was thinking the same thing. "He was supposed to be doing maintenance on the bus all day, but he could have found time to go down there."

"Check the cameras. See what he was doing all day."

"Good idea," Mariah agreed.

"How's Kylee taking the news?"

"Ugh," Mariah said, getting up. "Last I saw her was early this morning; I'm not even sure she knows what happened."

"Who have you told?" Zander asked. Mariah's face had a guilty look.

"You and Carmen." She again ran her hands down her face. "I should have told everyone what's going on hours ago."

"Ethan knew about it, so I guess Carmen told everyone."

"I better get downstairs and see what's going on. You coming to dinner?" The thought of food made his stomach wrench.

"I'm still feeling sick, so I'm going back to bed for the rest of the day."

"OK, I'll check in on you tomorrow and make sure no one bothers you."

"If Kylee wants to pop in, tell her it's OK. I'm sure she's worried that both her friends aren't feeling well."

"I'll let her know," Mariah confirmed. Zander started to leave, then said.

"Mariah, sorry, I don't want to be mean, but you might want to shower before you head down there. You seriously smell like sweat."

"Thanks a lot." Mariah said, sniffing herself. She picked up a pillow and started playfully hitting Zander. "Back to bed with you." She ordered. Zander grabbed the pillow, smacked Mariah with it, and then tossed it back in her room.

"I'll see you tomorrow," he said before going back to his room. When he shut the door, he again looked at the yellowing of his eyes. *What's happening to me? What's happening to me?* He thought, feeling himself starting to freak out. For a moment, he wanted to run back to Mariah's room, tell her what was happening, and ask her to drive him to the hospital. Soon, the thought dissipated. *My eyes have a yellow tint; big deal. I'll tell Mariah tomorrow sleep is more important now.* He had slept all day and still felt tired, like his body had no energy. He crawled in bed, pulling the covers over his head, and wrapped the covers around his body. The warmth from his cocoon covered his body, taking away the fever's chill. He listened to the dogs howling as he again drifted off to sleep.

CHAPTER 11

Mariah walked downstairs, wondering how far things had fallen apart since her departure. She had only been upstairs for several hours but knew a lot could have happened, especially under these circumstances. She hated the fact that she fell apart when her team needed leadership the most. She looked at the parking lot and saw that all the cars were still there. *At least no one left,* she thought, pleased. She checked the lobby to find it empty, so she put Blaze back in her kennel and went to the dining room.

"Mariah, you feeling better?" Carmen asked. She was sitting at a table with Kelly. Ethan and Kylee sat at a table across from them. Shawn sat by himself in the corner of the room. Mariah started to answer when Kylee ran up to her, wrapping her arms around her neck.

"Mariah, I'm so sorry about what happened. I thought about checking in on you, but…"

"Kylee, you're fine." Mariah said pulling away from the hug, not wanting to look weak in front of everyone. "I needed some time alone to think."

"Is Zander okay?" she asked.

"He's still feeling bad; hopefully he'll feel better tomorrow."

"I'll take him some soup. I'm sure he'd like that." Kylee said turning to go to the kitchen.

"Zander said he wanted to sleep; I wouldn't bother him." Mariah suggested. Kylee frowned and returned to her seat. Mariah tuned out the guilt she was feeling for lying and sat down with Carmen and Kelly. "How is everything?" She asked, worried what the answer might be. She thought Kelly would start berating her, but to her surprise, she remained slight.

"As you can imagine, Reggie's outraged. He wants that dam dog out of his kennel." Carmen answered. *Don't we all?*

"I assume he wants to talk to me?" Mariah asked, already knowing the answer.

"I answered most of his questions, so the heavy stuffs been dealt with. Some good news: Reggie called animal control and thinks he can have us opened by late next week." Carmen replied. *Some leader I am. When things get hard, I freeze up, letting other people handle the big problems.* Mariah reflected, feeling ashamed of herself once more.

"Mariah," Benjamin said, coming over to the table. "Sorry, this whole thing is my fault; if I didn't want to walk the dogs, none of this would have happened."

"No, Benjamin, this is my fault. I should have seen Matrix's gate wasn't latched." Kylee added.

"Kylee, don't blame yourself; we have no idea how Matrix got out." Kelly said. Mariah gave her a stunned look that Kelly noticed. "I changed my mind when he got out the second time. Sorry, Kylee, for accusing you so harshly."

"It's fine," Kylee replied, giving a small smile. "We were all upset at that time." *Wow, was not expecting that.* Mariah thought. She was worried Kelly and Shawn were going to give her the most problems; at least she was wrong about one of them. She looked over at Shawn, who seemed to be staring off into space. *Wonder what he's thinking about.* She thought about talking to him. *No, I can do that later.* She ended her thoughts and said.

"Ok, back to business. Have…?"

"Mariah, why don't you eat first? You haven't had anything since this morning." Kelly suggested. The mention of food caused Mariah to remember how hungry she was. Benjamin handed her a plate of spaghetti and meatballs.

"Have you called clients that have existing reservations?" Mariah asked as she twirled spaghetti around her fork.

"Carmen and I took care of that." Kelly assured.

"Honestly, as strange as this sounds, we were lucky we got shut down when we did." Ethan added coming over to the table to join the conversation.

"What do you mean by that?" Mariah asked.

"Looks like that storm that's going to hit tomorrow is going to be worse than we thought; it's probably going to bring travel to a near standstill. I bet most of the people coming were planning on canceling anyway."

"Things are looking up." Mariah said trying to sound strong in front of everyone. She looked over at Kylee. She was clutching her cup of coffee, and like Shawn, was staring off into space. Only Mariah knew what she was thinking about. That sent a wave of jealousy through her.

"Why don't you tell everyone that? Make a motivational speech." Kelly whispered. Mariah returned her focus to Kelly.

"Good idea." Mariah agreed. She stood up and clapped her hands.

"Hey, everyone just wanted to give a quick speech." Mariah looked around the room. Ethan and Kylee were giving her their attention. Benjamin walked out of the kitchen and sat down, and to her shock, Shawn also appeared to be listening. "I know things have been crazy around here lately, and all of us are worried about the kennel closing." Mariah made her voice more hopeful when she said. "But I have some good news. Reggie thinks we'll be reopened late next week, and many of the clients were going to cancel anyway because of the approaching snow storm, so the kennel hasn't lost much business. We still have lots of dogs in the kennel that need our care, so let's work just as hard as we always do and use any free time we have to make improvements around the kennel. If any of you have any questions or concerns, as always, you can come to me." Applause filled the room.

"Do we know when Zander is going to return to work?" Kelly asked.

"I talked to him earlier; he said he should be ready to get back to work tomorrow." With her speech finished, Mariah knew she had one more thing to do. Make sure Shawn is on the same page as everyone else. At first, she planned on getting in his face, making it clear that he was going to do as he was told without any backtalk. As she approached him, some advice her father had given her when she told her parents she had gotten the promotion entered her mind. *It's better to be respected than feared, Mariah.* "Good advice, dad." She whispered to herself. She changed her stance to more of a casual one when she reached him. "Doing OK, Shawn?" She asked in a normal voice.

"How do you think I'm doing?" He said in a less than kind voice. "Things have been going so great since you took charge. I mean, two dog bites, our phones were stolen, the facility got shut down. You're doing a great job."

"Are you done?" She asked seriously, managing to keep from shouting insults back.

"What if I'm not?" He challenged. Mariah momentarily closed her eyes, taking a moment to calm herself. Instead of yelling at him, she said in a calm yet commanding voice.

"Look, Shawn, we have a storm hitting tomorrow, and I need you to be on the same page with everyone. I know we don't get along, but I need you just as much as I need Kylee, Zander, and everyone else." Mariah noticed the tension starting to leave his body. *Have I finally gotten through to him?* She wondered.

"Yes, Shawn, we need someone strong to shovel the snow that's going to fall." Kelly added. Shawn snickered a little. *Do you have to get involved with everything?* Mariah thought, annoyed. Shawn was silent for a few moments then said.

"Heck, I have bills to pay and credit to rebuild. Fine, I'll play along."

"Good." Mariah complimented. "Before you go to bed, can you please make sure we have fuel for the heaters and flashlight batteries in case the power goes out and we're stuck here for a few days?"

"Already done." Shawn confirmed. "While you were upstairs, I took a trip into town and refilled the gas tanks, and we have enough batteries to last the winter." He joked.

"Nice job." Mariah complimented. "Alright, everyone, relax for the rest of the night. I'll take care of the few PM meds we have."

"Good speech." Ethan complimented before leaving.

"Yeah, you did really well." Kylee agreed coming over to her.

"Thanks." She looked at Kylee and said,

"We can hang out after I finish meds."

"If you feel up to it, sure. Want some help?" Kylee offered.

"I'm good, Kylee. I only have a few. See you in a bit."

For the next fifteen minutes, she went down the list, handing out the dog's medication. She gave the last dog on the list, Runway, an older brown cocker spaniel, her arthritis medicine, then did a final walk-through to make sure all the dogs were inside and all the gates were latched. When it was time to check the suites, she felt her stomach knot. She slowly walked down the wooden stairs, her heart jumping every time the wood creaked. Memories of what happened earlier that day came flooding back to her. She looked through the glass to make sure Matrix was in his cage. All the dogs were sleeping, including Matrix. When she heard the boards creak from the floor above her, she turned her attention towards them. *Wood settling.* She told herself. She looked at the dogs again. All of them were sleeping except Matrix, who was sitting next to his cot. She double-checked the latch on the gate. She felt Matrix's eyes watching her. He tilted his head slightly and winked.

"That's it!" She said fed up with his games. She looked him right in the eye and said.

"Look, I don't know who or what you are, but stop messing with me! I know you can understand me! Stop playing!" Part of her felt like she was doing the right thing, confronting a bully who was messing with her every chance he had. While another part of her was thinking how silly it was to be screaming at a dog, Matrix remained seated; he only raised his upper lip slightly. "Come on, show your true form! I know you're unlocking this door!" She screamed. Matrix put his head down, looking at her with half-moon eyes. Mariah put her hand on her face. She laughed. "Am I really in here yelling at a dog, accusing him of unlocking gates?" Mariah asked herself, questioning her sanity. Mariah looked at the suite entrance, expecting someone to barge in, wondering what all the shouting was about. *That would be fun to explain.* She thought sarcastically. She turned her body, putting the back of her head against the wall. "I'm going crazy."

"Let's play fetch." A voice from inside Matrix's cage said. Mariah shrieked. She turned, her feet tangling up as she stumbled backwards. She braced herself on the wall before falling. Again, a voice came from inside the cage.

"I'd love to play with you." Mariah looked at Matrix, her eyes wide with shock. *No, the dog couldn't have spoken to me.* Matrix was now lying on his cot, looking up at her. Mariah remained speechless, still not believing what just happened. *The dog talked! He actually talked!* Matrix moved his paw, revealing a black ball with red flames.

"Oh, my god." Mariah said feeling like an idiot, recognizing the toy. Matrix bumped it with his paw.

"Let's play fetch," it repeated.

"I need some time off. You're driving me crazy." Matrix looked at her and grinned. Mariah turned away from him, then heard.

"Come on, Mariah, it's been years since we spoke. Have you forgotten how to listen to me?" *No, this isn't happening.* Mariah felt her body starting to tremble. She closed her eyes and counted to ten when she opened them. Matrix was standing at the cage door. He started barking and growling, every so often parts of him started passing through the gate. Mariah screamed and ran. She ran up the stairs and down the now-darkened hallway. Several dogs started barking. When she neared the end of the hall, she slammed into something. Both she and the person in front of her stumbled. A dim source of light was coming from the kitchen, which allowed her to recognize Benjamin.

"Mariah, are you OK?" He asked in a slow voice. She looked into his eyes, which were empty sockets; his face was contorted, and the skin looked to be peeling off.

"Get away, get away!" She screamed. She moved her body to run when her left foot slipped in the drain. She fell backwards, her head hitting the back of a kennel gate. The nearby dogs started barking in excitement.

"Mariah, are you ok?" Benjamin again asked, trying to help her up. She looked at him again; his face was normal. Mariah began to regain her senses and realized she was in the client-dog section. She tried to think of something that would justify her actions, but her mind was blank. She got to her feet as she tried to clear her head.

"I'll go find Zander or Carmen and tell them what happened," Benjamin offered.

"No." Mariah said quickly that was the last thing she needed right now. Things were stressful enough around here without people having to worry about her, thinking quickly, she said. "I had a little scare with that scary dog, Matrix. He tried to bite me when I was checking his papers. Everything's ok now, though." She said giving him a wide smile, which she was sure looked fake.

"That dog is mean; I'll be glad when he's gone," Benjamin said, seeming to accept the explanation.

"Me too," Mariah agreed. "Benjamin, why are you even up here?" She questioned knowing he had no reason to be in the kennels.

"I saw the lights were still on and came to turn them off, then I heard you screaming and wanted to make sure you were okay."

"Well, thank you." Mariah replied. Believing his story, she turned the hall light back on. "I'm going to finish up in here and then join you guys.

"Can we play some games?"

"Sure can." Mariah replied. Benjamin walked away. Mariah opened the suite door to turn the light off. She put her hand on the switch, then saw the shadow of a dog at the bottom of the stairs. *It's not real. Mariah, get out of here and relax.* Without giving it another thought, she shut the light off and went down the stairs, hoping her deteriorating mental state would improve.

***

The large grandfather clock in the lobby struck midnight. The beautiful sound of the Westminster Chimes started playing. As the staff slept, a figure walked into the employee dog room. Kelly's dog, Bee, huddled under the cot, whimpering and shaking with fright as her room door was opened and shut. The figure stopped in front of the cot, throwing it to the side. Bee yelped in fright and ran around the room. The figure stood still, enjoying the small dog's yelps of fright as she ran across the room, fruitlessly jumping at the walls. The figure lunged forward. The cracking sound of bones breaking and the drips of blood smacking the floor were muffled by Bee's loud cries of pain. In seconds, it was over. The figure left the room ahead of the stream of flowing blood.

Kelly Linn was awoken by a tapping sound at her window. Her mind still fogged by sleep, Kelly opened the curtains. Large snowflakes hit the window, each making a small tapping sound. She got back into bed and looked around.

"Bee." She stated that she had not seen her dog. She tried to go back to sleep but couldn't shake the feeling that something was wrong. She turned her light on and couldn't see Bee anywhere. "Bee, where are you?" She said. "Bee, come here." She repeated this time, making kissing sounds. *Did I forget to bring her in the bedroom?* Kelly thought. Swearing, she did, but in her haze of sleep, she couldn't be sure. She checked under the bed, then the rest of the room. "I can't believe this." She huffed, put pants and a t-shirt over her pajamas, and walked downstairs. "Bee, I'm so sorry I forgot about you." She said as she entered the employee dog room. Once inside, she stopped in her tracks. A stream of blood was spreading out from under the door of Bee's room. "Bee!" She yelled in a frantic voice. She pulled the door open and screamed. Bee was lying in the middle of the room, mangled to the point of being nearly unrecognizable. "Bee!" Kelly yelled in horror as tears started to stream down her face. She crouched down. Her hand reached out to stroke a portion of fur that wasn't covered in blood. "Who could have done this?" She cried, wanting to pick up her beloved pet, but couldn't find the will to touch the mangled body. Anger filled her. She knew who did it. The same person who stole their phones. She thought about calling the police or, better yet, taking the hammer to Shawn. No, I need proof before I act. She looked at the ceiling; the camera was still intact. She didn't bother to wake Mariah or anyone else. She wanted to find out for herself who had done this unthinkable act. She grabbed the key and went to the office, not fully closing the door behind her. She sat down at the desk and opened the security video logs. She started playing the footage at ten p.m., around the time when everyone had gone to bed, and forwarded it. She watched until she saw Bee rush under the cot and the door swing open. She stopped the video, not sure if she was ready to see what she knew was coming. She grabbed a tissue from a box on the desk and wiped the tears from her eyes. "Ok, let's get this over with." She said softly. She hit play and focused on the video, not noticing the shadow against the wall disappear as its caster entered the room. The sound of the door shutting made Kelly jump. She stopped the video.

"Hello, is someone there?" she asked. "Ethan, that better not be you screwing around. I'm really not in the mood." No reply came. The monster that killed Bee entered her mind. A feeling of fear came over her. She looked around the office, trying to find something that could be used as a weapon. She grabbed the office lamp, not her first choice, but it was the best she had. She walked towards the door, the lamp raised above her head. She opened it slowly, looking both ways, only to see the dark hallways. After listening for several seconds and hearing nothing, her attention returned to discovering who had killed her dog.

She dropped the lamp on the desk before sitting down. "What the hell?" She said staring at the black computer screen. She hit the monitor button. Nothing. Did I kick the power cord loose? She looked under the desk. Her breathing increased as panic started setting in. The power cord was cut in half. Knowing someone or something was in the room with her, she slowly turned the chair towards the door and got up, getting ready to run. She let out a yelp of fear when she noticed an outline move between herself and the doorway.

"Who are you? What do you want?" She asked as she frantically grabbed the lamp again. A brief scream left her throat before the shadow leaped on her. The back of her head struck the desk before her body hit the ground. A wave of dizziness came over her. Dazed and confused, she felt a sharp pain in her left ankle. She let out another scream as her body was drug across the floor. Her arms flailed around her desperately, trying to grab something. She felt the cold outside air, then felt her body sink into the snow. Her screams were cut off by the smothering snow. She could feel the teeth in her ankle readjusting every so often, then suddenly they released. She moaned and cried in shock at what happened. On impulse, she slowly pulled her left pantleg up, expecting to see a massive wound. To her pleasant surprise, only a ring of small puncture marks that barely broke the skin were visible. She got up frantically, trying to get her bearings. *I'm outside in the parking lot.* She quickly realized this. She couldn't see her attacker, but she could hear the crunch of soft snow as her attacker circled her just out of sight. Her hands and face were numb. She looked towards the kennel, then towards her car. The car was closer, and she had a set of spare keys in a lockbox under the back bumper.

"Screw this; I'm getting out of here." She dashed for the car, hoping with every step, her attacker wouldn't return. When she reached the car, she bent down, her numb, burning fingers struggled to move the numbers on the lockbox as the frigid wind and falling snow picked up. She whimpered, hearing crunching snow behind her. She grabbed the keys and clicked the unlock button, then rapidly opened the door. She had one foot inside the car when her attacker slammed into her from the side. Her face smashed the side of the door before she fell. Kelly pulled her head up, seeing a stream of red dots forming on the snow. She started to scream, expecting the attack to continue, but to her surprise, it had again stopped. She looked around in the darkness, the wind and snowflakes limiting her vision.

"Why are you doing this?" In a daze, Kelly pulled herself into the car, quickly slamming the door. "Damn it!" she yelled, realizing her keys were gone. She started crying and moaning as she pleaded for someone to help her. A few minutes later, she was able to compose herself enough to reach into the glove compartment and grab a flashlight.

"Please..." She whimpered. Hoping the keys were somewhere in the car. After searching the car thoroughly, she found nothing. *I'm never going to find them.* She feared watching the snow fall. She shined the flashlight beam through the window. After several moments of searching by a miracle, she saw the key's metal reflection lying a few yards from where she fell. *I can't go out there.* She thought worried about what her attacker would do. *I can't stay here either.* Her thoughts continued, knowing her attacker was strong enough to break her car window by how effortlessly it dragged her outside. Having no choice, she breathed in heavily, opened the door, and ran for the keys. She reached down, praying her attacker wouldn't come upon her. With the keys in hand, she got back inside, slamming the door shut. "Please start, please start." She turned the key, and the car came to life. She turned the defroster and heater on and used the wipers to push aside the newly fallen snow covering the windshield. Her right hand put the gear in four-wheel drive. As she headed down the driveway, she looked back at the kennel, thinking about going in and getting the others. *No, I'll drive to the nearest town and bring back help. Everyone is safe in their rooms. I'll be back within the hour,* she thought, trying to justify her actions. Her free hand burned as the warm air blew against it. She stopped the car at the end of the driveway when she heard a growl in the back of the car. Kelly felt her heart racing, remembering she had left the door open when she ran out for the keys. She looked in the rear view mirror to see two dog-shaped outlines staring at her in the back seats. One had a short coat, the other a curly coat. The short-coated shape lunged forward, biting down on her arm. She screamed in pain, her foot letting off the brake as the jaws dug into her flesh. The car veered off the driveway, traveling through the snow for several feet before coming to a stop. The momentum caused her attacker to go forward, loosening the grip on her arm. Kelly opened the door and fell to the ground. She whimpered as she crawled through the snow.

"Help!" She cried weakly, then felt four feet land on her back, the weight burying her in the snow, muffling her screams. She felt a set of jaws bite down on the back of her neck. A snapping sound filled the area, and Kelly's lifeless head fell to the ground. Her body shook for several seconds, then remained still.

CHAPTER 12

The next morning, Mariah was awoken by the ringing of her alarm. She shut it off and felt Blaze jump off the bed.

"This is the second day you let me sleep in; I'm starting to like this," Mariah said, stroking her head. "I'll take you on a small walk." She attached Blaze's leash. When she left her room, she noticed Kelly's door was opened. Thinking nothing of it, she took Blaze outside. Snow was still falling at a rapid pace. The strong wind howled, whipping the snow around, limiting her visibility. Blaze leaped off the stairs into the snow. Mariah gasped when Blaze sank; soon only her head and neck reemerged. *It must have snowed two feet last night. Great,* Mariah thought, annoyed. Blaze leaped out of her hole and created another one. She looked like a swimmer as she dug through the snow, making herself a path she could walk through. Blaze was playing, rolling around in the snow, looking like she was having the time of her life. *We're not going on a walk in this.* "Come on, Blaze, let's go in." Moments later, Mariah put her in her kennel. *Poor Bee's going to have trouble out there.* She thought, looking in her kennel, and was surprised to find it empty. *She must be upstairs with Kelly or outside.* Mariah supposed, again thinking nothing of it. She noticed several tiny, dark brown spots on the floor. *Kelly, if your dog has the shits, clean it up.* Mariah thought, feeling amused, that she had a chance to preach to Kelly about cleanliness. Mariah showered, then went to the dining area. Zander and Ethan were already there.

"Zander! Feeling better?" Mariah asked in an excited voice, pleased to see him.

"Much," he replied.

"Some storm we got last night, Blaze nearly sank." Mariah said taking a seat next to Zander.

"Yeah, I thought we were only getting one to two feet; the weather man was way off this time." Ethan stated.

"What do you mean?" Mariah asked, grabbing a waffle.

"I checked my computer before coming down. The weather website says a state of emergency has been declared; we're expected to get an additional three to five feet." Mariah felt her mouth drop.

"Ethan, you're kidding, right?"

"No, I wish I was," he replied. *We could be trapped here for a couple of days. What happens if a dog gets sick?* Unintentionally, a look of concern came across her face. *What if I need to get my medication?* She feared. Regretting not getting it when her psychotherapist suggested it. Mariah got up before someone noticed she was nervous. "I need to see the most recent weather reports for myself." Mariah went to the lobby and looked out the window. Large portions of it were covered with snow; large snowflakes pounded against the clear glass. She heard the sound of an engine and saw Shawn driving the plow down the driveway. She turned on the computer and opened the weather website. She put a hand over her head and moaned. Everything Ethan told her was correct. The storm could last the next two days; heavy snowfall and whiteout conditions were expected throughout that time. Mariah saw that the office phone already had five messages, most likely from clients canceling their pickups. *If we're going to be shut down, now's the time for it.* Mariah thought.

"Hey." Carmen said, standing in the doorway. Mariah lifted a hand, still looking at the computer. Carmen walked over and looked out the window.

"So, what's the game plan?" Mariah stood up.

"I'm going to eat breakfast and think about it." Carmen snickered.

"Take your time; it's not like anyone is going anywhere." Mariah returned to the kitchen and grabbed a grapefruit to go with her waffle.

"There's a lot of snow falling." Benjamin said, pointing to the kitchen window.

"Sure is." Mariah replied. "Ready for a lot of shoveling?"

"I don't like the wind; it makes scary sounds." Mariah focused on the ghostly howl of the wind hitting the building.

"There's nothing to be scared of; we are safe inside; when you go outside, you won't hear that sound anymore." Mariah went back to the dining room, and to her dismay, Kylee had taken her seat next to Zander. Kylee saw her and happily said.

"Zander is back!"

"I can see that." Mariah replied, giving him a pat on the back, before sitting next to Kylee. "So, Zander, what should we do about the snow?"

"Shovel it." He replied, looking at her with a grin.

"I know that." Mariah playfully smacked him. "I mean, do you think we should do anything else besides that?" He thought for a moment.

"I'd have someone walk around the building every hour or so to make sure nothing is collapsing." Zander pointed to Kylee. "Kylee can do that."

"I'll sink and freeze to death." Kylee countered, mirroring Mariah's playful smack. Zander lightly bopped her on the shoulder. Kylee stole a sausage from his plate in retaliation. Mariah grunted under her breath.

"I'd also gather up flashlights and batteries just in case the power goes out and have Shawn check the generator to make sure it's working, and if you want to be really cautious, make sure we have dry firewood. That's all I got." Zander continued.

"Good ideas. I knew I should have asked you." Mariah complimented. "I've already made sure we have flashlights and the generators working."

"Have any of you guys seen Kelly?" Ethan asked as he reentered the dining room. "I haven't seen her since last night."

"Me either." Kylee said.

"Her room door was opened, and Bee wasn't in her kennel this morning." Mariah added. Now starting to worry.

"Well, she has to be around here somewhere." Kylee stated. Mariah noticed Zander had a spaced outlook; she could tell he had something on his mind.

"Benjamin, have you seen Kelly around?" Mariah asked.

"Not since last night; her car's gone through," Benjamin replied while he gathered the empty dishes.

"What!" Ethan asked, getting up to look out the lobby window. Everyone soon followed. Benjamin was right. Kelly's car was missing. Snow was up to the tires on the other cars.

"I hope she didn't quit because of the kennel closing down." Mariah said, not knowing what else to think.

"She would have told someone if she was." Ethan assured.

"Maybe it was a family emergency during the night?" Kylee suggested.

"I'm sure Kelly's fine, and there's a good reason she left." Mariah said trying to sound convincing despite knowing something was wrong. She glanced at the answering machine. "I bet one of these messages is her."

"I hope so," Ethan said, clicking the button. One by one, each message was a client canceling their appointment. The last one was from Reggie Donald, asking Mariah to call him back. Mariah nudged Zander, making a soft grunt. When their eyes met, she motioned for him to follow her to the other side of the room. When they were out of earshot, she whispered.

"What do you think I should do? This storm is stressful enough on everyone. I don't want everyone to start freaking out about Kelly."

"Have everyone start working to keep their mind off things." Zander suggested. *Good idea,* Mariah thought, than had to ask.

"Zander, do you think she's OK?"

"Honestly." Zander stopped, put his head down, looked back up at her, and said. "Never mind."

"What." Mariah whispered sharply. Her eyes widening with concern. *Please don't say she's dead.*

"I had... Mariah, it's nothing."

"Zander, please tell me." Mariah begged, needing to know what he was thinking. Zander looked reluctant but said.

"For the past few nights, I've had dreams about a wendigo, human-looking dogs mauling people, fun stuff like that," he said with sarcasm. Mariah was about to ask him what this had to do with anything when he continued. "Last night, it was like I was seeing through the wendigo's eyes. I killed Bee, then watched Kelly get attacked by two dogs near the road." Mariah felt a look of concern form on her face. "Like I said, it was only a dream."

"Yeah, you're right." She said trying to forget it. "Please don't tell anyone else about that. Speaking of eyes, what's up with yours?" Mariah asked.

"Nothing why?" Zander asked, surprised.

"They're more yellow than I remember them."

"Maybe it's the light." Zander suggested looking away from her. "We should probably get back to everyone else." Mariah saw everyone was starting to look their way. Probably wondering what they were talking about. *His eyes are a trick of the light, nothing more.* Mariah thought, then managed to find her confident voice.

"Alright everyone. I'm sure Kelly will be back when the storm clears. Right now, we still have dogs that need care, so let's get to it. I know the snow is still falling, but let's try to keep the outside runs as clear as possible. Prioritize snow removal in the smaller client dog's enclosures."

"How do you want the teams since Kelly's away?" Carmen asked. Mariah tapped her fingers against the table, then said.

"Kylee and Ethan will do the client dog wing; Zander you take sled dogs; Carmen you take the suite; then help Zander. I'll do feed then help whoever needs it."

"I take it, no walks today?" Carmen asked.

"What gave you that idea? It's not like there's three feet of snow outside." Unenthusiastically, everyone started to get to work. "Ethan. Kelly's fine." Mariah said seeing he was deeply troubled.

"I hope so." He replied.

"Let's get to work; she'll be back before you know it." Kylee assured. When she and Carmen were alone, Mariah put her coat and hat on.

"I'm going to walk to the end of the driveway. I want to see for myself how bad the roads are." Mariah said as she put her gloves on. *Mabey finds signs of what happened to Kelly.* Mariah continued in thought.

"Suit yourself, crazy girl." Mariah froze. *Does she know? Is she making fun of my illness?*

"You OK?" Carmen asked in a normal voice.

"I'm fine," Mariah replied, realizing she was talking about her going out in the snow. She pushed on the door. The wind made an eerie howling sound, the force of it slamming the door in her face. Mariah turned to Carmen with a grin, trying to make light of the situation.

"Push harder." She teased. Mariah put her weight into it this time and stepped outside. Her ankle sank into the snow. She took large steps until she got to the clear driveway. She looked toward the forest. The snow-covered trees rocked side to side as snowflakes danced around them. If it was a picture, she would have thought it was pretty. Mariah saw Shawn's truck coming up the driveway. The plow pushing large portions of snow to the side. He parked the truck and got out. He took out a cigarette and lit it. He gave Mariah a slight glance, like he was checking to see if she would complain. He was outside, so she had no plans to do so.

"Morning. Got the driveway cleared for a few hours at least."

"That's fine, thank you. Go in and warm up for a bit, then can you please get the snow blower and clear the sidewalks, and then walk around the kennel to check for damage?"

"Sure can." Shawn confirmed. "I'll dig everyone out after that."

"I'll have Benjamin come out to help you, then we'll join in once the dogs are taken care of." Mariah said pleasantly surprised they were getting along. "By the way, have you seen Kelly this morning?"

"No, I haven't seen her since last night. I thought it was odd that her car was gone."

"Did you happen to see anything down the driveway?" Mariah asked, hugging herself against the cold.

"Like what?"

"You know, like signs a car was buried in the snow or tire tracks." Mariah continued.

"I didn't see anything like that; if Kelly tried to leave and got stuck, she'd walk back to the kennel."

"That's true. What if she stuck on the road somewhere?" She continued looking toward it.

"I guess she will walk to the nearest house, or a passing snowplow will give her a lift." Shawn guessed.

"Your right." Mariah agreed, enjoying his positive outlook on things. She thought about asking him about it but instead said. "I'm going to take a walk down the driveway. I want to see what the road looks like."

"They're covered by at least a foot of snow."

"I want to see it for myself." Mariah stated. "You know how I am."

"Want me to drive you down?" Shawn offered.

"No, I'm good."

"Whatever you want," Shawn said. He was about to toss the cigarette when he caught himself; instead, he placed it in the truck's ashtray. Mariah gave him a pleased nod, then walked down the driveway, wondering what could cause Kelly to leave before the storm hit. She felt her face getting numb. Zander's dream again entered her mind. *It was only a dream*. Mariah assured herself. When she reached the edge of the driveway, she couldn't tell the road from the land around it. She turned to look at the pine trees that dotted the snow-covered meadow. Her eyes focused on a large group of seven that were clustered together. Large clumps of snow fell from the green needles and were quickly replaced. She noticed something crouched between the tree trunks. She thought it looked like someone was crouched down wearing a large fur coat.

"Hello. Kelly!" Mariah said, taking a few steps into the deep snow.

"Kelly, is that you? Hello." The figure's head turned to her, then she stood up. Mariah gasped, then found she couldn't catch her breath. Whatever was among the trees was eleven feet tall. The pine needles and branches hid most of its features. She could make out a large furry body and a human-like hand; she could tell it wasn't a bear standing on two legs. Mariah thought back to the sound she heard. She closed her eyes and repeated. *No, what you're seeing is not real; you're not seeing Bigfoot.* She opened her eyes, and the figure was gone. She thought she saw portions of disturbed snow where she had seen the supposed Bigfoot but didn't dare go investigate. *Mariah, you've got to calm down. Don't start seeing things at a time like this.* With no sign of Kelly and the cold and fear getting to her, she ran back towards the kennel.

CHAPTER 13

Zander shoveled the last of the snow away from the kennel entrance. Normally one to enjoy the snow, but this was even too much for him. He opened the door, letting Ethan and Kylee go ahead of him. Both were breathing heavily from the work. He barely felt tired, which he thought was odd. Normally, this type of work tired him out as much as anyone else.

"This storm's supposed to last till tomorrow. This is crazy." Kylee said, looking out the window. Zander joined her; their foot prints were already starting to disappear. "At this rate, the building's going to be buried."

"No, they won't." Zander assured. "We're only supposed to get five more feet."

"Only five feet! I'll sink." Amusing images of Kylee stepping outside and sinking went through Zander's mind.

"I'll clear paths for you." Zander promised. "Would hate to be stuck out there, though." Zander added, looking at the barren snowscape.

"I sure hope Kelly's alright." Ethan added joining the group.

"I'm sure she's fine." Kylee said moving away from the window. Zander felt the same way Ethan did. Kelly was a pain at times, but he never wished anything bad would happen to her. For some reason, the dream he had about Kelly dying stayed with him. He didn't dare tell anyone else about it, though. It was just a dream, and everyone had enough to worry about without him adding to it.

"I'm sure you're right; she's fine; I'm just worried about her." Ethan said in a concerned tone.

"We all are," Kylee assured, giving him a comforting hug.

"Well, let's get started." Zander suggested, wanting to break up the scene in front of him. "I hope none of the terrace covering caved in."

"That would be bad." Kylee agreed, following Ethan into the client dog room. "Wonder why it's so quiet?" *She's right.* Zander thought. Standing behind Kylee and Ethan He couldn't see what was going on, but Kylee was right: dogs should have been barking and jumping against the enclosures. Ethan switched on the lights.

"What is going on?" He heard Ethan say, startled. Kylee stopped in her tracks. Zander saw the look of fear forming on her face. He got between Ethan and Kylee. He felt the cold chill of fear when he saw what they were looking at. All the dogs were sitting calmly at the front of their cages, their expressionless faces slowly turned in unison as they looked at them.

"What's wrong with them?" Kylee asked.

"I don't know." Ethan wondered, taking a few steps down the hall. Zander watched the dogs' heads, following Ethan as he passed them, each one keeping its blank stare. *What da hell is going on?* He wondered.

"Hi Duncan," Kylee said to the Black Lab mix. Instead of him happily wagging his tail and doing his greeting dance, he remained still, continuously watching her. Zander saw the family of three Labs sitting in a perfect line.

"Would make a good photo if this wasn't so creepy," Ethan said. Zander had to appreciate him trying to use humor to break the tension.

"Dash, come on, boy, want to go outside?" Ethan asked a German shepherd a few cages down. The response was the same as Duncan's.

"We should probably tell Mariah or Carmen about this," Kylee suggested.

"Maybe we should wait a few minutes until we have a better idea of what's going on," Zander replied. Mariah had enough problems to deal with; he didn't want to bother her until he had something to tell her other then the dogs were sitting down.

"Why? In case you didn't notice, this is not normal dog behavior," Kylee said, motioning to all the dogs.

"I agree," Ethan added. Zander looked at the dogs again.

"Hold on, I want to check the sled dogs." Zander walked towards the sled dog section. Kylee followed behind him while Ethan walked back and forth down the hallways, trying to get one of the dogs to respond. "Ethan, don't touch any of them until we get back." Zander shouted from across the hall, hoping the noise would cause the dogs to get riled up. Not one of the dogs made a sound or moved; only their emotionless eyes followed his movements. After Ethan acknowledged the command, Zander and Kylee entered the sled dog room. He had hoped things would be different in here, but every sled dog was acting just like the client dogs, sitting near the cage fencing staring at them. "Zander, I'm getting worried; we need to tell Mariah!" Kylee said seriously.

"I agree." Zander conceded. In his four years of studying dog behavior and training, he never heard of anything like this ever occurring.

"Is it the same in there?" Ethan asked when they returned.

"Yes, exactly the same." Zander answered.

"Do you think they're sick? Maybe one of the newer dogs had a virus, and now they're not feeling well." Kylee suggested. Zander thought about saying what type of virus causes dogs to stand still and creepily follow you with their eyes. Everyone jumped slightly at the sound of the door opening. Mariah came in with a tray of meds in her hand.

"What's going on?" She asked. "Why do the three of you look like you've seen a ghost?" *Just look around you,* Zander thought before he could form his thoughts into words. Ethan said.

"Look for yourself."

"What the hell?" Mariah said just as confused as they were.

"All the dogs are like this," Zander said seriously. "I checked the sled dogs; they're the same way."

"Have they moved at all?" Mariah asked in a concerned tone.

"No, they're only doing that creepy head turn." Zander answered. Watching Runway's head follow Mariah.

"Runway, time for your meds," Mariah said, holding a hamburger ball and tossing it into the enclosure. The hamburger ball hit the cocker spaniel mix on the chest. The dog didn't move an inch or even look down at the food. From below, they heard the sound of a suite gate unlatching.

"Matrix got out!" Mariah screamed, rushing for the suite door. *I hope you're wrong.* Zander thought. Mariah was at the suite door, looking through the small door window.

"I'll check." Zander offered to get in front of her.

"Be careful." Mariah begged. He opened the door a crack and yelled.

 "Carmen!"

"Hey, Zander." Carmen replied in a normal voice, coming to the edge of the steps, which caused everyone to breathe in relief.

"Carmen, are the suite dogs acting weird?"

"Besides Matrix, no, they're actually pretty good; not one of them made a mess last night."

"Same as up here." Ethan added. "I don't remember seeing a single pile of poop or pee in any of these runs."

"Mariah, what should we do?" Kylee asked. Cupping her hands and putting them near her chin was something Zander knew she only did when she was really stressed.

"I don't know," Mariah replied, turning away from the group. Her back was to him, but Zander could hear her mumbling under her breath.

"Why do I have to be in charge? Why happening? Can't handle this." Hearing her complain about being in charge and misspeaking told Zander she needed comforted. He moved to her front and whispered.

"Mariah, you'll be OK. The dogs are acting weird but are safe and alive." Mariah smiled at him.

"I know. I need a few seconds to clear my head."

"Take your time then; tell us what you want us to do." Zander went back to Kylee and Ethan while Mariah walked down the aisle, looking at the dogs.

"Is she okay?" Kylee asked, concerned.

"She needs a minute to collect her thoughts."

"I mean, they don't look sick and don't seem to be in pain." Mariah said out loud.

"That's what I said." Zander agreed. "Though I've never read or heard about anything like this."

"I don't think anyone has." Mariah took another look at the dogs, breathed in heavily, and said, "OK, we monitor them for now. Let me or Carmen know if they eat or if any start acting odd." Zander saw Kylee give her a questioning look.

"I mean, look for signs that they're sick; check their stool for blood."

"I'll get started in the sled dog's hall." Zander said. Knowing getting back to work was the best and only thing to do right now.

***

Kylee watched as Ethan opened an enclosure door. *Please don't get bit, Ethan,* she thought. Watching intensely as he placed a leash around Dash, who remained completely still. The stillness and unsettling stare freaked her out, even more than if they were acting aggressive. At least with an aggressive dog, she knew what to expect, but she had no idea what to expect from the emotionless stares each dog now had. The blank look in their eyes made it seem like there was nothing behind them.

"Come on, boy." The normally hyper Dash calmly walked out and followed him. "Maybe this isn't so bad after all." He looked at Kylee.

"It's going to be a pain, though, walking every dog outside. I don't even think the walkways are shoveled yet," Kylee observed, looking at the layers of white through the slider. Ethan went outside, then came back in. White snow patches covered his pants up to his knees.

"There must be two feet of snow on the walkways," he said, putting Dash back. "You know what? Let's walk through and dump water bowls; we'll only take the dogs out if there's a mess."

"Sounds like a plan." Kylee cautiously entered a German shepherd named Clayton's kennel. *Please don't spin your head around to watch me,* Kylee thought. She whimpered when Clayton did just that. She hastily checked to see if the bedding was clean. Finding nothing, she dumped the water and left. She found her thoughts drifting to Zander. He was alone with the sled dogs, a bunch of large huskies that were acting strange. As she walked to the next enclosure, she started running through lists of dog diseases she had learned about in vet tech school. None that she could think of had any symptoms like this. She heard whimpering from an enclosure a few rows down. She walked towards the sound and gasped. A tan Doberman mix named Copper was lying on his side; blood was coming from his nose and mouth.

"Copper! Oh my God, baby, what happened?" Kaylee asked, opening the gate. Copper whimpered and gently wagged his tail. He tried to get up but only managed to lift his head.

"Ethan, get Mariah!" Kylee yelled. She took off her coat and rolled it into a ball. She gently lifted Copper's head, using the coat as a pillow.

"What happened?" Ethan asked, rushing over to her.

"He's hurt; get Mariah!" Kylee yelled, then continued to comfort Copper. "When did this happen?" Kylee wondered, knowing he was fine a few minutes ago. A terrible thought entered her mind. She looked to the enclosures across from her, where a hound mix was staring at her. *Was this going to happen to all the dogs?* She remembered watching nature documentaries about brain-eating parasites. *Did the dogs have parasites that were messing with their brains? Do I have them?* Kylee tried not to think about it; instead, she focused on helping the injured dog in front of her. She heard footsteps rushing down the hall.

"Kylee, what happened?" Mariah asked, getting on one knee to look at Copper.

"I don't know. I found him like this."

"We need to get him to a vet!" Mariah said, then shot a glance at the window and cursed.

"What about the snowplow?" Ethan suggested.

"Is the vet even open?" Kylee added. Knowing it was unlikely in this weather.

"I don't know!" Mariah snapped. "Ethan, find Carmen; tell her to meet me in the lobby!" Mariah ordered getting to her feet.

"Where are you going?" Kylee asked.

"To get Zander," Mariah answered before rushing away.

"It will be OK, baby; we'll get you some help; don't worry." Kylee said, looking down at Copper. Only yesterday she remembered playing fetch with him outside.

"What happened?" She heard Zander ask.

"We don't know." Kylee said, looking up at him. She was thrilled he was helping. He always managed to keep calm during stressful situations. A character trait she envied. Mariah appeared next to him, holding blankets.

"Zander, Kylee. I need you to carry him downstairs and lay him near the fireplace until we can get a vet appointment." Kylee could hear the doubt in Mariah's voice when she said vet appointment. Kylee took the cot out of the enclosure as Zander spread one of the blankets across the floor. Copper let out a loud whimper when they gently rolled him onto it.

"It's ok. It's ok." Kylee said softly, feeling terrible about causing the dog more pain than he was already in.

"Carmen's trying to get a vet appointment." Ethan said. Breathing heavily from running.

"On three," Zander said. He and Kylee lifted the blanket. Kylee felt herself struggling with the dead weight. Mariah went ahead of them to hold the door open.

"I can finish up in here, Mariah." Ethan offered.

"You sure?" Mariah asked.

"Yep, it's not like it's going to be hard." Ethan replied confidently.

"Ok, the client dog food is made up on the counter. I'll send someone back up to help you soon."

"Works for me." Ethan replied. When they got outside, Kylee and Zander rushed to get Copper out of the cold as quickly as possible. Kylee focused on keeping her footing, not wanting to slip on a hidden patch of ice. *Only a few more steps, only a few more steps.* She told herself. Soon, she felt the warmth of the fireplace. Carmen was sitting at the desk with a frustrated look on her face. That told Kylee everything she needed.

"Lay him down here." Zander said, standing near the fireplace. Kylee felt her muscles relax as she laid the dog down. One by one, the white snowflakes that dotted the blanket disappeared.

"Carmen, any luck on the vet appointment?" Mariah asked.

"No, I couldn't call anyone. The phones and Internet went out a few minutes ago."

"Use my cell phone," Kylee said, reaching into her pocket on instinct, then remembered it was gone like all the other cell phones. "Damn it. This isn't happening!" she cursed. Mariah had a blank look on her face. A look Kylee knew she got when she had no idea what to do. "I'm sure they'll fix the phones soon." Kylee said trying to cheer the group up.

"In this weather, Kylee, don't on it, not enough soon anyway!" Mariah snapped. Kylee looked at her oddly. *Why does she keep misspeaking?* She wondered.

"Mariah, she's just trying to help!" Zander added, coming to her defense. *Please don't get into an argument,* Kylee thought. Things were bad enough without her two best friends fighting. To her relief. Zander apologized for yelling.

"It's OK. Sorry Kylee." Mariah said, looking at her.

"We could take him on the minibus and hope we find an open office." Doubt crept into Carmen's voice when she said. "Though if we run into snow higher than a foot, I'm worried the bus won't make it." Kylee rubbed Copper under the ears.

"Everything will be OK; just hang in there."

"If anyone has other ideas, I'm open to suggestions." Mariah said in a worried voice.

"As bad as this sounds, there's nothing we can do, not until the storm passes, at least." Zander stated.

"Zander, what do you mean?" Kylee asked stunned by his answer.

"I mean, all we can do is keep Copper as comfortable as possible." Kylee hated what he was saying, but one look outside told her he was right.

"OK, Carmen and I will watch Copper and try to figure something out. Why don't the two of you go back to the kennel and help Ethan, then help Shawn and Benjamin?" Mariah ordered. Kylee couldn't stand the thought of leaving him like this.

"What about Copper? We can't leave him like this. I mean.." Zander spoke before she could finish.

"Kylee, there's nothing more we can do here." He gently touched the side of her head. She turned away from it, too upset to enjoy the pleasant feeling it normally would have brought her.

"Kylee, he's right. Go back and help Ethan." Mariah added.

"This is so messed up." Kylee replied, feeling herself tear up, knowing she was saying good-bye to Copper for the last time.

***

Ethan walked down the rows of enclosures, refilling water bowls and looking for any messes the dogs had made. At this rate, it was going to be the easiest cleaning ever. Ethan stopped at a golden retriever mix named Treasure when he noticed a small pile of poop behind the cot.

"First mess of the day." He opened the enclosure and started to put his leash around Treasure. Ethan turned his head, thinking he heard the suite or outside door open, then felt Treasure dart between his legs.

"Shoot, Treasure!" Ethan said, chasing after him. Treasure ran down the hall. Ethan followed close behind, shouting for him to stop. Treasure went through the half-open door that led to the kitchen. "At least you're back to normal." Ethan said in a happy voice. "I'll give you breakfast soon." Out of his peripheral vision, Ethan thought he saw two shapes moving down the hallway. He turned his head. While he was distracted, Treasure again ran past him. "Treasure no." Ethan said this again with annoyance in his voice. He ran out of the kitchen, seeing Treasure go into the batheing room. When he caught up, Treasure was at the other end of the batheing room lying down. He gave a playful bark as Ethan walked towards him. "OK, boy, enough games; where play later." Suddenly, Echo came out of the dryer crate and jumped on top of it. "Wow, how did you get out?" Ethan said surprised. Echo bared her teeth and snapped. "Hey, take it easy." Ethan said, stepping backwards, then heard a low growl from behind him. Fear crept through him as he turned. Matrix was standing in the doorway. "Alright, calm down, boy."

Ethan said, his voice now filled with fright. Matrix barked and walked towards him. "Matrix, come on, you know me." Ethan's head turned when he heard Echo growl, then she leaped at him. Ethan put his hands out, pushing Echo back. Matrix charged next, slamming into him. Ethan fell forward, hitting his head and jaw on the tub, before falling to the floor. "Help!" He managed to scream right before Matrix bit down on his face. Treasure ran out of the room. Echo got back to her feet and started ripping into his stomach. Ethan's screams were muffled by the blood pouring into his mouth. Matrix's jaws gnawed at his face. He tried to punch and rip Matrix off, but his blows had no effect. The loud crunch of facial bones breaking was soon added to the screams and growls. Ethan's flailing body soon slowed, and his muffled screams ended. Matrix released his hold on the mangled head. Echo chewed on an intestine; the fur around her face was now dark red. Matrix walked into the storage room and barked. Treasure, who was on two legs looking out the window, barked back. Matrix's head turned at the sound of footsteps. As commanded, Goliath, Neit, and Athena entered the room. Matrix gave a series of barks. The three dogs went into the bathroom. Goliath barked loudly at Echo, who was still munching on intestines. Echo jumped in the bathtub, getting out of the way. Goliath and Neit grabbed Ethan's legs, Athena grabbed his arm. The three dogs lifted his body, carrying him out of the bathroom. Ethan's free arm scraped against the floor. Matrix barked again. Treasure left the lookout position and placed the free arm in his mouth. Matrix went into the bathroom, ate a piece of intestine off the floor, and then jumped in the tub with Echo. Using his mouth, he turned the water on and grabbed the shower head. Echo went under the shower of water. The fresh blood flowed off her face. When she was cleaned, she grabbed the shower head from Matrix and washed him. When he was cleaned, he barked another order, then grabbed the shower head. He moved it along the floor. The red water started flowing down the floor drain. He looked at Echo, who was licking up any blood on the floor outside the batheing room. When the floor was cleaned of blood, Matrix turned off the water. His head looked towards the outside door, his ears moved up, and his head tilted as he listened. He put his mouth around the door knob, opening it, then rushed outside, disappearing in the whiteout.

CHAPTER 14

Discouraged and cold. Zander and Kylee walked back to the kennel. He saw the trail they had made was already getting covered. He couldn't understand why, but this storm seemed colder than the normal snowstorms that occurred this time of year. Kylee hugged herself and hid her face from the freezing wind coming at them. *There's no way anyone's driving in this.* Zander thought. He was barely able to see the kennel, which was only yards ahead of them. He stopped, thinking he saw something rushing from the building.

"Zander, what's wrong?" Kylee asked between chattering teeth.

"Nothing, thought I saw something."

"I'm freezing. Get moving." Kylee said with a gentle shove. He started moving again. He looked back, seeing Kylee trying to step in his tracks. He thought about tossing a snowball at her but decided not to, knowing she was getting into one of her whiny, stressed-out moods. When the two got inside, Kylee blew into her gloves. "It's freezing out there!"

"Well, we're inside now, where it's warm, buddy." Zander replied. On habit, he started taking off his coat.

"You're not?" Kylee asked, shocked.

"No, I'm not." Zander confirmed putting it back on.

"It's so messed up what's going on with copper." Kylee said moving under the heat vent.

"Were doing all we can, Kylee, you know that." Zander replied. Really not wanting to hear her keep repeating the reasons Copper needed to go to the vet. As much as he hated it, it only took one glance outside to know there was no way that was going to happen. "Come on, let's go help Ethan."

"Can I stay under the vent a second longer?" Kylee begged. Keeping her face and hands near it.

"Seconds up." Zander teased, giving Kylee a playful pull. "I think we should shut all the sliders. Maybe it's the cold that's making the dogs act strange." He knew the cold had nothing to do with it, but a possible solution to the problem might put Kylee's mind at ease.

"I hope so." Kylee replied as they walked into the client dog section. Zander could tell by her tone she wasn't buying it.

"Ethan!" Zander yelled, used to having to talk loudly due to the noise level. Still, not one of the dogs barked or reacted. As he walked, Zander looked into each enclosure, watching each dog's head follow them. Kylee called for Ethan with no reply. She looked at him and said.

"Zander I really don't like this."

"Neither do I." Zander agreed seriously as they walked forward. He occasionally tapped on the chain link to see if a dog would respond. Every dog remained still, keeping their unsettling stare on them.

"Maybe he's in the sled dog wing?" Kylee suggested. *Knowing Ethan, he was probably hiding around the hallway, ready to jump out and scare them.* Zander thought.

"I'll go check; you want to start closing the sliders?" Zander asked not wanting Kylee to be the victim of the prank.

"No, you're not leaving me by myself, Zander!" Kylee replied, walking close to him. She grabbed his hand like a frightened child would her parent. Zander gave her hand a gentle squeeze, which momentarily made her smile.

"Ethan's probably hiding, wanting to scare us." He warned.

"I hope that's where he is." Kylee added as they walked forward. "Your hands are warm." Kylee complimented.

"Thanks," Zander replied, enjoying the compliment. When they reached the end of the hall, Zander prepared himself for Ethan to jump out at them, but to his surprise, nothing happened. "Let's check the sled dog section," Zander suggested. When they entered, every dog turned in unison to stare at him. "I hate when they do that." Zander said now seriously wondering where Ethan was. He felt Kylee's sweaty hand grip harder. "Everything's going to be okay." He said for her sake. He pulled out the new walky-talky he picked up in the lobby and called Ethan several times with no reply.

"Everything ok?" Mariah's crackled voice asked.

"I think so. We're trying to find Ethan."

"Ask how Copper's doing." Kylee asked. Zander did as she requested.

"He's the same." Mariah replied. Zander thanked her for the information, then put the walky-talky away.

"Maybe he finished up and is shoveling snow." Kylee suggested. *That does make sense,* Zander thought, knowing the terrace canopy above the outdoor portions of the enclosures were most likely sagging under the weight of the snow. Outside, Zander took one step before his boot sank. Kylee stayed in the doorway. He saw no sign of Ethan or footprints he had left. As he suspected, the terrace canopies were heavily sagging. "Were going to need to get to that quick." He pointed out.

"We need to find Ethan first." Kylee added nervously, putting her free hand on her head. "Where could he be?" Kylee answered her own question with. "Maybe he was in the bathroom when we came in, and we've been missing each other, or he went down to the lobby?"

"Mariah would have said something." Zander pointed out. "Let's walk through again." The two again started walking down the client dog aisle. "Wait a second." Zander stopped in front of Treasure's enclosure. "Treasures gone; Ethan must have him outside."

"Why would he take Treasure outside during this?" Kylee asked. Zander looked through the slider to the outdoor portion of the enclosure, then remembered the snow on the canopy.

"He was afraid of the canopy collapsing and took Treasure to the play yard." Kylee looked at him like it was a dumb suggestion. Zander knew it was, but it was the only thing he could think of. Secretly, he worried that Treasure might have become sick like Copper was, and Ethan had taken him to the lobby, but again,

Mariah or Carmen would have said something if that were the case. "Let's check the play yard and see."

"And if he's not in there?" Kylee asked in a worried tone. Her frightened hand is still clinching his.

"We'll find him eventually." Zander assured as they walked. He opened the door that led to the play yard and felt his body freeze in place. Ethan's body was half covered with snow, and his face was mangled beyond recognition. Goliath, Neit, Treasure, and Athena were digging in the snow, sending it over the half-buried body. Kylee screamed. Zander covered her mouth, but it was too late. Goliath gave a grunt, all the dogs stopped digging, and they looked at each other as if thinking about what to do. *Is this even real?* Zander thought, hoping this was nothing but a bad fever dream. He glanced at Kylee; her eyes were wide with shock. Her breathing was rapid. Treasure started digging again, while the three larger dogs started walking towards them.

"Kylee, get back!" Zander ordered pulling her inside. He began to shut the door right before Goliath slammed into it. He tried to force it closed, but the snarling Tibetan mastiff shoulders blocked it from closing. The skinnier Neit leaped over Goliath's back; his head and upper body started squeezing through the doorway. Zander could feel his grip loosening. *Come on, push harder.* Zander thought, trying to will himself, then he heard a bark from behind them. Matrix stood in the hallway, blocking the exit. Zander tried to think over Kylee's frantic whimpers. No way I'm letting you get killed. He thought, looking at her. "Kylee, get to the sled dog area!" Zander cried, feeling his strength giving out. Kylee pulled the door next to them open. Having no other choice, he let go of the door and ran, thinking there was no way he was going to make it. The sudden release of pressure on the door caused Goliath to slip. Neit fell forward into the chain link of one of the enclosures.

"Zander hurry!" Kylee begged, grabbing for his hand. He ran past Kylee, who slammed the sled dog section door shut. He glanced at the door's window to see Goliath and Neit rushing down the client dog hallway. Athena started ramming the sled dog door while Matrix bit at the door knob. Zander watched in disbelief as it started turning. He put his hand on the knob and locked it. He started breathing in and out heavily, trying to process what happened, but couldn't. All he could think about was the fact that dogs had killed his friend and were trying to hide the evidence. "What do I do? What do I do?" He repeated. Kylee was looking down the hallway, probably in a state of shock. *Ok, get back to Mariah and Carmen. Safety in numbers. W*as the first thought that came to mind. He grabbed Kylee by the hand. "Kylee, we need to get out of here. Let's move." Kylee didn't move when he pulled on her. "Kylee, we need to go!" He stressed, hoping she hadn't completely frozen up. In a low, frightened whisper, Kylee said.

"Zander... The cage doors aren't latched."

"What!" He looked at the row of gates; every latch was sitting vertically. Zander saw Matrix standing on his hind legs against the window. He winked, then let out a single commanding bark. In near perfect unison, every dog stood up and grabbed the chain link with their teeth, pulling the gate backwards. One by one, they started to fill the hallway. None of them barked or growled. With a blank stare, they started slowly moving towards them. Zander felt his breathing once again increase.

"Zander, what do we do?" Kylee asked. Tears of fright now ran down her face. As luck would have it, the four enclosures closest to them had been empty. He pulled open the four gates into the hall, creating a flimsy wall. For a moment, he thought about shoving Kylee towards the dogs and leaping out the window. *Why am I thinking that?* He wondered, snapping out of it. What concerned him more was that his hand was on Kylee's back. The dogs in front of them were getting closer now, less than several yards away. The closest husky was trying to wiggle his way through the gate wall. Matrix and Athena continued to bark and pound on the side door. He knew it wouldn't hold forever. He grabbed the pooper scooper spade.

"Kylee, watch out!" He covered his face with his free arm and smashed the spade into the thirty-six by forty-eight window behind them. He heard the glass shatter, then hit the floor. "Kylee outside now!"

"What if there's a dog out there?" Kylee protested.

"It can't be worse than in here! Move!" He quickly brushed any bits of broken glass from the bottom of the window, helped Kylee through it, and then jumped out himself. When his feet hit the ground, he looked around the training yard. To his relief, he saw nothing, but he knew it was only a matter of time before the sled dogs would be swarming the yard. He had also not seen Hexum and Echo and knew they were around somewhere. They ran to the fencing; through the whiteout, he saw the outline of the staff building.

"Kelly's dead, isn't she, just like Ethan?" Zander didn't say anything. "Did that really just happen? What's going on?" Kylee continued in a spaced-out voice.

"I don't know." Zander replied, not sure himself if any of this was real. He again found himself hoping any second he would wake up from another lucid dream, then the muffled sound of wood splintering caught his ear. *Matrix must have broken the door.* "Kylee, start climbing!" Zander said, giving her a boost. Once Kylee was over, he started climbing, fearing he would feel the pain of a dog biting into his leg any second. He threw his body over the fence, becoming buried under feet of snow. He panicked, lifting himself out of the suffocating darkness, only to be greeted by bitter wind and snow striking his face. Kylee threw her arms around him. Her body felt cold compared to his, never the less, he leaned into the hug.

"Zander I'm scared."

"So am I." He admitted. He released the hug. "We need to get inside." He stressed. Kylee slowly shook her head in acknowledgement. He heard dogs barking, followed by thumping as they moved through the snow. He grabbed Kylee's hand.

"Zander, have you guys found Ethan yet?" Mariah's voice came over the walkie-talkie. Both Kylee and Zander screamed out loud.

"Zander, can you hear me?" Mariah called again. Zander pulled the walkie-talkie from his pocket, clicked the talk button, then the walkie-talkie went dead.

"Dam it." Zander cursed, turning it off and trying again. The walkie-talkies screen flashed red, and in the right corner, a low battery sign flashed. "Kylee, give me your walky!" Kylee fumbled with her pockets. Shawn's voice came over the radio.

"Mariah, you're not going to believe this. That dog, Echo, is running around out here."

"What?" Mariah replied in a shocked voice. "Are you sure?"

"Yes, she ran by just now. I tried to chase her down but lost track of her in the whiteout." *Don't go after him; it's probably a trap.* Zander thought.

"Kylee the walky. We need to warn them about the dogs." Kylee handed him the walkie-talkie just as a look of horror formed on her face.

"Copper's in with them." Zander pressed the walky-talky to his mouth and yelled.

"Mariah Ethan's dead; the dogs are going crazy!" Zander heard Mariah say what, followed by screams.

CHAPTER 15

Mariah sat at her desk, staring directly ahead. Had she heard Zander right? *Did he say Ethan was dead and there was something wrong with the dogs?* Fear began to creep back into her; she stood up, closed her eyes, and breathed heavily. She was hearing things again; that had to be it.

"Mariah, are you okay?" Carmen asked.

"You heard Zander and Shawn on the radio, right?"

"Yes, but I'm pretty sure I misheard what he was saying." Mariah was about to reply to Zander. When she saw a look of shock and fear form on Carmen's face.

"Mariah, look out!" She barely saw the shape before it was on her. She felt jaws bite down on her arm. She screamed in pain as she was pushed against the wall. Mariah briefly opened her eyes, and was able to process that it was Copper attacking her. *He was on his death bed a minute ago. Why is he attacking me?* The thought rapidly ran through her mind. Using her free hand, she punched at Copper's head. The dog responded by shaking his head back and forth. Mariah let out another scream of pain. She grabbed onto the wooden bookcase, trying to keep her balance. Mariah saw Carmen aim her bottle of pepper spray. She closed her eyes right before a stream of pepper spray hit Copper in the face. She expected to feel him let go, but instead she felt herself getting pulled forward. When she opened her eyes, the ground was coming towards her. She used her free arm to cover her face right before she hit it.

"Carmen!" She cried between screams of pain. She felt her arm getting wrenched and pulled. She tried to think of ways to fight back but couldn't focus on anything but the pain, then the attack suddenly stopped. Mariah felt the teeth release. She looked to see Copper lying on the ground with the fire poker embedded in his skull.

"Mariah, are you alright?" Carmen asked, kneeling next to her.

"I don't know." Mariah managed to get out as she gritted her teeth from the pain shooting up her arm. She moved her arm slowly back and forth. It hurt, but nothing seemed to be broken. She stood up and rolled her sleeve up to look at her arm. A steady stream of blood was flowing from three deep bite marks.

"Mariah." Mariah turned her attention to Carmen, who was visibly shaken. She held several towels and a medical kit. Mariah took a towel. Carmen opened the medical kit. "Mariah." She again said her focus on the window. Mariah turned and felt herself stumble. Matrix was looking through it. He looked at Copper, then at her. *He did this!* She didn't know how, but knew he was somehow involved.

"Go away, leave me alone!" Mariah yelled. Matrix lifted a front paw he was using to balance himself on the window, bit it, then whimpered. *You're mocking my injury, aren't you? You son of a bitch!* She thought still unsure if what she saw was real. The shocked look on Carmen's face confirmed she had seen it too.

Matrix gained the grin she hated. She moved closer to him, not wanting to back down.

"Mariah, be careful; he could break through the glass." Carmen warned. Both girls screamed when they heard the entrance burst open. Mariah felt her concern leave when Zander and Kylee rushed in.

"Zander. Thank God you guys are okay." Mariah said, rushing over to them. From the side, she saw Matrix drop down out of sight.

"Were not." Zander replied in a worried tone. "Every dog in the kennel has gone crazy."

"They killed Ethan." Kylee added tearfully. For once, Mariah hoped she was hearing things.

"Kylee, did I hear you right?"

"Yes, Ethan's dead." Zander added. "Where are Shawn and Benjamin?" Carmen grabbed a walkie-talkie and started begging them to come in. Mariah's head felt like it was going to explode. A million thoughts and fears were running through her mind. Zander had a spaced-out look. Kylee was grabbing for the phone. A moment later, she cursed in frustration because of the dead line. Mariah didn't know how much time had passed before Shawn came in, demanding answers.

"What da hell is going on?" He stopped dead in his tracks; his annoyed look turned to shock when he saw the dead dog and blood-splattered floor.

"What's going on?" He asked, concerned. Benjamin came in behind him, his face reddened from being outside. He screamed momentarily when he saw the dead dog.

"How did the dog die? I don't like blood." Benjamin added, looking away from it.

"I don't know what's going on." Mariah replied softly. A bark at the window got everyone's attention. *Dam him.* Mariah cursed, looking at Matrix.

"Is someone going to grab him?" Shawn asked, heading for the door.

"No, you can't go out there! The dogs killed Ethan and tried to kill us!" Kylee cried.

"What?" Shawn asked, confused. *Enough is enough. I'm ending this right now.* Mariah thought. She grabbed the fire poker and rushed for the window.

"No!" Zander stressed, grabbing her arm.

"Let me go!" Mariah demanded. The pain from her wound caused her to yelp in pain. Zander quickly released her.

"If you break the window, it will be easier for them to get in," realizing he was right. Mariah lowered the fire poker and handed it to Zander. "Let's get your wounds taken care of." Before Mariah could reply, Matrix barked and got down. She walked up to the window. Zander followed close behind her. They both froze in place. Matrix had become a ghostly outline in the whiteout. He was standing in front of Neit, Goliath, Athena, Hexum, and Echo; behind them, Mariah could see dozens of barely visible outlines. She guessed every dog from the kennel was there. She felt her body trembling. *This wasn't real; it couldn't be real.*

"Zander, do you?"

"Yes, I see it." He whispered. Everyone came over and had the same reaction. Matrix barked several times. A large St. Bernard mix started walking towards the window. "Shawn, help me move the bookshelf!" Zander yelled as the dog picked up speed. Mariah moved out of the way as Zander and Shawn shoved the bookshelf against the window. Moments later, glass shattered around the shelf. She heard a loud thud, then nothing. Zander hunched over, holding his forehead. "Shawn, do we have any wood, anything to barricade these windows?" He asked, pointing to the window between the lobby and waiting room. Mariah tried to get a look at his head, wondering if he was injured.

"No." Shawn replied, worried. He looked around the room. "I'll break apart some furniture. Someone want to come with me to carry tools?" Kylee followed as he rushed out of the room. Mariah rushed to lock both the lobby and waiting room doors. She was sure the dogs couldn't open them, but it made her feel safer.

"Zander cut you?" Mariah asked, rushing over to him.

"No, just got a little lightheaded, still feeling the effects of being sick." He admitted. The sound of wood shattering made Mariah's heart jump to her throat. She turned to see Shawn coming back with parts of a broken table. Zander and Carmen took some wood pieces from him. Kylee was holding two hammers and a box of nails. Mariah noticed Benjamin cowering near the fireplace. She wanted to say something to him, but there were much more important things that needed to be done first. *How long until one of them breaks through another window?* She feared. Thinking about the many first-floor windows and knew it was only a matter of time before Matrix tried it again. Her fear came true when she heard glass shattering, followed by Kylee's screams.

"One's in the waiting room!" Shawn yelled. Mariah helped Zander and Carmen hold a large table against the window that divided the rooms. "Kylee, give me the hammer!" Shawn said quickly, taking it and the nails. Mariah put her full weight against the barricade; every so often she felt a dog jumping against it. She leaned in and closed her eyes until she heard the hammering stop. "That should be good," Shawn said.

"What about all the other windows?" Kylee asked nervously. *Every dog in the kennel's probably in here by now.* Mariah thought worried. Shawn and Carmen gave each other a smile.

"Don't worry, Carmen asked me to close the storm shutters last night. Every window's secure." The lobby windows were the only ones we left open in case a crazy client showed up. Hearing that seemed to melt away the tension. The room seemed to light up as everyone smiled or laughed. *Why didn't I think of that?* Mariah regretted realizing she should have had that done last night. With the immediate danger gone, Mariah started to feel the pain of her bite wounds. She looked down to see blood was still running down her arm. She grabbed the medical kit and held a towel over the wounds.

"Zander, can you help me?" She asked.

"Of course I can." He replied. Removing items from the medical kit. *My knight in shining armor to my rescue.* Mariah thought.

"I'll help too." Kylee offered taking some gauze strips. Mariah lifted the reddened towel. Four large holes showed where the K-9 teeth had punctured; between them were smaller, jagged wounds. Mariah saw Carmen talking to Benjamin, and Shawn was checking the barricades.

"I'm about to spray bactine on the bites." Zander warned. She acknowledged that she was ready. When the pain of the bactine came, she focused on Zander, thinking about how their lives would be after this was over. As he and Kylee finished bandaging the bites, the look on Zander's face told her he was upset.

"Zander, are you okay?" She asked, wondering how sick he was really feeling. He looked her straight in the eyes and said with regret.

"Mariah, sorry to do this, but what are we going to do about Blaze?" She couldn't believe what she was hearing.

"Nothing!" Mariah replied, getting defensive. "No touching one, my dog!"

"Is that dog running around?" Shawn demanded.

"No, she kennel locked in her morning since wouldn't hurt anyone." Mariah assured. *Blaze is fine. Blaze is fine. She's the same loving, goofy husky she's always been.* Mariah was trying to convince herself.

"Mariah, what's wrong with you?" Kylee asked. She noticed everyone else was staring at her oddly as well. She looked away from them, knowing what was happening. She felt Zander's warm hand on her back.

"Mariah, it's ok. Calm down." She took several seconds to focus on the warmth and safety. Zander's presence made her feel, then returned her sight to the group. She noticed Shawn holding a hammer. She dreaded thinking about how he might use it.

"Mariah, we need to check." Carmen said.

"I'll go check on her." Mariah offered.

"Mariah, you can't go off alone!" Kylee protested.

"She's right, Mariah; it's probably better if we all go." Zander added. Knowing she had no choice, Mariah led the way to the staff dog kennels. "Let me go in first; I don't want everyone rushing in holding weapons." Mariah ordered.

"She's right. No need to become a lynch mob." Zander agreed. She gave him a grateful smile before opening the door, hoping and praying Blaze wouldn't be sitting down staring at her. To her delight, Blaze barked loudly, jumping in excitement. *Thank God.* She thought seeing Blaze acting like herself.

"Blaze got you a treat." Mariah said, grabbing one from a shelf. Blaze started spinning in circles barking. Without thinking twice, Mariah opened the enclosure, and Blaze ran up to her. She heard Kylee's frightened gasp as Blaze sniffed and licked her hand for the treat. Mariah petted her and kissed her on the head. She looked at everyone who had filed into the room. "She's fine, guys!"

"I still say we keep her locked up." Shawn suggested. As much as she wanted to argue the point and use Blaze as a source of comfort, for her team's sake, she knew he was right.

"We can do that." Mariah agreed. "I'll be back soon." Mariah said, kissing Blaze on the head a final time. She closed the slider, cutting off the outside portion of the kennel. "I'll come in to visit you soon." She whispered, wondering if Blaze had an idea of what was going on and was as frightened as she was. If she was, she wasn't showing it. Blaze gave a playful bark, looking at her through the window. Mariah waved bye and looked at her teammates. "Where's Benjamin?" She asked, realizing he was the only one not with them.

"I think he's still in the lobby." Kylee said. When Mariah returned to it, Benjamin was sitting against the wall, his head buried in his knees. Mariah started to sit next to him when a dog ran through the barricaded window. The rottweiler snarled as it ran around the room. Mariah screamed, grabbing a hammer.

"Mariah, what's wrong?" Zander asked.

"The dog!" She yelled, pointing to it, then wondering why Zander and the others weren't reacting to it. The dog slowly began to fade then disappeared. *No, not now!* Mariah put the hammer on the desk and smiled. "I thought I saw a shadow. Nerves, that's all." She said calmly, playing it off. "Zander, Kylee, let's go upstairs and make sure all the windows are closed."

"Are you sure we should split up?" Kylee protested, still clearly freaked out.

"Yes, we're not going far." She looked at the others. "We're going to check upstairs. Carmen, can you check on Benjamin? Shawn, Why don't you gather any supplies we might need down here?" She then went up to Zander and whispered. "I need to talk to both of you."

"Ok." Zander agreed. Mariah noticed the glazed look in his yellowing eyes.

"Zander, are you sure you're okay?"

"Still feeling sick, that's all. I'm fine." He gently patted Kylee on the back. "Come on, Kylee." Mariah saw Kylee reaching for his hand. She quickly moved her body between them. Kylee put her hand down and backed off. As they walked up the stairs, the surroundings got darker. "The storm shutters are closed at least." She said seeing no light coming from any windows, then went directly to her room.

"Why are we in here?" Kylee asked, confused. Mariah sat on her bed. Her voice became very serious.

"Kylee, Zander, I need to tell you something in confidence. It can't leave this room! Understand?" Both Kylee and Zander shook their heads, yes. "Ok." Mariah said taking a moment to get herself together. "Zander, you know this,

Kylee; you don't." Kylee gave her a puzzled look as she continued. "As a child, I was diagnosed with schizophrenia."

"What?" Kylee asked, shocked.

"Kylee, let me finish." Mariah interrupted. When I would get extremely stressed, I would get delusional, have word salad episodes, or see hallucinations. For the most part, medication and therapy cured it while I was still a kid. In high school, I was taken off my daily medication. I would still get slight episodes during stressful times and always had an emergency bottle of medicine for when my symptoms returned." Mariah paused to regain the strength to continue her story. *You can do this, she told herself.* "I have not had a serious episode for about a year and a half. Now, with everything going on, it has come back. For the past few days, I've been dealing with it, and I stupidly left my medicine at home."

"Why didn't you tell me about it?"

"I wasn't sure if you found out you would trust me or want to be my friend." Mariah admitted with regret. Kylee's face gained a hurt look of betrayal.

"You didn't have a problem telling Zander?" Kylee reminded.

"He only knows because I had an episode when we were hanging out at college." That's the only reason he knows." Kylee shook her head in disbelief.

"You didn't think you could trust me?" Mariah tried to think of an answer but couldn't.

"What do you need?" Zander asked in a caring voice. *Zander, you always get me out of trouble.* She thought gratefully.

"I don't know how much longer I'm going to be able to lead. I'm not sure how much longer I'm going to be able to tell the difference between reality and delusions." Mariah said doubt creeping into her voice. "Not that it matters; I'm not qualified to lead in a situation like this anyway."

"None of us are." Zander added. "How can we help?" Kylee sat next to her.

"Kylee I'm so sorry; I should have told you."

"You had your reasons; just know it wouldn't have changed anything." Kylee said still sounding hurt.

"Thanks Kylee." Mariah whispered, needing to hear it. She wiped the tears from her eyes. "Anyway, I need the two of you to have my back and help me figure out what is real if I start hallucinating."

"Mariah, you're my best friend; of course I'll help you." Kylee gave her a hug.

"Sorry, I didn't trust you with this sooner." Mariah again apologized.

"You're good." Kylee confirmed.

"We're here for you, Mariah." Zander added. Mariah gave both of them a smile.

"I knew I could count on the three of you." Kylee and Zander looked confused. Mariah pointed to Kylee. "You, Zander, and the elephant in the room." Mariah's smile turned mischievous to show she was joking. Kylee and Zander smiled and even laughed. Mariah heard a muffled yelp of pain from a dog. The lights flickered, then went out. Kylee started sobbing.

"Oh, no, no, no, no!"

"They cut the power," Zander stated, quickly walking over to a window. Mariah joined him as he opened the storm shutter. She saw a dead dog right near the severed power line. A group of dogs was around him. Neit was poking the dead dog with his paw. Matrix seemed to be examining the power line.

Zander cursed. "The generator should have come on by now. They must have gotten that too." As unbelievable as it was, Mariah didn't doubt that what he said was true.

"This can't be real!" Kylee yelled in a sobbing voice. "This isn't fair; these things don't happen to people." Zander went over to her and hugged her. Mariah felt jealousy come over her, but now wasn't the time to start anything. *He's just comforting a friend.* She told herself. She grabbed a flashlight from her dresser and turned it on.

"Kylee, everything will be ok." Zander promised in a confident voice. Mariah wondered how much of that he believed himself. Zander suddenly pulled away from Kylee and started coughing.

"Zander, are you okay?" Mariah asked. He coughed for several more seconds, bent down, and started throwing up. Dark streaks of blood were mixed in with the yellow vomit.

"Is that blood?" Kylee asked with a gasp.

"No, Zander I can't lose you." Mariah cried. Putting her hands on his back and shoulder. Zander continued throwing up for a few seconds; more blood seemed to come with every heave he made. *Please don't die.* She mentally begged. Zander moaned and sat down on the bed, putting his hand over his eyes.

"Zander I want to check your bandage, ok?" Zander weakly shook his head in acknowledgement. Kylee handed Mariah a pair of scissors. "Kylee, go grab another bandage from the medical kit, will you?" In tears, Kylee rushed out of the room. Mariah cut away at the bandage, bracing herself for an infected wound. Mariah turned Zander's arm over.

"How bad is it?" He asked. His tone told her he was expecting the worst.

"I'm..." Mariah tried to force words out but couldn't; in fact, she couldn't believe what she was looking at. She cursed several times.

"What?" Zander asked, looking at her. Mariah felt a new wave of fear and concern come over her. Hoping she was hallucinating, she slowly backed away from the glowing yellow eyes staring at her.

"Mariah, here's the bandage." Kylee said returning to the room. Mariah heard the medical kit hit the floor as Kylee gave a screech of fright.

CHAPTER 16

Zander looked down at his arm; the bite wound had fully healed. He already knew why Kylee and Mariah were freaked out; his eyes must have been yellowing again.

"This has been going on for a while, if that's any help." He said. Not knowing what else to say. *Please don't try to kick me out of the kennel.* Zander thought, fearing his friends were going to turn into a lynch mob.

"Why didn't you say anything?" Mariah demanded.

"The same reasons you didn't until now, I guess," Zander replied, pointing out her own secret she had hidden from the team.

"We need to get the two of you to a hospital!" Kylee said. *No hospitals Kylee,* Zander thought, fearing what they would do to him. He looked down at his arm, which had fully healed in only a matter of days. He noticed the dark parts of the upstairs had become brighter; if he focused, he could hear Kylee and Mariah's hearts racing. *Now it's affecting my senses. What's next?* He asked himself, dreading the thought.

"What can we do in this storm?" Mariah reminded.

"We have to do something! With all the dogs going crazy, it's only a matter of time before they get in or we freeze to death." Kylee stressed.

"Kylee, stop whining!" Zander shouted in a menacing voice. Mariah backed away from him; the look on Kylee's face was as if he had struck her.

"Are you guys ok up there?" He heard Shawn ask.

"Sorry Kylee I didn't mean it." Zander said feeling terrible. "I just want to lay down."

"We're fine; we'll be down in a second." Mariah replied. "Let's go down-stairs and regroup. We need to let the others know what's happening." Mariah said with a hint of fright in her voice. As they walked, Zander found himself fearing what the others were going to do. He could tell his own friends were frightened of him, so there was no telling what his co-workers, some of whom he didn't even like, would do. When they returned to the lobby, Carmen and Shawn were looking through the small, uncovered sections of the window. Benjamin was putting a plate of cookies together.

"The dogs seemed to have..." Zander's eyes met Carmen's. Her face gained a frightful, worried look.

"What the hell, man?" Shawn added.

"What's wrong with Zander's eyes?" Benjamin asked. *Here we go.* Zander thought. Fearing how easily things could get out of control.

"We don't know. This just happened." Mariah cut in. "I'm hurt, Zander's sick, and there's a bunch of rabid dogs running around. We need to get out of here."

"What about the storm? We can't see anything. People could get lost." Benjamin questioned. Zander saw Mariah looking into the fire. He could tell she was thinking, and then her face lit up.

"Shawn will drive in front with his truck, using the plow to clear the snow. The rest of us will ride in my SUV; it will be slow going, but we should be able to make it to Snowy Hills." *She's becoming a better leader with every minute,* Zander thought. Impressed with how she was able to still make smart decisions with everything going on.

"How are we going to get by the dogs?" Kylee asked. Zander looked out the window; he could see outlines of dogs running around.

"We walked down the fenced-in path to see how many dogs are around the cars. If it looks clear, we go out the side gate and walk to the cars."

"What if it's not clear?" Kylee stressed.

"We'll come back inside and figure something out." Zander added. In reality, he had a separate plan in mind. When they got to the cars and left the kennel, he was getting out before they got to the hospital, knowing they would have a field day with their new lab experiment. If the way wasn't clear, he'd act as a decoy so the others could escape. He wasn't confident his friends would remain his friends when the changes his instincts knew were coming occurred.

"What he said." Mariah agreed.

"Are we sure it's safe to ride with Zander?" Carmen asked. Her tone said she didn't like what she was saying, but knew it needed to be said. *Thanks for making me feel like a psycho, Carmen.* Zander thought, understanding, but hurt by her distrust.

"Zander's not acting dangerous." Mariah assured.

"And if he's contagious, we're all screwed anyway." Shawn added. Zander shot him a surprised glance. He had expected Shawn to be the problem, not Carmen.

"I'm ok riding with him." Kylee added.

"Thanks Kylee." Zander whispered. She managed a concerned smile.

"Seems like everyone's ok with the plan; let's get going." Mariah ordered. She looked at Carmen for confirmation. She made no protest.

"We'll need stuff we can use as weapons." Shawn said, putting the hammer on the table where he had already placed five flashlights, an emergency weather radio, and two pool sticks. Zander thought about other weapons they could use. He knew the only knives in the kitchen were safe no-cut and plastic knives.

"Do we have any utility knives around?" Zander asked.

"There in the tool box in the garage." Shawn reminded.

"What about snow shovels?" He continued.

"I doubt a snow shovel will do much." Mariah added.

"We could use them to keep the dogs at bay," Zander pointed out. Shawn returned holding two ice axes.

"I use these when I go hiking. Should be able to handle a dog." He kept one and handed another to Mariah. Zander reached for the hammer, but Carmen grabbed it before his hand could reach it.

"Zander, it might be better if you don't have anything." She said. Mariah placed a hand on his. Her way of showing she agreed with Carmen. Zander hated the idea of having to depend on the others if the dogs attacked; he should be helping fight them off, not standing in the back, but understood why she didn't want him to have one.

"Mariah, what's wrong?" He asked in a low voice. He could tell by the look on her face that something else was on her mind.

"I should bring Blaze."

"No way," Carmen said seriously.

"Mariah, she's right, you know." Zander agreed, feeling weird agreeing with Carmen over Mariah. Mariah started to gain an angry look before she could speak. Zander quickly said.

"Hear me out. Blaze is safe in the kennel with food and water; we're only going to be gone a few hours; she'll be fine." Mariah hesitated, then asked in a dry tone.

"Everyone ready?"

"We can't go outside." Benjamin protested, retreating back into the corner.

"Benjamin, we have to." Mariah added.

"Maybe he's right; maybe some of us should stay here until help comes." Kylee mumbled. She backed up against the wall. Terrified out of her mind.

"Kylee." Zander said in a gentle tone.

"Splitting up is not a good idea. We've seen enough horror movies to know that." He teased, hoping that would calm her. He saw and felt her body relax. He slowly walked over to her. Kylee moved her head to the side, still unable to look him in the eye. That hurt more than the others accusations or distrust. "I won't let anything happen to you, promise," Zander assured, gently stroking her hair. She breathed in heavily, managed to look him in the eyes, and gave a slight smile. He felt Mariah tug at his shirt.

"You ready, Zander?" She asked.

"Kylee." Zander continued.

"Ok, let's go." She said nervously, moving away from the wall.

"I won't go outside," Benjamin again protested. *Then stay here and die. My thoughts sure contradicted what I just said.* Zander thought as Carmen tried to calm him, and he understood why. He cared about Kylee. Benjamin, not so much. He looked outside as Carmen tried to get Benjamin to move. Mariah had gone to say goodbye to Blaze. The storm was letting up but still bad; even in the daylight, the wind and falling snow made it hard to see. He put his ear on the wood that covered the window between the lobby and waiting room. He heard nothing. *Where are they? What are they up to?* He hoped they'd run off, but he doubted it. Several minutes later, the group was gathered around the exit. Shawn was in front with his ice ax. He pulled a cigarette from his pocket.

"Sorry." He said putting it back as he looked at Mariah.

"Since when do you care about following the rules?" She asked. Shawn looked at Mariah and said.

"All the other supervisors were either dictators or pushovers. You're confident enough not to take crap, but also personal enough to make people feel like their valuable, and I respect that."

"Uh thanks." Mariah replied. Zander saw her surprised expression turn into a proud one. *I knew you'd be a good leader.* Zander thought. Carmen patted her on the back.

"Way to go, Mariah; you even got the respect of the asshole."

"I still have a problem with you, though." Shawn countered playfully. With a playful expression, Carmen raised her middle finger. "Everyone ready?" Shawn asked after the two shared a laugh. The momentary playful feelings were again replaced with tension. Zander walked behind Shawn as he opened the door. He felt Mariah grip his hand.

"Be careful." She whispered.

"You too, buddy." Zander replied, turning his attention to the outside. The group remained still, no signs of the dogs anywhere. Zander could see the outlines of their cars in the distance.

"Let's go," Mariah whispered. As they exited the safety of the building, Zander turned to look at Kylee, who looked scared out of her mind.

"Just follow my steps, Kylee."

"Thanks for caring about me." Mariah added, still clinching his hand.

"You too." He noticed two snow shovels resting against the lobby building.

"I'm going to get those."

"Zander, no, we need to stay together." He heard Mariah say.

"I'm probably dead anyway, and we need as many weapons as we can get." Zander reminded before releasing her hand.

"Zander, are you crazy?" He heard Kylee whisper as he opened the side gate. He stepped through the safety of the fencing, feeling his leg sink into knee-deep snow. He looked around for the dogs as his body waded through the snow; none were in sight. *Hopefully, they did run off somewhere.* When he reached the building's side, the snow was less deep. He hugged the wall. The wind picked up, causing his friends to become ghostly outlines behind the waves of snowflakes. He grabbed the shovels and made the easier track back to the group.

"That was stupid, but nice job." Mariah complemented. Zander kept one shovel, not bothering to look if anyone objected to it. He handed the second shovel to Kylee. She looked at the head; he knew what she was thinking a dog could bite right through this. Now at the front of the group, Zander started shoveling a path but quickly realized it was taking too long and making noise. Everyone walked in single file. Zander lifted his legs through the knee-high snow. He could hear heavy breathing and muffled whispers behind him. So many questions were running through his mind. *What is happening to me? Why had the dogs started acting vicious and seemed smarter?* After several tense minutes, he opened the side gate, stepping onto the recently plowed driveway, which only had about a half-foot of snow. Mariah's SUV, of course, was parked on the farther end of the lot. He scanned the area again as they walked, listening for a dog bark or howl between the crunching of snow. When he could clearly see Mariah's SUV, the snow was nearly touching the door handles; Carmen's truck was not much better; and his car was nearly buried.

"You sure your car can get through that?" He asked.

"It should be able to; the deep stuff looks to be only an inch wide," Mariah replied confidently.

"If there's no dogs around, I'll shovel around the wheels just to be safe." Shawn split off from the group, heading for his truck.

"We're going to make it." Zander whispered to Kylee. She gave an unsure smile as she held Benjamin's hand. Mariah pulled out her keys. Zander saw her finger moving towards the unlock button. Before he could say anything, Carmen quickly said.

"Don't! The noise." Mariah gasped, realizing what she had done right as her finger hit the button. Zander's body tensed, expecting the SUV lights to flash. To his surprise, nothing happened.

"I guess I didn't click it hard enough." Mariah said with relief.

"Mariah, I saw you click it," Zander replied, hoping he was wrong. He went up to the SUV, moved snow away from the front, and looked under it. He cursed when he saw several wires and parts hanging from the bottom. *Dam them! How are they this smart?* He thought. He looked back at Mariah.

"It's no good. The dogs destroyed the wiring."

"How?" Mariah asked in a loud whisper.

"How could they know to do that?" Kylee said louder than she intended.

"I don't know Kylee has anything that's been happening make any sense?" Carmen asked, worried and annoyed.

"Look!" Benjamin cried in alarm.

"SSSHH," Kylee said sharply, then let out a whimper of her own. Zander and the others turn to look in the same direction. Through the blowing snow, they saw Matrix standing alone on top of the stone wall. Everyone raised their makeshift weapons. Matrix tilted his head, shook the falling snow from his black and tan coat, then laid down, crossing his front legs in front of him. Mariah raised her ice ax. Zander grabbed her before she could walk forward.

"Don't. Somethings wrong." Echo came out of the tree line, dropping a dead rabbit in front of Matrix, then lied next to him.

"Guys, get in your car!" Shawn yelled. Suddenly, Kylee let out a yelp as she fell over. *Kylee no!* Zander thought, rushing over to her.

"Kylee you okay?" Zander asked.

"I slipped on something," Kylee replied, reaching for Zander's hand. She looked down; her brown eyes grew wide with fear as the head of a husky emerged from the snow. Zander heard Benjamin's cry of fear and saw him run towards Ethan's car.

"Shawn, look out!" Mariah screamed. Zander looked towards Shawn to see Goliath and Athena standing in the bed of the truck. *This was a trap.* Zander thought now understanding why the dogs had disappeared.

"You want to go!" Shawn yelled, swinging the snow ax in front of him. Zander raised the shovel over his head, ready to hit the husky moving towards Kylee. He saw two more emerge from the snow a few feet from him. Before he could swing the shovel downward, he felt a pain in his arm immediately, followed by something striking him. Zander managed to keep his footing as a fourth husky tore into his arm. Mariah was rushing forward, but the two huskies had moved between them, creating a wall. Her and Carmen's backs touched their weapons held in front. Kylee held her shovel in front of her, thrusting it like a spear as the black and white husky unburied itself. Zander heard her scream in fear when the husky tore the shovel from her hand. It leaped on her, knocking her to the ground. That sent a wave of anger through him. Yelling in pain, he swung his arm forward, sending the husky attached to it into the side of Mariah's SUV. He kicked his boot into the monster dog's skull. A crunching sound filled the air as the skull shattered and the dog fell limp. He brought his shovel down on the husky, trying to bite into

Kylee's throat. Again, there was the snap of breaking bones. He quickly pushed the body off and pulled Kylee to her feet. She was shaken but appeared to be OK. Shawn was still swinging his ice ax, keeping the two larger dogs at bay. Mariah and Carmen were trying to fend off the two huskies circling them.

"We have to help them." Kylee stressed despite being scared out of her mind. He couldn't blame her; he was the same way. Mariah swung at the husky closing in on her; it avoided the strike, using the opening to bite down on the sleeve of her coat. The ice ax flew from her hand as she was pulled to the ground.

"Mariah!" Zander yelled, knowing she was done for if he didn't get there soon. From behind, he heard Kylee scream. He turned to see her lying on her stomach. Hexum was on top of her, ripping at her coat. Zander froze, wondering who he should help. It took him less than a second to make up his mind. He struck Hexum several times with the plastic shovel. The Ridgeback seemed to barely feel the blows to the head. Then he remembered Mariah's ax, only a few yards from him. As he picked it up, he saw Mariah getting drugged around like a rag doll. Every time Carmen tried to help the other husky moved to attack her. Behind him, Kylee screamed and begged for help. Duck feathers from her torn coat mixed with the snow. *Is this what war is like? Having to choose which friend lives and dies?* Zander thought, lifting the ax. He turned, swinging the ax downward with all his might, bringing it down on Hexum's head. The sharp point came out of his lower jaw, ending him. Matrix let out a grunt, got to his feet, and charged. Zander again pulled Kylee to her feet, expecting her to be an emotional wreck. Instead, she let out a battle cry of frustration. She grabbed the shovel and ran at the dog, attacking Mariah.

"Leave my friend alone!" She yelled, swinging the shovel downward. The husky-attacking Mariah moved at the last second. The strike hit Mariah in the stomach and chest area. Mariah let out a gasp.

"Mariah, are you okay?" She cried. The husky jumped at Kylee, knocking her over. Zander moved between Carmen and the husky, attacking her. Carmen brought the hammer down on Kylee's attacker's back; she raised the hammer again, splitting the dog's head. The remaining husky stopped in her tracks, giving a few angry barks and growls before retreating. Shawn continued to back up. Goliath and Athena had left the truck bed; the two were moving to his left and right. Each time he swung the ax at one, the other would move closer. Zander saw Matrix leap onto Carmen's car. Before he could shout a warning, Matrix jumped on Shawn's back. Shawn screamed as his body hit the ground. Matrix bit down on his head. Goliath and Athena joined the mauling.

"Shawn!" Mariah yelled. Zander could still hear his screams, but with three large dogs on him, he knew there was nothing they could do.

"He's gone." Zander said with anger.

"We can still save him!" Carmen said. *She's right; we should try.* Zander thought upset he had given up on him while there was still a chance.

"Let's go!" Zander yelled, raising the ice ax. As if he understood him, Matrix got off Shawn and faced the four of them. Echo came to his side, licking the blood from his face. Matrix barked several times. From the tree line above them, other barks and howls joined in. Zander couldn't guess how many there were, but it sounded like at least thirty dogs. Neit appeared first, followed by huskies and other large dogs. Matrix gave his signature wink before barking. Neit led the charge.

"Back inside!" Zander cried, gently pushing Mariah. Shawn's screams had stopped, so there was no point even trying. *Where's Kylee.* He thought worried, frantically searching the area.

"Benjamin, come on!" He heard her cry as she tried pulling him from his hiding place.

"The dogs, no! I'm not going back inside. We need to get out of here!" Benjamin cried in a panic. Before he could reach them, Zander saw Benjamin break free of Kylee's grip.

"Benjamin!" Kylee and Mariah both screamed as he disappeared into the whiteout. Mariah started to run after him.

"Mariah don't!" Zander said, knowing it was pointless. Goliath and Neit rushed in his direction. "Back inside! Back inside!" Zander ordered.

"What about Benjamin!" Kylee yelled.

"We can't save him." He stressed pushing her in the direction of the staff building.

"He's right." Mariah agreed as she started running. Zander felt his heart racing as they ran for the fence. He turned to see the army of dogs in the parking lot. Some were around Shawn's body; some looked to be chasing after Benjamin; the rest were rushing at them. Kylee was the first to reach the fence. She struggled for a moment before pulling it open. Mariah and Carmen rushed in next. Zander flew through the gate; he turned to close it when a German shepherd lunged at him. He momentarily kept his balance before feeling his leg give out. He landed in a sitting position, his head and back hitting the other side of the fence. He screamed in pain when the German shepherd bit down on his chest.

"Zander!" He heard Mariah scream. Two huskies joined in the mauling; one bit his leg, the other bit down on his arm. He let out a cry of pain, feeling his flesh ripping. He tried to fight with his free limbs. The blows did next to nothing. Through the pain and watery eyes, he saw the gate was still open. *I need to shut this gate.* He thought through the agonizing pain. Managing to keep focused, he used his free arm to slam it shut. The dog's teeth continued to sink into him; there was nothing he could do. He heard a yell of fury, then felt a husky's mouth release his leg, then the German shepherd fell on his chest. He moved his head forward, seeing a large hole in its broken neck. "Zander, ok you? Be ok please!" Mariah cried, pushing the dead dog off him. He looked to his side, seeing Carmen and Kylee finishing off the last husky.

"I'm not dead yet." He replied weakly, feeling waves of nearly unbearable pain course through his entire body.

"Can walk you?" Mariah asked through teary eyes, offering him her hand.

"I...I should be able to." Zander replied, taking her hand. He looked at his left leg; a large chunk of his calf was missing. He tried putting weight on it; severe pain coursed through it, but he could still walk on it. Mariah placed his good arm around her shoulder, keeping pressure off his leg. "Thanks." He said gratefully. He turned to the fencing. Like a zombie hoard, the dogs started walking back and forth along the fence line, snapping and barking, trying to jump the eight-foot fence.

"Come on, guys, let's go!" Kylee begged. When Zander heard the sound of his boots hitting the wooden floor, it was one of the best sounds he had ever heard.

"Zander! God, your hurt bad." Kylee cried. *Thanks for pointing out the obvious.* He thought. Wondering how bad he was. He saw her eyes sparkling as she offered to take his other arm.

"Kylee I got him. Make sure the doors to the break room are opened, then get the first aid kit." Mariah ordered. She turned to Carmen. "Help me get to the couch. I'm not sure he can walk up the stairs."

"Good idea." Carmen whispered. Zander grunted as they moved.

"You ok?" Zander asked weakly. Seeing fresh blood coming from a bite mark on her left arm and right leg.

"Not as bad as you." Mariah replied, trying to manage a light smile as they reached the couch. Zander gritted his teeth as Mariah helped him get his coat off. He slowly laid down, being careful not to put pressure on any of his injuries. While Mariah pulled his boots off. Carmen headed back to the lobby to make sure the fire was going and to keep an eye on things. He looked at his chest; his blue shirt had black stains along his stomach and upper chest. Blood was slowly flowing from the wounds on his leg and arm. He gingerly pulled his shirt up. The wounds on his stomach looked to be the deepest. A mess of blood and mangled flesh. Kylee returned with the first-aid kit and a lantern. With the extra light, the girls must have seen the seriousness of his injuries. Mariah looked at his wounds, then at him, her eyes filling with tears.

"Mariah, what do we do?" Kylee asked with a sob.

"Water and towels get." Mariah said quickly. She huffed in frustration. Took a deep breath and said. "Kylee, get some water and towels." Kylee rushed out of the room. With them alone, Mariah let her tears fall. "Zander I don't know what to do." Mariah admitted. The look on her face told him she believed he was going to die. Looking at his injuries, he should have been thinking the same thing, but he wasn't. He remembered the bite Matrix had given him. The bite was now fully healed.

"Do what you can, Mariah." Zander replied, starting to feel very tired. Kylee returned with a half-filled bucket of water and three towels.

"The water stopped. Carmen said something about the pump not working." Kylee stated putting the towels on the table next to the first aid kit.

"I can do this." Mariah sobbed, dipping a towel in the water. Zander looked at Kylee, trying not to focus on the pain the cold, damp towel brought when she moved it across the wound on his stomach. When she made a second pass, Zander could see the flesh around the bite wounds bend to either side. Kylee started to cough. She turned her head and threw up on the floor.

"Kylee!" Mariah yelled. Knowing Mariah well enough to know she was about to unload all her worry and stress onto Kylee, he came to her defense.

"Mariah, it's not like she can help it." He said weakly.

"Sorry Kylee." Mariah apologized. "Thanks Zander." He heard her whisper. Kylee looked up; her face was pale, making the tears more obvious. Mariah went over to her. Zander heard Kylee whisper something about how he was going to die. *Not for a while, Kylee, not for a while.* He thought. "Kylee, can you go and get some blankets and see how Carmen is doing?"

"I want to stay." Kylee protested.

"Kylee I'll still be here when you get back." Zander said as loudly as his strength would let him, which only came out to a whisper. "She's going to finish cleaning the wounds. You don't want to see that."

"I'll be right back." Kylee assured. When she left the room, Mariah finished wiping down and cleaning his wounds. Zander heard a huff of annoyance from her as Kylee returned with the blankets and an extra towel, which she used to clean up the vomit. Mariah tossed the blood-soaked towels in the bucket.

"Kylee, take the bucket to Carmen and see what she wants done with the towels."

"Mariah, I want to stay with you two. I'll help you with the bandages."

"Kylee!" Mariah said sharply. She looked right at her, holding an intense stare. Kylee had a look of annoyance that told Zander she was sick of being Mariah's errand girl.

"For God sake, stop fighting you two." Mariah grabbed a towel and handed it to him.

"Put this on your stomach; keep pressure on it." Mariah ordered without breaking her gaze. Zander was about to tell them both to leave and send Carmen in when Kylee broke the stare.

"I'll leave you two alone." Kylee said meekly as she picked up the bucket. "Good bye, Zander." She added before gently running her hand through his hair. The way she said it, Zander knew she thought it was good-bye forever.

"I'm not going anywhere." Zander assured. "Come visit anytime."

"Come back when I'm done, Kylee." Mariah added. By her tone, Zander knew she was already feeling guilty about sending her away. When Kylee left, Mariah put gauze pads and medical tape around each wound. "Zander, I'm sorry; that's all I can do." He grabbed the blankets covering himself.

"Right now I just want to sleep." Before Mariah could answer, they heard loud banging on the roof and then the sound of feet moving across it. She looked at Zander like she wanted to know if he was hearing it too. "Good thing we closed the storm shutters." He said this before coughing.

"Maybe one will get his head stuck in the chimney and suffocate." Mariah joked.

"You know we used to love those dogs." Zander pointed out as he struggled to keep his eyes open. Finding it funny how quickly things had changed.

"You want me to stay with you?" Mariah asked.

"No, go with the others. I'm going to go to sleep. Take my mind off the pain." Mariah bent down and kissed him on the cheek. Zander tried to process what just happened but was too tired to feel either way about it.

"Let me know if you need anything. I'll check on you in a bit."

"Thanks mom." Mariah lightly smacked him on the head. "You sure you don't want me to stay?"

"I'm fine, Mariah; I just need some sleep." Mariah turned off the lantern when she walked out of the room. Zander pulled the covers over his head. The pain slowly faded as he drifted off to sleep.

<h1 style="text-align:center">CHAPTER 17</h1>

Mariah returned to the lobby. Carmen was sitting at her desk. Kylee was looking through the small section of uncovered window.

"How's Zander?" Carmen asked. Kylee turned her head.

"He's sleeping." Mariah replied, not wanting to remind herself of the fact that he probably wasn't going to wake up. "How are things here?" She continued as Carmen helped tend to her wounds. The heavy layers of clothes and boots had shielded most of the bite. Only a few small punctures from the K-9 teeth had broken her skin.

"As you can see, the fire is still going, but I'm not sure the wood we have inside will last more than the night." Mariah didn't reply; she sat down, staring into the flames. As if she read her mind, Carmen said.

"What happened to Shawn and Benjamin wasn't your fault, Mariah."

"Yes, it was." Mariah whispered. Despite having no love for Shawn, she still felt bad about his death, and innocent, caring Benjamin shouldn't have died. Now both were dead because of her mistake.

"No, it wasn't Mariah." Mariah looked at her, surprised that Carmen had heard her. "Who could have prepared for a situation like this?" *Still doesn't change the fact my decisions got people killed.* Mariah got up, placing her hands on the desk.

"I honestly don't know what to do. Zander desperately needs a hospital; we are trapped here, and I don't know how we are going to get out of this."

"One advantage we have is it's not like we're in a situation where no one knows where we are. Reggie knows we're here. You know he'll show up tomorrow to see how the kennel held up."

"He'll be in for a pleasant surprise." Mariah said sarcastically. The conversation was interrupted by more footsteps on the roof. "Let's hope we make it that long. What are they up to?" As the footsteps continued, she listened for wood or glass breaking; to her relief, she heard none of that, and soon the footsteps stopped. She joined Kylee at the window, who had a spaced-out, frightened stare. The storm was picking up again. Through the white sheet of snow, she could tell the sun was setting. Mariah dreaded the thought of what would happen at night.

"Mariah, I'm so sorry I hit you in the chest." Kylee said softly. "Are you ok?"

"It doesn't hurt." Mariah lied. She could feel the bruising every time she breathed.

"I don't know how much more of this I can take. Ethan, Kelly, Shawn, Benjamin, Zander are dead." Mariah felt like throwing her against the wall for saying Zander was dead.

"Kylee Zander isn't dead; you know he's just hurt. Tomorrow we'll get him to a hospital, and he'll make a full recovery." Mariah assured, trying hard to believe her own words.

"I hope so." Kylee replied. Mariah saw the dreamy look on her face.

"Kylee I know what you're thinking. Stop it." Mariah said in a low whisper filled with venom.

"What?" Kylee replied in a surprised voice. Mariah held her jealous gaze. For a moment, Kylee looked extremely uncomfortable. Mariah held her gaze until Kylee broke. "Ok, yes, I like Zander the same as you." Mariah breathed out heavily, trying to contain her anger. Kylee backed away, throwing her hands up in surrender. "What do you have to worry about anyway? Zander likes you better than me, and you're way more interesting and beautiful than me." Kylee put her head down, showing what little confidence she had in herself. "Do you really think I have a chance with him compared to you?" *Yes.* Mariah thought, knowing they were both equally pretty, and she came with her own set of demons. She looked to see if Carmen was paying attention; she was either focused on other things or keeping her nose out of it. Mariah got in Kylee's face and said in a serious voice.

"No, you don't; remember that!" Kylee backed away until her back hit the wall.

"Doesn't matter anyway. Neither of us are going to have him."

"What do you mean by that?" Mariah asked furiously.

"Mariah, you saw the way he looked, even before we tried for the car. What's happening to him?" Kylee gained a smug look before adding. "Or was your schizophrenia acting up and you didn't notice?"

"How dare you bring that up!" Mariah whispered loudly. Kylee's face gained an apologetic look. Mariah was beyond forgiveness, though. "Kylee, shut up!" She continued, shoving her against the wall and bringing her fist back.

"Mariah, stop it!" Carmen said seriously. Kylee said nothing, as if waiting for an apology. Her face still holding the hurt expression. Mariah lowered her raised fist and turned around. "Just because you both like a boy is no reason to treat her like that." Kylee gave a look of agreement.

"I was hoping you didn't hear." Mariah replied, embarrassed by her actions. "Your right. I'm scared, upset. I'm sorry I took it out on you, Kylee."

"You're good." Kylee replied, still sounding upset. Again, Mariah heard a dog walking on the roof, then heard Echo's long howl. The blowing wind against the building, mixed with the sound of the howls, created a haunting sound. Mariah's focus went towards the window, noticing a dim light coming from outside.

"I see something." She rushed to the window. Her eyes lit up when she saw the unmistakable sight of two headlights.

"Someone's coming up the driveway!" She yelled in a hope-filled voice. Right away, doubt started creeping into her. *Am I seeing things?* Kylee's happy shout of excitement pushed the doubt away. Soon, the outline of the silver truck became clear.

"It's Reggie!" Carmen said excited.

"We have to get his attention." Mariah said, knowing what would happen if he got out and started walking around. Mariah moved from the window to grab a flashlight and realized the howling had stopped.

"Oh no." Kylee gasped. "Reggie, don't get out of the car!" Carmen started yelling as well. Mariah went over to the window and saw the outline of Matrix sitting in the headlight beams. As she feared, Reggie got out of the truck and started walking towards Matrix. She could tell he was talking, but the wind made it impossible to understand what he was saying. Mariah turned the flashlight on and off, hoping to get his attention. Reggie continued to walk toward Matrix. He turned towards the window, seeming to notice the flashlight. His black dreadlocks swinging in the wind under his blue snow cap. Mariah and the others continued to scream warnings when Matrix rushed him, biting down on his right leg. Anger and pain filled Mariah as she listened to his screams, knowing there was nothing she could do. Neit and Goliath soon joined the attack, biting at his arms. Athena went up to the truck, seemingly checking for other people. The ghostly howls started again as Reggie fell into the snow.

"No! No!" Kylee cried in horror. Carmen picked up the hammer.

"Carmen, there's nothing we can do." Mariah yelled sadly. She let out a cry of frustration. This was the second time she had to watch someone die, and couldn't do anything to save them. Once Reggie's screams stopped, Matrix casually walked to the window. Blood covered his snout and upper chest. He let out a few happy barks, like he was gloating about his victory.

"They killed Reggie!" Kylee sobbed. "What are we going to do? What are we going to do?"

"I know don't." Mariah replied in a defeated voice. Reggie was the one person she was sure to come to check on. *Do we stay put and wait for a client to come pick up their dog?* Mariah asked herself. *And when someone does, will they end up like Reggie?* How many people were going to die until the authorities found out something was going on?

"Reggie might not have died for nothing; we can use his truck." Carmen suggested. Mariah closed her eyes to calm herself the best she could.

"Any idea how to get to it?" Mariah asked seriously. Matrix tilted his head, looked toward the truck then started barking. *No! Did he hear us and understand what we said?* Mariah thought in disbelief. Athena, soon followed by Neit, went under the truck. Matrix jumped inside. Goliath started biting at the tires. Matrix poked his head out and started barking at him. Goliath moved to the headlights. Soon the headlights went out, and the engine stopped. Once Athena and Neit came out from under the truck, the four dogs started to attack the tires.

"How could they? I can't take this!" Kylee shouted frantically, pacing back and forth. Mariah had had enough. She slapped Kylee, taking out her fear and guilt on her. "Kylee, stop whining for once and do something useful!" Kylee let out a hurt yelp, running past her as she left the room.

"Mariah!" Carmen scolded. Mariah let out a scream of frustration. Desperately needing a source of comfort or one of her close friends to share her thoughts with. Of course, she just hit the one person she could trust to listen. Mariah stayed silent for a few moments before saying. "Carmen I'm going to go apologize to Kylee; after that, would you mind if I brought Blaze up here? It would make me feel a lot better; we already know she's not acting like the other dogs." Carmen didn't answer for a few seconds, then said.

"Sure, I don't mind." Mariah could tell by her tone she was unsure about it, but she wasn't going to question the answer she wanted. Mariah grabbed a flashlight and noticed Carmen slide the hammer closer to her. On her way to get Blaze, Mariah stopped at the stairs, the guilt of how she had just treated Kylee sinking in. *She's either in her room or with Zander.* Mariah thought, hoping it was the former. As she walked up the stairs. The sound of footsteps on the roof and howls was even worse than downstairs. The cold and fading light coming through the slits in the storm shutters added to the unsettling atmosphere. Mariah turned the flashlight on, moving the light beam down the halls and over the windows, checking for signs that dogs had gotten in. When she reached Kylee's room, her flashlight beam went over her bed, revealing her outline under the blankets. She put the flashlight upright on a dresser.

"Kylee." She said gently touching her. Kylee pulled her head out from under the blanket. Giving her a blank, spaced-out stare. "Kylee, I'm so sorry about what I said and for slapping you." Kylee didn't say anything. Echo's ghostly howl came from what sounded like right above them.

"Make them stop! I can't take this anymore!" Kylee shouted, pulling the pillow over her ears. Mariah jumped at the sudden outburst before saying. "Why don't you come downstairs? We will be safer together, and you'll be warmer by the fire." She gave the blanket a soft tug. "I'll get you ear plugs." Mariah finished right before the howls started up. Kylee looked at the roof and slowly got out of bed. She didn't say anything; she just walked, clearly frightened out of her mind. Mariah felt even worse, knowing their fight didn't help things. When they reached the end of the stairs, Mariah said.

"I'm going to visit Blaze." Kylee let out a frightened whimper. "Blaze is fine. Kylee, go sit by the fire." Before getting Blaze, Mariah went to the recreation room. She turned her flashlight off, not wanting to wake Zander. Right away, she noticed someone was sitting on the chair near the couch. *Come on, Mariah, get with it*. Mariah closed her eyes and opened them. The figure was still there. As her eyes adjusted to the dark, she began to recognize the outline. "Benjamin." She said she was surprised. The outline turned slightly.

"Hi Mariah," he said softly. "I came in to see if Zander was alright." Benjamin turned in his chair. Mariah turned the flashlight on. Benjamin's eyes were black pits; bits of flesh hung from his face. "Why are you here, Mariah? Zander is resting." He spoke in a voice Mariah knew was not Benjamin's. She closed her eyes; none of her other hallucinations had been this bad.

"It's not real; it's not real." She repeated. Mariah swore she felt a boney hand touch her shoulder. "It's not real!" She screamed and opened her eyes. She breathed in heavily, seeing nothing.

"Mariah, what are you doing? Are you okay?" Zander asked from under the blankets.

"Yes, I'm fine. Sorry, I woke you." Mariah apologized. Feeling comforted by his voice. "How are you feeling?"

"Like shit." Zander replied weakly.

"Well, I'll let you get back to sleep then; let us know if you need anything. I'll come check in on you in a bit." Mariah went to the kitchen, the hallucinations of Benjamin still haunting her. Being in the kitchen wasn't helping things. She remembered the many times she came in to see him preparing the delicious meals he always made. She grabbed a box and put hotdogs and buns in it. She opened another cupboard and noticed gram crackers and chocolate. *This might cheer people up.* She thought grabbing them along with marshmallows. On her way back to the lobby, she sat her box of goodies down and went to the staff kennels. Blaze jumped up and down when she saw her, then gave a happy bark.

Mariah's thoughts went to Kylee, on how freaked out she was going to be when she brought Blaze into the lobby. *Kylee's going to have to deal with it. I need this.* Mariah thought before she opened the door. Blaze came rushing towards her, wagging her tail. In exhaustion, Mariah sat down, and Blaze laid down in her lap, giving her a kiss on the chin. A feeling of much-needed comfort came over her. She started thinking about the huskies that had attacked them. The ones she was forced to kill. One of them she knew was Sage, a dog she had raised from a pup. *Why had she suddenly attacked me?* As Mariah thought about the dogs and people that had died, she felt herself tearing up. Blaze seemed to sense her pain; she started gently licking her face. Mariah sat with Blaze for several minutes until she felt the cold biting at her skin. "Come on, Blaze, let's get you by the warm fire." Mariah left the room with Blaze by her side. "NO!" Mariah said it playfully as Blaze went for the box of food. "I'll give you plenty of treats in a minute." When they returned to the lobby, it was completely dark outside. The fire light casts shadows on the ceiling and walls. Kylee was sitting by the fire. Blaze went over to greet her, and she let out a gasp of fear.

"Blaze come." Mariah quickly ordered. "Kylee, it's ok; Blaze is fine." Mariah assured still seeing her look of fright. Kylee didn't respond; she gave Blaze an untrusting look, then went back to looking at the fire. Mariah placed the box on the counter and sat in her chair. Blaze lay next to her.

"I think Kylee's in shock." Carmen said, looking at her concerned.

"I know, and I have no idea how to help her." Mariah replied. "I've done a great job handling things so far." She continued with sarcasm in her voice.

"Mariah, you handled things as well as anyone could in a situation like this." Carmen replied, looking proud. *Three people killed, your boyfriend dying in the next room, bloodthirsty dogs running around, and no way to call for help, you're doing great.* Mariah thought, gently stroking Blaze. For several moments, no one spoke; only the sounds of the wind wailing against the windows and the occasional dog howl filled the room. Mariah saw Kylee tense every time a dog barked. Mariah opened a supply drawer at her desk, grabbed a pair of ear plugs, and handed them to Kylee. Kylee didn't react to them or her.

"I'm going to make us some hot dogs." Mariah said softly. The pleasant thought of a burning Matrix entered her mind. As she went through the box, she saw Carmen staring at a paper, seemingly in deep thought.

"You ok?" Mariah asked, hoping she would share what she was thinking about.

"Yeah, just thinking about what could have caused this."

"I'm still trying to convince myself it's real." Mariah replied as she opened the hotdogs. "Have any ideas?"

"I'm looking through Matrix and his pal's paperwork, hoping I might find something." Carmen held up the contract, which had the dog's information.

"Any luck?" Mariah asked pretty sure she knew the answer.

"No, everything here looks normal, and without the computers or phones, I can't check any of the addresses or see if the rabies certificates are real." Mariah sat next to her, becoming interested in the conversation.

"Do you think? Never mind, it's stupid." Mariah quickly backtracked.

"With what's going on, I doubt that."

"Do you think Matrix and the others are actually some type of military weapon and were being used as test subjects?" Carmen gave her a skeptical look. "Think about it: our phones go missing, the internet went down, we have no way to call out of here, and all the dogs suddenly became aggressive." She stopped for a moment before saying. "Then there's what's happening to Zander." Carmen still didn't look convinced. "You don't agree?"

"No, because the military could test this in a controlled secret environment, and if they wanted to see how effective the dogs would be in combat, it's not like we're good test candidates."

"Alright, smarty, what do you think happened?" Mariah asked in a non-serious voice.

"As far as we know, Matrix's owner is rich. I think he took his dogs to a remote location where one of them got a new strain of rabies virus that the vaccine doesn't stop, then he dropped them off here without realizing it." Carmen shrugged. "That's the best I got." Mariah nervously looked at her bitten arm. The thought of her and Zander slowly losing their minds started filling her head. She got up and looked out the uncovered part of the barricaded window. To her delight, the white-out conditions were now fading, and the falling snow seemed less intense. She could make out the outline of several of the huskies singing their eerie song. It had been a while since anyone had tried to get in or since she had seen Matrix. That worried her. *What is he up to?* She thought knowing it wasn't good, whatever it was. Her focus returned to what Carmen had said.

"I don't really care what caused this; I just want to get out of here and get Zander to a hospital." Mariah said, glancing in the direction of the recreation room.

"I was thinking all the dogs were probably outside by now. I could sneak inside the kennel, make it to the minibus, and drive to town." Carmen suggested.

"The dogs disabled the cars and set a trap for us." Mariah replied, not believing she said that or, worse, that it happened. "They probably got to the bus as well."

"I can try." Carmen offered. Inside, Mariah felt conflicted; she wanted to get out of here as soon as possible but also knew going back in the kennel with who knows how many dangerous dogs would more than likely get one of them killed. *I can't go myself because of the possible hallucinations.* Mariah thought frustrated. Knowing the stress and fear of walking through the kennel would bring them on in droves.

"I'm going to sit with Kylee a bit to think it over," Mariah replied, grabbing the ingredients for s'mores. "Blaze stay." She whispered, then sat next to Kylee, who ignored her. Mariah didn't say anything; she finished making a s'more, made sure Blaze was still lying down, and placed it on Kylee's knee.

"Kylee, come on, eat."

"We're all going to die." Kylee said softly, her gaze never leaving the fire.

"No, where not!" Mariah assuredly tried to keep confidence in her voice. "As soon as this storms over, someone will come to check on us, and we'll all get out of here." *I hope I sound convincing.* She thought. Making another s'more and handing it to Carmen.

"How do you know that? How do you know someone will come for us before the dogs get in here and kill us?"

"Because if we believe we're going to die, we will." Mariah finished her own s'more. "Come on, Kylee, it's not that bad; we have a fire and snacks, just like our camping trips." Mariah took a large bite out of the s'more, letting the melted chocolate and marshmallow run down her chin. Kylee smiled, and Mariah saw the fun-loving girl she had become best friends with. She gave her a playful pat on the back. A howl wiped the smile from Kylee's face. Her frightened, blank stare returned. "We're here for you, Kylee." Mariah assured before looking into the fire herself. Its warmth felt so good, which made her realize how physically and mentally tired she was. She laid down, using a sweater as a pillow. Blaze walked over and laid beside her. Mariah petted her and closed her eyes.

CHAPTER 18

The heavy snowstorm had turned into a lighter, more manageable snowfall. The residents of Snowy Hills exited their houses to begin the tedious task of digging the town out. The sound of snowplows and generators filled the night. At the mayor's office located in the middle of town, seventy-year-old Arthur Lawrence, the town mayor and majority shareholder of the Northern Alaskan oil refinery, watched his assistant Larry Crane push the snow blower down the sidewalk. The town's only snowplow, driven by Gregory Philips, drove by. Many of the town's people had trucks with plows on them, so he knew getting the snow off the roads would happen at an acceptable rate. Once the roads were clear, the priority would be clearing the driveways of older residents who couldn't dig themselves out. By morning, the roads should be clear enough to reach Snowy Hills Kennels to get his dog, Duncan. He looked at the sides of Main Street; the snow piles must have been nearing eight feet. *Going to be forever before we get street parking back.* He thought. He turned and saw something walking down the newly plowed road. He focused his eyes, trying to see through the blowing snow drifts.

"Duncan?" He said surprised. He moved closer, watching his steps on the uneven snow. Boom. In the distance, a gunshot rang out. The dog moved into the streetlight, close enough for him to see the dog and golden collar clearly. "Duncan, what are you doing out here?" He said. Anger forming in his voice. "Duncan, come here, boy. I'm sure your cold buddy." Duncan remained still, only giving a slight tilt of the head. Boom. Another gunshot rang out, followed by another. He heard the snow blower come to a stop. More shots rang out in the distance these days than before. "Larry, come over here." Arthur said starting to feel nervous.

"Yes, Mr. Lawrence. Is that Duncan?" He continued, his voice filled with surprise." Before Arthur could respond, they heard a loud guttural howl, followed by a rapid series of shots.

"Mr. Lawrence, what's going on?" Larry Crane asked nervously.

"I have no idea!" Arthur replied. "Duncan, come here!" Arthur said with more authority in his voice. Duncan continued to remain still. "Larry, go get him." Arthur ordered. The gunshots were becoming more frequent, and Arthur was sure he heard someone scream. Larry walked toward Duncan.

"Come on, Duncan, let's go in." Larry said in a nervous voice. Duncan let out a low growl when he reached for his collar. Larry jerked back slightly in confusion.

"Larry, what's wrong?" Arthur demanded. He heard the sound of a car turning quickly. He saw Gregory Philips snowplow driving erratically, swerving between lanes. Arthur thought he saw the outlines of dogs on top of the plow. The plow slammed into a street light, veered onto the sidewalk, and through the front of the Snowy Hills diner.

"My god!" Larry yelled, rushing towards the crash.

"Larry, watch out!" Arthur yelled, seeing the outline of a large dog emerging from the darkness. Before Larry could react, Goliath slammed into him from the side. Puffs of snow flew into the air as Larry's body rolled on the ground. Arthur watched in horror as Goliath and then Neit fell upon him. "Larry." On instinct, he took a few steps forward, but his courage soon left him. The snow around Larry was becoming red as the two large dogs tore bits of flesh from him. Duncan leisurely walked towards him, bearing his teeth. Arthur started walking backwards as Duncan advanced on him, bearing his teeth and growling. "Duncan, it's me. You know me." Arthur said in terror and confusion. Other distant screams started joining Larry's, replacing the sounds of gunshots. The guttural howl came again, joined by a chorus of husky howls. Keeping his eye on Duncan, Arthur pulled his cell phone from his pocket and slowly walked backwards to the office. From behind him, he heard a bark. He turned to see a large rottweiler standing between him and the office. Athena jumped on top of a nearby parked car. The frightened man let out a cry of fear. Duncan lightly bit his leg. Causing him to turn away from Matrix. When he did, Matrix bit down on his other leg. Matrix pulled backwards, causing Arthur to lose his balance. Arthur's hip took the worst of the fall. "Stay away from me! Stay away! Help! Somebody help!" Arthur screamed, swinging his fists wildly; on occasion, his hands would move to his broken hip. Athena leaped from the car, landing on Arthur's stomach. The man let out a gasp of air. Matrix let out an amused grunt before he leaped on the car and jumped on Arthur's stomach. Arthur felt his ribs crack as he screamed for help. Matrix barked several times, getting into a play stance. Athena jumped at him. Matrix got on his hind legs, knocking her back.

Arthur let out another painful gasp when Matrix's full weight again crashed down on him. Duncan attacked next. Matrix's head butted his jump, knocking him down. Matrix gave a victory bark for defending his hill. Arthur weakly punched Matrix, who responded with his own paw to the face. With Larry now a pile of mangled flesh, Goliath and Neit joined the game. Goliath began to circle Matrix. Matrix prepared himself for the challenge when gunshots rang out, getting Matrix and the others attention. A Malamute, chocolate, and black Lab ran from a side street onto the main street. A pickup truck was close behind them. Three men and a woman were in the truck bed. Another woman was in the passenger seat, firing a pistol. The black Lab hit the ground. Matrix looked at the truck then at the road in front of him. He started barking, Goliath and Neit rushed for Larry's body. Matrix and Athena drug the clinging-to-life Arthur to the middle of the street. Matrix barked several more times, then he and the other dogs scattered. Duncan ran right for the truck; a shot hit him in the chest. He yelled in pain but kept moving forward until he fell under the front right wheel. The truck veered to the left. Arthur screamed seconds before the truck ran over him. The unexpected turns caused the truck to slip on the ice and snow. The truck driver, Carl Mullins, clung to the wheel, trying to regain control. Neit rushed out of an alleyway. He ran around the front of the truck, then leaped into the opened passenger window. Before Rachel Ferguson could react, he bit down on her throat. Blood poured from the wound. Her gun went off several times during the struggle, one of the shots hitting the right tire. Carl cursed as he reached for his own gun. With the truck moving from side to side, Matrix gave a commanding barked signal, signaling the attack. Goliath jumped onto a large pile of snow. Standing above the truck, he leaped into the bed, knocking over two of the men. Steven Armstrong fell off the truck bed. Before he could get to his feet, he was attacked by the Malamute and chocolate Lab. Naomi Greaves moved her gun towards Goliath. Athena jumped on her back, the shot from her hunting rifle firing to the side. Naomi lost her balance, falling off the truck, the back wheel crushing her head. Matrix rushed the swerving truck, leaped onto the hood, then into the truck bed, attacking Jayson Wilkes before he could shoot either dog. He bit down on Jayson's head and throat. Goliath pulled his head up, his mouth full of intestines. Neit bit down on Carl's gun hand. The truck swerved onto the sidewalk. Matrix laid down right before it crashed into the town's grocery store. The truck continued to go forward, knocking over several shelves before getting stuck on them. Matrix barked for Neit, who pulled the dead man's foot from the gas pedal. Matrix barked again. Goliath and Athena returned barks, confirming they were okay. After Matrix double-checked the bodies of Jayson, Rachel, and Carl, making sure they were dead, he jumped from the truck bed. He put his nose in the air, sniffing, taking in all the wonderful smells. Athena started licking at broken jars of jelly. Goliath ripped open a bag of crab legs. Neit grabbed a pack of bacon from the shelf. Several other dogs rushed inside, helping themselves to the feast. Matrix walked over to the butcher shop after grabbing one of the finest tenderloins. He barked an inviting bark at a pair of beautiful female huskies ripping into a box of shrimp. He sat at the front window. The two huskies lied at his sides, one holding the box of shrimp, the other a bottle of grape juice. The fire that had started a few blocks down in the auto repair shop reflected in his eyes. A Pitbull and German shepherd mix fell upon a fleeing woman; the Malamute and chocolate Lab broke through the window of Arthur's office; dogs ran up and down Main Street. More gunshots from automatic weapons rang out in the distance, followed by the guttural howl. A smirk came upon Matrix as he watched the carnage unfold.

Chapter 19

Mariah opened her eyes, sat up, and looked towards the window. It was still dark out. Kylee was asleep a few feet from her. Carmen was playing a card game with herself at the desk. Blaze moved her head forward, giving her a kiss on the face. Mariah patted her on the head before quietly getting up.

"How long was I out?" she asked Carmen in a low voice.

"A few hours, not much happened, fortunately."

"How's Zander?" Mariah asked, fearing the worst.

"I checked in on him about half an hour ago; he's still sleeping."

"You sure he was sleeping?" Mariah continued needing to be sure.

"I can tell the difference between a sleeping and a dead person." Carmen said with a sarcastic smile.

"I believe you, but I'm going to check on him anyway." Mariah started to leave the room when she heard a familiar bark and then a tapping at the wooden barricade. Carmen huffed in frustration, then said.

"I'd hoped he ran off." *Of course.* Mariah thought, knowing exactly who it was. She went to the window, moving the curtains Carmen had put up to help keep the cold air out. As she predicted, Matrix was standing on his hind legs, looking in through the small portion of the window uncovered by the barricade.

"Having trouble getting in?" She teased. Mariah grabbed Blaze's collar when she approached the window, not wanting to risk anything happening to her. Matrix's head moved to the fireplace, then he looked at Mariah, giving her a wink. Mariah knew what he was doing. "Leave Kylee alone!" She said in a threatening voice. Her head turned to the fireplace when she heard a loud thump followed by loud yelping. Kylee awoke, startled, then screamed. She rapidly backing up as a burning Yorkie poo ran around the room. It pushed itself towards Kylee with its two front legs; its back legs broken in the fall. Mariah was about to rush it before Carmen hit it with her hammer, putting the little dog out of its misery.

"Da hell?" Carmen said. Then another thump happened. Mariah saw kindling and ashes fall on the floor; this time a toy poodle lay dead in the fire place. Kylee backed up against the desk. Mariah was momentarily stunned before she turned to Matrix.

"What's next?" She asked. "You going to send more little dogs to their death?" Matrix's face gained that grin she hated. "I'm going to kill you!" Mariah said bitterly. The toy poodle's fur caught fire, causing the flames to rise.

"Everyone get down!" Carmen screamed, then saw her rushing towards the fire.

"What!" Mariah asked, nearly tripping over Kylee's feet, who was backed up against the desk. Carmen grabbed the fireplace tongs and tossed an aerosol can onto the floor. A feeling of shock and disbelief came over her as Carmen tossed two more onto the floor. *The dogs were just cover for his bomb.*

"That looks to be the last of them." Carmen said still searching the fire. Mariah again brushed past Kylee, who was asking if the cans were going to explode. She went to the window. Matrix snarled and barked. She could see the look of disappointment on his face. Blaze leaped at the window, barking.

"Blaze, get down!" Mariah said worried. Matrix's look of disappointment turned to a look of surprise, which frightened her. No matter what he was thinking, she was not going to let him hurt Blaze. Matrix barked and ran off. Mariah kissed Blaze on the head. "You scared him off." She heard a thud, then movement in the waiting room.

"There inside, there inside!" Kylee wined getting to her feet.

"They can't get in!" Mariah assured. A third thump hit the fireplace floor.

"All my God!" Kylee yelled, covering her mouth in disgust. Mariah felt sick herself, looking at a chewed human foot. She knew she wasn't seeing things, not with how Kylee reacted. Carmen started poking around it when a severed arm came down. Mariah grabbed the fireplace broom to help Carmen search for anything else that might have fallen down. Mariah saw Blaze over at the waiting room door, sniffing." Blaze, get away from there!" Blaze got on her hind legs and bit on the door knob. Mariah felt her heart stop when she heard the click of the lock. Blaze rolled her body and head to the left, opening the door. *Blaze, no, you can't be one of them!* Mariah thought. Hoping and praying, she was seeing things.

"Run!" Carmen yelled. Matrix burst into the room, followed by Athena and two huskies. Blaze turned around, growling, giving her the blank expression she had seen with the kennel dogs earlier. Mariah felt like time was standing still. Blaze was no longer the loving dog she loved so much. Flashbacks of her and Blaze started filling her mind. Echo's haunting cries from above started up again. Mariah didn't know if she blacked out or if she forgot what happened; the next thing she remembered she was in the recreation room. Carmen was checking and locking the doors. Kylee sat on the floor, holding her ankle, which had red streams coming from a bite. Mariah started walking towards the recreation room door in a trance-like state. Blaze was still in her kennel, and her loving dog was waiting for her.

"Mariah, what are you doing?" Carmen asked, getting between her and the door. Carmen asked, getting between her and the door.

"I need to go check on Blaze. She's in the kennel." Mariah replied in a spaced-out voice.

"Mariah, you know what happened to Blaze." *It really happened*. She thought, feeling the drip of tears fall from her face as reality sat in. Carmen hugged her. Images of Blaze again started filling her mind. Images of how much fun and all the adventures they had gone on together. The images began to fade, replaced by Matrix's wink and grin. Mariah felt anger filling her body. He had done this. The huskies started joining Echo's cries, many of which sounded like they were right outside the room.

"Please make it stop! I can't handle this!" Kylee cried. *You did this. You took Blaze from me.* Mariah thought Remembering how Matrix got out on Kylee's watch, he must have bitten Blaze before walking to the sled dog's play yard. *You want Zander for yourself. You planned all of this to get me killed so you could have him.* In a rage, Mariah lashed out at Kylee, striking her across the face. Kylee's face turned to shock as tears continued to fall. Mariah grabbed her by the shoulders, throwing her to the ground.

"Mariah, what are you doing?" Stop!" Kylee pleaded. Mariah shoved Carmen against the wall, then grabbed the front of Kylee's coat, shaking her.

"I know what you're planning!" Mariah brought her fist down on Kylee's stomach. She raised it again when she felt a strong hand grab the back of her coat. She felt her feet leave the ground, then felt herself in the air, flying across the room. A wave of pain went through her back when she hit the pool table. Mariah looked up at Zander and felt her body freeze. His eyes were now a bright yellow, and his face was slightly disfigured. He looked like one of the people from the movies who were changing into a werewolf.

"I'm seeing things; this is not happening!" Mariah repeated. Hoping it was true.

"Mariah run!" Carmen said striking him with a pool stick. Zander seemed to hardly feel it; in a moment, he closed the distance with her, ripping the pool stick from her hand. His hand went around her throat, lifting her in the air. She kicked and gagged as he effortlessly held her a few feet off the ground.

"Zander, don't!" Kylee begged.

***

Zander remembered closing his eyes; he remembered being sure he would never wake up, but he had. Now he felt fine; in a way, he felt better than he ever had.

"Why were you hurting Kylee?" He demanded, looking into Mariah's frightened eyes.

"I don't...." Mariah tried to speak as she stared at him like he was about to kill her.

"Zander, please let Carmen go; don't hurt anyone." Kylee begged. The sound of Kylee's frightened voice lifted the cloud from his senses. *Why am I attacking my friends?* He thought, gently dropping Carmen, who hit the ground, coughing. Regret came over him, realizing how badly he could have hurt her.

"Sorry, I don't know what came over me." Zander said with sorrow. "Are you ok?" Zander asked in a concerned voice as Carmen got to her feet.

"What's wrong with you?" Carmen said in a hoarse voice, moving over to Mariah.

"I don't know." He looked at Kylee, noticing the bite on her ankle." Kylee, what happened? Let's get that taken care of." His voice filled with concern.

"No, please don't come near me!" Kylee said, shuffling away from him. Feelings of hurt and confusion came over him. *Why are they all looking at me like I'm some kind of monster?* Each of them had looks of pure fear on their faces. He could clearly hear the drumming of their hearts.

"I don't know why I acted like that; it was the sickness, not me. Please forgive me." Zander begged.

"Zander, do you know what's happening to you?" Mariah managed to spit out.

"Mariah cut it out. I know my eyes are yellowing, and I had an angry outburst. Why are all of you staring at me like I'm some kind of freak?" *Did something else happen to me while I was asleep?* Nervousness filled him as he looked down at his hands. His fingers seemed skinnier. Tuffs of gray hair were beginning to emerge along his arm. He pulled his shirt up. The wound on his chest was nearly healed.

"Zander, you should look in the mirror." He heard Mariah timidly suggest. *I don't want to.* He thought as he nervously made his way to the small mirror on the side wall. When he saw his reflection, he felt a wave of fear like he had never felt before go through him. His eyes were now a bright yellow, and his lower and upper k-9s looked to be becoming fangs. The bones in his face looked to be pushing outward under the skin, slightly elongating his jaw. No! This can't be real. This isn't happening. He punched the wall, then let out a scream of terror. In a rage, he pushed the cabinet next to him over. What's happening, and how is this possible? He thought. He noticed everyone was gathered near the door, looking at him with terrified faces. They seriously think I'm a monster, don't they? I guess because I'm acting like one.

"You guys know I would never hurt you, right?" Zander asked, feeling tears fall on his deforming face. He sat down on the sofa, not knowing what to do.

"What should we do?" He heard Carmen whisper.

"I don't know." Mariah replied. Zander saw her put her hands over her face. "Everything is happening so fast."

"You know I can hear you." Zander said with humor in his voice. Everyone looked at him at once. The looks of confusion and distrust remained. *I can't be around them like this. I don't know what I'm becoming.* Zander mentally admitted recalling his actions from minutes ago. It took a few tries, but he finally managed to get out. "I don't blame you for not wanting me around. I'll...I'll leave."

"No, Zander, we don't want that at all." Mariah said, taking a cautious step closer. Kylee and Carmen remained near the door. "We need to get you to a doctor and find out what's happened."

"Thanks for stating the obvious, Mariah." Zander replied, trying to add some humor to his voice in order to lighten the mood as much as possible. He looked at his hand again. "I'm not sure a doctor can fix what's happening to me anyway."

"Zander of...of course they can. You're sick, that's all." Kylee added, still sounding scared out of her mind.

"What kind of sickness does this cause someone?" Zander stared at Kylee, who didn't respond.

"Zander, when did you first notice this change was happening?" Carmen asked.

"A few hours after, I got bit." He admitted. *Might as well tell them everything.*

"And you didn't say anything?" Carmen snapped.

"I was scared, ok? I thought if I ignored the problem, it would go away or something." Zander replied, knowing how foolish it was to do that.

"Great, is this going to happen to everyone who got bit?" Carmen said out loud. Kylee's face turned pale as she looked down at the wound on her ankle. Mariah pulled back the bandage on her arm from the bite from Copper. Dried blood covered her skin. Soon, fresh blood started flowing from the bite. Mariah put the bandage back in place. You seem to be okay, Mariah; that's good. Zander thought, recalling how quickly his wounds healed.

"Zander, you're sure you noticed the first signs a few hours after getting bit?" Mariah asked, her tone serious with hints of fear. Grudgingly, he explained the situation again.

"Carmen, only you haven't been bitten, right?" Mariah asked. She nodded her head, yes." Kylee, how do you feel?"

"Fine." Kylee said before quickly adding. "Besides freezing, my ankle hurts, and I'm worried about the dogs running around outside." Zander saw her send another fearful glance his way.

"Kylee, if I wanted to kill you guys, I would have already." Zander said, not wanting her to fear him.

"I know that." Mariah stepped in, trying to smile. "I'm just trying to get used to your new look."

"We need to get out of here and figure out what caused this." Carmen added.

"How did the dogs get in here anyway?" Zander asked, trying to move the topic away from him. Mariah only said Blaze before turning away; Zander knew she was tearing up, so he left the subject alone.

"Guys, we can't stay here. If this is rabies, we need to get to a hospital right away." Carmen again insisted.

"It's not rabies!" Kylee said. She looked at her wound, then looked at Zander. He went over to the couch and ripped a piece of cloth from his blanket.

"Kylee, put this on your wound." He said tossing it to her. For a moment, a smile broke her look of fear." Carmen, why do you think this is rabies?" Zander asked, wanting to hear her thoughts. Carmen explained the theory she told Mariah earlier.

"Rabies would explain the aggressive behavior, but it doesn't explain this."

"Or how their acting smarter?" Mariah added as she helped Kylee with her bandage. Zander heard her whisper an apology to Kylee, which she accepted." Also, if what's happening to Zander is a symptom of the dog bites, why is it only happening to him?"

"Maybe it reacts differently to male and female bodies." Zander suggested. Carmen threw her hands up.

"Like we're going to figure this out!" She shoved a pool ball across the table. "We need to figure out how we're going to get out of here. I say we try to get to the minibus. It's only a matter of time before the dogs get in." On cue, one of the dogs jumped at the storm shutter, causing a loud bang to fill the room. Kylee whimpered. Mariah started a counterargument against the idea. Kylee remained silent. Zander stayed focused on the previous subject. He started to recall something he had seen in a fictional documentary. The idea seemed completely crazy, but another glance in the mirror made it seem more and more likely.

"Guys." Zander said in a serious voice, getting their attention. "As crazy as this may sound, what if that dog Matrix is a werewolf or some type of shape shifter that would explain..." Zander stopped instantly regretting what he said, knowing it would probably cause his friends to think he was losing his mind. To his surprise, Mariah and Carmen didn't make counterarguments; in fact, they looked to be at least entertaining the idea. Kylee was the first to speak.

"Zander, no, there's no such thing as werewolves. We'll get you to a doctor; there, find out what's wrong, and everything will be ok." Kylee's voice shook with every word, sounding like she was trying to convince herself more than him.

He could tell by the look on her face and the way her eyes were moving toward him then her wound she was seriously thinking about it. Now he really regretted saying anything. The last thing he wanted to do was scare her more.

"Zander Kylee's right; there's no such thing as werewolves, but you might be on to something." Mariah added, looking like a light bulb had just gone off in her head. "You're the only one who got bit by Matrix. What if only his bites have this effect?" making sense to him, Zander added to her theory.

"I bet you Matrix or one of the other dogs he came with got out and bit the other kennel dogs; that's why they started acting crazy." Mariah huffed, looking frustrated.

"We have no way to prove if any of this is true." She added.

"Enough of the brainstorming." Carmen cut in. "We need to be focusing on getting out of here, not acting like scientists trying to figure out what caused this."

"Alright, Carmen, how are we going to get to the minibus?" Mariah asked with frustrated sarcasm. Zander could feel the tension in the room growing; he knew it was only a matter of time before another fight broke out.

"Those dogs are going to break in; once they do, we'll be sitting ducks in here, and even though he's the Zander, we know at the moment we don't know how whatever's happening to him will affect his mind," Carmen replied.

"And when we're attacked, what then? You're the only one that isn't hurt." Mariah countered. Another bang came from a west-facing window, then the left door. The wood on both buckled.

"If we stay inside the fencing, it won't be an issue; it's only a few feet from here." Carmen reminded her, pointing to it. "Then we get inside the kennel and rush for the minibus." Zander thought Carmen's plan over. He knew they could get inside the fencing. The problem was that her plan was banking on no dogs being inside the kennel, which he highly doubted was true, plus most of them were hurt, which would make running and climbing more difficult.

"There are dogs outside at least one of the doors, and Kylee and Mariah are hurt." Zander reminded. "We need to leave, but we'll never make it with all the dogs." A hint of fear entered his voice when he said. "The only way this is going to work is if one of us acts as a decoy to lead the dogs away while the other's escaped."

"Zander, you can't! We can't separate!" Mariah shouted. *She knows me too well.* He thought.

"Mariah, I've accepted the fact I'm dead already. No need for the rest of you to die." Zander replied, his voice filled with regret when he said. "You saw how I acted earlier; if I'm around everyone, I might end up hurting one of you."

"No! Zander, we'll figure out another way!" Mariah promised with a serious look on her face.

"Yeah, Zander, we try for the minibus or hide in here until help arrives. Kylee added. Mariah looked at Carmen, signaling for her to say something.

"Zander is right; it's the only way." Carmen answered sadly. Mariah looked right at him, her eyes visibly tearing up.

"No, it's not happening. I don't want to hear another word about it." As Mariah spoke, a dog rammed the door. Zander saw small cracks beginning to form. *There isn't much time.*

"I'm going," Zander said, grabbing the ice ax and heading towards the door. "You girls, get ready to run."

"Zander, you're dead if you go out there!" Mariah yelled, getting between the two of them.

"Mariah, I'm doing this." He said, determined not to let her pleas change his mind.

"You're not actually going to go through with this, are you?" Kylee asked in a pleading voice. Zander tried to tune her out. He grabbed a stick. There was a loud crack when it broke over his knee. He snapped some pieces off the ends of the break, making a rugged wooden spear. He handed one to Mariah and one to Kylee, which she immediately put against the wall.

"Take care of them." He said quietly to Mariah, putting his arms out for most likely their last embrace.

"You want to go through with this fine?" Mariah yelled, pushing away from him. She walked towards the left-side recreation room door.

"Mariah don't!" He yelled, realizing what she was doing. Before he could grab her, she pulled open the door. Kylee screamed. Zander readied himself for the charging horde; instead, he saw an empty hallway. The lobby door closest to the waiting room was still closed. Carmen slightly opened the storm shutter of a nearby window.

"I don't see any dogs in the walkway between the two buildings."

"If we're going, let's go now." Mariah ordered. *I might not have to die after all.* Zander thought thinking about how lucky they were Mariah's carelessness led to something positive. He again looked at his transforming hands. *Death might be a blessing compared to what's in store for me if I survive this.*

"You coming?" Mariah whispered. Carmen picked up the broken pool stick and walked over to Mariah.

"Kylee, come on!" Zander said. She reluctantly followed. "We have to walk by the kitchen and the staff dog kennels." Zander reminded that if there was going to be an ambush, it would come from there. He could still hear the dogs barking and hammering at the recreation room's other door. He walked slightly ahead of the group. As luck would have it, both the kitchen and kennel entrances were closed. When they reached the entrance to the fenced-in walkway, everyone held their weapons up. Zander slowly pulled the door open, just like Carmen had said nothing in any direction. The earlier whiteout conditions were now a mild snowfall. He took a step outside; the snow on the recently plowed path was just below his ankle. Mariah and Carmen stepped outside. Kylee stood at the door, looking for dogs on either side of the fence. Zander walked over to her.

"Kylee, we need to get going." He tried to gently move her forward, and she stepped back with a whimper of fright.

"Kylee I'm going to get you out of here; you'll be safer with the group." Mariah added. Walking over to her. Kylee still didn't move. Zander decided to take a different approach.

"Kylee, it's only a matter of time before the dogs at the other end of the hall find us here. Do you really want to be standing here alone when that happens?" As he suspected, she started walking down the path.

"Thanks." Mariah said, then gasped.

"What?" Zander asked. Looking to where she was staring. He didn't see anything and knew what was happening.

"No, Mariah, not now." She whispered to herself. Zander wrapped his arms around her and embraced her.

"You OK?" he asked.

"I am now," she replied.

"Let's get moving." Zander suggested. As they walked, Zander kept looking for dogs, but there was nothing. *I don't like this; it's some sort of trap.* He could still hear Echo and several huskies howling. *Maybe they were so focused on getting inside they missed us. Wishful thinking.* Zander thought, recalling the earlier trap. He was beginning to seriously doubt whether this escape plan was a good idea. Everyone walked as carefully as they could. Eyes and hearts raced every time snow crunched under someone's boot. Finally, they reached the kennel building. Zander put his hand on the metal kennel door knob.

"Everyone ready?" He asked.

Chapter 20

No matter what happens, don't scream. Mariah told herself. Holding her, make shift spear in front of her. Knowing the overwhelming fear and stress she was feeling was causing her to hallucinate and act irrationally, she couldn't believe she had attacked Kylee earlier. *We can do this; just stay strong and focus on making rational decisions.* Something she had failed at since that monster took her dog from her.

"Zander, hold up." He and the others gave their attention to her. "If there's too many dogs in there, we turn around and go back. We lost enough people; I'm not losing any more."

"Mariah, we can't go back; the dogs probably made it into the recreation room by now. If that happens.

"I know." Mariah quickly said, knowing he was right. If that happened, there would be nowhere to go. She closed her eyes for a moment, then said words that nearly broke her heart.

"If we get overwhelmed, go along with your plan, Zander." She placed her hand on the side of his face. "But only as a last resort." She quickly added.

"It really doesn't matter. I'm dead either way at this point." Zander replied casually. Mariah felt like slapping him for saying that. Before she could verbally respond, Zander again placed his hand on the door. Mariah raised the ice ax, fearing a zombie-like hoard would come charging out at them. When he opened it, Matrix came charging at them; the only reason she didn't scream was because he ran through Zander to get to her. She closed her eyes, and he was gone. Inside the storage room, it was pitch black. Knowing any dogs inside could hear or smell them, Mariah and Carmen turned on their flashlights. Mariah expected to see everything destroyed, but to her surprise, except for a few knocked-over bottles and towels, everything looked normal. Carmen checked the dog batheing room, while Zander checked the human bathroom.

"Anything?" Kylee whispered, standing in the doorway.

"No." Carmen replied in a low whisper.

"Let's keep moving." Zander suggested. Despite none of the flashlight beams pointing in that direction, Zander moved towards the kitchen like it was brightly lit. Mariah held her breath as the flashlight beam moved across the room. Shadows seemed to jump from every direction; some came to life, trying to attack her.

"It's all in your head; it's all in your head." She repeated. She saw Kylee still standing in the doorway. "Kylee, come on. We won't let anything hurt you."

"You did." Kylee said with a hurt glare. Mariah put her head down in shame.

"Kylee I'm so sorry I hit you back there. I was scared and took it out on you." Kylee rubbed her eyes, then replied in a defeated tone.

"Sorry, I'm so useless."

"You're scared, just like the rest of us. Let's just get out of here; we'll both feel better then." Mariah handed her the flashlight." Here, I have the pool stick; why don't you light the way for us?" Kylee nonchalantly took it, and Mariah grabbed her free hand like a mother would a frightened child. To her delight, Kylee walked with her. They rejoined Zander and Carmen, who had entered the sled dog wing. She felt Kylee squeeze her hand.

"Are dogs hiding in the kennels?" Kylee asked, shining her flashlight down the dark hallway. The enclosures white walls, preventing the beam from showing what was inside. All the front gates were pushed inward, leaving the hallway eerily clear. Mariah readied herself as the beam went over the front gate of the closest few enclosures, revealing only beds and toys.

"Everything looks clear up ahead." Zander said, coming out of the darkness.

"How do you know that?" Mariah asked. Kylee was pointing the flashlight in the opposite direction he was facing; she could barely see anything without it.

"Turns out now; I can see in the dark." Zander said smartly. At first, she thought he was kidding, then realized he was serious.

"What does it look like?" She asked curiously.

"Pretty much like how normal people see in the daytime."

"We should head to the minibus." Carmen suggested getting everyone back on track.

"What if they're in the garage waiting? They destroyed the cars; why not the bus?" Kylee reminded. *Don't say those things.* Mariah thought, not wanting to think about them reaching the minibus only to find it destroyed and then be attacked by a group of dogs.

"All the doors to the garage are shut." Carmen reminded.

"Let's get going then." Mariah suggested.

"Mariah wait." Carmen said. The tone of her voice told Mariah she was about to say something she wasn't going to like.

"Carmen, what is it?" Mariah asked, knowing she was holding something back. Carmen hesitated a moment before saying.

"Zander, I'm sorry." She paused. Sadness entered her voice. "I don't think it's a good idea if you come with us." Mariah felt a wave of shock and anger go through her. She felt like putting the makeshift spear through Carmen's head.

"No, we can't leave him!" Kylee cried.

"SHHH." Mariah stressed, then coldly said, "Carmen, I'm going to pretend I didn't hear that."

"She's right." Zander agreed. Mariah gasped. *Zander, no, don't you dare agree with her.* "I can't just walk into a doctor's office." Dogs started running between the enclosures, some changing colors as they ran. Mariah closed her eyes, using all her mental strength not to break down.

"Zander, you're coming with us. That's the end of it." Mariah commanded.

"Sorry Mariah I can't listen to that. Who knows what's going to happen to me next? I can't risk losing my mind and attacking someone." Zander opened the closest enclosure gate. "I'll bunk down here until you bring back help." Mariah closed the gate.

"Zander, this is not a good idea. I can't leave you here." Mariah said in a last-ditch attempt to change his mind. She was already starting to feel the pain of possibly leaving him. Despite his appearance, she still loved him.

"Last I checked, the dogs can't bite through steel. I'll be safer than most of you." Zander pointed to the blankets. "I'll turn in for the night; maybe grab a snack from the kitchen; you girls will be back before I wake up."

"You're not really going through with this, are you?" Kylee asked in disbelief, shining the flashlight at Zander, causing his yellow eyes to appear to glow. Zander shook his head, yes. He put one foot in the enclosure, then paused his face briefly, showing signs of deep thought.

"Screw it; I'm probably going to die anyway," Zander said. Mariah felt her heart rate increase as he turned around. This was it. Zander was finally going to tell her how he truly felt about her. Mariah managed a giddy smile. Expecting Zander to grab the back of her head and give her a big kiss. Mariah slightly outstretched her arms as feelings of excitement filled her. Zander brushed past her. He put a finger on Kylee's chin, gently moving her head up, then kissed her lips. Mariah felt her heart break. *Zander, how could you do this to me? It was me you loved, remember?* Mariah thought. Zander released the kiss. Kylee had a surprised look of disbelief; her light brown eyes were sparkling. "Sorry, I never told you how I felt sooner." He said softly. Mariah put her head against the fencing as feelings of anger and disappointment set in. The more she thought about it, the more the signs had always been there, but she chose to ignore them, replacing reality with her own fantasy. Kylee remained speechless and appeared much calmer. "When this is over and we get out of here, I'm going to take you out on a proper date," Zander continued.

"I'd like that." Kylee replied, then seemly remembered the situation. She looked at the enclosure, then at Zander. *Get in there and die, Kylee.* Mariah thought bitterly.

"Kylee, trust me, I'll be fine. Now I have a reason to want to live and get better." Zander slowly released Kylee's hand. He gave Carmen a quick hug, then turned to Mariah. She managed to smile, but didn't know how well she was hiding her feelings of disappointment.

"Keep them safe while I'm gone." Zander said, hugging her tightly.

"I will." Mariah replied in a near-robotic voice.

"And sorry." He whispered. Mariah tried to find the right words but couldn't. She separated from him, and as much as she tried to prevent it, she couldn't help but give Kylee an angry glare. Kylee either didn't notice or didn't care. Before Zander could shut the gate, Kylee jumped into his arms and kissed him.

"I'm holding you to your promise. You...you want me to stay with you?"

"It's too dangerous, Kylee. This will be over before you know it. And I mean to keep my promise," Zander said confidently. Kylee closed the enclosure door. Carmen placed the clip on the gate.

"Just in case the dogs try to jump up and open the gate, you can still get out if you need to," Carmen assured. Zander moved the clip around. It would take a while, but he could unlatch it if he needed to. Mariah watched Kylee's starry smile. *I want to wipe that off your face*, she thought, still bitter. Down the hall, outlines of phantom dogs were walking across the hall, disappearing through enclosures.

"Piss off." Mariah said seeing the shape of a rottweiler move between the enclosures. Kylee's expression went from dreamy to concerned. *I didn't say that out loud, did I?* Mariah thought.

"Mariah," Kylee started to say.

"We'd better get going." Mariah interrupted, motioning for Kylee to move forward. *Calm down.* Mariah told herself wanting the phantom dogs to leave. Several sat inside enclosures, fading in and out of existence. Carmen looked through the door's window, then opened it. Mariah gave the middle finger to the rottweiler before following.

"We're nearly there." Carmen said as the girls left the sled dog kennels. Kylee, who was in front, stopped.

"I can't leave Zander," she said, turning around.

"Kylee, we'll only be leaving him for a few hours; we'll be back before you know it," Carmen assured.

"I'm going back to him." Mariah shielded her eyes as the flashlight beam went by her. Everyone froze when they heard a bark. Kylee stopped frozen in place. The flashlight beam danced in her trembling hand. She turned the beam down the hallway that led to the garage and suites' stairs. Mariah turned her head. Matrix was standing only feet from her.

"Run!" Carmen yelled. Barks and howls started coming from in front of them and from the side hallway, blocking the way they came. Horrified, Mariah tried to focus; her phantom dogs were mixing with the real ones. She shrieked when a dog leaped at her, causing her to drop her spear. Seconds later, it disappeared. Kylee screamed as three real huskies rushed down the hall at them. Matrix walked towards them in no hurry to catch up to them. Deciding to run instead of try to fight, Mariah shoved Kylee into the play yard door. She felt the wind from Matrix's closing mouth right before the door pushed open, sending her and Kylee forward. From the corner of her eye, she saw Carmen run back into the sled dog area. Mariah used her feet to keep the door closed. The door opened a fourth of the way when Matrix slammed against it. With all her might, Mariah kicked her feet forward, closing it. Kylee put her full weight against the door. Mariah got to her feet and helped push against it. Matrix continued to slam into it, but it didn't budge. Matrix jumped at the small window, his white saliva covering it as he barked. Having escaped the trap, both girls turned away, breathing heavily.

"Kylee, watch out!" Mariah yelled, pointing to the two dogs coming through the fence.

"What?" She cried, looking around, confused. Mariah saw the dog starting to fade.

"Never hallucination mind." Realizing how her words came out, Mariah closed her eyes, mentally focusing on her speech.

"Are you OK?" Kylee asked, concerned.

"No," Mariah snarled.

"Can we worry about that later?" Kylee suggested. Mariah could hear multiple dogs at the door barking and running around. Mariah acknowledged she was right.

"Carmen and Zander?" Kylee said in a worried tone.

"Zander is fine." Mariah said, not wanting to think about him. "I saw Carmen get inside the sled dog kennel. I'm sure she's okay." Mariah added, hoping she was right.

***

"Carmen, are you okay?" Zander asked, trying to keep his voice low.

"I'm fine," she replied. "Zander, do you see or hear any dogs at the other end?"

"No, I don't see or hear anything. Are Kylee and Mariah OK?" His voice filled with concern.

"There, fine, I saw them get outside." Carmen replied, lying about knowing if they got away or not. She didn't trust the new Zander and didn't want him coming out of the enclosure.

"I'm coming out to help you guys."

"No, let's stick to the plan. I'm about to make a run for it." Carmen replied. Hoping Zander would play along. She slowly walked towards the door window and looked through. Matrix and the others were barking at the outside door. She moved back, not wanting them to see or hear her.

"Good luck getting to the bus." She nearly shrieked at the sound of Zander's voice. She quietly sprinted to his enclosure.

"Thanks," she whispered. To her relief, he was sitting down calmly. Despite his appearance, she started to see the same friend and co-worker she had worked with for the last few years. "Zander, I promise we are going to bring back help and get you back to normal."

"Don't make promises you can't keep." Zander replied. "If I do make it out, the government is going to lock me away and use me as a lab rat." Carmen swallowed, fearing he was right. His yellow eyes seemed to look right through her.

"Zander, we won't let that happen."

"Good to know you have so much influence in the world," he sarcastically remarked. "Just get Kylee to safety; that's all I ask." Carmen looked away, not sure she could keep that promise.

"I'll be back. I promise," Carmen replied. She again went to the window. Matrix and the others were gone. She cautiously stepped halfway out of the room. She turned on her flashlight, shining it down both hallways. She moved it across the top of the enclosures. A day ago, she would have called someone crazy for thinking dogs could plan ambushes, but she had seen it for herself. She banged the spear slightly against a metal pipe, then listened. *Did they all chase after Kylee and Mariah?* She worried, wondering and hoping they had gotten to safety. Deciding things were as good as they were going to get, she walked forward. She could hear her heart beating as she held the spear in front of her. She walked gingerly down the hall; every time she passed an enclosure, she opened the door to block the hallway behind her. She could see the door to the garage only a few feet in front of her. In excitement, she rushed for it, and when she passed the open suite entrance, a shadow leaped at her. She hardly saw it before the impact knocked her against the wall. Carmen fell, dropping the flashlight, but managed to hold onto the spear. She felt a set of jaws clamp down on her leg. She swung the back of the spear, striking her attacker in the head. The dog yelped; she felt the jaws release her. She got to her feet as the dog recovered from the attack. The flashlight had rolled into the water drain. The dim light illuminated the outline of the black Newfoundland she knew was Teddy.

"Teddy, easy boy," she said. He was between her and the garage. During the standoff, she carefully squatted down and picked up the flashlight. She shinned it in Teddy's eyes, hoping to blind him. Teddy sprinted at her from the left. Carmen moved to the right, hoping to get around him. Teddy jumped in front of her and again charged at her left. Carmen again moved to the right, then felt her foot slip. Too late, she realized what was happening: he was herding her to the suites, then Teddy leaped at her. Carmen felt her feet fall from under her, then she was tumbling down the stairs. Her world spun until, seconds later, she hit the suite floor. Carmen moaned. She moved her legs and arms. Everything hurt, but nothing seemed to be broken. She heard the sound of heavy footsteps rushing down the stairs. She saw the flashlight beam and grabbed it. The beam of light moved across the room, searching for the spear. *Please don't let it be on the top steps.* She thought, knowing she was dead if it was. The light found the spear sitting in the drain next to the kennels. Carmen heard Teddy's feet coming down the steps. Having no time to get up, she rolled her body towards the spear. She grasped it in her left hand. She could hear the dog rushing towards her. She tilted her head sideways. The charging dog was only feet from her. Carmen twisted her body, holding the spear in front of her. Teddy yelped as he fell on top of her. Blood from the wound flowed on her shirt and pants. Still on her back, Carmen screamed as the crushing weight pushed her against the kennels. As best she could, she shielded her face from the coming attack, then realized the dog had stopped moving. The massive dog fell next to her, the spear embedded in his chest. Carmen took several deep breaths, knowing how lucky she was. She looked at Teddy, and a feeling of deep sadness came over her. He was always a sweet, loving boy who had gone crazy because of this virus, or whatever it was. *At least I ended his suffering,* Carmen thought, trying to make herself feel better. She pulled herself up by the chain link, and the fencing pulled out at the bottom, nearly causing her to fall again. *What the hell?* She thought, getting to her feet, and pulled on the chain link again. The chain-link fencing on the bottom half of the door was no longer connected to the frame. *So that's how you were getting out.* She thought. Looking at Matrix's homemade dog door. Instead of dwelling on the discovery, she gingerly walked up the stairs, hoping more dogs had not reentered the building by then. She turned the flashlight beam down the hall. The beam shone on Blaze, and several dogs rushing towards her. Carmen rushed into the garage, slamming the metal door behind her. *I made it!* She thought with relief, looking at the bus in front of her. She pulled the garage door open slightly, checked for dogs in the fenced-in area, then opened it all the way. The cold air and falling snowflakes never felt so good to her, then she heard what she was expecting. The barks and howls of approaching dogs. Soon they came into view. Most of them were huskies, but several German shepherds and mixed breeds were among them. Carmen guessed there were ten to fifteen of them in total, either rushing along the fence or on their hind legs, barking and snapping. From behind her, she heard Blaze's familiar husky bark at the garage entrance, followed by the doorknob rattling. Then she saw Matrix, flanked by Echo and Athena, rushing towards the fence. Matrix looked around, seemingly getting a feel for the situation, before barking several times. Half the dogs started climbing the ten-foot fence, while the other half started to dig. The doorknob behind her started to rattle more intently. "Too late for you guys." Carmen said, reaching into her pocket.

"Shit!" She shouted, feeling no keys. *They're in the lock box in the lobby,* Carmen realized, cursing herself for making such a stupid mistake. Several of the dogs were halfway up the fence, while others heads and upper bodies were coming under the fence. *The spare key.* Carmen remembered. She reached under the front bumper and pulled the box off the magnet. She looked toward the garage door. Echo was climbing; her front paws were on the top of the fence. Carmen saw Athena standing sideways next to the fence. *What is she doing?* Carmen wondered. Matrix gave her the answer when he rushed the fence, using Athena as a ramp. He leaped on her back, then over the fence. Seeing that momentarily stunned Carmen, she would have even found it cute in a different situation. She quickly snapped out of it, unlocking the bus, and slammed the door shut moments before Matrix reached her. She saw Blaze had gotten the door opened. She and the other dogs were jumping against the bus, causing it to shake. Other dogs were climbing over the fence or coming from under it. She heard the scraping sound of dogs biting and clawing at the aluminum. Carmen turned the key, knowing it wouldn't be long before one of the dogs got to the break or fuel lines. She exhaled in relief when the engine came to life. Matrix leaped on the front of the bus and lied down on the hood. Blocking her vision, he tilted his head sideways as if he were again examining the situation. She could hear several dogs on top of the bus biting at something. Carmen beeped the horn, hoping the noise would scare some of the dogs off. Matrix didn't move an inch. He barked and snarled, white frost fell from his mouth onto the window. "You think this is going to stop me?" Carmen said out loud to Matrix, who was still barking at her. She turned her head to see Blaze and another dog go under the bus. She again locked eyes with Matrix. "Nice try. Sorry Mariah." She said getting ready to put the bus in drive. Matrix gave a commanding bark, then winked at her. Carmen heard something moving above her. It sounded like something was moving inside the aluminum body. She saw Echo fall from the bus roof. She dangled in midair, holding the radio antenna in her mouth. Suddenly, the radio wires from below came rushing towards her, getting tangled around her neck and chest on the way to the roof. Echo's feet pushed against the bus as she continued to pull. Carmen struggled for breath as she pulled at the wires tangled around her throat. Matrix again laid down on the front of the bus, crossing his front paws. A look of satisfaction formed on his face, like he was admiring his plan coming together. His taunting look sent a new wave of strength through Carmen; she couldn't die here, not like this, not to him. She pulled with all her might. She felt air enter her lungs as she pulled the wires away from her throat. Matrix got to his feet and got closer to the glass, barking again. Athena leaped on top of the bus, biting down on the wires. Carmen started choking as the wires once again wrapped her in their deadly embrace. As hard as she tried, the wires wouldn't budge this time. Matrix's face gained a grin, knowing he had won. Seconds later, Carmen's coughs and gagging stopped; her eyes rolled to the back of her head, her long tongue moved to the side of her mouth as her arms fell to her sides. Matrix got up and let out a soft grunt. Athena and Echo released the wiring. The moment Carmen felt the pressure release, she pulled the wires from her throat and chest. Matrix let out another grunt. She could see the look of shock in his eyes. "Yeah, I played possum," she said in a raspy voice. Matrix barked in fury as the bus started to move. The wiring moved again; this time she moved her head back, causing them to miss her. Carmen moved the bus forward. Matrix leaped on the roof, and then she saw him land outside the gate. The bus slowed down as it crashed through the fencing; she saw Athena, Blaze, and Echo retreating too. She could still hear dogs biting at the frame below her. *What are they up to?* Carmen thought worried about Matrix's sudden retreat. A husky leaped onto the hood. A small can of gasoline was in his mouth. He dropped it. *All no.* she thought as the gasoline spilled everywhere. From the side mirror, she saw two large mixed breeds dragging a larger gas can under the bus. For a second, she heard a rumble, flames surrounded her, and then everything went black.

CHAPTER 21

Mariah and Kylee rushed into the staff building. They had tried for the garage only to find several dogs between them and it, forcing them around the other side of the kennel to the safety of the fenced-in path, which they followed to the staff building. Mariah grabbed her ice ax as they entered the lobby. No dogs were inside, and all the doors were intact. Momentarily out of danger, she put the ax back on the desk, then moved the bodies of the dead toy poodle and yorkie poo to the waiting area. She could hear dogs roaming around in the recreation room. Whether they were real or imagined, she was unsure. She looked at Kylee, who was sitting near the fireplace, the fire still pleasantly burning like nothing was happening. Mariah sat as far from her as possible, trying to control her anger and sadness. She thought about going to her room and locking the door; her mind focused on and played back as best she could remember every time she, Kylee, and Zander had hung out. The more she thought about it, the more reality was confirmed for her. Zander had always preferred Kylee. She tried to hold onto the hope that Zander kissing Kylee was nothing more than another symptom of his illness, but deep down she knew the truth.

"Hey," Kylee said.

"What?" Mariah asked, turning around, agitated. Kylee took several steps back, putting her hands up defensively.

"Look Mariah I had no idea Zander felt that way about me; I knew how much you liked him." Kylee said franticly. Mariah gave her a bitter look. "It's not like I planned this; I never met to break your heart." *Too late,* Mariah thought.

"Kylee, what's your point?" She asked, getting up.

"I just wanted to make sure there's no bad blood between us." Kylee gave a slight shrug. "You know we're still friends?" *The only way that was going to happen was to tell Zander you're not interested and give him to me,* Mariah thought. She closed her eyes and took a minute to think.

"Do you feel the same way about him?"

"Yeah, I always liked him, but never thought I had a chance with him. Mariah, please don't let this get between our friendship." Kylee begged. "I've lost enough friends today. I couldn't stand losing you." As much as she wanted to stay mad at Kylee, her words were getting to her. After a long, tense pause, Mariah said:

"Kylee, it's not like Zander and I were dating and you stole him from me. I'm not happy about what happened." She stopped trying to hold back her anger and got out the last words. "But Zander chose you, and I have to live with that." Mariah again hesitated, then held out her index finger. Kylee extended hers and twisted it around Mariah's. "Don't worry, Kylee, I won't get in the way of you and Zander. I truly hope you live happily ever after."

"If we make it out of here alive." Kylee replied in a worried tone. "Do you think Carmen's ok?"

"Carmen's probably getting the bus right now. She'll either go get help or pull up next to the fence to get us," Mariah replied, trying to sound convincing.

"If we leave, we have to go back for Zander!" This was the last subject she wanted to talk about. *Not this again, Kylee* Mariah thought. She didn't want to leave Zander either, but he was as safe as anyone, and there was probably no way they could get back in the kennel.

"He's safe in the kennel; we'll send a doctor back for him when we get back to civilization." Mariah assured, but was secretly worried they were going to use him as a lab rat, like he feared.

"Mariah, we can't leave him; he's our friend," Kylee added.

"Kylee, please don't start an argument about this. I really can't handle it right now." Mariah begged. "Zander's sick, and I can't do anything about it." Before Kylee could answer, they heard a loud explosion. Mariah grabbed the ice ax and rushed to the fenced-in pathway. In the distance, she saw the bus engulfed in flames, slowly sliding down the hill. Howls and barks of victory filled the night.

"No! How could they do this? There's no way he's that smart!" Kylee cried.

"I don't know!" Mariah shouted, dropping the ax, feeling her hope fade. Matrix stood in front of the burning bus, staring right at them. "That bastard!" Mariah cursed.

"Leave us alone!" Just leave us alone!" Kylee screamed before breaking down into tears. Mariah felt the same way. Athena came into sight, holding something in her mouth. Mariah took another step outside, trying to make out what it was.

Some snow from the roof hit her on the shoulder. Mariah looked up to see two large mixed breeds on either side. She cursed, not knowing if they were real.

"Kylee, do you?"

"What!" Kylee yelled. Mariah pointed up. Kylee barely got out a scream before both dogs leaped down. Mariah fell backwards into the building. Kylee fell just short of the front of the door. "Mariah!" She screamed as one of the dogs bit down on her left leg; the other was standing on her, biting down on her shoulder and back. Mariah frantically got to her feet. *This is the end of your problems. Sorry Zander Kylee was killed by the dogs.* For a moment, the thought formed a wicked smile across her face. Kylee's screams and pleas for help quickly brought her sensible mind back. Despite not having a weapon, Mariah charged forward, kicking at the dog biting dangerously close to Kylee's neck. The first kick did nothing. When she reared back again, the dog bit down on her boot. Mariah grabbed the nearby fencing, trying to keep her balance on one leg. She could feel the dog's teeth working their way through the thick leather. She managed to get her foot out of the boot, and the dog stumbled back at the loss of resistance. Mariah rushed back inside, grabbed the snow ax, and brought it down on the charging dog's head. She pulled it free and struck the other dog across the neck. The dog fell, her teeth still latched onto Kylee's leg. Mariah yanked the dog's jaws free.

"Please don't, Kylee. Please don't die." She repeated as she bent down to help Kylee, who was a sobbing mess. The all-too-familiar red snow was forming around her leg and shoulder. She went to one knee, using her arm as a makeshift pillow for Kylee's head. "Kylee, it's OK; it's over; we need to get inside." Mariah said, trying to pull her to her feet, then she heard the bark she had learned to dread. Matrix was sitting outside the fence with Blaze by his side. He gave Mariah a wink, then started licking Blaze across the ears and face. A wave of anger filled her. He had taken Blaze from her, and now he was taunting her with it. Mariah imagined him saying:

"I've already taken two of the things you love most. Blaze is mine, and soon Zander will be." Wanting to end it right then, her left hand gripped the ax handle. The sound of Kylee's moans of pain stopped her. Rushing to him was probably just what he wanted.

"Kylee, we're going inside. Can you walk?"

"I don't know." Kylee moaned in pain.

"We'll treat your wounds inside. Mariah held out her hand, ready to pull her to her feet." Matrix barked again. "Shut up!" Mariah screamed. Four other dogs were now at the fence; three started digging, and one started climbing it. Matrix turned his head, looking towards the kennel. Athena was coming down the hill, followed by Thunder and two other dogs. Each dog was holding something, but she still couldn't tell what the objects were. When they walked by Matrix, she saw Athena and Thunder holding cans of gasoline. A black and yellow lab followed behind, carrying a propane tank. Echo was several yards behind them with a piece of wood in her mouth, flames dancing on the top half. Mariah and Kylee's disbelieving eyes met. "There not." Mariah whispered. One by one, each dog disappeared into the building. "Get to the kennel!" Mariah yelled, pulling Kylee up. She screamed in pain as she was pulled to her feet. Mariah rushed forward, holding onto Kylee's shoulder, who was limping and doing her best to keep up.

Mariah saw the German shepherd mix was nearly halfway up the fence. She heard barking, then the explosion she knew was coming. Both girls fell forward as the world around them seemed too lit up. Mariah got back up, hoping pieces of falling wood and bricks had crushed Matrix. She couldn't see him, though she was sure he was around somewhere.

"Mariah," Kylee moaned, sitting on the ground. She pointed to the fencing. The shepard mix's front paws had reached the top of the fencing.

"Get inside!" Mariah screamed as she helped Kylee to her feet. The shepherd mix jumped into the gated path. Mariah raised her ax.

"Mariah, come on." Kylee said, weakly unlatching the door. The door abruptly flew open, striking her on the side of the head. A brown pitbull named Coco bit down on Kylee's arm. Mariah cursed, striking him in the neck with the snow ax, then felt something strike her in the back. She fell forward against the fence, losing her grip on the snow ax. The shepherd mix bit down on her shoulder. Mariah's hands went around the dog's head, trying to pry its jaws from her trapezius muscle. Mariah grunted in pain, feeling her flesh tear every time the dog chewed. Suddenly, the dog yelped and fell off her. The snow ax was lodged deep inside its rib cage. Kylee again brought the ax down on the dog's head, ending its suffering.

"Thanks Kylee." Mariah said in a voice filled with pain. Mariah put Kylee's arm around her good shoulder, each girl supporting each other. They had one foot inside when Mariah heard the unmistakable sound of dogs running on the floor. "Shit!" She screamed, slamming the door shut. Seconds later, a malamute was snarling at them through the glass. Mariah looked towards the burning building;

the digging dogs were nearly under the fence. Mariah felt her strength leaving. *Is this it?* She wondered.

"Zander, help us!" Kylee screamed. Mariah frantically looked around, searching for a way out and a place to hide, then she saw it.

"Kylee, we have to get to the suite basement door!"

"We'll die if we go out there!" Kylee screamed.

"We'll die if we stay here!" Without discussing it any further, Mariah opened the side gate. She started tracking through the knee-high snow; Kylee hesitated but followed. Mariah kept her eye on the entrance, only yards away. Her right sock was soaked, and her foot burned. Mariah cursed herself for leaving the boot. "Take another step." Mariah repeated moving as fast as she could, not wanting to know how close the dogs at the fence were. Finally, she broke through to plowed ground, where the snow was only ankle-high. When Kylee walked out of the deep snow, Mariah saw blood still dripping from her wounds. Both girls leaned against the chain link. Mariah was mentally and physically exhausted. The suite door was only a few yards away. Mariah pointed to it. "We're almost there, Kylee."

"I'm coming." Kylee said in a dazed, spaced-out voice. The blood loss clearly affecting her. *I've got to stop our bleeding.* Mariah thought, looking at her own bleeding shoulder. She dreaded looking at her foot more, fearing how frostbitten it was going to be. "No." She heard Kylee say defeated, then saw why. Matrix was casually strolling towards her. Blaze, Goliath, and Athena followed close behind. The three dogs that were at the fence joined the group. *No, we're almost there,* Mariah thought, knowing that in their exhausted and wounded condition, there was no way they could outrun them even a few yards from the door. Mariah walked with Kylee, keeping an eye on the dogs, who were steadily moving closer. Matrix walked ahead of the other dogs; he stopped right at the edge of the deep snow. *It's like he's taunting me and challenging me,* Mariah thought as they continued forward, wondering why the dogs weren't attacking. *He started this. He's the leader, and I'm the leader; if I defeat him, I'll end this.* In her mind, she could clearly hear him saying.

"I don't want to end the game too soon, Mariah; defeat me, and I'll give you your precious Zander and Blaze back." Mariah didn't know if she was imagining it or if he was somehow taunting her telepathically. Kylee reached the basement entrance, frantically kicking the piles of snow away from the door.

"Come on, Mariah," she said, grabbing her hand. Mariah limped to the opened suite entrance, keeping an eye on Matrix as Kylee rushed inside.

"Let's go; we made it." Kylee said exhausted. Mariah looked right at her.

"Sorry Kylee." Mariah said, putting her hands on her shoulders, then pushed her to the ground.

"Mariah, what are you doing?" Kylee screamed, getting to her feet.

"I'm cutting off the head of the snake; it's the only way to save Zander and Blaze."

"Mariah, have you lost your mind? Get in here!"

"Stay inside, Kylee." Mariah ordered, slamming the door. "You!" Mariah continued holding the blade out at Matrix. "I know you can understand me; we're both leaders. I accept your challenge. Let's settle this right now, me and you." Matrix and the other dogs didn't move. He tilted his head slightly in confusion.

"Mariah, get in here!" Kylee cried, opening the door. Mariah swung the ax, the blade stopping inches from Kylee's shoulder.

"Kylee, get back inside, or this blade goes through you." Instead of backing down like Mariah expected, Kylee stood her ground. A look of determination formed on her face.

"Then do it. I'm as good as dead anyway." Mariah remained motionless, having no idea what to do now that Kylee called her bluff. While the two girls were in their standoff, Mariah felt a chunk of snow hit her shoulder. Before she could say or do anything, Echo jumped onto her from the roof. The girls' heads knocked together. Kylee's head hit the ground as the force of the fall sent the tip of the ax blade into her already wounded shoulder. Mariah saw Echo rushing towards her face. Mariah closed her eyes when she heard Matrix bark loudly. Echo stopped, and she danced in place, letting out several barks herself. Matrix let out a more vicious bark. That caused Echo to reluctantly back away.

"Kylee!" Mariah spoke in a concerned voice. Kylee, who now looked to be barely conscious, moaned. "Kylee I'm going to pull the ax out." She put her hands right where the ax blade and handle connected. She quickly tugged upward, pulling the tip out. Kylee screamed momentarily, gasping and whimpering as she clinched her shoulder. Mariah saw Matrix slowly walking towards her. She kept an eye on him as she pulled Kylee inside. "Kylee, stay here. I'll be in soon." Kylee, who seemed completely zoned out, let Mariah lead her inside. Mariah closed the door and took a deep breath. "I can do this." She focused on the hope that if she killed Matrix, the other dogs would back off, and scientists could find out what was wrong with them and help cure Zander and Blaze. Mariah walked ahead.

Goliath, Athena, Echo, and Blaze started to form a circle around her. She looked at Blaze and smiled. *You're still in there; I know it.*

"Mariah!" She heard Kylee's muffled yell. Goliath and Athena stood between them, preventing Mariah from retreating or Kylee from coming to help. Mariah felt herself feeling glad they were there; it would stop Kylee from doing something stupid. She and Matrix began circling each other, the light from the fires making it possible for her to see clearly. Mariah held the ax slightly above her left shoulder. Matrix slowly circled closer. Mariah kept an eye on the dogs around her, even though they weren't moving at the moment. There was no guarantee they wouldn't make a move. Matrix growled and lunged forward. Mariah swiped her ax sideways, missing. Matrix slowly started to advance baring teeth. Mariah stepped back slightly and looked over her shoulder as she walked towards the kennel. She wanted to keep him in the deep snow and her back to the kennel, making it harder for him to move quickly or get behind her. Mariah felt her back bump chain-link. For a moment, the two remained in a standoff. Matrix trampled through the snow every time he tried to get to the plowed area. Mariah attacked with the ax. *If I keep this up, I can win.* She thought trying to tune out Kylee's cries. Matrix again tried to charge; Mariah swung the ax right before he could leave the deep snow. Wanting to press her advantage, Mariah ran forward, quickly closing the distance. She swung the ice ax as hard as she could, aiming for Matrix's side. Matrix leaped away, sinking up to his chest in the deep snow. *Now.* Mariah thought as she rushed him; she raised the ax. Matrix tried to move, but the snow trapped him. Right before Mariah could swing it down, a sharp pain came from her ankle. Mariah stumbled forward as Echo continued to bite at it. The deep snowbank braking her fall. Mariah spun her body, aiming the ax for Echo's head. She retreated the moment she swung it forward. From the side, she saw Matrix charging. Mariah hardly had time to think before he was on her. He bit down on the hand holding the ice ax. She cried in pain as it fell from her hand. Matrix pulled her to the ground. She felt her body impact the fencing as Matrix yanked and thrashed her around. Mariah tried to fight back, but there was nothing she could do; her arm felt like it was getting pulled from its socket, then Matrix released her. Slipping into unconsciousness, Mariah could hear Kylee yelling, the sound of a door opening, and Goliath slamming against it. She tried to feel for the ax, but her fingers only felt the cold touch of snow. Mariah watched the snowflakes fall from above. Strange, wonderful shapes of all different colors started to appear in the night sky, more beautiful than the northern lights, but Matrix's black and tan fur blocked them out. He put a paw on her chest. He looked her in the eye, giving her a wink as if gloating that he had won. Mariah turned her head and caught a glimpse of Blaze standing in her spot, feet from them.

"Blaze...Help me." She weakly begged. Blaze looked right at her. Soon, Matrix's face was the only thing Mariah could see. *I failed.* Mariah thought, knowing she only had seconds left to live. *Sorry Kylee, sorry Zander, sorry Blaze.* Her thoughts started lingering on the future home, husband, and children she would never have. Matrix's jaws opened, moving downward, covering her lower face and throat. Suddenly, he yelped in pain, his head pulling back. She heard loud barks and snarls. Mariah rolled to her stomach, wondering what had happened. Despite her pain, she managed a wide smile. Blaze was on him, biting down on the side of Matrix's neck. Large clumps of snow kicked up as the two dogs battled. "Blaze, you saved me." New feelings of hope and joy seemed to open her reserves of strength. Mariah got to her feet, grabbing the ice ax. She walked towards the fight, keeping a close eye on Goliath and Athena, who were still occupied with Kylee. *Keep them there, Kylee.* Mariah thought. Echo and the three other dogs were nowhere in sight. Matrix put his right paw on the back of Blaze's neck, pushing down on her. He tore loose from her grip, then bit down on her head. Mariah moved to a sprint, and Matrix lifted Blaze's body off the ground, slamming her back down. He shook his head back and forth, rag-dolling her through the snow. Blaze let out yelps of pain, clawing at the larger rottweiler with her back legs. With Matrix's back to her, Mariah swung the ice ax down with all her might. Matrix released his grip on Blaze, turned his head, and then dashed to the right. The blade grazed the side of his face, then went down into Blaze's neck and chest.

"Nooo!" Mariah cried in horror. *This has to be a hallucination. Please, God, let this be a hallucination!* In tears, Mariah got to her knees, reaching down to touch Blaze, hoping her hand would go through her. Instead, her hand touched soft fur. Blaze whimpered, still alive, panting heavily. Tears formed in Mariah's eyes as she removed the ice ax as gently as she could. Blood squirted from the wound, soon becoming a heavy flow. Mariah pressed down on the wound, trying to stop the bleeding. She threw the ice ax and started screaming in fury as uncontrollable anger came over her. "I'm so sorry, my darling." She said placing her left hand under Blaze's head and gently stroking it with her right, wanting to give her as much comfort as she could in her final moments. Blaze pulled her head up, giving Mariah a final lick as if saying, I'm sorry, I forgive you. Mariah cried uncontrollably as the light in Blaze's blue eyes dimmed, and then the shadow of death loomed over her, a shadow called Matrix. Still on her knees without a

weapon, Mariah turned her head. A look of pure anger was on Matrix's face; white

foam dripped from his mouth. His black fur highlighted the line of fresh blood

that ran from the top of his head to his right front leg. In a final act of defiance,

Mariah spat at him, then looked down at Blaze, remembering her beloved dog.

CHAPTER 22

Kylee watched in horror as Matrix pulled Mariah down, and both disappeared from her line of sight. *What was happening? Why had she sat down?* She thought. More than anything, she wanted to rush out and help her friend, but the dogs in front of her prevented it. Weaponless and bleeding, there was nothing she could do. *Mariah has the ice ax; she's going to hit him and get up. The heroine always wins, right? Even if it looks like she's losing,* Kylee thought, clinging to any hope she could. *Then we get Zander and walk to safety.* Kylee waited, hoping and praying a silent prayer. Only it was Matrix who arose over the snow bank with something in his mouth. He tossed it through the air several times, then kicked it through the snow with his paws, acting like a friendly dog playing with his favorite toy. The other dogs started barking in excitement. Matrix got on a pile of snow, holding his trophy in victory. Kylee tried to focus on it. Her body began to tremble when she realized what it was. Mariah's severed head. *No, she can't be dead!* Kylee thought in horror. But there was no denying what her eyes were seeing. Kylee started coughing, bending down to throw up. Tears filled her eyes. She slammed her fist against the window, screaming and cursing at Matrix. Her outburst was ended by Goliath striking the door so hard that the glass shattered. Kylee screamed and stepped back. Echo started to howl. Goliath and Athena took turns ramming the door, the middle wood flexing back and forth. "Leave me alone!" Kylee screamed. "What do I do? What do I do?" Kylee asked, looking around for anyone to answer. Her eyes grew wide with fear, her breathing stopped as the realization that she was alone dawned on her. "I can't be the last one." Kylee said out loud, trying not to accept her reality. "Mariah, Zander, Carmen, Ethan! Help me! Someone help me, please!" *Zander is still alive.* Then she remembered the dogs were in the kennel; they had gotten through the enclosure and killed him. "I can't be alone. I don't know what to do! I don't know what to do!" Kylee repeated, covering her eyes. She was dizzy, freezing, and becoming increasingly tired. "This is a bad dream. That's all I'm going to wake up any second." Kylee told herself. The sound of wood shattering brought her back to reality. Goliath's head was coming through a hole in the door. Kylee screamed and ran for the stairs. She briefly turned her head to look at Goliath; he was pulling his head back for another ram. She tried to run faster, then felt her foot trip on something. She stumbled, breaking her fall on a suite gate. She gasped in fear when she felt her leg brush thick fur. "No! No! Please!" Kylee yelled. Before realizing the dog was dead, she heard dogs above her, their footsteps rushing towards her. *I can't go upstairs; there's nowhere to run.* Thinking of Zander, Kylee pulled the gate open and locked herself in a suite. She sank as low as she could against the wall. She grabbed the cot, placing it between her and the outside world, then put a blanket on top of that. As a little girl, she would hide under the blankets when she was scared. She heard wood breaking and dogs moving on the floor above her. *I'm going to die. I'm going to die.* She closed her eyes and imagined herself in her mother's arms. She listened to her mom's voice, to what she would say to her as a little girl when she was frightened by thunderstorms.

"It's ok, Kylee; the storm will pass, the sun will break through the clouds, and everything will be ok." Kylee felt blood still dripping from the wound on her arm. "Don't kid yourself; you're not getting out of this alive. You know that, right, Kylee?" She let out a sobbing grown of frustration. "Why can't I be a stronger person? Why did I spend my life always getting help from others?" Dwelling on her thoughts, she put her head against the wall and closed her eyes, not expecting to ever open them again.

When she awoke, she stretched her legs out, knocking over her makeshift tent. *Where am I?* She thought, then remembered everything. Her entire body felt weak. Waves of pain pulsed in her forehead. Without thinking it through, she pulled the small flashlight from her pocket and turned it on. Fresh and drying blood covered most of her body. *I've got to get a med kit; I need water.* Kylee thought, feeling an intense thirst. She slowly got to her feet. Her legs wobbled, and dizziness struck her. Kylee hugged the suite wall. She shined the flashlight beam on Teddy's body, noticing the spear. *It's going to be too hard to bend down.* Kylee thought, hardly able to stand. Her only focus was getting to water then to a warm bed. She exited the suite and turned on a water hose. A few drips fell into her mouth, then nothing. She dropped it, not noticing the water valve was turned off, and walked towards the stairs. Her legs wobbled under her. She tried to walk straight but could only manage to stumble forward, falling against the wall at the side of the stairs. She hugged herself, trying to keep warm. "You can do it, Kylee; be strong for once." She clung to the wall, put one foot forward then heard a growl. A brown pitbull mix walked through the destroyed door, followed by a gray pitbull mix and a white samoyed. She looked towards the suites, knowing there was no way she could make it back to them. She sat down. She let out a half-crazed laugh, half-cry of fright. The three dogs snarled, moving towards her. Knowing what was about to happen, she put her back against the wall and covered her face. She pulled her arms away from her eyes when she heard something hit the ground in front of her. Kylee felt herself smile widely, seeing Zander crouched in front of her. The three dogs growled. She let out a helpless scream as the three dogs leaped at him. *No, I can't lose him.* Kylee grabbed onto the stair railing, trying to pull herself up. Her weak arms gave out, and the dizziness caused her to stumble back against the wall. Zander reached out, grabbing the tan pit by the head and neck and slamming him to the ground. The samoyed jumped on his back, taking him off balance. He fell to one knee, and the brown pit mix jumped at him. He pushed both his hands forward, striking the dog in the chest, sending him crashing into the side wall. The dog got up, limping into the darkness. Still on his hands and knees, Zander fought with the other two dogs. They jumped and snapped at him, preventing him from getting up. Kylee watched in amazement. Zander's reflexes seem faster than those of normal humans. Zander managed to get both dogs off him, but they charged again. Zander rolled on his back, kicking the Samoyed, then wrapped his clawed hand around the grey pits head, slamming it into the ground. Zander leaped up, breathing heavily. Kylee got to her feet, watching both dogs retreat. He turned toward Kylee. For the first time, she noticed the rips in his clothes and half a dozen bite wounds. Not sure if she could trust him, she looked for an escape route.

"Kylee, did you see what I did to those dogs?" He asked in a pleased voice. Kylee tried to talk, but the words seemed to be stuck in her throat. Zander looked the same as when she last saw him, but the sight still unnerved her.

"Yes.... Yes." She finally managed to say. Fearing his next words were going to be. *I'm going to do the same to you.* She didn't know why, but she felt there was something evil hiding deep inside him. He seemed to sense her fear.

"If I wanted you dead, don't you think I would have attacked you by now? I'm still me; you know that." Kylee desperately wanted to run over to him, to fall into his arms and cry, but she was still unsure if she could trust him.

"Zander, we're going to get you some help; this disease must have been created somewhere. Whoever made it must know how to fix it."

"We'll worry about that when the time comes. Right now, I'm worried about you. Where's Mariah?" he asked, concern entering his voice.

"She's dead." Kylee managed to choke out, new tears rolling down her face.

"Dam them." Zander said with anger and sadness in his voice. "Before I came here, I checked what was left of the bus. Carmen's dead too." He slammed his fist against the wall. Seeing how upset he was about his friend's death caused some of her fear to go away. She warily walked over to him. She noticed the small tufts of fur on his hand when he stroked her hair. The feeling of the gentle touch and knowing she was no longer alone brought a calming sensation. "Kylee, you probably already know this, but you're a mess." *At least he hasn't lost his sense of humor.* Kylee thought finally managing a smile. "Let's get you upstairs and patched up, then we worry about getting out of here." Zander, you're still in there. Before she knew it, Zander lifted her off her feet.

"What if we run into dogs?" Kylee asked, wondering where they had gone.

"Don't worry, it took a while, but I killed about a dozen or so after I heard the explosions." The confidence in Zander's voice made her feel safe. She pressed her head against his warm body and closed her eyes. Kylee could feel them going up the stairs, then down the halls. She thought she heard dogs walking past them, but she dared not look. She heard a bag ruffle, then a door opened and close. "Kylee, I'm going to put you down." Before she had time to protest, she was sitting in the dog tub. Zander opened the medical kit, pulling out Bactine, gauze, and medical tape.

"What if there's a dog in here?" Kylee asked again.

"Don't worry, there aren't." Zander assured. He hung a blanket on the door frame, covering the windows, then turned on a lantern. Kylee squinted her eyes at first, but soon she was grateful for the light. "Let's get your coat and boots off. Kylee gingerly removed her torn-up coat, being careful not to put any pressure on her right arm. She winced at the feeling of dried blood being pulled from her skin when she took her shirt off. Her white bra was covered in blood stains. While Zander unlaced her boots, she looked at the wound on her shoulder. Dried blood covered most of her body, but a steady flow of blood still streamed from the large gash in her shoulder. The wounds on her wrist and left ankle were mostly clotted. She moved her hand through her hair, feeling matted portions due to dried blood. Kylee looked at Zander's appearance then at her wounds.

"Zander, how did you feel after you got bit?" Kylee asked, worried she was going to suffer the same fate as him.

"I had a fever, wanted to sleep. My eye change occurred a few hours after the bite." Zander looked at her seriously. "Have you...?" Kylee cut him off before he could continue.

"NO! I'm thirsty, feel weak, and have a bad headache."

"That might be from blood loss? I'm not sure, though." Zander admitted.

"Well, I am." She added. Hoping she was right. "The symptoms are from blood loss, and I hit my head pretty hard."

"I can tell. Like I said, you're a mess." Zander teased. "Your face is ok, at least." Normally, Kylee would have shot back with a sassy remark, but she only managed an amused smile as Zander gently felt the back of her head. "I don't feel any blood, but you have a bump. You probably have a concussion." *Great.* Kylee thought. Zander placed a large bowl under the bath spigot, then turned the water on.

"How are you getting water? I thought I used it all." Kylee questioned.

"The Kennel and staff room have two different water tanks." Zander placed a cup under the stream of water and handed it to her. Kylee slowly drank, grateful to have it. He then put a bag on her lap with two cups of Duncan's yogurt and a box of dog treats. "Eat; it will help get your strength back."

"You want me to eat dog treats?" Kylee asked, giving him as much of a playful look as she could muster.

"I've tried one before, remember? They don't have any flavor, but they don't taste bad." Zander grabbed a green bone and ate it. "Kinda tastes like those soup crackers." Kylee pulled a red bone from the box. *Goodbye, dignity.* She thought before biting the end off. Zander was spot on with his description of the flavor.

"Thanks," she said, opening the yogurt.

"No trouble; let's take care of these wounds." She dipped the dog treat in the yogurt, covering it, before taking another bite. She tried to ignore the frigid cold on her skin and the unpleasant feeling of the damp washcloth moving over her shoulder. Kylee turned her head, and the deep gashes were even clearer. She quickly turned away. "I'm going to put Bactine on." Zander warned. Kylee grimaced from the sting.

"Zander, say something funny." Kylee said trying to keep her mind off the jolts of pain that occurred every time bactine seeped into a wound.

"Finally got you alone with your shirt off." That made Kylee laugh.

"If I wasn't injured and you weren't sick, I might want to take it a step farther." Kylee added.

"When we're out of danger, I'll take you up on that." Zander promised as he covered her wound with fresh gauze. "You're going to need a million stitches when we get out of here."

"I figured that out." Kylee said, not looking forward to the process.

"Ok, shoulder's done." Zander said cutting the thick medical tape. I'm moving onto your wrist. As she rested her hand on the side of the tub, Kylee found her thoughts drifting to Mariah. All the fun memories and dreams they shared came flooding back to her. Now she was gone, no new memories would ever be made. Mariah's dreams would never be fulfilled. Kylee found herself tearing up. "Let me know if you need a break." Zander said, pulling the towel away.

"I was thinking about Mariah." Kylee said sadly.

"I should have been there to help you two. It was stupid of me to let myself get talked into staying behind." Zander's voice was filled with regret.

"None of us could have known the plan would fail that badly. Zander, do you mind if I ask you something?" Kylee asked, wanting to keep her mind off the subject.

"Go for it." He replied.

"Mariah." She hesitated a moment before continuing. "Had a crush on you since we started working together."

"I know." Zander acknowledged with some sadness. "But I always thought of her as a close work friend." The fact that Zander knew surprised her.

"Mariah was a beautiful, confident, fun, adventurous girl. I was always the shy, quiet girl with no confidence; why did you choose me?" Zander finished bandaging her wrist and arm, then moved to her leg.

"That's honestly what I liked about you. When you were around new people or in public, you'd never talked to anyone, but when you were with Mariah, you were a silly, fun-loving girl. So I wanted to learn more about you. After a while, I got to know you, and you started to act the same way around me, and I've been hooked ever since." *That's so sweet.* Kylee thought, feeling flattered.

"Why didn't you say something sooner?" Kylee wondered.

"I guess I was afraid."

"You?" Kylee said surprised. "Of what?"

"I was worried you'd say no." Zander paused and gave a shy smile. "And I could never build up the courage to ask you out."

"It only took nearly turning into a werewolf to find it." Kylee teased. Zander gently put his hand on the back of her head and kissed her. A feeling of joy and safety came over Kylee as she leaned into it, wrapping her arms around his neck. For a moment, nothing in the world mattered or existed to Kylee until the sound of something crashing into the door made her yelp.

"Zander?" Kylee whispered. Concerned, neither of them had a weapon.

"Kylee, go near the window; get ready to run!" Zander ordered, putting his hand on the blanket.

"What are you doing?" Kylee asked. Slipping into her boots.

"They already know we're in here. I want to see how many there are." Kylee quickly put her shirt and coat back on. *Please be careful, Zander.* He dropped the blanket. Matrix was lying in the middle of the room. He winked, pushing Mariah's head between his front legs.

"You son of a bitch!" Zander shouted.

"No!" Kylee yelled, seeing his hand was on the doorknob. "It's a trap; it has to be!" Zander stared at her; his face showed he was debating what to do. Kylee felt the breath leave her when she saw Goliath rushing towards them. "Look out!" She cried. Goliath crashed through the glass, sending large shards over him. "Zander!" Kylee screamed as Goliath fell upon him. Zander groaned, holding Goliath's massive head back, but Kylee feared he couldn't keep it up for long. She grabbed the shower head and started hitting Goliath with it, which only seemed to annoy him.

"Kylee, run!" Zander ordered, still straining to keep Goliath at bay. She started to move forward, then noticed Athena was next to Matrix. "Kylee, there's nothing you can do. Run!" Athena sprinted forward. Kylee's thoughts were frozen, not knowing what to do, but her body was moving for her. She had one leg over the window ledge when Athena leaped at her. Kylee shielded her face; through her fingers, she could see Athena's mouth only inches from her, then the dog was pulled backwards. Zander was holding onto her leg with one arm and using his other to hold Goliath back. *No Zander, please.* Kylee's thoughts begged. She started to get down when Zander screamed in a strained voice. "Kylee, there's nothing you can do! Please get out of here. For me!" Matrix had now entered the batheing room. Not wanting his sacrifice to be in vain, Kylee let out a cry of anguish and climbed out the window. Her ankle flared in pain the moment she hit the ground. *Where do I go?* She thought, looking around for a safe place. The kennel was overrun, the staff house was burning. She thought about trying to run and make it to Snowy Hills. *I'll never make it.* Kylee knew, already feeling her gloveless hands going numb. *There's a radio station nearby.* She cursed, remembering it had burned down. *The garage. I can hide there until help comes.* Kylee moved her damaged body as fast as she could. Behind her, she heard a bark; she turned her head to see Matrix casually sprinting towards her.

CHAPTER 23

Zander moved his head left, Goliath's jaws narrowly missing. His right arm was burning as he tried to hold the massive dog back. Athena pulled him forward, trying to get her foot free. *I need to hold them off a little longer. Give Kylee time to escape,* he thought, hoping she could find the strength and courage to grant his dying wish. Matrix victoriously walked up to him, holding his trophy in his mouth.

"Dam you!" Zander cursed him, knowing there was no way he could stop him. Matrix dropped the mangled trophy on his chest. He loomed over Zander, giving him a wink. His mouth opened. *Please, Kylee, get somewhere safe.* Zander thought, knowing this was it. Matrix's jaws were only inches from his face when they slammed shut. Matrix pulled his head back. He looked towards the window, his ears went up, and his head tilted from side to side.

"Leave Kylee alone!" Zander cried, cursing Matrix. Athena turned around, biting down on his arm. Zander let out a cry of pain. Matrix got up on the window ledge and barked. Goliath stopped his attack and followed Matrix out the window. "No Kylee!" With the other attackers gone, Zander delivered strike after strike to Athena's head, finally she released his arm. The cane corso stumbled back, dazed. Zander noticed the broken pieces of glass behind him, so he walked backwards towards them. Athena again charged. Zander leaped to the side, then grabbed two large icicle-shaped shards of glass. Athena stopped right before she hit the wall. She turned around, growled, and leaped at him. He waited until she was in midair, then plunged both glass shards into her eyes. The raging dog fell at his feet. Zander looked at his mangled arm, knowing in a few days it would be as good as new. As he quickly bandaged it, he wondered. *Matrix had me dead to rights. Why did he run off like that?* He thought about how Matrix looked and acted right before running off. It was a look he had seen before. The look a dog gets when his master calls. That worried him. His thoughts quickly returned to Kylee. He went out the window, following her trail in the snow.

***

Weak and out of breath, Kylee reached the garage fencing. Matrix and Goliath were trotting closer to her. *Why are they playing with me?* Kylee thought tired of their sick game, knowing they could have easily caught up with her if they wanted to. Sections of staff building debris and the minibus were still burning around her. As she got inside the fencing, she tried to close the gate behind her; the left side easily moved into position, but the right wouldn't budge. Kylee saw a piece of metal wedged between the fence and gate corner, preventing the gate from moving. She pushed on it, trying to force it closed, but her numb, tired arms were too weak to budge it. She saw Matrix and Goliath walking across the fence line.

"This is a game to you, isn't it?" Kylee moaned, wondering when Matrix would decide to finally kill her. She gave up on the gate and limped into the garage. The fire from the outside created an orange glow inside. She closed the garage door and locked the door connecting the garage to the kennel. Inside, the gas and propane lockers had been ripped open. Spilled gas cans and propane tanks littered the floor. Outside, she could hear Matrix and other dogs walking around. *So your idea was to get me in here so you could cook me alive?* Kylee thought remembering what they did to the employee building. With nothing else to do, she sat down, taking the weight off her burning ankle. Thoughts of Zander, Mariah, and the others filled her head. How they had tried their hardest to get everyone out of this situation alive. All of them had died trying to save their friends, and what had she done? Cower in a corner. A feeling of regret came over her. *How many of them would still be alive if I had done more*? She questioned. On the other side of the room, she heard something hit the floor. She noticed the large shadow on the wall moving towards her. The dog that made it was hidden behind the knocked-over shelves and lockers. *A husky.* She could tell by the cropped ears. Kylee got up but didn't move. She was done running; she looked around the room for a utility knife, hammer, or something in arm's length to fight with. The shadow was getting smaller. *Here we go.* Kylee thought she was preparing for her death. The shadow got smaller until a chihuahua came around the sections of knocked-over shelves. The frightened look left her face when she recognized Sparky. He showed his teeth, gave a warning yip, and then charged. Kylee yelled in fury and kicked her foot forward. The kick hit Sparky's head, sending him flying against the wall. A new feeling of rage filled her. If she was going to die, she was at least going to take a few of them with her.

Matrix and Goliath circled the building, barking and jumping at the walls, waiting for their prey to come out of hiding. Matrix lifted his ear when he heard the sound of a large door opening. He and Goliath moved through the opened gate to the open garage door. Kylee let out a battle cry. She rushed out of the building holding a burning digging shovel. *Now it's your turn to be scared,* she thought, swinging the shovel at a charging Goliath. The blow struck him in the face, knocking him to the ground. Kylee pulled the shovel up and locked eyes with Matrix. She could see and hear other dogs in the area, but she was going to end him before she died. She screamed in rage, running at him, her wide strides kicking up snow in every direction. Instead of fighting, Matrix ran. "Run, you coward!" Kylee yelled, feeling her confidence grow. Matrix made it onto the tracks the bus had made. Kylee broke through the knee-high snow on the bus tracks. The snow was more compact and easier to walk on. Matrix waited on the other end. The burning bus concealing him in shadows. *This is for you, Mariah, Zander.* Kylee thought. Fueled by rage, she ran at him, doing all she could to ignore the burning pain in her ankle. In the back of her mind, she wondered why he was sitting there waiting for her. It didn't matter; she had to strike now before the other dogs overwhelmed her. She raised the shovel when she was only a few yards from him. For a moment, she felt the slippery feeling of ice, then felt her feet leave the ground. Her back struck the ground hard as she slid on the newly frozen ice, stopping only inches from Matrix, who let out an amused huff. *No,*

I have to beat him. Kylee rapidly thought. Her hands moved, trying to find the shovel. Her left hand found the shovel; she grabbed it, trying to pull it towards her. Matrix bit down on the other end. Kylee struggled to maintain a grip on the handle as Matrix easily pulled her to the bus. Kylee felt the bitter cold replaced by unbearable heat as Matrix pulled her into the burning wreckage. Kylee released her grip on the shovel handle, rolling away from the fire until she was in an area with a pleasant temperature. She started breathing heavily. Her wave of courage was quickly fading, replaced by the fear of the death she knew was coming. She saw Matrix circling her in no hurry to finish things. Like he had with Mariah, Matrix placed a foot on her chest, giving her a victory wink. Kylee gave him a frightened, defeated look. *Sorry, Zander, I tried. At least I'll be with you guys soon.* Kylee thought, regretting that she couldn't finish him. Matrix's attention abruptly turned from her; he looked up, barking in rage.

"Here's your friend's head."

"Zander!" She cried and saw Athena's severed head hit the ground beside her. Matrix stared at it, then glared at Zander with half-mooned eyes. With Matrix focused on Zander, Kylee slammed both her fists across his face. Matrix grunted as his feet staggered. Kylee shoved him on his side, knocking him off her. He recovered in an instant. He growled and charged Zander, biting down on his mangled arm. Zander thrust his clawed hand onto Matrix's head, digging into his flesh and moving his hand down to his eyes. Matrix whimpered and jumped back. Kylee watched the two circle each daring the other to attack. She got to her feet, grabbing the shovel, whose flames had nearly faded. She saw a German shepherd mix running at her. She swung her weapon across her body, striking him on the side. The dog yelped and tumbled over. Kylee brought the shovel over her shoulder, hitting her attacker again and again until he was dead. Zander and Matrix were still circling, getting in an occasional bite or scratch. Kylee could see the outlines of other dogs moving around in the dark. *We're going to be overwhelmed.* Zander jumped back toward her. Matrix followed close behind.

"Kylee," he said, keeping an eye on Matrix and motioning for her to come closer. Kylee listened as he quickly whispered instructions in her ear.

"Please be careful." Kylee whispered as she rushed for the garage door. The outlines of other dogs were still moving around, like they were waiting for their leader to command them to attack. She got inside the garage and hid on the side wall, watching Zander and Matrix continue their deadly dance. Zander overextended on a strike. He fell forward, landing on all fours. She gasped when Matrix took advantage of the mistake. He quickly darted around Zander, leaping on his back, then bit down on the back of his shoulder. Kylee winced. "Please don't die." She begged. Zander brought his free arm around, grabbing ahold of Matrix's body, then got to his feet, rushing for the garage. Kylee's body was filled with anticipation. The moment Zander got inside, Kylee pulled down on the garage rope. The door slammed shut, trapping the three of them inside. Zander ran backwards, Matrix jumped off him before his body hit the concrete wall. Matrix looked at both closed doors. Kylee thought she saw a look of worry on his face, making her feel the best she has felt since the attack started.

"Yeah, we tricked you. How does it feel?" Kylee taunted. She could hear dogs at the garage and side door barking and slamming against them. Zander ran at Matrix, his claws extended for a swipe. Rushing past him, Matrix avoided the strike. Kylee saw him charging towards her. She swung her shovel. He moved to his left, the shovel head making a loud thud when it struck the floor. Matrix leaped at her. Both his front paws hit her in the chest. Kylee stumbled backwards, yelling in pain, when her back struck the wall. Matrix turned his attention back to Zander, who had knocked a tool chest to the floor. He reached down, grabbing a hammer and a utility knife. Matrix looked at both of them, then ran to the garage door. Kylee gasped when he bit down on the pull rope. *No, I have to stop him!* Kylee thought, moving as fast as her body would allow, knowing if he opened the garage, it was over for both of them. Zander got there first; he swung the hammer at Matrix, who avoided the blow, getting a quick bite to Zander's right leg before backing up out of Zander's striking range. The three were in a near-triangular shape, with Matrix at the front. Kylee and Zander moved closer, trying to box him in. *We can do this.* Kylee told herself. She looked over at Zander, his one finger occasionally pointing towards Matrix. She figured he wanted her to attack first; she didn't know what he had planned but trusted his judgment. Kylee limped towards Matrix, thrusting the shovel head in front of her like a spear. Zander didn't move. Kylee thrust the shovel head again, and with half her focus on what Zander was doing, Matrix took advantage. On one thrust, he darted left, avoiding it.

"Zander!" Kylee cried as Matrix bit down on her leg, knocking her to the ground. Kylee held the shovel across her body. She looked at Zander, who was still in the same place. *What was he doing? Why isn't he helping me?* Then a new, horrifying thought came to her. *Had the disease affected his mind, turning him into one of Matrix's followers?* Matrix bit down on the shovel. Kylee could hear the wood cracking under his jaws. She didn't know how much longer her weak, sweaty hands could hold onto it. "Zander!" She desperately cried out. Matrix's jaws were nearly to her face; she could see the splits in the shovel handle getting larger. She screamed when she heard a loud cracking sound, but it wasn't the shovel breaking. It was Zander's hammer hitting Matrix's skull. Everything was moving in slow motion now. Matrix's head reared up, howling in pain. His body wobbled for a moment, then fell to the ground. Kylee watched him closely. *It's over,* she thought, breathing in relief when his eyes closed. A steady stream of blood came from the top of his skull.

"Kylee, I'm so sorry." Zander said, picking her up. "I needed his focus off me for a few moments and couldn't tell you my plan."

"It's OK," Kylee assured. "We're both alive, and that's all that matters." Kylee kicked Matrix a few times, getting her frustration out. She could still hear dogs running around outside, but the main threat was gone.

"What do we do now?" She asked.

"Were safe for now. Let's relax for a moment." Zander replied, giving her a smile. Kylee wrapped her arms around his neck, and then their mouths locked. After a long kiss, Zander moved his mouth away. Kylee closed her eyes and moved tighter into his embrace.

"What's going to happen to us?" Kylee wondered. Tears of relief, sadness, and exhaustion fell on her cheeks.

"You're going to the hospital to get better." Zander paused for a moment before saying. "I don't know what's going to happen to me."

"I won't let anything happen to you," Kylee assured in a serious voice. She opened her eyes, and through the haze of tears, she saw the outline of Matrix standing near the garage door, his mouth on the pull rope. *No, he can't be still alive! There's no way he could have survived that!* "Zander!" Kylee screamed, pulling away from him. Matrix winked with a smirk that seemed to return Kylee's taunt from earlier. He pulled back on the cord. The garage door seemed to be moving in slow motion as it moved to the halfway point. Zander ran towards Matrix. Several huskies and other dogs began flooding in. In Zander's panicked attack, Matrix easily moved to the side, causing him to miss. Zander landed outside the garage door. Kylee saw several dogs leaping onto him before Matrix released the rope, closing the garage. "Damn you, this isn't fair!" Kylee shouted, not believing how quickly he turned the tide on them. With no hope of winning against six dogs, Kylee limped to the door that led to the kennel. *Get out, regroup with Zander.* Any hope of escape left her when she saw at least four dogs on the other side. She looked right at Matrix. *No, I won't let you win.* She saw the tools scattered all over the floor. She went over to them. The other dogs inside started to charge, but a bark from Matrix stopped them. One by one, they sat down. Only Matrix, slowly taking his time, moved in closer. Kylee fell, whimpering as she picked up a screwdriver. She put her free hand on a propane tank to lift herself, then weakly fell into the propane locker. She sat down, holding the screwdriver out. She watched as Matrix moved closer. A look of fright formed on her face. He was only a few feet from her now. *It worked.* Kylee's look of fright turned to a sly smile; she raised her right hand, holding a lighter. Matrix let out a shocked bark and rushed at her; the other dogs did the same in a last-ditch attempt to stop her. Kylee dropped the lighter on the propane tank she had opened. Her thoughts went to Mariah and all the other friends Matrix had killed. She saw the lighter hit the gasoline-covered floor. Flames quickly traveled in all directions. One by one, the dogs became engulfed by the flames. Matrix's body caught fire. He yelped in pain but kept charging in a desperate attempt to kill her. Portions of his fur burned away, leaving boils and charred skin. The fur on Matrix's face seared, making him look like he was becoming a hellhound. Kylee closed her eyes. Her thoughts went to Zander, imagining the life they could have had. It was a bright summer day. Her and Mariah sat on lawn chairs, relaxing after finishing a summer picnic. She held a sleeping baby girl in her arm while Zander and Mariah's husband played soccer with their two young sons. She felt Matrix's hot breath strike her face; intense heat surrounded her. She briefly heard a loud bang, and then she was permanently in her dream.

Chapter 24

Zander slowly got up from the explosion; the three attacking dogs he had been fighting were dead. In the distance, he could hear the sound of an approaching helicopter. The remaining dogs were running around wildly, like they didn't know what to do now that their leader was dead. "Kylee!" Zander approached the burning building; the garage door had been blown several feet from the blast. He carefully navigated through the maze of flames. Dead dogs lay across the floor. "Kylee, where are you?" Zander cried, knowing he had to act quickly before the garage collapsed. He continued to call her name, his worry increasing with each unanswered call. Then he saw Matrix's body, which made him smile in delight. Half his face was burnt off, pieces of metal were impaled in his skin. He listened carefully and watched closely for any sign of him playing dead. You're not getting up, are you? He thought with delight. "We did it, Kylee." He said spitting on him. He sniffed the air; he could smell blood mixed with the flower-scented perfume she always wore. He noticed the propane locker was knocked down, the opening facing the ground. He began to lift it, and right away he felt the extra weight inside. "Hang on, Kylee." He said slowly moving it on its side. The doors swung open, and Kylee rolled out motionless. "Kylee, are you OK?" She didn't answer or move. "Kylee!" Zander said, turning her over. Her mouth was halfway open. Blood was flowing from a wound on the back of her head. "It's OK," he said in tears, gently picking her up. "I'll get help, and everything will be OK." He kicked the door to the kennel open and carried her to the batheing room. He held her in one arm, lining the bathtub with blankets, and rolled up several towels to use as a pillow. Then he laid Kylee down. "You'll be OK." He said touching her hand. Right away, he noticed it was unusually cold. Fearing he knew what it meant, he touched the side of her neck, checking for a pulse. He looked into her eyes; they stared back at him, but there was no life in them. He let out a cry of rage, feeling deeper pain than any wound he had received. "No, Kylee!" he cried, pounding on the side of the tub. Outside, Zander heard dogs coming through the broken windows, followed by barking and growling. *They must have regrouped.* Zander thought, realizing Goliath, Neit, and Echo were still alive. Matrix may have been killed, but there were probably at least fifty dogs still running around. Zander looked at himself in the mirror. *I can never have a normal life. My friends are dead.* He smiled an evil smile. *Might as well die avenging Kylee taking as many of these monsters with me as I can.* "You still want to play; let's have some fun." Zander pulled the door open. At least ten dogs were in the room: four huskies, five mixed breeds, and a pitbull. Zander scraped his claws against the wall, ready to go down fighting. The sound of gunfire erupted outside. The dogs looked towards it, then towards him. Zander saw a flash grenade come through the broken window. He backed into the batheing room, his new reflexes allowing him to look away before it went off. He heard the bang, the dogs yelping in confusion, then the sound of machine gun fire. *Whoever opens that door's going to be in for a surprise.* Zander thought amused. Wondering if they would shoot him on sight or leave the room screaming. Zander kissed Kylee on the forehead, placed a blanket over her head, then sat on the dryer. The door yanked opened. A soldier stood in the doorway, holding a submachine gun.

"Hey, glad you're here," Zander said. It was the only thing he could think of at the moment.

"Holy shit! Max, get over here!" The soldier yelled. Her face was covered by a gas mask, her neck-length black hair was wrapped in a ponytail. "Stay where you are, dogman." She added, pointing her gun at his face. Zander acknowledged that he understood her order. "What's under the blanket?" She asked, sounding like she already had a pretty good idea what it was.

"I was trying to save my girlfriend; she didn't make it." Zander sighed with anger and regret.

"Liz, what is it?" He heard another soldier ask.

"Either a dog became a human or a man's becoming a dog," Liz Tayler replied.

"I like your sense of humor," Zander praised. Hoping it would lighten the mood.

"Thanks." Liz replied. She moved to the side to let the other soldier in. His reaction was similar to Liz's.

"Did he say how this happened?" Max Varian asked.

"I got bit by the rottweiler; you can find him dead in the garage. I might be starting to look like a werewolf, but I'm still sane." Zander assured. Wanting the new soldier to know he was human and would cooperate.

"This could be worse than we thought." Max said, then called for a medical unit. He turned his attention back to Zander. "That's good to know. As I'm sure you can imagine, we're going to have a lot of questions for you. We're going to take you to our base of operations on Niihau."

"To do what?" Zander asked in a serious tone. Recalling his fear about the military wanting to use him as their lab rat. Zander's options raced through his mind as he waited for a response. *If they sound deceptive, should I charge them? Better to be gunned down than spend the rest of your life as a lab rat.* He mentally decided.

"Find out what happened to you and hopefully get you back to normal." Max answered with no hint of deception. Zander didn't like the idea of going with them at all, but he couldn't continue his normal life either, and with guns pointed at him, he doubted he had a choice.

"Why this place, Niihau, and not the CDC?" He asked, knowing Niihau was an uninhabited Hawaiian island. A *place where the military hides things. He mentally answered.*

"It's our base of operations. We specialize in bizarre cases." Max's cryptic answer worried Zander.

"We've had one," Liz added. Max looked at Liz. Zander could tell he was glaring at her through the mask.

"And what case was that?" Zander asked.

"We can't tell you about it now. I'll explain when we get there." Zander shrugged.

"Guess I have no choice. I have two requests, though." Max and Liz's body language showed they were listening. "First, let my folks know I'm alive and make up whatever story you want about why I'm in quarantine. Second, he pointed to Kylee's body. "I want Kylee Campbell's and the rest of my friend's bodies returned to their families."

"I take it; they got bit." Max asked. Concern was forming in his voice.

"Yes, but I'm the only one who got bitten by Matrix." "Besides a movie, who's that?" Liz asked. Zander snickered at the comment. *I could get along with her.*

"I'm guessing patient zero. He was the first dog infected, correct?" Max added.

"As far as I know, like I said before, he's dead by the garage." Zander heard muffled radio chatter come from their headsets.

"Try to capture one of the dogs alive if we can." Max replied. "Is the medical team ready? Ok, we'll bring him down now."

"Can you grant my requests?" Zander asked, having no idea what he was going to do if they refused.

"I promise we will do our best to fulfill them."

"That's not good enough." Zander stressed. Readying his body for a fight.

"Well, we don't run the world, so it's the best we can do." Liz added. Her finger tightened around her gun's trigger.

"Fair enough." Zander admitted relaxing.

"I need you to turn around." Liz said, her hand reaching for her belt.

"You're not handcuffing me. Zander said it seriously. "I'm trusting you; you can trust me." Zander stretched his arms out. "Otherwise, shoot me."

"I left my silver at home," Liz replied.

"Why didn't you say so? I would have ripped you to pieces earlier." Zander could tell both of them had cracked a smile.

"Great two people with a weird sense of humor." Max said. "Ok, just walk ahead of us."

"I can do that." Zander said, moving in front of them. When he got outside, it looked completely different. The area was lit up with spotlights, and army vehicles formed a perimeter around what used to be the kennel. Above Zander saw a helicopter and soldiers rushing around the area, putting large, bright flags near the bodies of dogs. Occasionally, gunshots joined the sounds of engines running and soldiers radio chatter. *I hope they kill them all.*

"We obviously don't have anything set up here, so we're going to take you to a station at Fairbanks Memorial Hospital." Liz said. Zander was about to speak when he heard.

"Max, Samuel's with the Delta team trying to capture some dogs."

"What the hell is that?" Ashly Cross yelled in alarm.

"Name's Zander Conri. Nice to meet you too." Zander replied with sarcasm.

"Wait, the virus does this to people!" Ashly asked, worried.

"From what I saw, only a bite from Matrix does this." Zander again reminded.

"And what are your qualifications to know such things?" Ashly asked. *Who does she think she is?* Zander thought bitterly.

"I lived through the attack and watched my friends get killed; that's how I know." Zander replied, giving her a snarl. Ashly's hand went to her sidearm.

"Both of you stop it." Max ordered.

"We have at least thirty-three reports from five different countries of dogs acting the same way." Ashly replied as she entered some information into her iPad. *This is happening everywhere.* A million questions ran through his mind.

"Ashly, regroup with Samuel; I'll join you guys once we get him settled." Max ordered. Even with her gas mask, Zander saw distrust in Ashly's eyes before she turned away, and then he noticed two men carrying a black body bag coming from the kennel.

"Hold on." He pointed toward it. Max and Liz ordered the soldiers to stop. Zander approached the bag. Emotions filled him as he slowly unzipped the first half of the bag. Kylee's eyes were now closed, and the color was leaving her skin. Zander again kissed her forehead, saying a final goodbye. "I'm done." He said closing the bag.

"Max, right?" Zander said to the male soldier as the three walked to a military truck.

"That's my name."

"You seem like the science type; what are the odds of getting me back to normal?" Zander asked now, clinging to the hope that there was a chance.

"To be honest, I don't know. I'm an animal behaviorist and trainer, not a medical scientist."

"That's comforting," Zander said, looking at his clawed hand. They walked for several more feet until they reached the military truck with a closed canopy. When he reached the back, four soldiers were sitting in the truck bed. They must have heard about him because none acted surprised at the sight of him.

"They'll take you to the hospital; from there, you get on a flight to Niihau. All I can promise is that you'll be treated well." Max assured.

"Thanks for being honest." Zander said sincerely. Liz handed a phone to Max, and the two walked away. Zander pressed his ear to the canopy, listening as Max spoke.

"I don't know. I believe we're dealing with a mutated strain of the rabies virus." The truck's engine started. Zander felt himself jerk forward when the tires moved. He gave his new companions a look-over. Their guns were trained on him, but none of them appeared to have ulterior motives. He looked out the back of the truck. He saw five soldiers loading a cage with a husky inside into a silver helicopter. *Wonder how many are left?* Zander thought, doubting they could have killed or captured all the dogs. His thoughts were interrupted by several gunshots, and then nothing; the soldiers near the helicopter came to alert. *Last desperate attack?* He wondered, seeing them move towards where he thought the gunfire came from. The truck came to a sudden stop. The spotlights all moved in the same direction. He could tell the soldiers with him were hearing something on their radios. *What's going on? He* wondered. His answer came when a human-looking shape flew into the sky. Zander cursed in surprise, watching the searchlights move on it. Twin horns protruded from the forehead, a long dragon-looking tail twisted side to side, and gargoyle-like wings effortlessly moved it through the sky. What worried him the most was that in its arms, he clearly made out the body of Matrix. Before anyone could get a shot off, it flew into the night sky and disappeared in the darkness. *What was that?* For a moment, he hoped and wondered if it was Kylee. A bite from Matrix changed him; why not her? His dream quickly faded. Kylee was dead, and whatever it was didn't come from the medical truck her body was in. He had been watching it the entire time. He laid his head back and closed his eyes, wondering what his new life had in store for him.

Epilogue

Alaskan National Guard Sergeant Allen Moore watched the X-7 lift off. He had no idea why an American and Japanese task force came to assist in the operation. He guessed they were somehow involved with the dogs going crazy, but at the moment had no proof. He watched two of his soldiers load body bags into the back of the truck, then looked at the two charred buildings, thinking about how he would bring justice to whatever science division was messing around with viruses and dog DNA. If not now, then in the future. He was quickly working his way up the military ranks and was on the career track of becoming a captain.

"Sir," Private Swanson said, coming to attention.

"At ease, private, what do you have to report?"

"All the dogs in the area seem to have been killed."

"Seem?" Moore replied. A slightly nervous look formed on Swanson's face. She stuttered a moment before saying.

"Well, sir, we don't know how many dogs were staying here, and the Alaska State Troopers haven't yet reported how many dogs were killed at Snowy Hills."

"Get a chopper with an infrared camera in the air. I want a circular area of one hundred miles searched. I don't want one of these dogs to escape; we can't let whatever they're carrying infect other pets or, worse, wildlife." The thought of that brought him chills. It would be a horror movie brought to life. He watched Humphreys and Lloyd loading a dog's body into a truck. He had sent Corporal Velasquez and three of his troops to escort a survivor to the hospital, leaving him with five soldiers. He was about to dismiss Swanson when he heard Private Rice yell from near the burned building.

"We have a survivor!"

"Come on, Private!" Sergeant Moore commanded. The two of them rushed through the broken framework to where Rice was standing. Private Humphrey and medical officer Private Osborne followed close behind them. The man was sitting on a burnt pile of wood; his hands covered his face as he sobbed and muttered what sounded like.

"Everyone's gone." *How did we miss him, and why didn't he come out sooner?* Moore thought. Osborne unstrapped her medical kit and walked over to him.

"What's your name, son?" Moore asked. Keeping his rifle at the ready.

"Benjamin," he said in a low voice.

"Can you repeat that?" Moore asked.

"He said his name's Benjamin." Osborne repeated, putting a gentle arm on him. "We're here to help. Are you hurt?"

"Benjamin...." His voice went from soft and meek to deep and cruel. "Has been dead for about a month." Moore saw the unmistakable look of pure fear in Osborne's eyes. Seconds later, he saw why. Most of the man's face was half decayed; unusually long bones protruded between the bits of flesh and muscle around his mouth. The parts of skin that remained looked like a torn mask. Before Moore could give the order to fire, the abomination thrust his arm into Osborne's chest. Rice and Humphrey's screamed and cursed. Before they could raise their guns, Goliath leaped on Rice. As Humphrey turned to shoot the attacking dog, Neit bit down on his foot. Echo leaped on him from above. Moore heard Private Lloyd's rifle get several shots off, followed by screams. He raised his rifle, putting the crosshairs on Neit. His hand was about to squeeze the trigger when he felt a knife at his throat. He felt the steel dig into his flesh. His body went numb. He tried unsuccessfully to move his trigger finger. He let out a gurgle of blood before he dropped to the ground. On his back, he saw two people in winter camouflage standing over him. The last thing he saw was Lloyd's severed head and mangled body lying on the ground.

"That's the last of them." Rein said, pulling off her mask. She shook her head, causing her dark black hair to fall past her shoulders. The large man next to her adjusted the heavy machine gun slung over his shoulder.

"We're finished here," The abomination said getting to his feet.

"Finished?" Rein questioned. "What about that guy going to the hospital? And why didn't you have us shoot that chopper down? They captured a few of the dogs in case you didn't notice." The abomination shot a warning glare at her.

"Quit questioning about the operation, Rein. You know he doesn't want to hear them. Zeke Reminded, still wearing his winter-camouflaged mask. Rein wiped her knife on a burnt piece of wood.

"Well, this makes no sense. We destroy a radio station." Rein looked up, staring behind the abomination. "My gun shot and crying at the window joke was pretty funny, right?" She got an annoyed grunt in response. Her attention went back to the abomination. "We encircled the area." She made a circular motion with her finger. "To monitor how Matrix and his infected dogs would perform, then help attack the town, then we…"

"Rein!" The abomination sneered. He walked right up to her, bits of flesh falling from his face. Zeke took a few steps away from her. The three dogs began snarling at her. "Do you want your tongue or vocal cords ripped out?" Rein looked down with a look of fear on her pale face. The abomination put a bony finger on her chin, lifting her head until her frightened eyes met his cold gaze. "You have potential, Rein; don't waste it." He moved his finger across the bottom of her chin, leaving a small cut. "Zeke, where's the other two members of your team?" He asked, turning from her. Rain let out a gasp of relief.

"Jasper and Trinity are still observing the Snowy Hills clean-up. Jasper was asking, if you want them to take the dog corpses once the police gather them?"

"We need to keep our enemies guessing. Attack the vehicle carrying them, take a few dog corpses from it, and leave the rest. Be sure any documentation pertaining to the number of corpses remains intact and with the vehicle."

"Yes sir." Zeke replied. "I take it you don't care what happens to the dog bodies we take?"

"Correct." The abomination looked up at the outline of the twelve-foot, hairy humanoid figure standing outside the ruined building. Its baboon-like snout sniffed the air, then looked down at him. He pointed in the direction of the town of Snowy Hills. The figure grunted and walked in that direction.

"Speaking of enemies, sir…" Zeke continued. The abomination breathed heavily.

"I know one of his accursed followers was here." Pure hatred formed on what remained of the abomination's masked face.

"You had to take the most important piece from me, didn't you?" he said under his breath. Zeke and Rein remained silent, leaving their leader with his thoughts. After a short amount of time passed, the abomination reached down. Pulling a lollipop from Osborne's pack, he tossed it to Rein, a sign she had been forgiven this time. "Finish up here, then you will head to your next assignment."

"Where's that, sir?" Zeke asked.

"We have business at Lake Champlain."

"Finally, someplace warmer." Rein muttered happily.

"Understood sir. If you don't mind me asking, will this be a capture or kill operation?" Zeke wondered.

"Both. It's more than likely our operation will attract unwanted attention. Ignore and avoid our friends. We don't want unnecessary conflict just yet." Rein took the lollipop out of her mouth.

"Like, we have to worry about them. They could barely handle an oversized water cat." Rein said in a cocky voice, staring at the large human footprints going into the forest.

"We understand, sir." Zeke added quickly.

"I'll fill you in on the details later." The abomination replied, dragging the bodies into a pile. "Now rejoin the others; these soldiers will be missed."

"We'll find a place to hide the bodies," Rein offered.

"I'll handle that," the abomination said with a grin, his now-boney face beginning to elongate. "It's been too long since I had a decent meal."

ABOUT THE AUTHOR

Vance Albright has been writing in some form or another since he was five. Throughout high school he wrote several book drafts but always fell into the trap of never finishing them. During college, he temporarily gave up on fiction writing to focus on his studies. After graduating, he renewed his love for writing and started Light and Dark Novelizations to begin creating his own universe of characters. Vance believes compelling storylines and believable characters that capture the reader's interest are the keys to a great novel.

Vance graduated from high school in 2008, and in 2016 he earned a B.S. in Environmental Science and minored in Biology. He is currently working in the environmental technician and horticulturalist fields.

Vance always has been an animal lover. He currently has two cats, Luna and Nova, three parakeets, and a tropical fish tank.

Vance's hobbies are watching football (Steelers and Packers are his favorite teams), martial arts, hiking, video gaming, collecting Godzilla figures, and 90s toys.

Thank you for reading Eyes in the Dark. If you enjoyed this book, please consider leaving a review on your favorite online book purchasing site.

9 781734 062847